THE HORUS HERESY®

RUINSTORM

Sanguinius drew the *Blade Encarmine* from its sheath. Raldoron, in his office of equerry, approached and handed him the *Spear of Telesto*. Behind him, the doors of the bridge opened and Azkaellon led his Sanguinary Guard out to surround the command dais. At the sight of the gathering might of the Blood Angels, the human crew drew courage. The moans quieted. The officers worked their stations, holding the course of the *Red Tear* as true as they could in a realm where truth drew the blood of reason.

Claws scratched at the hull. They scraped along it, as if it were a thin wall of tin. The shutters bulged again, and yet again, with the rhythm of strange lungs.

The breach came in the bridge's vault. It snaked in sharp angles down the height of the wall. It vibrated with the hum of a million flies. It began to peel back, metal framework and marble cladding turning flesh-red, flesh-supple, flesh-weak. The buzzing of the flies filled the command deck. The taste of the sound was foul on Sanguinius' tongue. He felt the crawl of legs and the flutter of wings.

A bell tolled, and with the chanting of a thousand festering tongues, the tear split wide.

THE HORUS HERESY

Other Novels and Novellas

*Many of these titles are also available as abridged and unabridged audiobooks.
Order the full range of Horus Heresy novels and audiobooks from*
blacklibrary.com

Also available

Download the full range of Horus Heresy audio dramas from
blacklibrary.com

THE HORUS HERESY®

David Annandale

RUINSTORM

Destiny unwritten…

BLACK LIBRARY

For my mother, Eleanor Anne Annandale (1935–2016). In loving memory.

A BLACK LIBRARY PUBLICATION

Hardback edition published in 2017.
This edition published in Great Britain in 2018.
Black Library,
Games Workshop Ltd.,
Willow Road,
Nottingham,
NG7 2WS, UK.

10 9 8 7 6 5 4 3 2 1

Produced by Games Workshop in Nottingham.
Cover illustration by Neil Roberts.

A CIP record for this book is available from the British Library.

ISBN 13: 978-1-78496-672-0

See Black Library on the internet at

blacklibrary.com

Find out more about Games Workshop
and the world of Warhammer 40,000 at

games-workshop.com

Printed and bound by CPI Group (UK) Ltd, Croydon, CR0 4YY

THE HORUS HERESY

It is a time of legend.

The galaxy is in flames. The Emperor's glorious vision for humanity is in ruins. His favoured son, Horus, has turned from his father's light and embraced Chaos.

His armies, the mighty and redoubtable Space Marines, are locked in a brutal civil war. Once, these ultimate warriors fought side by side as brothers, protecting the galaxy and bringing mankind back into the Emperor's light.
Now they are divided.

Some remain loyal to the Emperor, whilst others have sided with the Warmaster. Pre-eminent amongst them, the leaders of their thousands-strong Legions are the primarchs. Magnificent, superhuman beings, they are the crowning achievement of the Emperor's genetic science. Thrust into battle against one another, victory is uncertain for either side.

Worlds are burning. At Isstvan V, Horus dealt a vicious blow and three loyal Legions were all but destroyed. War was begun, a conflict that will engulf all mankind in fire. Treachery and betrayal have usurped honour and nobility. Assassins lurk in every shadow. Armies are gathering.
All must choose a side or die.

Horus musters his armada, Terra itself the object of his wrath. Seated upon the Golden Throne, the Emperor waits for his wayward son to return. But his true enemy is Chaos, a primordial force that seeks to enslave mankind to its capricious whims.

The screams of the innocent, the pleas of the righteous resound to the cruel laughter of Dark Gods. Suffering and damnation await all should the Emperor fail and the war be lost.

The age of knowledge and enlightenment has ended.
The Age of Darkness has begun.

~ DRAMATIS PERSONAE ~

Ultramarines

ROBOUTE GUILLIMAN	Primarch
VERUS CASPEAN	Chapter Master of the First
TITUS PRAYTO	Librarian
TURETIA ALTUZER	Shipmaster, *Samothrace*
DRAKUS GOROD	Commander, Suzerain Invictus Bodyguard
IASUS	Chapter Master of the 22nd, Destroyers
JUNIXA TERRENS	Vox-officer, *Samothrace*
NESTOR LAUTENIX	Lieutenant, *Samothrace*
HIERAX	Captain, Destroyers
LUCRETIUS CORVO	Captain, *Glorious Nova*
MNASON	Destroyers legionary
TEOSOS	Destroyers legionary
BYZANUS	Tech-priest
KLETOS	Destroyers legionary
APHOVOS	Sergeant, second squad, Destroyers
GORTHIA	Sergeant, third squad, Destroyers
ANTALCIDAS	Dreadnought, Destroyers
EMPION	Chapter Master of the Ninth

Blood Angels

SANGUINIUS	Primarch
CARMINUS	Captain, temporary Fleet Master
RALDORON	First Captain, Equerry to Sanguinius
MKANI KANO	Librarian

MEROS	The Red Angel, Herald
VARRA NEVERRUS	Vox-officer, *Red Tear*
AZKAELLON	Captain, Sanguinary Guard
AMIT	Flesh Tearer, Fifth Company
JERAN MAUTUS	Lieutenant, auspex officer, *Red Tear*
OREXIS	Sergeant
VAHIEL	Sergeant

Dark Angels

LION EL'JONSON	Primarch
STENIUS	Captain, *Invincible Reason*
HOLGUIN	Voted Lieutenant, Deathwing
LADY THERALYN FIANA	Chief Navigator, *Invincible Reason*
TUCHULCHA	
FARITH REDLOSS	Voted Lieutenant, Dreadwing
VAZHETH LICINIA	Mistress of the astropathic choir, *Invincible Reason*

Iron Hands

KHALYBUS	Captain, *Sthenelus*
RAUD	Sergeant
CRUAX	Iron Father
SETERIKUS	Legionary
DEMIR	Legionary
KIRIKTAS	Helmsman, *Sthenelus*

Raven Guard

LEVANNAS

Word Bearers

TOC DERENOTH	Unburdened
GREL KATHNAR	
PHAEL RABOR	Captain
QUOR VONDOR	Chaplain
YATHINIUS	Navigator, *Annunciation*
NEKRAS	Navigator, *Annunciation*

Others

KONRAD CURZE	Night Haunter
ELESKA REVUS	Colonel, Imperial Army commander, Episimos III
MADAIL THE UNDIVIDED	Daemon

PROLOGUE

I sing the carnage of faith rewarded.

By verse of eight and chorus of four, with choir of bone and chords of pain, I am the celebrant of ruin.

By path of eight and praise of four, I bow to excess and to blood, to change and to plague.

With sight of eight, by command of four, I am weaver and reaper, the shaper of souls and their devourer.

I lead the congregation of slaughter. I bring the revelation of skulls. My path is deluge, my wake is holocaust, and my march is fealty. I am the servant. I am the priest.

I am the undivided.

The web of storms shakes and moans. Its strands convulse. Down their lengths, the prisoners struggle in bonds they do not truly perceive. Fate shackles them. By power of eight and will of four, they are caught in the design. It pulls them towards me. I take up the web. I gather it in. The prey rushes forwards, blind in the arrogance of false hope.

They are three, coming to be ground and torn by jaws of eight and edict of four. They believe in the illusion of choice, in the ragged dream of their struggle. The disciple of reason, the holder of secrets, and the winged nobility, they are infused with fire. It will burn them.

I will burn them.

They are no more than ash.

But by knives of eight, for the glory of four, of the three there is the one whose pyre must be the galaxy. I pull the web, and shape his fate. The riven must stand before the undivided.

He will embrace the majesty of ruin.

PART I
THE TEMPEST

ONE

The Redemption Leap

My sin is the greatest, the Angel thought. *And so my need is the greatest. Father, hear my cry. Bring me to you.*

His great wings folded, one hand resting on the pommel of the *Blade Encarmine*, the Angel stood as a towering, meditative statue on the central command dais of the *Red Tear*'s bridge. By his word, a fleet went to war. The power of a Legion flowed from him, and his decisions, his acts, had brought the sin to all his sons. His must be the power now to wash away that sin.

From the dais' forwards, elevated position, Sanguinius had a panoramic view through the battleship's windows. He watched the warp-torn agony of the void for a few final seconds as the shutters began to close. The view of the Ruinstorm narrowed, and the tension of the crew increased. The humans had survived the madness that had fallen upon the fleet on the jump to Signus Prime, though they bore the psychic scars, memories like shards of glass digging at their courage. But they looked at him and drew strength, and performed their duties. A navigation officer began counting down. Her voice was steady, committed. One after another, officers called from their stations, announcing the readiness of the vessel.

A tremor ran through the decking as if the machine-spirit of the battleship were bracing itself. The *Red Tear* had fallen on Signus Prime. *Like so many of us,* the Angel thought. It had risen again. The years at Macragge had been time enough to repair the venerable ship. It was battle-worthy once more, but its scars ran as deep as those of the crew, as profound as the spiritual wounds inflicted on the Legion. Much had been lost. The lines of the battleship ran true. Its halls and bays were intact. Its weapons systems were fully operational. But the statues, the art and the manuscripts that had been burned were gone forever. The *Red Tear* had been the proud embodiment of the culture of Baal. Each destroyed artefact was a vanished piece of Blood Angels history. Sculptures, tapestries and tableaux still lined the corridors. Those that could be restored had been. Sanguinius had given orders that the others stay in their places. They were memorials now. And they were reminders that the IX Legion fought on, no matter its wounds, no matter the flaws that threatened to shatter its fundamental nobility.

The shutters closed. The Ruinstorm vanished from Sanguinius' view. It remained before his mind's eye. The rage of madness tore at the materium. It hid the stars. It was a howling promise of destruction, an endlessly twisting slashing at reality. Yet this bloody pyre of existence was just a foretaste of what waited in the warp itself. The warp that Sanguinius knew held worse than just the breakdown of sanity. There were deeper forces there, powers with sentience and will.

He had fought them. He and his Legion had fought them, and they had triumphed. If it was time to fight them again, then he and his sons were ready.

Yet he felt the wounds. He felt them in his crew, in his ship, in his Legion, in his soul.

Seated on the *Red Tear*'s command throne, Carminus called out. 'My lord,' he said, 'the jumps of the First and Thirteenth Legions are confirmed.'

'Thank you,' Sanguinius said to the captain of the Third Company. He had made Carminus temporary fleet master during the exodus from the Signus System. There had been time to find a mortal officer suitable for the command, but the Angel had decided Carminus should lead the fleet again. Even if all went well, the journey through the warp was going to be a long one. After what had happened at Signus Prime, Sanguinius needed a genhanced human at the post, someone with a stronger resistance to the attacks of madness.

At the Angel's side, Raldoron said, 'May we meet our brothers again at journey's end.'

'We will,' Sanguinius told him. The First Captain had been in favour of the combined forces of the three fleets striking out together. Even if the primarchs had been of the same mind, their approaches to the journey were too different. *We each have our hopes, our convictions, and our sins,* he thought. Guilliman's fleet was attacking the warp in a systematic manner, seeking to batter the storm into submission with the brute force of reason. As for the Lion...

Sanguinius did not know his strategy. He did not know how the Lion would travel through the warp. But in their last meeting together in the Fortress of Hera, where Roboute had looked determined, the Lion had appeared confident. He fully expected to reach Terra.

Sanguinius envied his brother's confidence at the same time that he distrusted it. Certainty had brought catastrophe to the Imperium. Sanguinius had been certain of Horus. And what was Curze, if not certain of the truth in whose name he had slaughtered?

The Blood Angels had been lost in the Ruinstorm when they tried to reach Terra after Signus. There was no reason to believe the passage would be any easier now. Sanguinius knew to hold fast to the certainty of uncertainty. All there was to take the Legion through the storm was urgency.

Urgency, and the need for redemption.

There had been no ceremony to mark the departure of the fleets from Macragge. There had been no formal taking of leave by the Triumvirate. The Emperor, the Lord Warden and the Lord Protector had left, each taking two-thirds of their fleets. Those who remained would guard

Ultramar under the regency of Valentus Dolor. Imperium Secundus no longer existed, except as a fiction Sanguinius despised as much as he understood its necessity. Some form of continuity had to be maintained to preserve what order had been restored to the Five Hundred Worlds. Until Terra was found again, until the Emperor was proven to be alive, the Angel's official status could not change. For the billions of Ultramar, he was the Emperor Sanguinius. His sin could not be erased by edict. It could only be forgiven by his father.

My sin is the greatest.

The Angel was the usurper. He had sat upon a false throne and been called Emperor. Not even Horus had managed to go so far.

Father, hear my cry.

Urgency drove all three fleets. Urgency to reach Terra and confound Horus. The traitors had done their work well, convincing three Legions that there was no Terra to aid. The Ruinstorm was not just a barrier, it was a veil concealing the truth and had led to the lie of the Imperium Secundus. The lie was over now, but the barrier remained. To purge the sin of usurpation and save Terra, the task was clear.

Break through the Ruinstorm.

'The fleet is ready, lord,' Carminus said. 'We jump at your command.'

Father, bring me to you.

Sanguinius sent his need towards hidden Terra. He could not call it hope, the thing that would travel with his fleet through the warp, this convulsion in his soul that the galaxy felt too small to contain. He could not expect it would guide them to his father. But he reached out as if it would. In the exodus from Signus, anger and military priorities had been the driving needs. They were still present, but the desperate reach for redemption was even more powerful. If Sanguinius stretched out his arm, surely he should be able to grasp the path to Terra.

The need was that strong.

But there was no certainty, and he would not fall to the illusion.

He turned to Mkani Kano. The Librarian stood at Raldoron's right hand. 'Your men are at their posts?' he asked. Sanguinius had ordered a Librarian be stationed in the Navigation chambers of every vessel in the fleet. They were to do what they could to protect the fragile humans from the forces that would come for them in the immaterium. There was no more certainty they would succeed than there was of reaching Terra.

'They stand ready,' said Kano.

Sanguinius turned his back on the shutters. He faced his sons and the human crew. Below the dais was a squad of Raldoron's Sanguinary Guard. With them was the Angel's herald. This was his sacrificial son, the legionary whose identity Sanguinius had necessarily hidden from himself, who had become the Angel's voice in the Imperium Secundus. It was he who had been the figure most of the supplicants to the throne had seen, and not Sanguinius. The Angel now saw this son's sacrifice as all the greater for having been part of an immoral folly. His presence on the bridge, close to Sanguinius, was in recognition of his service, and as a visible reminder of the need for atonement. The sacrifices his sons had made weighed heavily on his mind. On Signus Prime, Meros had taken his place to become the Red Angel, giving up all nobility and humanity to become the worst of the Blood Angels' savagery. The herald lived, and remained human, but the price he paid was a high one. His helm kept his face hidden, and would until the legionary's death. Sanguinius was no longer Emperor. There was no need for the role of herald any longer. Yet the legionary's identity remained subsumed by his duty.

What you have created, you must not destroy.

The instinct was imperative. The herald had a significance that Sanguinius could not see yet. The role was needed. There was something in it he had created that was pure, that was the best of what the Blood Angels could be.

'Let us strike forth to Terra,' Sanguinius pronounced, and the power of his voice made the walls of the bridge thrum. 'Shipmaster,' he said to Carminus, 'signal the fleet. We jump.'

'So ordered, lord,' Carminus replied.

Father, hear my cry.

Reality, bleeding and savaged by the Ruinstorm, tore wide open. The Blood Angels plunged into the vortex of the warp consumed by rage. A klaxon sounded as the *Red Tear*'s Geller field shrieked with strain.

Then reality collapsed. Only Sanguinius felt it from within his perceptions. He saw the shutters ripple and bulge. They flowed like liquid. The shapes of his legionaries smeared into nothing. Then the command deck vanished from his sight.

Blows hammered his frame and stabbed his mind. His eyes were filled with a colossal figure in sin-black armour. Crimson eyes blazed. Fratricidal hate battered the breath of life from his body. Horus was the shape. Horus was killing him. The Angel's death fell on him with a piercing immediacy. Blood soaked his sides and poured through rents in his armour. His hearts lurched under the agony of the terminal vision. The future grasped Sanguinius, a future where his hearts no longer beat, where the pain and fire of a lost, final battle dropped him into the endless dark.

Here was certainty.

Here was the end of all doubt.

Sanguinius had thought he had come to terms with the inevitability of his death. If it was the price of saving his father, he would be the willing sacrifice. Yet now, as the attack sought to buckle him under its fury, as the maw of the dark gaped wide to swallow him, he did not feel the acceptance of the good death. He answered the rage with his own. It was rage at betrayal, at treachery and at crime that surpassed all understanding. Destruction took him, and he howled at the night, howled with a hate greater than he had ever known, yet was his completely, as much a part of his identity as the light he embraced. As the pain dragged him down, his howl filled the dark, becoming one with it. The howl grew, echoing, redoubling, shattering time and reason and hope.

Death was his destiny. So too, was the howl.

Father.

My cry.

Sanguinius fought back. He hurled his will against the wall of night and pain. Horus was not here. Horus was not looming in triumph over him. The reality of his death was not now. The future had not come. Not yet. Not yet.

The Angel clenched his fists. His body responded to his will, and he took hold once more of his present self. He denied the pain of his ending. He pushed through it, rising as if from the depths of a molten ocean. He spread his wings in defiance and in the assertion of victory. The vision broke up. It did not vanish at once; it fragmented, its shards stabbing him to the last. Jagged patterns of black and blood and silver flashed and shimmered. They burned his vision, then fell like scales as he forced his way back to the real. The bridge reappeared, first as an uncertain transmission, then gathering substance, and at last the vision faded.

Sanguinius exhaled. He had been in the grip of his death for the space of a single breath. Across the bridge, mortals and Space Marines struggled with psychic injuries. The warp storm was so furious that strands found minute weaknesses in the Geller field and forced their way through them. Servitors flailed at their stations, their limbs jerking chaotically, energy sparking out of the points of fusion between their flesh and machinic components. Officers clutched their heads. Some were screaming. Some were on their knees, jaws clattering hard enough to splinter teeth.

But the damage was less than it might have been. The crew was strong. It had been tempered by Signus. Every man and woman on the bridge had survived the insanity that had taken so many of their comrades. They had been braced for the jump. In the midst of the siege of insanity, the command deck continued to function. After a few moments, someone shut down the klaxons. Medicae personnel pulled the incapacitated and the raving from the bridge.

Raldoron looked shaken, but was standing firm. Kano was doubled over, a hissing snarl of pain and anger escaping from his clenched teeth.

A nimbus of unlight flared at the edges of his psychic hood. Sanguinius placed a hand on the Librarian's shoulder. Kano felt his presence. He straightened. The dark glow dissipated, and his eyes cleared. He looked at Sanguinius with deep anguish. 'My lord,' he said, 'I saw…'

'You saw what has not come to pass. It does not matter.' *For now,* he added to himself. 'What matters is how the present moment tasks us.'

Kano nodded, strain visible on his face. He was holding off the immaterium's attack, but it had not ceased.

Sanguinius turned back to Carminus. 'Shipmaster,' he said, 'what is the status of the fleet?'

'All vessels accounted for, but communications are breaking down,' said Carminus.

'Are there reports from the Navigators?'

'No, though there have been no casualties among them.'

The best we can hope for, then. With Terra invisible, there was no clear course to take through the warp, but if the coherence of the fleet was holding, the Navigators were managing, for the moment, to cleave to the course he had set them. The grand flotilla had direction. He could only hope it also had a destination.

The Angel moved to the command dais' hololith plate. 'I will speak to the fleet,' he said. While communications still functioned, he would impart what strength he could to his sons.

Carminus pulled a lever on the console next to the throne, and the plate crackled to life. The hololith caster in every bay and hall of every vessel projected his image to the Blood Angels and to their mortal crews.

'The transmission quality is erratic,' said Varra Neverrus. The vox-officer barely looked up as she worked the controls at her station. 'I don't know how long it can be sustained.'

Sanguinius nodded. He thought he could feel the dissolution of his image as it reached through the warp, the claws of the immaterium tearing apart the transmissions, fracturing the self he was sending to his sons.

He had spoken to the fleet before the jump to Signus. That had been the Blood Angels' last moment of true hope, and the last moment of delusion. They had been through the fire of ultimate treachery and of destroying revelation. There was no hope to speak of now. No promise of a cure. He would speak instead of strength and faith.

'My sons,' he said. 'Legionaries of the Ninth, our war for Terra has already begun. The storm is our enemy as surely as Horus is. We know the nature of our foes much better than before. We know the truth of the danger they present. We are attacked on fronts far beyond the physical. We have seen how they might destroy us. But they have failed, and we are the stronger for it. Your armour is more than ceramite. You know what is in your blood. You know what you are capable of.' He chose his words deliberately. Every Blood Angel would hear the two meanings of that sentence. He needed them to. The flaw he had cursed them with had almost destroyed them. 'You know what you must guard against. Make that defence a sword. Its blade is the forged adamantium of our noble selves. Let us burn our way to Terra with the flames of our loyalty to the Emperor.'

He stopped speaking. He knew the hololith transmission had broken down before Neverrus told him it had.

Furious waves of unreality slammed against the hull of the *Red Tear*. The hololith plate screamed.

The edges of the Angel's vision cracked. Filaments of darkness coiled. The endlessly repeated moment of his death stabbed inwards to his consciousness.

Sanguinius strode to the edge of the command dais. The hull groaned. The empyrean's convulsions were roars and whispers that battered the ears and slid into the veins.

'We fly on righteous wings,' he thundered, defying the storm. 'We cannot be stopped.'

The warp seemed to answer him. A massive surge struck the fleet. Even shielded by the Geller field, the auspex readings fell into shrieking madness. Pict screens shuddered, and their images suddenly looked too much like flesh. Vox-casters squawked and rasped with incoming transmissions, as broken and static-disrupted as they were urgent.

'The *Encarnadine* has a Geller field breach,' Neverrus said. 'Incursions on the *Scarlet Liberty*, *Sable* and *Requiem Axona*.'

Sanguinius pressed his lips together. An instinct, deep and ancient, insisted that the apparent response of the warp to his challenge was no illusion. The fleet was not just battered by the vortices the traitors had summoned into being. This attack was directed.

Directed at him.

I do not accept this, he thought. The implications were too grotesque. He was deluding himself with sinful pride. It was the same hubris that had convinced him the Imperium's salvation depended on his taking the throne. Would he now decide the empyrean itself was attacking him?

No.

And yet. And yet.

The *Red Tear* shuddered. The huge battleship was tossed by the fury of the warp.

The death vision pressed harder, a bare membrane of consciousness holding it back. Beyond the vision, there was something else. A hint of shadow, the weight of a huge displacement wave, the thing that pushed the vision upon him, that used the storm against the fleet.

You are watched. You are targeted.

Again, he tried to shake the delusions off. His mind must be clear. There were threats enough that were real without him clouding his decision-making with hubristic anguish. Whether or not he, personally, was the subject of the attack, something was coming. The threads of unreality were already reaching into the ship. A serious breach was imminent.

Sanguinius drew the *Blade Encarmine* from its sheath. Raldoron, in his office of equerry, approached and handed him the *Spear of Telesto*. Behind him, the doors of the bridge opened and Azkaellon led his Sanguinary Guard out to surround the command dais. At the sight of the gathering might of the Blood Angels, the human crew drew courage. The moans quieted. The officers worked their stations, holding the course of the *Red Tear* as true as they could in a realm where truth drew the blood of reason.

Claws scratched at the hull. They scraped along it, as if it were a thin wall of tin. The shutters bulged again, and yet again, with the rhythm of strange lungs.

The breach came in the bridge's vault. It snaked in sharp angles down the height of the wall. It vibrated with the hum of a million flies. It began to peel back, metal framework and marble cladding turning flesh-red, flesh-supple, flesh-weak. The buzzing of the flies filled the command deck. The taste of the sound was foul on Sanguinius' tongue. He felt the crawl of legs and the flutter of wings.

A bell tolled, and with the chanting of a thousand festering tongues, the tear split wide.

TWO

Divisions

His name had been Toc Derenoth. He still accepted the syllables as a designation of his physical presence, but they were no longer the sum of his being. He had once marched in the Third Hand of the Word Bearers, but he had transcended that role. He had once served the Chaplain Kurtha Sedd. He had transcended that role, too. He had become the greater truth of the Word. He was two and he was one. He had cast away limits of flesh and the lies of old existence.

He was Unburdened.

He had resisted the coming of his transformation. In the profound depths of Calth, Kurtha Sedd had brought the gift upon him, and he had struggled to hold on to his trivial humanity. He had sinned against the Word. He had spurned the will of the gods. And so, there had been penance.

He was Unburdened, yet he was imprisoned. He sat in the command throne of the battle-barge *De Profundis*. Psychic and physical chains bound him there. His nerves and the power conduits of the ship were one. Throughout the halls and chambers of the vessel, a ritual was proceeding, binding his being and the ship's more and more tightly.

He welcomed the duty of his chains because they presaged his bloody redemption. They were an agony as sublime as his transformation. Arrogance and selfish designs had, in the end, doomed Kurtha Sedd, who had sought his own transformation too late. Toc Derenoth had learned obedience. He had learned to submit to goals greater than his own, and he had been rewarded. A being had come to him on Calth. It called itself a celebrant of undivision. It took him from Calth. It brought him to the *De Profundis* to take part in a great hunt.

When the ritual was complete, he would be unleashed upon the prey.

Not long. Not long.

His jaws parted in the long, slavering smile of truth.

'WE'RE LOSING FORMATION coherence,' said Verus Caspean, Chapter Master of the First.

So soon. Guilliman kept the frustration from his face. This jump was even shorter than the last, and the storm was about to force his squadron back into real space.

The strategium of the *Samothrace* could be sealed off from the bridge and its distractions of moment-to-moment demands. The doors were closed now, turning the chamber into a sanctuary of war governance. Here the theoretical was tested. From here, the practical issued. The dome of the strategium was lower than that of the bridge, the darkness of its stone illuminated by a hololithic projection of the regional star chart. The relative closeness of the walls and the constant presence of the immediate battlefield focused the mind.

The star chart was a complete blank during the transition through the warp. That was the one note of grace as the operation continued to break down. Guilliman took in the essentials of the onrushing, overlapping reports. The hololiths on the tacticarium table were a patchwork of approximations, guesses and darkness. It mocked Guilliman. It was the evidence of his campaign's theoretical devolving into a pointless exercise, one that no practical could salvage.

He had divided his fleet into strike forces, each powerful enough to annihilate a system. He had ordered tight formations. If the warp storms pulled the ships away from each other, their jump was to cease and the strike force reassemble before a new attempt was made. The wrenching apart was already occurring, and Guilliman's cohort had barely started this jump.

The deck heaved as the *Samothrace* ploughed through the storm. The Ultramarines officers gathered in the strategium did not shift with the motion. They were solid as marble columns. From the corner of his eye, Guilliman saw a ripple crawl down one side of the doorway. The materiality of the ship was less stable than his sons.

'Theoretical,' said Titus Prayto, speaking over the droning vox-speakers solemnly announcing the formation's disintegration. 'The increased resistance is evidence that this route is the correct one.'

'An inviting theoretical,' Guilliman told the Librarian. 'One dangerously close to wishful thinking.'

Prayto nodded once. 'Admittedly so.'

'And we have no choice but to verify it,' Guilliman said. 'Shipmaster,' he voxed Turetia Altuzer, 'end the jump.'

'*So ordered, my lord.*'

Deep in its core, the *Samothrace* shuddered. The tremor swept along the length of the ship. It passed under Guilliman's feet. He grimaced in sympathy for the great vessel's pain. A moment later, there was a change in the air, a more assured reality. They had returned to the materium.

After a series of flickers, the star chart appeared in the vault again. Guilliman glanced up.

'Apologies,' Prayto said. 'That *was* wishful thinking.'

The stars were a scattered few. There was even more cogitator extrapolation than with the fleet positions. The Ruinstorm made even the most basic navigational measurements uncertain. Entire star systems, even ones that were theoretically in the near vicinity, were as invisible as Terra. There was still enough data for Guilliman to see the strike force's position. The *Samothrace* and its escorts were on the north-western fringe of Ultramar, a bare few light years from their previous position.

They had moved laterally along the border. If there had been any progress towards Terra, it was well disguised. The nearest system was Anuari, and it was on the western edge of the chart, hardly close enough to register. The strike force had emerged in the deep void.

'We're scattered,' said Drakus Gorod, commander of the Suzerain Invictus bodyguards.

The tacticarium table blinked and rearranged its runes to reflect the new positions of the strike force. The ships had been thrown like a handful of bones across the region. Only the strike cruiser *Cavascor* was still attending the *Samothrace*.

'Your theoretical may still be worth pursuing,' Guilliman said to Prayto. He tried to push away the suspicion he was grasping at straws. Self-doubt had become an unwelcome, frequent companion. He had believed he had thought through all the possible consequences of Imperium Secundus. He had included, at its very inception, the contingency that his father was still on the throne of Terra. He worried that had been lip service to something he had not really believed was possible. If he had thought there truly was a chance that Horus had not conquered Terra, he wondered if he would have made the crime of Imperium Secundus a reality.

He didn't know.

The Imperium Secundus had been a practical in response to a theoretical whose foundations he could not trust.

Prayto's idea engaged with active conditions, and proposed a possible course of action. The search for a way forwards had failed so far. The signals from the other strike forces were becoming more broken and erratic, and they were no closer to finding the path to Terra.

'We regroup,' Guilliman said, 'and then we make another attempt following the last route.'

'And the other strike forces?'

Guilliman scanned the parchments chattering out of servo-skulls hovering over the table. They were transcriptions of astropathic communications arriving from the other battle group. They were more and more vague. The distances were taking their toll. The Ruinstorm was becoming a wall between his ships. He had gone as far as he dared down this path. 'Signal them,' he said. 'We'll gather the fleet and start the search again, spreading outwards from this position.'

The tacticarium table blinked.

'Contact,' said Caspean. 'Not ours.'

'Analysis and theoreticals now,' Guilliman ordered. 'Doors open.'

The strategium opened up to the bridge. Guilliman strode through the doors while they were still grinding apart. The primary oculus revealed the Ruinstorm in full anger. Searing vortices and uncolours exploded in the dark. There were no stars. The void screamed, and in the insanity to the fore of the ship, other vessels were closing.

'I want energy signatures and I want identities,' Guilliman said. 'Shipmaster, set an attack vector. Communications, get me Chapter Master Iasus.'

One step behind him, Prayto said, 'This cannot be a coincidence.'

'It isn't,' Guilliman agreed. 'It's an ambush.'

'The alert has been sent to all ships,' Altuzer said, anticipating his order.

'If we rush the enemy with only two ships...' Prayto began.

Guilliman cut him off. 'Theoretical – if it's an ambush, our retreat will already be accounted for. Practical – disrupt the enemy formation with maximum aggression.'

'We have Chapter Master Iasus,' said Junixa Terrens, the vox-officer.

Guilliman turned to a vox-unit on the pulpit that overlooked the bridge.

'*The* Cavascor *stands ready, lord,*' the commander of the 22nd Chapter said.

The companies of Destroyers would be straining at the reins to bring their violence to the traitors. By the standards of Guilliman's Legion, they were brutal, even under the moderating command of Iasus. He would be glad to unleash them today. 'It will be our two ships,' Guilliman said. 'The others are too far away to reach us in time.'

'*So I presumed.*'

'Forwards elements identified,' Nestor Lautenix at the auspex array station called. 'The lead ship is the battle-barge *De Profundis*.' The grey-haired officer frowned. 'I think,' he said. 'There are anomalies…'

'There would be,' Prayto said. 'Trust your initial judgement, lieutenant.'

'Word Bearers,' Guilliman breathed. His right cheek twitched once.

'More contacts,' Lautenix said. 'Another squadron coming in below the ecliptic, thirty degrees to port. Elements of the Twelfth Legion. Battle-barges and strike cruisers closing at ramming speed.'

'To be expected,' Guilliman said, dismissive. 'The World Eaters wouldn't think of anything beyond a brute force attack.' The holo-lithic display of the tacticarium table became populated with signals. Guilliman stared at the rune of the *De Profundis*. His fists clenched. 'Take us at full speed into the vermin of the Seventeenth.'

'The World Eaters won't expect recklessness from us,' said Prayto approvingly. 'And this will take the *Samothrace* and *Cavascor* out of the direct line of the attacks.'

'And tear the heart out of the Word Bearers,' Guilliman snarled.

Battleship and strike cruiser accelerated towards the Word Bearers formation. Guilliman watched through the oculus for the enemy to emerge from the Ruinstorm. He felt the rising power of the engines as an expression of the *Samothrace*'s wrath.

Then torpedoes slammed into the stern shields.

THE CROW HAD haunted the bowels of the *Invincible Reason* before. He had been the spectral shadow, a thing of darkness and talons, tearing apart any who hunted him. He had claimed an entire region of the capital ship as his own, taunting his brother by stealing what was his.

It was fitting, then, the Lion thought, that Konrad Curze should be deep in the night of the *Reason* once more. If he liked it so well, he should dwell in it. His domain was much smaller, though. It was a cell, isolated at the end of a long corridor, two hundred feet from the rest of the prison. An iron chair sat against the left wall for the Lion's use. The chamber's ceiling was low, not much more than ten feet above the deck. It was high enough, though. High enough to keep the Night Haunter suspended above the floor. Adamantium manacles the length of his forearms held him to the wall, his limbs outstretched. The crow's wings were spread, but he would not fly. The door to the cell was ten feet thick. The walls were twice that. The cell was a vault. The crow was caged. There was nothing for him to haunt except memories.

And yet he smiled when the Lion entered the cell. Black lips stretched over black teeth. His white flesh was the colour of drowned hope. His eyes were dark as rotten blood. They glittered with madness, with pain, and with amusement born of perfect despair.

'Do you really think it will be that easy?' Curze said.

The Lion made a point of ignoring him. He walked past his brother and sat in the chair, judge and gaoler, forcing Curze to turn his head awkwardly to see him. Curze did, still smiling.

'Do you?' said Curze.

The Lion remained silent.

'You are not going to Terra,' Curze said.

The ship jolted, struck by a series of huge waves in the immaterium. The Lion waited for the deck to settle, then finally spoke. 'You think not.' He was not amusing himself. He was not here for petty reasons. He wanted to see what knowledge he could make Curze let slip. The Night Haunter's vision was twisted, but he also saw further than any of his brothers. If the Lion could parse the lies from the hints, he might be left with fragments of the future to use in the struggle ahead.

Curze glanced up, as if looking through the ceiling. He frowned slightly, touched by curiosity. 'My sense of wonder died long ago,' he said. 'And there isn't much for me to wonder about any more. I know where everything leads. I know the truths you try to hide from yourself, brother. Even so, I wonder how you travel.' He paused. The grin became an insinuation. 'You do get around. Much more easily than Roboute or poor, suffering Sanguinius.'

'I'm sure you have a point, Konrad.'

Curze could not shrug. Instead, he cocked his head to one side. 'I just think this secret of yours is interesting. You are on a journey with it. Your destination will be fascinating.'

'My destination is Terra.'

'Did you come here just to wilfully misunderstand me?'

'You claimed I would not reach Terra. I tell you that I will.'

'No. You are wrong.'

The statement was unusually direct, coming from Curze.

'I see,' the Lion said. He permitted himself a small, grim smile. He showed his mad brother his lack of concern. 'You know this as an immutable fact, do you?'

'I do.'

'Then where are we arriving?'

'That would be telling, wouldn't it?'

There was still the icy glint of mockery in those abyssal eyes, mockery lashing out from the depths of the most profound anguish. But the Lion caught Curze's hesitation. It was tiny, a fragment of a fragment of a second. It was real, though. Curze's facial muscles contracted in a microscopic gesture. The change would have been invisible to anyone except the Lion. He knew about secrets, how to keep them, and how to detect them. He saw one now. The Night Haunter had just shown him uncertainty.

You don't know, the Lion thought. *There is something you aren't sure about, and that bothers you.* For a moment, the thought of Konrad's bloody conviction being shaken at all was satisfying. Then the emotion shaded into concern. Curze rattled, however minutely, was an omen. The question was how to read it.

The ship jolted again, this time with the hard shock of the translation to the materium. The Lion forced down a grunt of surprise. This was too soon. He had not expected the jump to end now.

His vox-bead buzzed for his attention.

Curze laughed, his breath a foetid wheeze. 'News!' he rasped. 'News! Enlightenment is upon you, brother. Will you stay and share the moment with me?'

'I was not to be interrupted,' the Lion said to the vox.

'*Your pardon, my lord,*' said Captain Stenius. '*But your presence is needed on the bridge.*' The urgency of the request lurked beneath its flat delivery.

The Lion stood. 'On my way,' he said.

At the entrance to the cell he paused and met Curze's eyes. 'I think you're curious, Konrad,' he said. Then he slammed the vault door behind him.

'HAVE WE ARRIVED at Terra?' the Lion asked Stenius as he marched towards the grav lift that would take him to the bridge.

'*We have not.*'

'Then where are we?'

'*We don't know.*'

'THE IDENTITY OF the *Samothrace* is confirmed,' said Grel Kathnar. The Word Bearer bowed his head and returned to his station.

'Will he be on board?' Phael Rabor asked Quor Vondor.

'That is his flagship,' the Chaplain answered. 'He'll be there.' His hand went to his belt and touched the hilt of the athame. He saw Phael Rabor make the same gesture. *We are nemesis,* he thought. Guilliman had not died on Calth, because his death had been reserved for the two of them. They had earned the blessing through trial and through faith. The proof of the favour granted them sat on the transformed command throne of the *De Profundis.*

The entire bridge had undergone a profound change. It was barely recognisable as the command deck of a battle-barge. The walls and the oculus rippled like curtains. Curving columns radiated from the throne, crossing the floor and rising up the walls, partitioning the bridge as if it were gripped by a great talon. The claws were outlined by glowing fissures. The cracks extended through the entire length of the *De Profundis.* The empyrean was pressing through, splitting the ship and holding it together.

Below the throne, the workstations had become shifting sculptures.

Their shapes were ornate, slowly waving flames. The silhouettes were laden with meaning. They were the manifestation of truths unutterable by human tongues. They were another form of the Word, speaking truth to the real, eroding the illusions of the universe, each movement another razor wound opening the way to revelation. They could no longer be operated by unaltered mortals. Word Bearers were at the posts, at one with the lethal truths as they governed weapons systems and prepared attack vectors. But Quor Vondor recognised the actions as the dying echoes of the former being of the ship. The *De Profundis* would not attack as it once had.

The oculus twitched. Streaks of light appeared, heading for the blue glint of the *Samothrace*. The World Eaters' attack. Quor Vondor sniffed in contempt. The World Eaters were useful, but barbarians. The Night Lords, even now launching the rear assault, were closer in their beings to the primordial truth, even though their faith was lacking. They had their uses, too.

'The Eighth and Twelfth Legions might finish him off before we get a chance,' Phael Rabor said.

'They won't.'

'There are only two Ultramarines vessels.'

'Do you think Guilliman is going to die so easily?'

'No,' the captain admitted.

'No,' Quor Vondor repeated. 'Do your doubts come so easily?'

'I have none,' said Phael Rabor.

'That is well.' There could be no more doubts. Not after Calth.

Not with Toc Derenoth sitting on the command throne.

The Unburdened turned his horned head to look at Quor Vondor, as if he had heard the Chaplain's thoughts. The elongated jaws gaped in anticipation. Before his ascension, Toc Derenoth had been a mere legionary. Now Quor Vondor had to look at him as a wonder.

The underworld war on Calth had been raging for years before he and Phael Rabor had encountered Toc Derenoth. The ascended Word Bearer had fought on since the destruction of Kurtha Sedd, killing

Ultramarines without rest. But his transformation had also been a continuous evolution, an ever more complex fusion of the daemonic and
the human. He had communed more and more deeply with the gods.
And he had gone deeper and deeper into the darkness of the planet.

He had touched the octed.

He had learned.

And in the end, through him, Quor Vondor and Phael Rabor had
completed their penance too. They had brought their forces to the
octed in the purity of worship and devotion to Chaos. They were present without thought of ambition or rivalries.

The octed tore open the night of stone, and swallowed the devout.
And in the warp, the celebrant appeared. It was a being of the immaterium, yet Quor Vondor had seen something of his own calling in it.
The celebrant was a Chaplain, though of a kind and of an order far
beyond anything human.

The celebrant brought them a mission. Quor Vondor still wondered
if the mission was a sign that he and the others with them had purged
the weakness of their failure, or if the gauntlet of Calth had instead
been the proving ground. Perhaps it had been the fire through which
he and Phael Rabor had been destined to walk so they might reach this
point, this moment, when at last they would unsheathe the athames
they had been given on Davin and drive them home.

The spark of Guilliman's vessels grew brighter. The two ships became
visible. They were rushing in, as if eager for the doom awaiting them.
The ships flashed.

'Torpedo launches,' Phael Rabor said. 'A sound strategy, trying to
break up our formation with a hard run.'

'It would be,' said Quor Vondor. He looked at Toc Derenoth once
more. The Unburdened had withdrawn into himself. Shadows gathered
around his monstrous form. He was feeding on the ritual performed
by the faithful throughout the ship. His lidless eyes burned with the
intensity of his concentration. He was the conduit of what was coming. His role was as precise as the one given to Quor Vondor and Phael

Rabor. They would wield the blades. Toc Derenoth would bring them to Guilliman.

The Unburdened had the power to do this because the *De Profundis* had also earned a gift from the celebrant. It had been badly damaged in the battle over Calth. It had limped out of the system, and existed as a raider in the years that followed. Its injuries grew worse, more and more of its crew died, until at last it was a husk, its machine-spirit raging impotently in the void. The warp had taken it at last, and its faithful service to the Word was rewarded with this last mission.

Quor Vondor had found himself aboard the battle-barge in the midst of its transfiguration. In the midst of the changes, he had looked out between the gaps in the vessel's being. He had caught glimpses of the Intercessor, and of the vastness that brought its blessing to the *De Profundis*. That such things had being had brought him and Phael Rabor worshipfully to their knees. In these visions, the truth of the faith was confirmed. The sublimities were the agents of the Word's fulfilment.

'The Ultramarines are increasing speed and rate of fire,' said Grel Kathnar.

A wave of torpedoes and missiles cut through the void towards the *De Profundis*. A warning klaxon sounded, its voice a moan that rose and fell. There was nothing machinic about the sound any longer, and the cry was one of celebration, not distress. Culmination was at hand.

'We are at the centre and the head of our formation,' Phael Rabor said. 'He is right to target us.'

'You mean he would be,' Quor Vondor said, 'if this ship and we were as we had once been.' He grinned. His jagged, curving incisors drew blood from his lips as they pulled back.

Phael Rabor nodded. 'As you say, Chaplain. And he is behaving as you predicted.'

'Rushing onto the point of our blades.' He drew the athame.

Phael Rabor followed his example. 'The moment is upon us?'

'It is.' Quor Vondor gestured at the columns on the walls. The glow of the warp was blinding. The structure of the ship trembled.

Toc Derenoth hissed. The Unburdened seemed to grow bulkier. The tendons of his arms, running along armour and flesh without distinction, were rigid and thick as chains. His monstrous head reared back in the ecstasy of his great work. He was the conduit for the force that held the *De Profundis* together, and that was shaping its final attack.

Quor Vondor and Phael Rabor moved to the fore of the elevated platform that held the command throne. Quor Vondor stood in the pulpit. 'Faithful of the Word,' he called, and the legionaries below turned from their stations to look at him. 'Your mundane work is done,' he said. 'Now there is only glory. Prepare, and bear witness to the glory of Chaos. We go to kill a primarch.'

The Word Bearers bowed as one, then turned to face the oculus. They took up bolters and chainswords. The bridge rang with the clank and growl of weapons being readied. The klaxons shrieked in a frenzy as the Ultramarines ordnance closed in. From aft, on all sides, the Word Bearers fired back. The attack would not be enough to kill the battleship and the strike cruiser, but it would strain their void shields.

The Night Lords maintained pressure from the rear, and Guilliman's ships were lit by the throbbing aura of flaring energy. The World Eaters squadron was altering the course of its run, having overshot the Ultramarines. The ships were making their turns, slow as continents. Quor Vondor pictured the fury of the captains aboard. Their cannons lashed out in anger, lines of fire cutting across the spirals of the Ruinstorm.

The torpedoes hit. Toc Derenoth shouted with two voices. A daemon laughed in triumph, and a human exulted in the joy of revelation.

The *De Profundis* had no shields. It welcomed the impacts. They completed the ritual. Explosions blossomed on its bow and across the face of its superstructure. The bridge took a direct hit. The fissures blazed, ignited by the blast. Toc Derenoth reached forwards with both arms, his claws spread, lunging for prey. The fissures yawned wide.

Quor Vondor roared, his voice drowned in the screaming thunder of the sundering of the *De Profundis*. The illusion of hull integrity vanished. The battle-barge shrieked its last. Adamantium tore apart.

Conduits split and split again, filling disintegrating halls with streams of burning plasma. The engines raged, then fell silent in a blinding flare that incinerated the light cruiser *Levana*, which had strayed too close to destiny.

The *De Profundis* screamed, and it screamed in victory. It streaked towards the *Samothrace*, its course as unalterable as prophecy. Its crew was dead, but the splinters were not mere shrapnel. They had coherent form. They were daggers. Inside scores of them, Word Bearers crouched, hurtling towards their prey.

The physical self of the battle-barge disintegrated, but its soul and its purpose did not. The *one* of the ship ceased to be. It transformed into *legion*.

It became the undivided swarm.

THREE

Dark Unities

'WHERE ARE WE?' the Lion demanded.

'Still unknown,' said Holguin, voted lieutenant of the Deathwing. He observed the fury in his primarch's eyes. There was far more than frustration there. The Lion had truly expected to reach Terra. He was reacting to the failure and confusion with anger reserved for betrayal. Holguin could guess why. He wished he could not. He felt the urge to speak, to sound a warning. He knew how it would be received. He said nothing. The right moment might never come. This, though, was the worst.

The *Invincible Reason* shuddered, straining to keep to its course. Roiling gravitational forces battered the Dark Angels fleet almost as violently as the tempest in the empyrean. The vessels had translated into the materium on the edge of a system caught in a maelstrom. The boundary of the system was marked by a barrier of furious warp flame. Ahead and to port, billions of miles of madness exploded and stormed.

The wall was an aurora of blood. It billowed with such violence that the Lion could hear the roar of tortured existence in his soul. Cyclonic currents the size of gas giants collided, merged and broke asunder. The engines of the fleet strained to move the ships away from the embrace of disaster.

Beyond the barrier, the Ruinstorm boiled across the void. A violent bruise of eye-searing colours filled the darkness. No stars were visible. The auspex officer was in communication with Lady Theralyn Fiana, the Chief Navigator, in her cell. They were struggling to get a fix on the fleet's location with almost no viable data.

'Your disapproval is deafening, Lady Fiana,' the Lion said.

'*I have not spoken, my lord,*' she said over the ship's internal vox.

'Even so.'

'*I have no control over our journey,*' she said. '*I therefore have little to go on to discover where we are. I think the means of our jump would be the first place to turn for answers.*'

'I want your evaluation first,' said the Lion.

He doesn't trust it, Holguin thought, and was glad. Some distance between the primarch and the thing in the dark chamber would be welcome.

In the near space of the barrier, between it and the Dark Angels fleet, was a graveyard of ships. Metal corpses tumbled slowly, caught in the random currents and bursts of gravity. Holguin saw two ships collide. They disintegrated, fragments spinning lazily off, glinting dully in the glare of the Ruinstorm. 'Do we know anything about this wreckage?' he asked.

'*The craft are not warp-capable,*' Fiana said. '*Beyond that, we can't tell. If we could identify where they came from, proximity might suggest where we are now.*'

The Lion's gaze was fixed on the warp storm. Holguin could not look at the vortex for more than a few moments at a time. The colours and movements ate at his mind, filling his thoughts with monstrous irrationalities, the fragments of waking nightmares. The Lion stared at the storm as if he would pierce through its secrets by will alone.

'This system,' said the Lion. 'It is so far gone. The event here is immense. Its traces must be felt from this location.'

'I agree,' said Fiana. 'If we had any readings at all of other stars, we might be able to factor in the distortion and form a hypothesis. The upheaval might even be detectable by others, much further away.'

'A dark beacon,' Holguin muttered.

'Exactly. But we are too close.'

'So there is nothing you can tell me,' the Lion said.

'That is correct.'

The primarch glared at the oculus a few moments longer, the green of his eyes going beyond ice, becoming sharp as a rapier. 'Keep at it,' he ordered. He turned on his heel and strode from the bridge.

Instinct urged Holguin to follow the Lion and be present when his lord confronted the thing that had brought the fleet here. Wisdom told him to stay where he was. The Lion in his fury would not tolerate any other presences at this encounter.

THE SERVITOR-PUPPET WALKED towards the Lion as he entered the chamber of Tuchulcha. The stench of the degrading body wafted before it. The boy-thing's gait was stiff. The puppet was already halfway to the entrance when the doors slid back. Tuchulcha's anticipation of his arrival was unpleasant. It was too knowing.

'I read anger in your face,' said the boy. 'But that is too easy a task to count as progress, I think. Your expression at this moment is not a challenge.'

'I told you to take me to Terra,' the Lion said. He looked past the puppet and addressed Tuchulcha itself. The gold flecks in the black-and-grey sphere moved more quickly for a moment, as if they were the shifting thoughts of the artefact.

Cables linked Tuchulcha to the spinal implants of the servitor. A split second after the burst of movement in the gold, the boy smiled, revealing blackened gums. It had lost more teeth during the passage through the warp. A clump of lank hair dropped from its mottled scalp to the deck. 'True,' the boy said. 'You did ask me to take you there.'

'You disobeyed me,' the Lion snarled.

'Did I say that I would bring you to Terra?'

The question gave the Lion pause. Before every other jump, Tuchulcha's puppet had confirmed the destination. This time, the boy had said, 'I will make the necessary jump.'

'Your sophistry will be your doom,' the Lion said. He drew his chainsword and it growled. It was an ancient weapon. Too large to be wielded by any son of Caliban except the Lion, it had been forgotten in the depths of Aldurukh, waiting for the Lion to appear and claim it. Its provenance had been lost. It had had no name before his coming. For the Lion, it would always be the *Wolf Blade*. With it, he had carved his way through the Knights of Lupus, ending their challenge to the Order and their corrupt use of the Great Beasts. The blade was a dull black except for the silver inlay of runic teeth. The chainsword was a brutal exterminator. It had none of the beauty of the *Lion Sword*, and there was no artistry in its kills. There was only finality.

The Lion raised it now, a single provocation away from cutting down the servitor. He did not know how to destroy Tuchulcha, but he was ready to explore every method.

The servitor cocked its head at the snarl of the *Wolf Blade*. The expression on its decaying face was simple interest. 'I did not betray you,' Tuchulcha said.

'Then why are we not at Terra?'

'That journey is too far, the storm too great. It is beyond my reach.'

'I find that hard to believe.'

'It is the truth. Do you prefer to believe I am omnipotent?' the thing mocked. 'Is that more comforting?'

The Lion lowered the chainsword, though he did not silence its engine. The teeth whirred around the edge of the blade. 'Tell me what you have done,' he said.

'I have taken you where you must go, if you wish to find Terra.'

'Have you?' He was suspicious, but he had not known Tuchulcha to lie to him yet. 'So where are we?'

'Pandorax.'

The puppet smiled, and the Lion's vox-bead buzzed for his attention. *'My lord,'* said Holguin, *'a warship is approaching.'*

THE BELLS TOLLED, and the daemons chanted. They spilled through the tear in the real and onto the bridge. Their voices were thick with phlegm and the buzzing of flies that flew in streams from between their lips. They were bulbous, rotting monsters. Their stench was an assault, a wall of gas emanating from ruptured organs and weeping innards. Clusters of open sores covered their flesh. The daemons were diseased. They were shambling creatures in the full blossom of decay. Yet their chanting, low and liquid and hollow, was also a kind of laughter, an expansive celebration of their condition and a promise to the universe that they had come to share the gift.

The abominations were joyful. Their joy was a horror, but it was also freely exultant in a way that Sanguinius could barely imagine any more. Joy had been foreign to him for so long, he was not sure he had ever truly experienced it. What happiness he could remember was a shadowed thing, haunted by the curse his blood had brought to his sons.

That monsters could revel in such unbridled joy was intolerable. In fury, Sanguinius launched himself across the bridge, wings opened wide, and came down in the midst of the daemons. Azkaellon called out to him as the Sanguinary Guard rushed forwards. Sanguinius barely heard him. He allowed himself the luxury of this moment of rage. Even then, he attacked with precision. The Angel struck the daemons midway between the front of their horde and the rear. A daemon burst apart under the impact of his descent. Bile, pus and rotting ichor splashed wide, liquid plague tainting the *Red Tear's* bridge. Sanguinius swept the *Blade Encarmine* before him. It sliced through daemonflesh as if through air. Its purity burned the bloated tissue and boiled ichor to steam. Decapitated horrors fell, their pitted blades clattering to the deck.

'Begone from my ship!' Sanguinius bellowed. He thrust the *Spear of Telesto* before him. The blast from the tip cut a swath through the daemons, incinerating them in a line that reached to the mouth of the breach. The edges of the fissure trembled as if recoiling from the Angel's wrath.

Iron blades clashed against his armour from behind. Sanguinius ignored the attacks, and in the next instant, the daemons turned away from him to confront the advance of the Sanguinary Guard through their ranks. Sanguinius marched forwards, destroying abominations with sword and spear, cutting short the obscene chants.

'We destroyed worse than you on Signus Prime,' he shouted at the daemons. 'You insult us with your presence.' His anger was mixed with contempt as he slashed the monsters apart. Even so, he did not lose himself in the battle. *Be cautious,* he thought. He had not seen these daemons before. They were distinct in kind from the ones the Blood Angels had fought on Signus Prime. The difference was important. It spoke to the very nature of these beings. They were embodiments. Sanguinius had a vision of disease itself become sentient, become divine. He wanted to deny the vision and the horrors it implied. He knew better than to give in to the impulse. Gods were real, and they were malign.

The Sanguinary Guard reached him. 'My lord,' Azkaellon began, an edge to his voice stopping just short of chiding.

'I know,' said Sanguinius. 'I make your task difficult.' He loosed another blast from the *Spear of Telesto,* turning a rush of daemons to ash. 'You are at my side now, Azkaellon. Destroy the foe with me. These things are fit only to be trampled.'

'They are still dangerous.'

Blood Angels were containing the plague daemons in the vicinity of the warp breach. But the traces of their foulness were reaching the wider area of the bridge. Officers had collapsed at their stations. Some vomited and shook with bone-wracking fever. One man was still, his face a mass of overlapping boils. Servitors were slumped, liquefying flesh drooping from their machinic parts. Illness marched ahead of the battle, laying claim to the *Red Tear.*

'Hurl them back!' Sanguinius shouted as two squads of Blood Angels thundered onto the bridge to join the Sanguinary Guard. 'Their taint goes not one step further. Tear them from reality.' *Send them back to the darkness of myth*, he was about to say. But there was no going back to that state of history. Daemons walked the galaxy. The myths had flesh and drew blood.

We should have known, Sanguinius thought. *We should always have known. My sons and I most of all. How could we believe there could be angels without daemons?*

He thought of the inner monsters his Legion had long fought, and how the horrors of the warp had brought them to the surface, almost destroying him and all the Blood Angels.

My father told us there were no such things, and because we believed this to be true, we were vulnerable to them.

Enough. These doubts were unworthy. If he did not know why the Emperor had denied the existence of gods and daemons, then the reasons were not his to know. Yet. He must have faith that he would learn in time. And he had faith. Faith that would burn the galaxy with its purity.

He charged deeper into the daemons, and the plague withered before his wrath. He brought light to the darkness, a purging, incinerating light. It blasted from the head of the *Spear of Telesto*. It blazed from the length of the *Blade Encarmine*. But it came, too, from his being. He was in the centre of a blinding fire. He *was* the centre. The daemons cried out. They fell, they burned, they disintegrated. Their existence was an insult to him and everything he had given his life to forge.

Yes, he would return them back to the darkness of myths. He would expunge even the memory of the myths.

Bolter shells screamed on both sides. They were a destroying wind, ripping the abominations apart. Sanguinius marched towards the rift. He was inexorable. The daemons' advance halted. It reversed. He waded through a dissolving mass of bodies and disintegrating weapons. The bell still sounded, but he thought he heard alarm in its toll now, a frantic, futile call to arms.

At the mouth of the rift, daemons still tried to force their way onto the bridge. They were hampered now by the immobilised crowd of their kin. Behind them, howling in the writhing darkness and infernal colours of the warp, still more daemons raged to break through. There were other kinds of monsters there, alongside those the Blood Angels had fought on Signus Prime. Mingled with the daemons of rage and change were creatures whose movements were sinuous, corrosive invitations to unnameable sensations. The tear in the bridge was a glimpse into an abyss of every foul hunger. It was an eye that opened onto the reality of souls, and that reality was hideous. '*I deny you!*' the Angel shouted. He scythed through the daemons.

He slashed the *Blade Encarmine* across the front of the rift, from edge to edge. '*I deny the lies. I deny the madness. My father's kingdom of reason will triumph!*'

Sanguinius cut through unflesh. A gash opened wide in the invisible veil between the materium and the warp. Blood erupted out of the air. The outline of the rift trembled. Sanguinius aimed another burst of the spear's power into the centre of the tear. He bellowed a curse and defiance as the cleansing lightning enveloped the abominations. They burst into flame and fell to ash before they could manifest themselves on the bridge. The daemonic horde fell back. Around him, his sons battered the plague monsters out of existence. The smell of burned fyceline filled his nostrils, the clean sting of battle cutting through the viscous stench of bodies bursting like overripe fruit.

The breach trembled violently. Its edges lost definition. The space beyond became vague. The forms of the daemons smeared into one another, and then into the contusions of the warp. Whorls of unreality swept over them. The wall of the bridge became visible behind the breach, and then, with the hiss of a wounded serpent, the rift vanished.

Sanguinius paused, reining in his anger. He turned around to survey the bridge. Many of the diseased crewmembers had stopped moving. Most of the officers were still at their posts. From the other side of the sealed doors, he heard bolter fire and the ululations of daemons.

'The *Encarnadine* has repelled its incursion,' Neverrus called, her voice unwavering. 'New breaches on the *Nine Crusaders* and the *Victus*.'

'The *Victus*,' Azkaellon said. 'Amit will welcome the chance to exact some vengeance for Signus Prime.'

Sanguinius picked up the undercurrent of concern in his voice. Of all the Blood Angels, the Flesh Tearer and his Fifth Company were the most vulnerable to lapsing into the savagery of the Thirst.

'We will all wreak that vengeance,' Sanguinius replied. *I have faith in you, Amit*, he thought. *I must.* 'We shall seal every breach with the blood of abominations.'

He strode towards the door, the Sanguinary Guard flanking him.

The *Red Tear* shook again. The deck heaved as if the battleship were cresting an immense wave, and then dropped, gravity tilting at a sharp angle. The Blood Angels kept their feet. The mortals had to cling to their workstations to stay upright.

'New contact,' said Jeran Mautus. The auspex officer sounded worried.

'Identity?' Sanguinius asked.

'I don't know, my lord.' Mautus frowned at his screen. None of the adjustments he was making to the scans were satisfying him. 'It's a shadow. I can't get anything more precise than that.'

'Is it attacking?'

'Approaching, but as for a vector…' Mautus trailed off.

Sanguinius grimaced. The immaterium was not space. Even to speak of relative distance between ships was to attempt to impose an illusion on the indescribable. But the human mind needed its frames of reference.

'It's big,' Mautus went on.

'You are being vague, lieutenant,' Raldoron warned. 'At least tell us if this is a ship.'

Sanguinius placed a calming hand on the First Captain's pauldron.

'I'm sorry,' said Mautus. 'I can't. It's very big. It… I don't know. It's too big.'

'Train our weapons on it,' the Angel said. 'Fleet master, the command to fire is yours.'

'As you will, my lord,' said Carminus.

Sanguinius nodded, and headed for the doors. They opened before him, and he rushed out to cleanse his ship of invaders.

As he ran towards the sounds of combat, he felt a shadow press in. It was just beyond the edge of his consciousness, yet it weighed on his hearts like a planetary mass. He knew, beyond the excuses of reason, that it was the same shadow that Mautus had detected. And it was immense.

THE DE PROFUNDIS splintered, and there were no good practicals.

'Our first volley did that?' Caspean said. 'Too easy.'

'We didn't destroy it,' said Guilliman. 'We did exactly what they wanted us to do.'

For several moments, the fragments of the Word Bearers vessel stayed close enough together that they preserved its silhouette. It seemed to expand, the space between the pieces gradually widening. As the De Profundis closed with the Samothrace, it finally looked like what it was – a hail of jagged shards, a ship turned into shrapnel. Every sliver stabbed towards the Ultramarines battleship.

Guilliman read the contours of the trap, and cursed what he saw. The Word Bearers had closed off his options. If he redirected any power to the forwards void shields, he opened the ship to destruction by the Night Lords or the World Eaters. If he didn't reinforce the forwards defences, he was going to be hit by hundreds of boarding torpedoes at once. All he had left was weapons fire.

'Cavascor,' he called on the vox. 'Coordinated fire on the De Profundis. Cut down that swarm.'

'So ordered,' Iasus answered.

The Samothrace was already redirecting its artillery. The batteries of plasma projectors and macro-cannons threw up a wall of incandescent destruction. Torpedoes streamed towards the intact shapes of the rest of the Word Bearers fleet.

'Up thirty degrees,' Guilliman said. It was too late to evade. The impacts were seconds away. But evading even a few shards could make a difference.

The bow of the *Samothrace* began to rise above the ecliptic. The splinters of the *De Profundis* ran into the storm of fire from the two Ultramarines ships. The void flashed with the disintegration of fragments. The *Samothrace* drove into clusters of explosions. It shuddered as more Night Lords torpedoes struck the stern. The *Cavascor* tightened up with the battleship, trying to interpose its bulk with the long-range fire of the World Eaters. Guilliman heard Iasus over the vox, roaring defiance at the XII Legion. At this moment, the Chapter Master, one of the most thoughtful of Guilliman's commanders, sounded more than ever like he was one with the aggressive companies of Destroyers he led.

Void shields strained. Through the oculus, their pulses seared the eye. Bursts of ignited plasma marched along the flanks of the warships. The splinters hit, and still more of them blew apart as they collided with the shields.

But there were scores behind them, and the forwards shields of the *Samothrace* collapsed under a hail of impacts. The swarm smashed the bow. Shards broke up against the ablative armour. They came in at a shallow angle on the upper hull, streaking it with rolling fireballs. And they hit the superstructure. The change in the ship's orientation was enough to destroy still more. If they did not hit directly, they could not pierce the alloy of the ship's hide.

Some did pierce it. Guilliman felt the blows even before the breach klaxons sounded. Needles stabbed into the body of the *Samothrace*, and poison flowed from them into its veins. One hit just below the bridge. The vibration of the impact was a quiver of pain, the spirit of the *Samothrace* reacting to a wound worse than the drawing of blood.

'With me,' he said to Gorod and Prayto. Gorod and the squad of bodyguards on the bridge formed up around their primarch. To Caspean, Guilliman said, 'The bridge is yours.'

Caspean slammed a fist against his breastplate. 'They won't set foot on this deck.'

The *Samothrace* had already borne the insult of the Word Bearers' presence over Calth. Guilliman would not see it suffer the same indignity.

'All breached halls sealed,' said Altuzer.

The splinters of the *De Profundis* were not true boarding torpedoes. They did not have the means to close rents in the hull with foam. The bleed of atmosphere to the void had triggered the automatic defence protocols.

Guilliman drew the *Gladius Incandor* and the *Arbitrator*. He held the combi-bolter before him as he marched out of the bridge, finger on the trigger and ready to deliver judgement.

THE ULTRAMARINES RAN into the enemy one level down from the bridge. The splinters had pushed the outer walls in when they hit, narrowing the corridors and filling them with wreckage. Guilliman waded into the first clutch of Word Bearers. His lips were pulled back in hate. He pulled the trigger of the *Arbitrator* rapidly, the shots echoing the furious beat of his pulse. The traitors sprayed the halls with bolter fire. They were responding to his presence too quickly. Their shots smacked into his armour. The shells were nothing to him; a slight wind, a failed distraction. He ignored them. His shells hit the traitors like warheads. He shot the Word Bearers through their helmets. Their heads burst, painting the walls with blood, gouging them with ceramite shrapnel. Guilliman marched past the first splinter and over the bodies. Though his actions were unhurried, he had slaughtered a squad of Word Bearers before Gorod and his men could find a target.

Ahead, the bulkhead was twisted and had failed to seal. A stiff wind of escaping atmosphere blew against his cheeks, pulling at him, calling him towards the next fight. Legion banners hanging from the ceiling swayed and flapped. The walls of the *Samothrace* rang with gunfire.

'We have numerous breach points,' Gorod said.

'We will repel them,' said Prayto. 'Our numbers far exceed those the enemy could possibly have inserted.'

'Then why make the attempt?'

'*Lord Guilliman*,' Altuzer voxed. '*The enemy has ceased bombardment of the* Samothrace.'

'And the *Cavascor?*' Guilliman asked.

'*Still under attack.*'

'Tell Iasus to take the offensive,' he said. 'Close with the nearest enemy ship. Use it as a shield and launch assault rams. Turn Captain Hierax and his Destroyers loose on its bridge.'

As he reached the ruined bulkhead, Guilliman paused. 'Theoretical,' he said to his warriors. 'This is more than a simple boarding attack.' He looked at Prayto. 'Are you sensing anything?'

Prayto was frowning. 'Not a build-up, exactly. Nothing in our vicinity to suggest they're planning a...' He grimaced. 'A *sorcerous* assault.' The word still did not come easily to anyone in the Legion, even the psykers. 'But there is something. A presence, I think. Not far.'

'Then we're forewarned,' Guilliman said. He kicked at the buckled door, knocking it out of its frame. He advanced into the corridor more cautiously. Shattered ferrocrete cladding littered the deck. Another splinter had broken through fifty yards down, but there did not appear to be any Word Bearers nearby. Guilliman glared at the shard as he moved past it. It protruded through the hull of the *Samothrace* as a thing of jagged diagonals and broken lines. Its shape was crystalline. He shared a look with Prayto.

'This result was not achieved by technological means,' the Librarian said.

'But this isn't the source of what you're detecting.'

'No.'

The wind's keen was high and savage. The twitching light of the Ruinstorm leaked through the fissures between the splinter and the broken hull.

Past the shard, the corridor curved as it approached the port corner of the superstructure. From the bend onwards, the lumen globes in the ornate bronze wall sconces had been smashed. Here, the shadows had breached the *Samothrace*. They waited for Guilliman. He knew it, and was ready. He raised the *Arbitrator*. He held the *Gladius Incandor* low at his side, blade angled outwards.

'It's close,' Prayto said.

'Is it… human?' Guilliman asked. His reason still rebelled against the word *daemon*.

'I'm not sure. It seems grounded in the materium.'

'But it isn't a Space Marine.'

Prayto hesitated. 'I don't know,' he admitted. 'I'm picking up thoughts. It knows you are coming.'

'That is hardly surprising.'

'It is eager.'

'Noted.' Guilliman was eager too. He anticipated a trap, but he would not deny his anger. The ambush had happened on the edges of Ultramar, but still Ultramar. The boarding of the *Samothrace* was another insult. He would seek redress in traitor's blood.

'Theoretical,' said Gorod. 'If the boarding assault has no practical chance of taking the ship, its target must be a narrower one.'

'Me,' said Guilliman.

'Titus' evidence points in that direction.'

'I agree. Your practical had better not involve me leading from the rear.'

'I'll revise it.'

'See that you do.'

They reached the shadows and the curve. The corridor stretched several hundred yards in darkness. Sparks from ruptured electrical conduits created a feeble glow around the *De Profundis* splinter at the far end. When Guilliman rounded the corner, rasping, inhuman bellowing erupted from inside the shard.

The darkness around the splinter deepened, and the wind grew stronger. The shadows began to bubble and smoke. Cracks appeared in the decks and walls spreading outwards from the shard. The thing inside was taking apart the reality of the *Samothrace*.

Guilliman ran. The Invictus guards and Prayto charged forwards with him. They hurtled down the corridor, *Arbitrator* and bolters sending a mass-reactive barrage ahead of them. There were no visible targets, but they had to be there.

This is a trap, Guilliman thought as he pounded deeper into the shadows. *The enemy knows I have to respond. The threat is real and I must counter it, so this is when they will spring the ambush.*

He understood that the ships of three Legions, and the void war in its totality, were the means to the end that would come now. *I should be flattered*, he thought.

The shadows were thick as pitch. They pressed against Guilliman, trying to slow him. Even with his enhanced vision, he couldn't see more than a couple of paces ahead. The spreading red cracks illuminated nothing except themselves. The splinter seemed to hunch lower, melding itself into the fabric of the *Samothrace*. Guilliman cut through it with *Incandor*. He shot it as though it were flesh. The Ultramarines' gunfire hit home. Dying Word Bearers materialised from the dark. Their brothers, giving up on futile concealment, retaliated. Guilliman took the return fire seriously. He snapped off shots at every muzzle flash. His focus flicked back and forth from the attacks in the blackness to the spreading disintegration and the splinter at its centre. Neither was the true assault. Either could be its source.

On his right, Prayto stretched an arm. A blast of psychic lightning tore through the darkness. It burned through the gorget of a Word Bearer and set his head on fire, but still the darkness intensified.

The roars from inside the splinter grew louder. They were mocking, triumphant. As Guilliman reached the shard, two squads of Word Bearers erupted from the dark. They surrounded him, attacking with chainswords and powerblades. He parried and slashed with *Incandor*. He exploded helms and skulls with the *Arbitrator*. Gorod and the others cut into the Word Bearers, trapping them between Guilliman's cold rage and his bodyguards' lethal precision.

This is still not the real attack, Guilliman thought. He plunged the *Gladius Incandor* through ceramite marked with spidery runes of such density they seemed to crawl. He drew the blade to the right, cutting armour and muscle, disembowelling the traitor. The front of the shard was open, and he moved inside, leaving the struggle at the entrance behind.

He advanced three steps, seeing nothing at first. There was only the cloying black. Then the monster lunged out of the night. It was massive, spined and horned. Its jaw was long and powerful enough to snap iron. It could never have been human, but the remains of Word Bearers armour clung to its tree-trunk limbs. The old markings were still there, to be read, as if the powers that had transformed the Word Bearer desired all who saw it to know what it had once been, and know despair. Warp-fire tendrils arced from its body to the sides of the splinter, turning into webs, then cracks. This thing was the source of the disintegration.

In the distortion of form, the complete desolation of anything human and the mockery of the preserved armour, Guilliman saw the distillation of the perversion and treachery of the XVII Legion.

He jerked back, firing the *Arbitrator* as the monster lashed out with a massively clawed hand. The blow threw off his aim, and the shell punched through its left shoulder, disintegrating flesh and spines. The monster snarled and lunged. It was fast, and its movements slid between the real and the immaterial, hard to track and counter. Guilliman blocked a strike with *Incandor*, but then the claws were suddenly coming from a different angle, and the creature seized him. It was huge, half again as tall as he was, and its flesh was still shifting, mutating, growing in the glory of its ascended state.

'*I am Toc Derenoth,*' it boomed with a double voice. '*I am Unburdened. And I will unburden your ship.*' It bent Guilliman backwards, acid dripping from its jaws.

Guilliman heard the first cracks in his armour. He resisted, and the monster grew even larger, fed by the warp. Toc Derenoth's eyes were a milky white, but patterns swirled in them, forming and dissolving runes.

Guilliman tore his arms free. He fired and stabbed into Toc Derenoth's chest. The stream of shells blasted a hole a foot wide in the monster's chest, breaking its hold and hurling it back. Guilliman drove the gladius deep into the wound, puncturing things that had once been organs. Toc Derenoth howled, the twinned voices wrapping around Guilliman's mind in pain and fury.

Guilliman poured bolter shells into the thrashing beast. The web of disintegrating unreality began to withdraw. The crimson light dimmed, and the substance of the splinter became more stable. It began to resemble a fragment of a void ship's bridge once again. Undulating mounds became the wreckage of cogitators and pict screens. The floor shifted from tissue to ferrocrete. The shape of a command throne began to appear in the centre of the darkness.

'I want you off my ship,' Guilliman said. He advanced, emptying the *Arbitrator*'s magazine into the monster, driving the deathless thing back, reclaiming reality inside the splinter. He measured every step, calculating his position with respect to the outer hull. The sounds of battle behind him grew quieter and more distant.

The splinter was long, many times longer than any boarding torpedo. Guilliman had thought of it as a dart striking the battleship. He was wrong. It was a worm that had worked its way into the body of the *Samothrace*. He moved deeper and deeper into the dark maw, until he reached a point where the splinter extended beyond the outer hull. He forced the Unburdened back even further, then trained the *Arbitrator*'s fire on the floor of the splinter. The shells blew huge rents in the material. Guilliman arced the shells from the deck to the walls, carving out a circular fissure in the shard. No longer battered by the combi-bolter, Toc Derenoth moved forwards. The Unburdened was slow at first, so much of its mass lying shredded on the deck. But darkness fed it, embraced it, and gave it rebirth. Bones re-formed. The chest sealed. The shattered jaw was whole again. The monster charged, shaking the deck. The splinter began to come apart. Toc Derenoth was a few paces away when Guilliman finished sawing through the shard.

He blasted away the last of the splinter's integrity. Metal snapped and tore. The void appeared through the gap. The fierce wind of escaping atmosphere blasted through the narrow tunnel. Guilliman stood strong against it, but Toc Derenoth stumbled.

The rear portion of the splinter fell away, carrying the Unburdened with it. The monster clung to edges of the gap, already too distant to leap. It stared at Guilliman with its white eyes. Its crocodilian jaws opened and closed, opened and closed, snapping in frustration as its prison took the Unburdened further and further into emptiness.

Guilliman turned away and marched into the wind. He was almost halfway down the length of the splinter when he realised he had misread Toc Derenoth's reaction. The Unburdened had not been raging. It had been laughing.

Understanding came too late. He had relaxed his guard. The shadows ahead and behind parted.

Guilliman saw the dull blades in their hands, and cursed the depths of his foolishness.

FOUR

The Lure of Revelation

'WE HAVE BEEN hailed,' Stenius said when the Lion returned to the bridge, 'by a frigate of the Tenth Legion.'

The Lion gazed at the ship visible in the oculus. 'You've its identity?'

'We have. It's the *Sthenelus*. A vessel of the Eighty-fifth Clan-Company.'

The frigate's shape was battered. It looked like an ancient iron ingot, eroded and gnawed by rust and time. The hull was scarred by las-burns and patched repairs over torpedo hits. Some of its cannon batteries were gone, leaving behind wounds like broken teeth. The architecture of the upper hull was not much more than a functional ruin, yet the ship still conveyed the strength of a clenched fist. It was bloodied, but had not fallen.

The Lion thought of the Iron Hands he had encountered on Macragge. They bore the loss of Ferrus Manus and the shattering of their Legion with a mix of stoicism and brooding, vengeful silence. And those were the fortunate ones. They had reached Ultramar. They could become part of a multi-Legion alliance against Horus. This ship was alone. Its warriors must have been fighting a war of skirmishes since Isstvan V. The Lion doubted they had had any chance of resupply. Their survival was impressive.

'Captain Khalybus has asked to be received,' Stenius went on.

'We will welcome him and his escort aboard,' the Lion said. 'With all due ceremony.' Meaning all due caution.

'Understood,' said Holguin.

An honour guard would receive the Iron Hands captain in the landing bay, and in the hall leading from there. There would be full respect and full security. The Lion accepted that the ship was the *Sthenelus*. After this long in these storm-wracked regions, so close to the Maelstrom, there was no assurance that what walked the frigate was what it claimed to be.

He waited until a Thunderhawk pulled away from the *Sthenelus*. Then he withdrew to the ship's council chamber to wait.

The hall was a large, solemn space, dimly lit as if jealous of its secrets. Six iron chairs were placed in an arc around the Lion's throne, three on each side, one for each voted lieutenant of the Hexagrammaton. The circle took up the centre of the chamber, and left a vast expanse of shadows between it and the walls. The banners of the Six Wings hung from the high dome. They were barely visible in the gloom, whispers of strength. They swayed with slow, deliberate movements in the ventilation currents.

The Lion took his throne, flanked today only by Holguin and Farith Redloss, voted lieutenant of Dreadwing. The chamber was a long march from the landing bay. By the time Khalybus arrived, the primarch had received a full security evaluation of the captain. He was who he said, and there was no taint of the warp around him.

Khalybus entered the chamber accompanied by two other legionaries. One was his sergeant, Raud. The other was a Raven Guard, Levannas. The Lion was struck by the choice Khalybus had made for his escort. The Iron Hands would not include the Raven Guard out of politeness. Relations between the two Legions had sometimes become heated on Macragge. They shared the trauma of Isstvan V, but the Iron Hands held the tactical decisions of Corvus Corax as being in part responsible for the death of Ferrus Manus. Levannas' presence spoke to an unusual level of trust. The Lion wondered about the length and cost of the campaign that had forged this kind of a bond.

The appearance of the three legionaries suggested much. Their armour was as pitted and scarred as their ship. It was polished, and clearly treated with honour. But the means to repair it were lacking. The cost of the war was also in Khalybus' face. By the faint hum of servo-motors, the Lion could identify the captain's legs and right arm as bionic. That was no surprise. He had known Iron Hands who had even less flesh prior to Horus' treachery. But Khalybus had lost more flesh recently, and it had not been replaced by the strength of metal. His head had suffered what looked like severe plasma burns. His hair and eyebrows were gone. His skull was mottled black and angry red. The flesh looked melted, and it shone as if varnished.

'Captain Khalybus,' the Lion said, 'well met.'

Khalybus dipped his head forwards in respect. 'Our thanks, Lord Jonson.' His larynx was evidently still organic, though his vocal cords had been damaged. He spoke with a voice of stones rubbing against each other.

Levannas said, 'The sight of the strength of your fleet revives our hopes.'

Khalybus grimaced slightly at the mention of hope.

'What forces do you have?' the Lion asked.

'The *Sthenelus* is all we have left,' Khalybus said.

'We have been hunting the enemy since Isstvan V,' said Levannas. 'We have hurt the traitors. But over time...'

'It has been years,' Holguin said, impressed and sympathetic.

'Does the Emperor yet live?' Khalybus asked.

'We believe so,' said the Lion. 'We are making for Terra.'

Khalybus cocked his head. 'By way of Pandorax?'

'The size of our fleet does not change the difficulties of navigating through the warp,' the Lion said, his tone cold.

Khalybus seemed to realise he had spoken disrespectfully. 'I had hoped your experience was different from ours,' he said.

You're right, the Lion thought. *It was.* He waved the question aside. 'I misspoke. We seek the way to Terra. And what about the *Sthenelus.* Is Pandorax your hunting ground?' It seemed unlikely. There were no warships in the wreckage outside the warp storm.

'No,' said Khalybus. 'We came hoping to find my brother-captain, Atticus. We know his strike cruiser, the *Veritas Ferrum,* reached this system and made for the world of Pythos. We know he left at least once, and carried out a raid that destroyed the Third Legion's battle-barge *Callidora.* That is the last evidence we have of him.'

'Why do you think he would have returned here?'

'In our last communication with him, he was tracking an anomaly, one that made transmission impossible, but provided the mistress of his astropathic choir with unsurpassed awareness of the sector.' Khalybus was clearly dissatisfied with his description. 'He knew little when we spoke. The effect seemed to be the reverse of the Astronomican.'

The Lion nodded. After the Pharos, he found the concept easier to accept than Khalybus did. 'You think he was successful.'

'He was able to ambush the *Callidora* and its escorts,' Levannas said. 'A single ship destroyed them.'

'And you have heard nothing since then?'

'Nothing,' Khalybus confirmed. 'We expected that, as long as he was on Pythos, he would be impossible to contact. But there has been only silence since the *Callidora.* That was years ago. We can no longer be effective against the enemy, not with a single frigate. We have been unable to find any of our other brothers. So we came here.'

'Our choices have been reduced to desperate ones,' Levannas added.

'That is true for us all,' the Lion said. 'Have you found any sign of him?'

'No,' said Khalybus. 'Though that is hardly surprising, given that we cannot enter the system. The presence of wreckage outside the warp storm is curious, though. Atticus sent us the *Veritas Ferrum*'s auspex scans of Pandorax before communications ended. He did not encounter these ships.'

'Do you know where they came from?'

'That is what we've been trying to determine. They are all civilian, antiquated, and appear to have been in poor condition long before they met with disaster here. Much of the wreckage we have examined shows signs of having been patched up repeatedly and badly.'

'Have you boarded any of the hulks?'

'We had only just identified a few promising targets when your fleet translated.'

'I see.' The Lion thought about Tuchulcha's words. *I have taken you where you must go.* There was a confluence of too many events at Pandorax to be ignored. He did not trust Tuchulcha, but it had never lied to him yet, at least not in any way he had been able to detect. He would act, for now, as if what it said was true. 'I cannot say if your captain is to be found here,' he said. 'I believe, however, that there is a secret here, one we must uncover.' *Somehow, Pandorax is the gateway to Terra.* 'We will examine your target vessels with you, captain.'

Khalybus nodded once, his acknowledgment curt but respectful. 'I did not think the task worthy of such resources.'

'It may prove to be vital,' the Lion said.

THE GOLD-PLATED DOUBLE doors of the Exaltatio Angeli librarium had been ripped from their hinges, and their engravings bubbled, the shapes of heroic war transformed into a nightmare tangle of insectile limbs. Plague daemons stumbled down the aisles, their rotten swords hacking at books, turning them into liquefying pulp. In the centre of the great hall, there were other abominations. They were vortices of flesh and flame, headless cones of screaming mouths that breathed the fire of nightmare against the towering shelves. They whirled from lectern to lectern, and rampaged through the marble bookcases. Vellum or data-slate, metal or stone, whatever they touched burned and changed.

The Exaltatio Angeli had been badly damaged in the *Red Tear*'s fall to Signus Prime. Hundreds, perhaps thousands, of irreplaceable tomes had been lost, swaths of the history of the Blood Angels and the culture of

Baal swept into oblivion. Sanguinius regarded what had been salvaged as even more precious. These books were more than records now. They were survivors in their own right, every scar and burned page a mark of the new chronicle, and of the cost it exacted. Now they were dying, and worse. The corpulent monsters, their bodies leaking decay, were killing the memory of Baal, turning it into a rotten swamp. Fungus and mould sprouted on the spines of books at their passage. Tentacles and grasping fingers grew from the volumes. Data-slates spread wings and flew about the wide central space of the librarium. Scrolls became tongues. They slipped off the shelves like long white slugs, babbling words that belonged to no tongue in the material galaxy. As they chanted, the air flaked into ash around them.

A squad of Blood Angels led by Sergeant Orexis fought the incursion in the librarium. Two five-man teams had taken up positions on opposite sides of the bronze-railed gallery that ran around the centre. They had a wide field of fire and were pumping bolter shells into daemons on all six levels. Each shot was sniper-precise. They fired in short bursts, keeping firm control over the spread of their projectiles. They were trying to preserve the Exaltatio Angeli as much as purge it of the daemonic presence.

The Angel swept his gaze over the first level of the Exaltatio and had to transmute despair into anger. The mutations were worse than the destructions. What had rotted was dying, already gone. What was changed was more insidious.

On the first level, Sanguinius slashed the *Blade Encarmine* across the torso of a spinning abomination. Pale blue daemonflesh parted. Two halves of grotesquery twisted away from each other, their mouths wailing anguish. The Angel charged to the centre of the floor, wading deep into the spawn of the warp. Jawed arms snapped at him. Unnatural flame washed over him, and he felt his bones try to change. He hurled the madness away. The destiny of his visions waited for him in the future. He was not going to fall here.

Beneath the peak of the Exaltatio's dome he paused. As Raldoron and the Sanguinary Guard formed a cordon around him, he struck the ground with the end of the *Spear of Telesto*'s shaft, splintering a flagstone. The spear's blade glowed brighter and brighter. 'Put everything to the flame,' Sanguinius ordered, his voice thunder over the din of battle.

Raldoron looked at him sharply. 'Everything?'

'*My lord,*' Orexis voxed. '*We might yet save part of the archives.*'

'We have already lost them,' Sanguinius replied. 'We cannot know the full extent of the corruption. The changes we cannot see are the most dangerous. History altered is worse than history forgotten. The poison must be excised. Burn it. Burn it all.' He fired the spear in anger, in anguish, and most of all in righteousness of purpose. Purity blazed magnesium-bright. The beam sliced through clusters of whirling daemons. Their babble turned into a choir of screaming distress, and then they were consumed. The blast took out five shelves at a stroke. Flame raced through the histories, the treatises and the literature of Baal. The untouched and the corrupted alike burned.

Raldoron's gasp was almost as subtle, and as deeply felt. Azkaellon's agony came through in the anger with which he ordered flamers deployed. 'Give me fire!' he yelled. 'Give me flames as high as the dome!' There was a desperate fury in his voice that was closer to the violence of Amit than Azkaellon normally allowed himself to come. The Sanguinary Guard obeyed. Three of the legionaries stepped forwards with heavy flamers. Streams of burning promethium arced across the space of the librarium, igniting a firestorm around its periphery. They marched around the ring formation, gradually raising their weapons' nozzles, creating a spiralling conflagration. Daemons lurched and danced through the blaze. They resisted the burn, but it devoured the archives before the warp flame could transform them further.

The other Blood Angels sent mass-reactive hell into the fire. There was no more restraint now, and the full-auto bursts of shells shredded the monsters of disease and flux. From beyond the veil, the dark bell tolled and tolled, and its clamour sounded angry now.

We defy you, Sanguinius thought. *And we deny you. Defeat is insupportable to you. You will come to know it well.*

The bell tolled and tolled. The daemons rushed the Blood Angels and fell back, rushed and fell back again. When their forms lost coherence and they could no longer fight, the fire burned their remains faster than they could deliquesce. The Exaltatio Angeli descended into a tempest of devastation. Sanguinius hurled blasts from the spear without cease, mourning the knowledge and the art he destroyed, but made resolute by the necessity of what he did. The flames rose, and he was standing in the heart of a furnace. It roared, destroying what should not exist, bringing absolution to the tainted space of the *Red Tear.*

In the midst of his sorrow and anger, Sanguinius sought the solace of victory. He spread his wings. They beat the air, sending smoke curling in violent eddies. He rose straight up through the rage of flame and battle until he reached the dome of the Exaltatio. He wheeled around its circumference. The firestorm reached up for him and he looked down at the struggle between his sons and the daemons. At this height, the figures were small, yet the majesty of the Blood Angels shone brightly. They cut down the abominations with resolution and glory. There was anger in their attacks, but it was controlled, honourable. There was no sign of the blood thirst. He saw only discipline. He saw his sons as they could be, as the best part of himself, and for a short while he could believe in the illusion that the flaw was not just beneath the surface, waiting for its chance to erupt again.

He gazed at the daemons with contempt. There might always be new horrors for the warp to reveal, but the Blood Angels had the measure of these, and they would all be destroyed. *We have faced worse,* he thought. *We have defeated worse.* The loss of the librarium was a blow, but Baal still lived. The Imperium still lived. There was hope, and so the chance to rebuild, to create new art, new knowledge, new chronicles. He vowed there would yet be a new dawn. And from the peak of the dome, he sent the beams of the *Spear of Telesto* stabbing down into the abominations, fuelling the fire. The Exaltatio's pyre blazed with purifying light.

The shadow came for him. The immense weight on his hearts suddenly moved to crush them. 'Mautus,' Sanguinius voxed, about to ask if the *Red Tear* had engaged the contact. But the darkness attacked before he could speak again. It was not a presence. It was the mere approach of the thing in the warp that hit, a bow wave catching him and drowning him. His wings folded under the blow and he plummeted from the dome. He fell into the mouth of the fire vortex. Daemons leapt for him, the mouths at the ends of their limbs snapping in hunger. Then they were gone, and he was falling in a blackness that was absolute, but not empty. Its substance knew him, and at a level beyond the conscious, he knew it. Before he could think what it was he recognised, the dark was gone.

Sanguinius wasn't falling any more, and he wasn't on the *Red Tear*. He was running down the hall of another ship. He knew this hall. He knew the tapestries that had once hung here. He knew the runes and monstrous carvings that had replaced them. And he knew what chamber waited at the end of the hall.

He was aboard the *Vengeful Spirit*. He was about to enter Horus' throne room. He was going to fight his brother and die.

This was no vision. It couldn't be. It was too real. He had no consciousness of his body being elsewhere. He heard the hammering thuds of his feet against the deck. He smelled the foulness of the ship's corruption. He felt his wounds. He was bleeding, and his armour had been damaged in earlier fights. He had slipped from time. The future had come for him, and the time of visions was finished.

As Sanguinius closed in on the throne room, the *Red Tear* slipped away. Its reality faded and became a memory. The present was the *Vengeful Spirit*, and Horus was waiting.

Sanguinius burst into the throne room. A colossus in black armour stood before him.

There was a roar, and the chamber shook so hard it blurred.

Then it was gone.

Sanguinius was dropping through the firestorm of the Exaltatio Angeli again. He was not in the future. The roar had travelled with him, or it had summoned him back. It was louder than any of the explosions in the librarium. The *Red Tear* shook as the *Vengeful Spirit* had. A massive thrum rang the length of the hull. The dome of the Exaltatio cracked, and bookshelves twenty feet tall collapsed.

Sanguinius spread his wings wide and held them rigid, breaking the speed of his descent. He regained control of his flight and landed in the centre of the Sanguinary Guard formation. Above, the gallery was collapsing, the railing dropping into flame. Orexis and his squad jumped down onto the sloping wreckage and made their way to the ground floor, trapping the plague daemons between them and the Sanguinary Guard.

The roar came again, and a shudder that sickened Sanguinius. It was the mark of a profound wound to the *Red Tear*. 'Mautus! Report!'

'*The contact, lord. It's hitting us.*'

'With what? Is it a ship?'

'*Unknown. But it's overwhelming the void shields. We're firing. No way to tell if we're causing any damage.*'

Sanguinius opened his mouth to answer, the roar came again, and the *Vengeful Spirit* forced itself onto his consciousness. He didn't believe himself to be on Horus' flagship this time. His perception flickered between the *Spirit* and the *Tear*, and when Horus' blade struck him, the intensity of the vision almost brought him to his knees.

This is a vision, he thought. *Only a vision. It has no reality. Not yet.*

He turned his spirits away from the experience of his death. The effort was so great, the taste of blood flooded his mouth.

'My lord!' Azkaellon was at his side. 'What is happening to you?'

'A psychic attack,' Sanguinius rasped. Giving it a name was necessary. It was a means of regaining control, the truth as counterstrike. He straightened. 'We finish here, and we return to the bridge.' He had to see the enemy in the warp. He had to lead the struggle against it.

His mind kept slipping back to the *Vengeful Spirit*. His mind, only his mind. He looked out upon the burning Exaltatio, and focused his anger on what had been taken from the Blood Angels here. He held tightly to the loss he felt *now*, and the future's grip on his spirit slipped just enough. With the Sanguinary Guard forming a wedge behind him, he brought the final flames to the abominations in the librarium. As he fought, the shadow began to pull away. He saw more clearly. The oppression lifted, and the hull shudders ceased. When he turned from the ashes and smoke of the purified hall, he knew before he reached the bridge that the enemy had pulled away from the *Red Tear*.

Carminus was speaking with Mautus when Sanguinius arrived.

'I'm sorry, fleet master,' Mautus said. 'There is nothing more we can tell. There is *nothing*.'

'What is it?' Sanguinius asked. 'Has the foe retreated?'

Carminus looked grim. 'It left us for different prey,' he said. 'The *Sable* is gone.'

THE CORRIDOR HEADING towards the bridge of the Word Bearers strike cruiser *Annunciation* was heavy with shadows. Walls, floor and vaulted ceiling were black marble veined with crimson runes. Muzzle flashes lit the hall as the defenders were cut down. Two Word Bearers, slow to retreat, tried to hold back the Destroyers while the rest of their squad pulled back quickly up the corridor. Hierax's squad rushed them, each legionary wielding two bolt pistols. The hail of mass-reactive shells punched through armour and blew apart the flesh inside. The traitors staggered and fell, blood splashing out behind them.

Leading the charge, Hierax fired after the other traitors, alternating blasts with his pistol and his volkite serpenta. The shells cracked open one Word Bearer's helmet. The serpenta's heat ray incinerated his skull. Flame burst from inside the helmet, followed by the cloud of ash that had been the legionary's head.

The rest of the squad reached an intersection. As they turned off the main hall, one of them pulled a detonator from his belt.

The corridor flashed white before Hierax could shout a warning. A series of demolition charges blew out the sides of the vaulted ceiling. Tonnes of marble and ferrocrete crashed down. Hierax threw himself back with his men. They were at the edge of the destruction and narrowly escaped being crushed. A chunk of the upper decking struck Hierax's shoulder. It was a glancing blow, but still hard enough to smash him to the side. He hit the starboard wall and shattered the cladding. When the dust settled, Legionary Kletos said, 'We aren't getting through that.'

The rubble blocked the corridor completely. The charges had gone off down a length of more than a hundred yards. There was no point trying to punch through the wreckage with melta bombs. There was no corridor at all, only compacted decks.

Hierax cursed. His squad had moved fast since the three Caestus assault rams had struck the upper levels of the *Annunciation*'s superstructure. He estimated they were a few hundred yards from the bridge. The strike cruiser had undergone dark transformations, but the layout of the decks was familiar enough. As close as he had come to the goal, though, he might as well be miles distant now.

'Aphovos,' Hierax voxed the sergeant of the second squad, 'we're blocked. Tell me you have the bridge in sight.' Hierax and Aphovos were leading attacks along parallel paths, port and starboard, direct runs straight to the bridge.

'The Word Bearers just tried to drop a ceiling on us, captain. We can't go any further in this direction.'

The simultaneity of the demolitions made the tactics look less crude. 'Hold your position, sergeant,' Hierax said. 'We need to understand the trap they're trying to set for us.' He opened a channel to the third squad, advancing two decks below. 'Gorthia, has the enemy demolished your way forwards?'

'No, captain. We have reached a sealed door. It's very large. From its markings, I believe there is a fane on the other side.'

'Lorgar's wretched sons want to funnel us into their hall of worship,' said Hierax.

'They want to bring the destruction of battle into their shrines?' Aphovos asked.

'More likely they think to make a sacrifice of us.'

'*Let them try,*' said a slow, grindingly mechanical voice. Antalcidas, the ancient Deredeo-pattern Dreadnought, marched with Gorthia's squad.

'I think we will.' Hierax looked again at the rubble. 'Gorthia, I want the precise dimensions of the door and its wall.'

'*Do we make for his position?*' said Aphovos.

'No. Stand by.' The trap was effective. If there were other routes to the bridge, it would take time to find them, time the Word Bearers could use, and the Ultramarines did not have. The traitors knew the Destroyers would have no choice but to enter the fane, where the ambush would be waiting. But if the hall was as big as Hierax suspected it was, there was another option.

Gorthia relayed the data, and Hierax compared it to what he knew of the deck plan of the superstructure. He couldn't know the length of the hall behind the door, though it was clear it ran parallel to the blocked corridors. More crucially, the fane appeared to be at least three decks in height.

Hierax turned to the starboard wall and punched it, breaking off more marble. 'Prepare melta bombs,' he said. 'We're going through this wall. Aphovos, we're moving laterally. Break through the wall to port. Gorthia, take the door on my signal. We'll make the ambush ours.'

The bombs ate through the wall, turning stone and metal to smoking rivulets. The tunnel glowed with heat, and Hierax had the impression of moving through the flesh of a living thing. The ship's hull groaned with the rhythm of the *Annunciation*'s guns and the impacts of the *Cavascor*'s assault, but the walls here trembled too much like wounded muscle.

The second set of melta bombs broke through to the other side of the wall. 'Go,' Hierax voxed Gorthia. 'Hit them now!'

He rushed forwards. He was prepared for the breach to be forty feet up a vertical wall. Instead, it opened onto a high gallery. The Word Bearers' temple was larger than he had expected. His and Aphovos' squads had entered twenty yards forwards of the main door, and the huge hall extended several yards to Hierax's right. Its ceiling was another fifty feet up, and was ribbed, stained armourglass. The sick light of the Ruinstorm shone through, refracted into rays that touched on the altar and pews like the blessings of a corrupt god. The wide central aisle sloped upwards until the forward doors, leading to the bridge, were two decks above the aft entrance. The altar stood ten yards from the top of the slope. It was a massive slab of granite, etched deeply with designs that taunted the eye with the suggestion of squirming movement. Dried blood stained the engravings, and a huge, eight-pointed star of iron surmounted the altar. A triforium ran the length of each wall, sloped like the floor. Hierax had to fight off a wave of vertigo as he stepped into the gallery before him. The fane felt more than oddly sloped. Its angles seemed to be adrift from the precepts of architecture, as if the space were floating in its own poisoned reality.

Across from Hierax's position, melta bombs seared away the shadows of the triforium's arches and Aphovos' squad broke through. Aft, a massive explosion blasted the great doors off their hinges and Antalcidas marched into the fane. He was a colossus in black. His sarcophagus bore the same grim colours as the armour of the Destroyers. The blue of the XIII Legion was a splash on the pauldron, a vertical streak down the helm, a mark of honour and allegiance in the midst of the black. The Destroyers were the company of war at its most brutal, the Ultramarines of last resort, and their colours spoke of their grim purpose.

Antalcidas fired straight ahead with his twin-linked hellfire plasma cannonade at first, destroying the central aisle with the flame of suns. Then the Word Bearers retaliated, and he turned his weapons up to the triforia. The traitors had taken up positions in the arches and in the four corners of the fane. Had the Destroyers entered as a single unit, they would have been caught in a withering crossfire. As it was, the Word Bearers outnumbered the Ultramarines two to one, but Hierax and Aphovos' squads disrupted the cohesion of the ambush.

Antalcidas moved forwards, shaking the floor with his steps, weathering the bolter fire coming in from all sides, shielding Gorthia's men. The Word Bearers had only a few seconds for a concentrated volley.

Then the Destroyers were among them. Antalcidas took on the starboard side, sweeping the cannonade from the triforium to the corner of the fane. Word Bearers and the structures of the hall alike melted and vaporised in the inferno. Gorthia and his squad charged the traitors on the port side. Rows of pews exploded in the exchange of fire. Hierax and Aphovos took their squads forwards, sending a steady barrage of bolter shells ahead of them down the narrow confines of the triforia. The Word Bearers' superior numbers did them little good here in the initial moments of the struggle. There was barely space for three legionaries to march abreast, and the traitors could not bring their fire to bear effectively on the intruders on the upper level.

Hierax used the momentum of surprise, blasting through a full squad of the enemy. 'This is for Calth!' he snarled, pumping shell and flame through the head of another traitor. Then a huge shape barrelled through the next line of Word Bearers. Its armour still bore the insignia of the Serrated Sun Chapter, but the ceramite had mutated to contain the form of the swollen monster. The legionary's hands had split his gauntlets and turned into huge claws. His face was inhuman, his mouth a raging beast's maw. Fangs as long as mortals' fingers parted as he attacked. He fired his bolt pistol past Hierax, blasting Kletos in the chest. He seized Hierax, his claws punching through the captain's armour, and swung him against an arch, slamming him through stone and suspending him over the drop.

Hierax fired his serpenta into the Word Bearer's face. The creature staggered back, roaring, as flame engulfed his flesh. His claws convulsed, digging deeper into Hierax's armour. Flesh burned through to bone, but the beast did not fall. He hurled Hierax against the far wall again and again, fighting now like a wounded animal, his eyes blazing with unnatural fire brighter than the flame that consumed his skull.

Masonry crumbled around Hierax. Ferrocrete girders rammed into his back as the Word Bearer drove him deeper into the wall. Beyond the monster, the clash between the Destroyers and traitors was a maelstrom of chainblades, lightning claws and power fists. Bursts of warring energy tore the gloom of the triforium. Hierax tried to fire again, but the monster batted aside his pistols. The Word Bearer seized his arms, pinning them to his sides. His armour began to buckle under the grip of the distorted talons. The light from the Word Bearer's eyes now enveloped his entire body in a shimmering, scarlet aura. The skull had shed all burned flesh. It was a howling death's head, animated by something utterly beyond the human.

Kletos swung his chainsword against the Word Bearer's back. Mechanised teeth ground through the armour. The Word Bearer hurled Hierax down and whirled, striking Kletos a blow that knocked him back against the triforium's balcony, then turned on Hierax again.

The Destroyer was already on his feet. He slapped a melta bomb to the creature's chest plate. The fiery eyes flickered with dawning comprehension. The claws hesitated. Hierax crouched low, and his auto-lenses clicked shut against the flare of the blast. Damage runes flashed warning as the heat washed back over him, further disintegrating the wall. The full force of the explosion went through the Word Bearer. An inhuman thing shrieked. The sound took too long to fade, as if whatever had screamed were falling into an abyss beyond the materium. A pool of molten armour and charred fragments of bone lay where the Word Bearer had been.

Hierax lunged out of the ruined wall, guns in hand once more. The death of the monster had killed another Word Bearer, and the traitor's squad had retreated a few yards, laying down heavy suppressive fire. The forwards doors of the fane burst open, and reinforcements poured in. The Destroyers had survived the ambush, but their advance was stymied.

'Venerable Brother Antalcidas,' Hierax voxed, 'two missiles to the forwards doors. Destroyers, pull back and take cover.'

The rockets streaked from the Dreadnought's Aiolos launcher. Hierax grinned tightly as they roared across the fane and exploded just past the altar, blasting the eight-pointed star to shrapnel.

'Burn,' Hierax muttered. 'Burn, you treacherous scum.'

The missile warheads were phosphex shells. A cloud of burning mist erupted at the far end of the fane. Currents roiled within it as streamers latched on to the movement of the Word Bearers. It crawled over them, covering them in the white-green flame. The cloud billowed down the central aisle and along the triforia. It moved like a living thing, leaping and crawling over its prey. It burned armour, stripping it away layer by layer until it devoured the flesh beneath. The Word Bearers' barrage faltered as the phosphex cloud moved down the forwards half of the fane, a grasping hand of agonised death. The traitors tried to escape. Many stumbled blindly, human torches of chemical fire, and spread the horror with them.

In the triforia and in the central aisle, the Destroyers formed a black wall. With bolter and plasma fire, they drove the Word Bearers back into the phosphex and cut down those who staggered out.

'Scorch this hall,' Hierax ordered.

Antalcidas advanced, rotating left and right, blanketing the fane with cannonade fire. Legionaries from all three squads fired rad missiles into the cloud. Nothing could live in the forwards half of the fane. Hierax's auto-senses tracked the spiking rad levels. The phosphex cloud flowed closer, swallowing the last of the Word Bearers, edging towards the Destroyers. When the leading edge was less than ten yards away, he spoke to the Dreadnought again.

'Time to cleanse the battlefield, venerable brother. We still have to reach the bridge. All squads, prepare for atmospheric voiding.'

Antalcidas aimed the cannonade towards the ceiling and opened fire, vaporising the armourglass. A gale shrieked upwards. Deprived of oxygen, the phosphex burned itself out. Flames extinguished and smoke rushed into the void. The space of the fane became clear and cold, an irradiated waste of incinerated corpses.

The doors to the bridge were still open. The Ultramarines advanced as an impassable wall of black death. 'Burn everything that moves,' Hierax said.

'Not the controls?' Kletos asked.

'No. We have a use for this ship.'

The Destroyers crossed the threshold, and bathed the bridge with flame.

THEY CAME AT Guilliman with their dark blades.

The Word Bearer in front of Guilliman was an apostle of madness. The grey flesh of his face and clean-shaven skull was covered in a dense inlay of runes. The bones of his head were beginning to distort, sprouting growths that might develop into horns, or into more eyes. Left hand outstretched, he unleashed a blast of warp flame at Guilliman's face and lunged forwards, bringing the athame up to stab at the seam of the primarch's armour beneath the arm. At Guilliman's back, he sensed the other attacker springing to plunge the knife into the back of his neck.

His mind raced ahead of the actions. The ambush was strong. The absolute certainty was injury. The absolute need was to avoid being hit by the athames.

Practical: choose your wound.

Guilliman threw himself into the blast, turning his face to the side. His flesh burned and rippled. His skull rang like a bell. In the depths of the fire, there was a voice, inhuman, knowing, a speaker of blood and ruined fates, a whisperer of bones.

Your path is chosen.

Needle-sharp, precise as doubt, the words sank into his mind, a sliver shooting past his defences as surely as the *De Profundis* splinters had struck the *Samothrace*.

Deep in the blaze, moving forwards, half blinded by flames, Guilliman fired the *Arbitrator*. In the same instant, the rear attacker slashed at his neck. The passage of the athame breathed against his skin, the nature of the blade so powerful, so toxic, he could feel its presence even through the pain of the warp fire. The Apostle's primitive blade scarred ceramite and cut through layers of ablative armour.

Guilliman's bolt shell struck. The Apostle grunted in pain. Guilliman dropped below the flames and spun, thrusting with *Incandor*. The blade shattered the right poleyn of the other Word Bearer's armour and punched into his knee. The traitor stumbled and threw himself back. The defensive move, trained into instinct, spoiled his opportunity for a suicidal second attack with the athame.

Guilliman tore the gladius free of the Word Bearer's leg and rose with his back to the wall of the splinter. The Apostle, hit in the right pauldron and sent into a spin, recovered a few yards away. His arm hung limp, and he held the athame in his left hand now.

The Word Bearers hung back, a few paces on either side of Guilliman. He held them at bay, his attention switching back and forth between them. They were still fast enough that if he shot one, he would leave himself open to a suicidal attack by the other. 'Do you know us?' the Apostle asked.

The markings on their armour were familiar. So was the distorted face of the Apostle. 'Quor Vondor and Phael Rabor,' Guilliman said.

'Good,' said Quor Vondor. 'You should know the authors of your fall.'

Guilliman sniffed in contempt. 'You are authors of nothing,' he said. 'You are messengers at best.'

Phael Rabor growled, but Quor Vondor looked past Guilliman to where the ragged end of the splinter marked where the Unburdened had vanished, and he smiled. 'We are undivided,' he said. 'Chaos acts through us.'

'Then it fails through you,' said Guilliman. 'Now let's be done. Hurry up and die.'

'He doesn't realise he's already lost,' Quor Vondor said to Phael Rabor. The captain didn't reply, as if unconvinced. But then he charged with a speed and confidence that belied his wounded leg. He held the athame before him. Quor Vondor attacked at the same time. He hurled the athame at Guilliman's face.

Guilliman read how they would move before they did. His counter was so fast, it was as if he had attacked first. He crouched, and Quor Vondor's athame passed over his head. It buried itself in the wall.

Guilliman fired a sustained burst into Phael Rabor's chest and head. The rapid concussion of shells blew his armour open like an eggshell. Still clinging to the athame, Phael Rabor took three more steps. He was dead after two.

Guilliman whirled on Quor Vondor. Eldritch lightning crackled around the Word Bearer's hands and head. Guilliman flung *Incandor*. It thudded into the centre of Quor Vondor's forehead. The Apostle went rigid. His lightning lashed out with his death spasm. It struck with flashing violet light. A bolt hit Guilliman in the chest. He bore it. He stood, immovable, until Quor Vondor's throes ended.

The wind of escaping atmosphere shrieked through the ship. Bolters chattered at the corridor end of the splinter. To Guilliman, a deep silence had fallen. He holstered his weapons, then pried the athame from Phael Rabor's grip and jerked Quor Vondor's blade from the wall. He held a knife in each hand; they were unnaturally heavy. He stared at the dull black edges. He remembered the feel of another athame, its blade against his throat. Kor Phaeron had barely nicked his flesh. An insignificant wound. Guilliman had mocked Kor Phaeron for his error. Back then he had not placed much importance on the blade. It was Kor Phaeron's powers that had made the Word Bearer dangerous. Analysis of the conflict after leaving Calth had shown Guilliman his mistake. The knife had cut his flesh. It had drawn blood. But Kor Phaeron had not tried to kill him. He had tried to *convert* him.

The truth will shock you, Roboute, Kor Phaeron had said.

Embrace this.

This is the beginning of wisdom.

The athames were dangerous. Yet blades like the ones in his grasp had destroyed a powerful daemon on Calth.

Theoretical. The weapon of the enemy can be turned against him.

Practical...

He hesitated. So many unknowns getting in the way of evaluating risks and opportunities.

Practical...

Practical...

Guilliman's vox-bead buzzed, jerking his attention back to the imme-diate. He hadn't contemplated the athames for more than a second or two. He flinched, guilty as if he'd been in a fugue state for hours.

Altuzer was on the vox. *'We are in contact with the rest of the fleet,'* she said.

'Our ships?' Guilliman asked.

'Widely scattered, but close. Arriving from all directions.'

'How long before they reach us?'

'Minutes.'

In no time at all, then. But no time would be what the *Samothrace* and *Cavascor* had once the bombardment began again.

Theoretical. The enemy is holding fire to facilitate my assassination. Once they know I am still alive, the attacks will resume.

Practical. Do not show yourself to the Word Bearers. Let them think the struggle continues. Gain enough time for the fleet to arrive.

He made a conscious decision to consider the attack an assassination attempt. He refused to contemplate the idea of conversion.

He doesn't realise he's already lost.

He saved himself from introspection by considering how the gather-ing fleet should attack.

Practical. Use the advantage of our apparent weakness. 'Then we are sur-rounding the enemy,' Guilliman said. 'Send the command to attack and engage as soon as the assaults can be coordinated. The fleet is a fist. Close it. Crush the foe.'

'So ordered.'

Guilliman looked at the athames, and thought again about using the foe's tools for his own purpose. 'Shipmaster,' he said. 'What news from the *Cavascor?'*

'It engaged the strike cruiser Annunciation. Captain Hierax's Destroyer company boarded, as you commanded.'

Hierax would leave nothing behind but ash. The *Annunciation* was a dead ship even if the Word Bearers aboard believed otherwise. 'Signal

Chapter Master Iasus,' Guilliman said. 'Captain Hierax is to take the *Annunciation*'s Navigators alive.'

'Understood.'

Guilliman sheathed the athames in his belt. He felt their presence as a cold pressure. He would store them securely as soon as he could. He drew his own weapons again and made his way back down the splinter, towards the sound of battle. He stopped while he was still out of sight. He listened to his sons purge the traitors from the *Samothrace*. He was the light in the shadows, holding back though instinct urged him to join the fight. The correct practical was to wait for the right moment, and then he would bring his avenging light to bear on the traitors.

What choice, ever?

The wait was a short one.

'*The fleet is here, primarch,*' Altuzer voxed.

'Begin,' Guilliman ordered.

THE NIGHT LORDS were the first to react. The World Eaters were too focused on the chance to destroy the Ultramarines ships before them, so consumed with frustrated anger that the athame mission was taking so long, they barely noticed the first contacts on the auspex array. The Word Bearers vessels, in the centre of the operation, realised what was coming sooner, but the concentration of the squadron around the *Samothrace* and the *Cavascor* slowed their manoeuvre to face the approaching threat. The Night Lords, already hanging back, took the first contact seriously. Their squadron turned away from the *Samothrace* immediately.

The next contacts showed how big the threat was. Now the World Eaters reacted too. New contacts appeared with every second.

Wise heads on each ship realised what was happening. They had known this was a possibility. They had trusted in the prophet and the captain of the *De Profundis* to make the kill before now.

The squadrons were stronger than the two ships they had trapped. But they were not a fleet, and it was a fleet that came for them.

The Night Lords accelerated quickly. The strike cruisers *Vitam Mortem* and *Night Revelation*, with the frigates *Infinite Fall, Phosphene* and *Descent from Hope* did not look for a fight they could not win. They raced to translate into the empyrean while there was still time. The *Glorious Nova* fell on them, and with it the strike cruisers *High Ascent, Cornucopia* and *Triumph of Reason*, and almost a dozen frigates. At the command of the *Glorious Nova*, Captain Lucretius Corvo muttered thanks to the fates when he saw the Legion markings of the ships he was about to destroy. The streaks of hundreds of torpedoes carved the void with light, and every strike was an act of justice for the dead of Sotha.

The *Night Revelation* was at the head of the squadron, pulling even further ahead. The Ultramarines torpedo barrage hit it as its warp engines were spooling up to make the jump. Further back, the *Vitam Mortem* lowered its bow below the ecliptic, its angle with respect to the rest of the squadron becoming more and more steep. It was as close to an evasion as a vessel of its magnitude could muster.

Seventy-three torpedoes hit the *Night Revelation* in a matter of seconds. Its void shields collapsed immediately. The blasts that lit up the length of its hull fused into a single river of fire, a lava flow devouring the integrity of the strike cruiser. The warp engines went critical, and a sphere of unreality expanded from inside the hull. The shape of the vessel bulged, distorted and rippled as the shimmering bubble burst from its confines. The shimmer spread. The entire ship refracted fire and reality, a fragmenting mirror. Then it exploded. Ignited plasma and uncontrolled immaterium lashed out. The phantoms of the night perished in the heart of a new star. The killing light grew, and in its hunger it swallowed the *Infinite Fall*. The frigate's hull melted as it drove through the fireball, and then it too became part of the purging dawn.

The *Vitam Mortem* went lower, and lower yet, until it was running perpendicular to the plane of the squadron's flight. It sustained torpedo hits on its stern, and flames swept through its corridors, cutting off the enginarium from the superstructure. Primary power flickered. The void shields went down for a full two seconds. But then it was past the initial barrage, and still accelerating.

The *Phosphene* and the *Descent from Hope* tried to follow it. The *High Ascent* and *Cornucopia* took the *Descent from Hope* apart, moving forwards to trap the vessel between themselves, hammering it with batteries of cannons and macro-lasguns. It hit back, punishing the larger ships on either side, but it took many times the damage it could inflict. It was a flaming ruin when it emerged from between the two ships. It moved off into the void, a crematorium for all aboard.

On the bridge of the *Glorious Nova*, Corvo watched the *Vitam Mortem's* evasion. The *Nova's* course was changing to put it on a pursuit heading. 'Are you seeing the craven flight?' he voxed.

Aboard the battle-barge *Magisterial*, Chapter Master Empion of the IX answered, 'We are.' The *Magisterial* was only now coming into range of the battle. The ship and its escort were approaching from the direction in which the *Vitam Mortem* sought to flee. '*The traitors are running into our teeth,*' Empion said.

The World Eaters did not try to run. Their formation attacked the Ultramarines as if the fleet had been drawn into a trap, and the traitors were not surrounded by a closing gauntlet. The strike cruisers *Bellatorus* and *Creuisse* led the charge. They were up against the battle-barge *Gauntlet of Glory*, the grand cruiser *Suspiria Majestrix*, the *Chronicle*, the *Glory of Fire* and twenty more ships beyond them. The World Eaters fired all their forwards guns at once. The barrage was a roar of defiance that cut through the *Chronicle*. The cruiser became a cloud of ignited gas and debris, moving forwards on momentum. Its kin repaid the attackers in kind; the *Suspiria Majestrix's* nova gun hit the *Creuisse* head-on. The blast split the ship in two, the halves parting like jaws, then peeling back from the gathering eruption.

In the midst of the Word Bearers formation, the *Annunciation* turned against the flow of the retreat. It accelerated as if it sought to escape from the cluster of ships. It had ceased to respond to hails shortly before the arrival of the Ultramarines fleet. The *Cavascor* pulled away from it, and the *Annunciation* drove straight for the *Orfeo's Lament*. The light cruiser was still turning when the larger ship closed in on it. It abandoned its manoeuvre and tried to accelerate on a tangent. The *Annunciation* struck it just forwards of the stern. It broke the *Lament* in half. It barrelled through the hull in a storm of explosions. Statuary from both ships, colossal embodiments of metaphor and the lessons of the dark, flew off from the collision in a swarm of tumbling fragments. The *Orfeo's Lament* howled its last, and the plasma cry swept over the *Annunciation*. The strike cruiser's bow was a ruin after the collision, twisted and fused. Tremors swept the hull, damage feeding damage until the ship was a bomb awaiting the signal for detonation. The signal came from the *Cavascor*, when Hierax remotely triggered melta charges he and his Destroyers had left behind. The raging holocaust grasped at the retreating squadron, scraping the void shields, striking at the vessels with a foretaste of the XIII Legion's anger.

The full measure of this wrath came from the *Ultimus Mundi*, and the *Gauntlet of Glory*, and the *Praetorian Trust*, and the *Triumph of Espandor*, and the *Unbroken Vigil*, and the *Aquiline*, and scores more. The fist of the Ultramarines closed with convulsive fury. Not a single ship of the Night Lords, the World Eaters or the Word Bearers translated to the immaterium. Overwhelming force turned them to fire, to ash, to the dissipation of gas, and to the silence of dust. Cold, devastating precision annihilated the warriors of terror and of rage. But when it came to the sons of Lorgar, there was a shout that echoed on the bridges and in the halls and in the weapon bays of every ship involved in their destruction.

'For Calth!' went the cry. The Ultramarines fleet had been reduced by that betrayal, yet it was still the largest of any Legion. Many of the ships that had survived that day were present now. Their legionaries, hungry for victories and for justice, took their measure of revenge, and rejoiced.

'For Calth! For Calth! For Calth!'

GUILLIMAN OVERSAW THE extermination of the squadron from the bridge of the *Samothrace*. He stayed focused. He monitored every action, and approved of the decisions of his sons. But the athames pulled at him. When the last of the enemy ships were guttering torches, he returned to his quarters alone. He sealed the door. A twenty-foot vault dominated the starboard wall. He opened it, revealing compartmentalised stasis chambers. He placed the athames in an empty one, engaged the field and stepped back. The air between him and the blades shimmered slightly. The vault door boomed when he shut it. Hexagrammic circuits locked the vault down tight. It would open to him and no one else. The athames were secured now. They were beyond doing harm.

His hand rested on the wheel of the door.

They can be studied now, he thought. *Maybe they can be used.*

In the lower levels of the *Samothrace*, cells held the Navigators captured from the *Annunciation* and transported by Thunderhawk from the *Cavascor*. They, too, might be used.

Theoretical. The tools of the enemy subverted from their purpose can be among the most effective weapons against the foe.

Theoretical. These tools may be dangerous in their own right. Any attempted use may invite disaster.

His analysis was incomplete. He couldn't tell which theoretical was the most valid.

What choice, ever?

He thought he heard the voice in the flame laugh.

He doesn't know he's already lost.

FIVE

Chorale

THE LION'S STORMBIRD approached the rent in the hull of a mass conveyer. The ship was one of the largest in the graveyard. Apart from the breach, which extended almost a third of its length, it was intact. Pict and vid screens displayed shifting views of the freighter. The Lion sat on an elevated throne, eyeing the images, trying to pierce the ship's secret. The gunship's lights picked out its name above the breach, a quarter of the way back from the prow. It was the *Chorale*. The marlins were faded, almost invisible. The ship had been in a poor state of repair long before its end.

The Lion frowned. He turned to Khalybus. 'You said the ships were not warp-capable. A conveyor of this size would be.'

The Iron Hands captain looked at the centre pict screen a moment longer. Then he tapped it, freezing the image. 'It would be,' he agreed. 'Normally. But look at the engine.' He pointed. 'It's been modified. I suggest the warp engines have been removed.' He waved his hand, taking in the whole of the ship. 'So much patchwork,' he said. 'Layers of it. I would say an accretion of centuries. This is a vessel that was rescued from the scrapheap and used for short journeys, by many owners.'

Khalybus glanced back at the Lion only once as he spoke. If he was curious about the primarch insisting on leading the exploration of the wreck himself, he said nothing, and his ruined face was unreadable. If he resented being a guest on the Dark Angels mission rather than leading one himself, he kept that hidden too.

Holguin, though, looked no happier than he had on the *Invincible Reason*.

'I must see for myself,' the Lion had told him, putting a stop to the voted lieutenant's objections. 'I will verify what I have been told.'

Holguin had opened his mouth to ask, *By whom?* He stopped himself. His eyes narrowed, though. He knew.

Very well, then, the Lion had thought. *So you know why I need to be sure. If the secret of the way forwards is contained in these wrecks, I will not see it through an intermediary.*

Now he asked Khalybus, 'Can you extrapolate what killed the ship?'

'I see no sign of collision. The engine looks intact. The work on the hull is poor. I suspect metal fatigue. Internal pressure finally burst the hull.'

'Just as it reached this location. At the same time that disaster befell all these other ships.'

'I do not trust the coincidence, either,' said Khalybus.

The Stormbird flew inside the *Chorale*. The breach was over a mile long and a hundred yards high. Multiple levels of cargo bays were open to the void. The gunship came in for a landing in the most sternward of the upper bays, the closest to the ship's superstructure and bridge. The Lion donned his helmet and pulled open the Stormbird's side hatch as the retro exhaust nozzles vented gas, manoeuvring the ship to the deck in the absence of gravity and atmosphere. The Lion pushed himself down. His boots maglocked to the bay decking.

The five-man squad selected by Holguin spread out, bolters ready. Holguin's helm lights were the first to pass over the inner wall of the bay. 'This is an enemy ship,' he said.

The Lion joined him. The wall was covered in runes. Some had been burned into the surface, others had been daubed in blood. The Lion's lip curled. Their forms were becoming familiar in all the worst ways. Repeated exposure did nothing to dull their obscenity, or their uncanny nature. If he looked at any one of the runes for too long, the conviction grew that it was about to start moving. Human hands had marked the walls, and they had used a language that had no origin in the materium, and that no sane being should ever contemplate.

The eight-pointed star held dominion over all the other signs.

'Matters are becoming clearer,' Khalybus said.

'You have had dealings with these cults too, then,' said Holguin.

'And the beings they worship, yes.' His voice, thick with hate, grated more harshly than before. 'We have established a base on Thrinos,' he went on, naming a moon in the neighbouring Anesidorax System. 'There are refugees there, from many worlds. This plague is widespread in the subsector.'

'Do you think any of them have come from the same location as these ships?' the Lion asked.

Khalybus shook his head. 'We have examined all ships as they've arrived. They have been free of this taint. And none have been of the same vintage and disrepair. None of these vessels should ever have left their home system.'

They moved on. Once they left the region of the breach, they started to encounter bodies that had not been sucked into the void when the atmosphere vented. They passed corpses tangled in ruined bulkheads, caught in half-closed doors, and lying in sealed rooms. The Lion paused at one closed chamber and looked through the plasteel. He wrenched the door open and stepped inside. He examined the corpses. 'These did not die from suffocation,' he said. The room was a scene of mutual slaughter. Torsos had been cut open, throats slit. Runes had been carved on every forehead. Many of the dead clutched primitive blades. More than a few appeared to have cut themselves open, perhaps after all the others had been despatched.

'This was not murder,' said Holguin.

'No,' Khalybus agreed. 'It was sacrifice.'

'So the breach was deliberate?'

'I would wish to examine it,' Khalybus said. 'But that seems likely.'

'Too many ships dead at once,' the Lion said. 'We know how it happened. The question remains why.'

'The warp storm would seem to be a result,' said Holguin.

'To what end, though?' the Lion asked. 'And why here?'

The path to the bridge was littered with more corpses. All of them bore self-inflicted ritualistic wounds. The faces of the dead were ecstatic in the frozen moments of their last suffering. The ship was a tomb, and it was a monument to triumph. The dead of the *Chorale* were degraded things even in life. The Lion observed their clothing and their tools. He saw hides that would have been still bloody when worn. He saw icons of human flesh and bone. Their weapons were crude, though crafted with horror as their intent. He was surprised that these people were capable of piloting void ships, no matter how poorly maintained. They seemed to be a feral people. They were so in thrall to the gods of the warp, they should have had no ability to reason.

Just outside the entrance to the bridge, Holguin stopped and kneeled beside a brace of corpses. They had died with the runes incomplete on their foreheads. They had been gouging their flesh with their fingernails when the end came for them. 'Those look rushed,' Holguin said, pointing to the wounds. 'And the clothes are different.' There were none of the perverse icons. Their robes were still primitive, but unobjectionable.

'They were meant to pass,' said the Lion.

'An infiltration?' Holguin asked.

'Perhaps. You are sure of all your refugees on Thrinos?' the Lion asked Khalybus.

'As sure as we can be of the flesh,' the Iron Hands legionary grunted.

The Lion nodded. He turned his attention back to the bodies. 'They were not meant to die here,' he theorised. 'When they realised they were going to, they tried to complete their ritual. But the sacrifice was supposed to occur somewhere else.'

'On Pythos,' said Khalybus.

'That does seem to be the only destination in this system.' A destination closed to everyone. There the warp storm was ferocious. Nothing could cross the frontier of the Pandorax System.

The Dark Angels and the Iron Hands legionary entered the bridge, and found the heart of the *Chorale*'s self-contradictory madness. There were many more bodies here, and they had all fallen in the same kind of mutual suicide that had consumed the inmates of the previous chamber. A stone altar on a dais occupied the front of the bridge. It was stained brown by blood. A brass eight-pointed star rose above it. A human head was mounted on each of the eight arms. Each spike end punched through the bridge of the nose, caving in the skull. The last victim of the altar lay across it, a man whose gaze had frozen into a sublimity of horror.

The altar faced workstations, and each of them had its own crew. They were clad in the same primitive rags; there was nothing to differentiate them from their kin. Yet they had known how to bring the *Chorale* out to this heading. There was no data to salvage here. The cogitators were burned wrecks and the screens at every workstation were smashed. The crew had destroyed the bridge before killing themselves.

'Where did you come from?' the Lion muttered.

He moved through the rows of gutted pict screens until he was before the altar again, much closer now. His helm lamps swept over the carvings on the stone. He walked around the altar, sensing the risk he incurred in trying to understand what he saw, yet knowing that risk was necessary. On each side of the slab was a crawling density of runes. Lines of the figures had been chipped out of the rock with care and frenzy around the periphery of each face. They captured the eye, forcing the gaze to travel on insect legs. They circled engravings that the Lion recognised as star charts despite the presence of other lines suggesting monstrous beings and a galaxy caught in the claws of horror.

The Lion returned to the front of the altar, then walked around it again, counter-clockwise this time. The crawling of the runes was worse, and the engravings flowed one to the other. The altar stone was a narrative of travel. 'This was a *pilgrimage*,' he said. The word almost stuck in his throat. Its accuracy enfolded layers of perversity.

The Dark Angels and Khalybus gathered at the altar. They looked at the stone with a dispassion possible only through discipline.

The Lion pointed at the chart on the front of the stone. 'Pandorax,' he said. The positions of the stars were unmistakeable, despite the crude work and toxic embellishments. The work embodied the same paradox as the *Chorale* itself. The people aboard it appeared too primitive to pilot a void ship, yet they had. The Lion wouldn't have believed they could map the positions of the stars in their home system, let alone their destination. Yet they had.

The Lion circled the altar again. Khalybus followed. They traced the corrosive vectors leading from Pandorax back to the first system. The effort made claws scratch at the Lion's chest. The surface of reality felt a little thinner each time he walked around the obscenities. The charts would not click into place in isolation, though. He had to subject himself to the narrative.

Khalybus hissed in disgust as they walked the circuit. He was silent again as they looked at the start of the *Chorale*'s journey. Khalybus crouched, looking closer.

'Do you recognise it?'

'I do.' Khalybus reached out to tap the world at the centre of the engraving. He stopped himself just before making contact, his bionic finger recoiling. 'That,' he said, 'is Davin.'

ALONE IN HIS quarters, the Lion thought about what he had seen on the *Chorale*. He faced signs without referents. The origin point of the cultists was important, but he did not know why. He did not like the idea of approaching Tuchulcha without having some knowledge beforehand. He believed in the utility of the artefact and was willing to use it to travel, trusting it only one jump at a time. What he did not wish was to rely on it for information. He would not have what he believed to be true shaped by something inhuman.

By the time the Dark Angels fleet anchored in orbit over Thrinos, he was no further along. He could imagine Guilliman remarking about his singular lack of data, that he had absolutely nothing concrete to go on. And that was without Roboute knowing about Tuchulcha.

In the end, though, he entered Tuchulcha's chamber again. The meat puppet was facing the door as if it had been waiting for his appearance.

The Lion had thought through his questions before coming. He was not going to commit the fleet to a jump based on a deliberate half-truth this time. The creature would answer him, and it would answer him well.

'Davin,' the Lion said.

'Are you asking me something? That is a name and not a sentence.'

What did you expect? the Lion wondered, irritated with himself. *A guilty start? A refusal to meet your gaze?* Laughable. Every expression that crossed the servitor's face was a deliberately constructed imitation of the human. 'Can you take us to Davin?' the Lion asked.

'No,' said Tuchulcha.

That was interesting. The being had never answered in the negative before. 'Why not?'

'There are obstacles. Ones that even I cannot breach.'

'Can they be crossed in some other way?'

The servitor cocked its head. The Lion was becoming used to reading this as a signal of amusement from Tuchulcha. 'Shouldn't that be my question for you?'

The Lion ignored the jab and took another approach. 'Can you take us part of the way?'

'Yes.'

'As far as the nearest barrier?'

'Yes.'

'And if we succeed in crossing it, can you take us further?'

'I can.'

'As far as the next barrier.'

'That is correct.'

'Let us be clear. If we wish to reach Terra, we must reach Davin, is that correct?'

'It is.'

'Why?'

'The current flows that way,' Tuchulcha said.

The answer was enigmatic again after the plain speaking. The Lion knew he would not learn anything more.

When he left the chamber, Holguin was outside the doors. His face was respectful. His presence was concerned.

'Speak your mind, voted lieutenant.'

'Have you learned something, lord?' Holguin asked.

'I am told that Davin is the key to Terra.'

'Do you believe what it tells you?'

'Provisionally, yes.' He did not need to justify himself, but he chose to answer fully. He decided that he wanted Holguin to understand the actions he was going to order the fleet to take. 'Tuchulcha cannot take us all the way to Davin.'

'Obstacles imply importance,' Holguin said.

Good, the Lion thought. He sees. 'Precisely,' he said. *The same is true for Terra, if only we had realised it sooner.*

'What will you command?' Holguin asked.

'The astropathic choir must contact my brothers. Let the word be sent. We have found the way.'

THE ORDER WAS given. The word was sent. It did not go easily.

They will kill us all yet, Vazheth Licinia thought. The mistress of the *Invincible Reason*'s astropathic choir wasn't sure who she meant by *they*. She did not question the order from the primarch. She did not doubt its necessity. She would give up her life to see it transmitted.

Even so, the thought sprang to her mind. It was beyond her control, a flare of dark truth she could not suppress. *This war*, she thought. It tore apart the galaxy, and it tore apart every understanding of reality. The impossible march across the void, and the impossible demanded of every one.

The impossible was asked of her choir now. The message itself was simple and urgent. *The way is found. Come to Thrinos.* Its conversion into mental imagery was not difficult. To send it, though… That was a different task. That was the impossible.

Licinia stood in her pulpit. An articulated framework attached to her chest held her upright, its servomotor-driven legs giving her mobility when she had to walk. The curved rows of iron astropathic pews before her formed an amphitheatre. Though Licinia was blind, it often seemed to her that she could perceive the chamber as a vague grey space. The first row of astropaths were a hint of phantoms, a false dawn of sight. When she opened her inner, psychic eye, though, the hall became a tempest of energy. Each astropath was a blazing node. Beyond the choir was the non-space of the warp, howling with the Ruinstorm. The mere awareness of the convulsion was a dagger to the mind. Transmitting a message meant staring directly into the madness. It meant being completely vulnerable to its torments.

'We call to the Ultramarines and to the Blood Angels,' Licinia said to her choir. 'We call them to us. We call to them across the infinite.' Her words were command and invocation. As she instructed the astropaths, bringing them to the single-minded concentration on their duty, she conjured the collective power of the choir. Unity was its strength. Unity was the means by which the individual might survive. 'We call to them through the bonds of loyalty. We call to them through our bonds to the Emperor.' The ankle manacle each astropath wore was a symbol of the soul-binding to the Emperor. In the midst of transmission, when the individual became part of the whole, but also courted the risk of annihilation on the dream-storms of the warp, the anklet was a physical grounding, a lodestone for the self and its purpose.

As the transmission began, Licinia fell silent. Her guidance became entirely psychic. She reached out with the combined force of all the astropaths, and they reached out with the focus of her will.

They reached out to their counterparts in the IX and XIII Legions. They did not know where or how far away the Blood Angels and Ultramarines were. Location and distance were meaningless. The call went to the infinite.

But madness ruled the infinite. The call encountered the Ruinstorm, and the Ruinstorm answered with fury. Its winds sought to shred the coherence of the message. Its waves crashed upon the minds of the choir. The roar took Licinia. It plunged her perception into the maelstrom. She pushed back, urging the chorus to greater heights, summoning strength from determination. And as the storm raged harder, it reached into the minds of all to shatter the core of the collective.

A great distance away, blood ran warm from Licinia's eyes and ears.

She cried out, again and again, hurling herself and her charges against the storm, until at last, there was a sudden crack across the non-space. It was a fissure, and the call went through it, travelling now on its wave of dreams, independent of any sender. It was also lightning, and it struck the choir. It was as if something in the warp welcomed the message at the same time that it punished its senders.

Licinia screamed, psychic vision blinded by shrieking silver, as she was slammed back into her physical self. She choked on the smell of ozone and burned flesh. She clenched her psychic vision shut against the pain and the feedback of energy. She was in the amphitheatre once more, surrounded again by the false sight of grey and phantoms. There was light in the grey now. Even with her inner eye closed, the psychic energies lashing out in the chamber were too strong to shut out completely. Some of the nodes were burning. People were screaming. An echo that might have been thunder or might have been laughter rolled away, fading with the dissipation of the energy.

Licinia breathed in and out, her lungs wheezing and gurgling. She would have collapsed, but her framework held her up. Her face and neck were sticky with her blood. She forced calm back into the storm in her head. When she felt she could stand it, she opened her perception by the smallest crack, and took in the tally of the dead.

Bright lights had gone out. Many pews held slumped, broken shapes.

The message had been sent. Almost a quarter of her astropaths had died in the process.

They will kill us all, yet.

SIX

The Convergence of Fates

Datum: that was an ambush.

  Corollary: they knew where to find us.

  Corollary: they travel the immaterium at will.

  Theoretical: their Navigators are able to do what ours cannot.

  Practical: use them.

There were two Navigators from the *Annunciation*. That was unusual. Perhaps it had something to do with success of the ambush. They stood in chains and manacles in the interrogation chamber. The space was spare, the walls unadorned. A bank of focused lumen globes shone from the upper wall directly onto the prisoners. It illuminated them in a hard, unforgiving white light that bleached every shadow from them. They could hide nothing in the brilliance, and they could see nothing. To them, Guilliman knew, he was nothing but a huge silhouette. The guards at the four corners of the chamber would be dark masses. Lead bindings, thick with hexagrammic circuitry on their foreheads, covered their third eyes. The function of the Navigators was to see what others could not. Now they were blind.

Guilliman had the bitter sensation that they still saw more clearly than he did.

He studied them before speaking, surveying the field of battle to come. They were a man and a woman. Their names were Yathinius and Nekras. They were Terran, scions of important families of the Navis Nobilite. Guilliman made a note of their ancestry and the need to purge the families, root and branch, when the time came.

The two Navigators were old before their time, with only a few strands of lank hair hanging from their scalps. They were so weak the manacles had no strategic necessity. Their robes, burned and frayed when Hierax's Destroyers took the *Annunciation*, were the crimson of their Legion, and threaded with passages from Lorgar's writing. Guilliman had once seen that work as tragic, a philosophy of error consuming his brilliant brother uselessly. He knew better now. It was not futile. It was monstrous.

Yathinius opened his eyes wide into the light, daring it to burn his retinas. He smiled. Blood gushed from his mouth. He parted his teeth, and the front half of his tongue, bitten through, fell out.

Do you think you can use this creature? Guilliman asked himself. 'You see through the Ruinstorm,' he said.

Yathinius kept smiling while Nekras spoke. 'We do,' she said.

'Tell me how.'

'By the blessings of Chaos.'

She was being too forthcoming. Guilliman did not trust the eagerness with which she answered his questions. It felt like mockery.

Experimentally, he said, 'You will serve my Legion now. You will take us where you are ordered.'

'Of course,' said Nekras. Yathinius' laugh was wet and gargling. He started to choke on his blood, then laughed again.

This was all mockery. What was worse, though, was that Guilliman did not think Nekras was lying. There were no telltale micro-expressions on her face that might suggest evasion. Instead, when she agreed with his demand, her face became even more open with a fanatic's enthusiasm.

'You would serve your enemy so easily?' Guilliman probed.

'We would,' Nekras said, and Yathinius nodded, drooling blood. 'What choice do we have?' Nekras continued. There was a pause, during which her features shifted. 'What choice do any of us have?' she asked. The humour was gone from her voice now. She spoke with cold fire, a disciple enraptured by the sublime. Her gaze turned to Guilliman. She did not blink. Though her pupils had almost vanished, it was as if she was seeing him clearly. Or seeing through him to an even greater clarity. 'We all walk the assigned path.'

There was something wrong with her voice. There was a distortion, a very slight echo, as of a second voice entwined like a parasite around hers. It was the voice from Quor Vondor's psychic flame, striking out at Guilliman again through another willing instrument. The thing was an infection that had entered the ship with the splinter. It was poisoning his blood, flooding his mind with doubts. He could feel it building into something larger. There was the seed of a cancerous revelation, and he did not know how to excise it. It attacked and grew through truth, damnable truth. Nekras would not stop speaking the truth even under torture.

A heavy tread stopped just outside the interrogation cell. Guilliman turned from the prisoners. The door rattled as it slid aside for him, its sensors keyed to respond at once to his proximity, then closed behind him with a deep clang. Prayto stood in the hall. 'You wanted no vox communication,' he said.

'Yes,' said Guilliman. And he had chosen to conduct the interrogation personally. He told himself that to form the practical for the fleet's movements, he needed the data first-hand. That was all. 'What is it, Titus?' Guilliman asked.

'An astropathic message from the Lion. The Dark Angels have found a way through the storm. They are calling on the fleets to muster.'

'I see. We are not surprised that my brother was the first to forge the path, are we?' The Lion had been able to find his way through the warp before the light of the Pharos had been lit.

'No, we are not. Though I would give much to know how he accomplishes these feats.'

'So would I. We must be wary of secrets. We have all been guilty of keeping them, and we have seen the disasters their corrosive power can bring.'

Guilliman thought about the athames in his quarters. He knew what the Lion would have to say about those. He was troubled by his own hesitation to deal with them one way or the other. The possibility of turning the enemy's weapons against him stopped him from destroying them. The threat they presented made him keep his distance from them. Uncertainty was a state inimical to his being. It was through certainty that he had forged Ultramar. Certainty was the bedrock of action, the fulcrum that pivoted the theoretical into the practical.

Imperium Secundus had not been an act of certainty. That was the flaw that marred its foundations, that changed it from salvation to heresy.

'Do we have the Lion's location?' Guilliman asked.

'We do. Thrinos, in the Anesidorax System.'

Guilliman frowned. 'That is not on the most direct route to Terra.'

'No.'

'Your thoughts?'

'We do not know how the Lion comes by some of his knowledge. We...' Prayto hesitated.

'Say it,' Guilliman told him. 'We're both thinking it.'

'We don't trust those sources, whatever they may be.'

'No, we don't.'

'But we trust in the Lion's loyalty.'

'Completely.' No matter how great the hostility had grown between them on Macragge, loyalty had not been the question. They had fought over the correct prosecution of the war. And the Lion had humbled himself before Guilliman in the end, in the desperate act of showing that the Emperor must still be alive. For a man with his brother's pride, bringing himself to beg was a truly heroic feat.

'Theoretical. Broadcasting an astropathic signal from that distance through the Ruinstorm would be a very costly effort. The Lion would not engage in it without a strong conviction. Practical. We should treat his conviction as justified.'

'And make the jump to Thrinos.'

'Yes.'

'I agree. Getting there will be costly for us too.' Anesidorax was further than anyone had travelled since the beginning of the Ruinstorm. It would take many short jumps, draining the Navigators. Unless he used the Word Bearers' Navigators.

'Less costly than not going,' Prayto said.

Guilliman glanced at the interrogation cell. His jaw clenched in frustration. 'I want you to see something,' he said. 'Come with me.'

He led Prayto into the cell. The Navigators smiled their mock greeting.

'Anesidorax,' Guilliman said. 'You will take us there.'

'We will,' said Nekras. 'So it is willed by the gods.' She answered quickly, and with ferocity. Yathinius laughed.

'Your willingness to sacrifice yourselves surprises me,' Guilliman said.

'You mean you distrust us,' Nekras said. She leaned forwards, as if daring the searing light to burn her. Guilliman had not identified himself. Even so, the size of his silhouette would leave the Navigators in no doubt as to who stood before them. They showed none of the awed terror that shook most mortals in the presence of a primarch. They were too much in ecstatic thrall to beings much more powerful.

'No,' Guilliman said. 'I don't trust you.'

'We will take you to Anesidorax,' said Nekras. 'I swear it.' Yathinius' braying turned into a moaning howl of worship. 'We will get you there in a single jump,' Nekras continued. She smiled, caught up in a beatitude so foul, Guilliman saw the guards stir in disgust. 'I see Thrinos already.'

'I said nothing about Thrinos.'

'No matter. That is where the gods decree our path must lead. You are going to Thrinos.' She stretched the name of the world, as if the sentence were incomplete, as if she were going to add *whether you wish to or not*.

Guilliman exchanged a look with Prayto and left the cell again. Once on the other side of the door, he said, 'Their stated eagerness coincides precisely with what the Lion asks of us.'

'Worrisome,' said Prayto. 'I stand by the practical, though. Her words could easily be attempts at misdirection.'

'I agree with the practical. But I don't think she's lying... Theoretical. A single leap through the warp will be far less costly than many.'

'Theoretical. There will be unanticipated costs that will be far worse.'

Guilliman nodded, musing over what he had seen in the Navigators. So much fanaticism, and that was a form of honesty. 'They were telling the truth,' he said. 'Their reasons are what they are, but they will find the way to Thrinos.'

'We're going to use them?' Prayto sounded horrified.

'We need to reach Thrinos. The Word Bearers wish to take us there. When your goals align with the enemy's, let the enemy labour for you.'

The interrogation chamber doors opened for him one more time. 'Prepare them for their task,' he ordered the guards. He looked at the Navigators. 'I will put your vows to the test,' he said.

'The gods will see you to your destiny,' Nekras called out to him as he turned to go. 'You walk your assigned path.'

The doors slammed shut, cutting off the hall from any sound in the chamber. Guilliman strode down the corridor with Prayto. The walls rang with the echoes of their boots, and not with Nekras' last taunt. Her words were not following Guilliman. They were not becoming a refrain in his head.

For almost fifty yards, Guilliman managed to hold fast to this lie.

'WE'VE CONFIRMED THE foe is a ship,' said Carminus.

On the bridge of the *Red Tear*, Sanguinius eyed the pict screens. Their displays were erratic, streaked with interference. Every few seconds, the effort to present coherent information about the intruder would become too much. The images would vanish for a moment. Sometimes, they would distort instead, and the hololithic representations

and data summaries would become something else. A hint of a screaming, inhuman face. A shiver of claws.

The *Red Tear*'s Geller field was holding, at least. The incursions had
been repelled. The rest of the fleet was not as fortunate. Battles still
raged on numerous ships, but control had not been lost. The Blood
Angels formation was as intact as Sanguinius could expect it to be in
the empyrean's tempest.

'What ship, though?' said Sanguinius. Much of the information he
saw on the screens was nonsense. It had to be.

'We don't know,' said Carminus. 'We can't even get a precise fix on
its size, never mind its configuration.'

Huge, the pict screens said. The ship was a colossal black shadow in
the warp. The *Sable* had fought it, and the *Sable* had gone.

'How close did the *Sable* get?' Sanguinius asked.

'We can't tell with any certainty, lord,' Mautus said, apologetic and
frustrated. 'Closer than we were when it bombarded us, that's all we
can say.' He paused for a moment. 'The *Sable* lasted less than a minute against it.'

So powerful, Sanguinius thought. 'That implies it did not use its full
force against us.'

'That was my thought, too,' said Carminus.

'Unless it was farther away than we thought,' Mautus suggested.

Sanguinius looked at the screens again. The picture they presented
was incomplete, but there were brush strokes to the impression that
were clear. The ship was immense, and it carved a clear swath through
the warp. Sanguinius seized on the sign of the monster's passage. It was
a direction for the fleet to take, the only one to appear since the Ruinstorm's warp aspect had taken them. 'Pursue it,' Sanguinius said. 'All
ships. Form up, and get into the foe's wake. Close with it.' He paused
for a moment. 'Destroy it.' That command was an illusion. He knew
it as he said it. At the same time, he rejected the fatalism. 'Destroy it,'
he repeated, his voice booming across the bridge, a call to action and
to retaliation.

'So ordered,' said Carminus, and the fleet master sent out the command to the fleet.

The contorting empyrean sent another huge wave slamming against the *Red Tear*. The flagship groaned. It heaved to port like a terrestrial ship caught in a swell. The artificial gravity could not adjust. It was fooled by the madness of the warp, and when the deck canted violently, officers and servitors slid from their stations towards the port wall. Another wave hit, this time from an imagined below, knocking the prow high. The huge vessel tossed and dropped, a leaf in a whirlwind. The mechadendrites of the command throne linked Carminus to the ship's guidance systems, and he bellowed orders to the secondary guidance operators. They were fighting to right the ship in a realm where space was meaningless, where all directions were none. But even a substanceless dream can be fought, and the immaterium had substance. It was more and less than matter, and it was hostile. It was a foe to be fought as much as the dark ship.

His jaw clenched, Carminus brought the *Red Tear* to a level bearing, directly in the wake of the huge vessel. The battleship gave chase, and behind it, the rest of the fleet moved into formation. Sanguinius listened to the messages as they came in. Numerous ships were still struggling with daemonic incursions, but no helms had been lost, and even the *Chalice*, the most hard-pressed by breaches, managed to join up.

'We're going faster,' said Mautus.

'That is an illusion,' Sanguinius corrected him. He understood the misperception, though. The ship did seem to be running more smoothly. The wake of the enemy was calmer, and the stuff of the immaterium appeared to be hurrying the *Red Tear* forwards, as if millions of spectral hands were hurling the vessel along its destined path.

And illusion or not, the conceptions of speed and direction were the only ones available.

'Range to the enemy?' Sanguinius asked.

'No closer than before,' said Mautus.

Far from ideal. Only now the entire fleet was pursuing the target.

'All ships, open fire,' Sanguinius said. 'Destroy that phantom.'

THE XIII LEGION fleet lost two destroyers on the first jump. The cruiser *Praetorian of Ulixis* vanished in the warp during the second. By the third, almost a quarter of the fleet was reporting episodes of madness afflicting Navigators. Guilliman ordered the fleet's formation held even tighter. The risk of collisions was high, but he was willing to take it. The communications were better, and the diminished isolation of the ships was a lifeline of sanity to the crews and struggling Navigators.

The practical worked. But as the *Samothrace* shuddered its way through the warp, the measure felt inadequate. The tempest of the immaterium clawed at the ship. The decks and walls groaned with the strain of holding fast to their reality. Nightmares pressed at the hull, seeking purchase, seeking entry. The Geller field was holding, though the air Guilliman breathed felt wrong, as if tainted by invisible filaments, a twitching nest of insect legs.

We might get there faster. The thought assailed him through the leaps. It grew more insistent with every casualty to madness. It undermined the practical, shaking its foundations with the loss of each ship. One jump, Nekras had said. The practical of distrust was sound. He knew this to be true. Prayto had concurred. Yet there had been no sign that Nekras was lying.

And? What of it? You have been blind before. You did not see this war coming. You did not see Lorgar's betrayal coming. And with a bitter pang, he thought back to before the war, to Thoas, and to the history of human civil war he had found and ordered expunged. The lessons had been there, and he had wilfully turned his eyes from them.

We might get there faster. If we use the enemy's tools.

The concept should have been unthinkable. It was not. He confronted it, but could not put it aside. He left the bridge of the *Samothrace* and returned to his quarters. He needed to face what he was contemplating in a form that was not abstract. In the main chamber, he advanced to the stasis vault. It opened with a groan of metal and a hiss of escaping air. He stood before the two compartments that held the athames.

Theoretical. You postulated that careful study might lead to the successful use of these tools. Would the same not be true of the Navigators?

The train of logic was seductive. It would be easy to agree with it.

'No,' he whispered. 'The theoretical is flawed. It ignores realities. It shapes itself to irrational hope.'

The truth did not have the convincing effect it should have had. The blades mocked him with the lethal secrecy of their being. They seemed to answer him with Nekras' words. *You walk your assigned path.*

Guilliman's right hand came up in an involuntary gesture. His fingers touched the point on his throat where Kor Phaeron's dagger had pierced his flesh. He had been wounded, but he had resisted the power of the blade. He had not been corrupted.

Weren't you?

He closed his eyes for a moment, then, staring at the blades, made himself work through the darkest theoretical. Perhaps he had deluded himself. Perhaps the athame had infected him. Perhaps every decision he had made since then had been shaped by the shadow that had entered his blood.

He looked back with horror on the Imperium Secundus, at its arrogance. The Lion and Sanguinius had been right to mistrust it. Yet he had insisted upon its necessity, and dragged them into his delusion.

He wondered how many of his brothers had been brought to make war on the Emperor in exactly the same way.

The conclusion of the theoretical was appalling. Corrupted, walking the assigned path, he had become a corruptor in his turn.

He wished Tarasha Euten was there. He wanted her counsel now, more than any other's. He needed to hear her dismiss the premise of his corruption.

Is that what you call making a mistake now? He could hear her voice in his head. He could see her wry expression as she spoke those words.

Only she was on Macragge, not the *Samothrace*. She had not spoken.

The words belonged to his wishful mental constructions. They served no purpose. They were an attempt at self-absolution.

They were meaningless.

The edges of the athames cut the light of the vault. They were darkness staring back at him.

The *Samothrace* shook again. The tremors were taking on a new violence, as if the hunger outside the hull sensed the blood pouring from the psychic wounds within.

A FLEET'S ANGER streaked through the empyrean to the shadow, and did nothing.

'Auspex,' Sanguinius called out. 'Have we hit or not?' On the primary tactical screen that had descended before the window shutters, the hololithic renderings of the battle had shown him the arcs of cannon fire and the trajectories of torpedoes, all heading directly into the vague mass of the enemy. The *Red Tear*'s cogitators struggled to create a logical representation of the unreality beyond the hull.

'I can't tell, lord,' Mautus replied. 'If we did, there is no visible effect, but I can get no readings at all on the ship. It may even be outside our range... I mean...' He paused, frustrated over the uncertain meaning of the word *range* in the warp. 'I don't think we are closing with it.'

Yes we are, Sanguinius thought. Distance was a lie, space was an illusion, and yet there was a truth to proximity. The *Sable* had come near enough to die, and the *Red Tear* was nearer too. The weight of the phantom's shadow oppressed him. The bridge felt insubstantial, and time was slippery. The halls of the *Vengeful Spirit* tugged at him. If he let them, they would pull him into them. His fist tightened around the *Spear of Telesto* with the effort of holding his consciousness in the here and now. Micro-visions of his final moments flickered across the surface of his mind. They stabbed him, each blow like the jab of a monomolecular blade. And as the shadow's weight grew heavier, it took on a new character. It became the inevitability of fate. It was the grasp of his doom. That which had not yet occurred took on the certainty of the past. Sanguinius stared at the black shape on the tactical screen as if it would resolve itself not into the form of an identifiable ship, but into his death. His end was coming. It marched towards him, the one absolute in an ocean of flux. It was almost upon him, and it would not tell him if his death would have any meaning, or simply be miserable, pointless, his corpse just one more added to the heap piled up before Horus' victory. He could know nothing except how he would die.

Fate would not be changed. Destiny was unalterable.

The fist clamped tight around him. The shadow of hopelessness spread across his sight.

The fleet's barrage continued without pause. The power to destroy civilisations reached out for the phantom, and found nothing. The pict screen shuddered, ship positions realigned and the cruiser *Laudem Sanguinum* was far ahead of the formation, in the lee of the great shadow. The phantom lashed out, its weapons fire represented by the hololiths as dark, streaking claws. The *Laudem* vanished.

The shadow grew again. The abyss of foretold death opened up before Sanguinius. It was ready for him. It would not be denied. Choice and hope died in its maw.

Unless...

The possibility had no shape. It barely had existence. It was no more than a sliver, a thin, trembling slash of silver in the darkness. It flashed at Sanguinius, a glimmer so slight he might have missed it, yet so insistent he had no choice but to turn to it.

Unless...

Unless what? The sliver trembled like hope. He could not articulate it. He did not know where the embryonic thought came from, or where it might go. If he looked at it too closely, it might vanish. But it was there, real, a silver scratch in the night of destiny. *Unless, unless, unless...* A seed of possibility. The tiniest deviation in the march of the inevitable. His spirit lunged for it, cutting through the phantom's grip with razored wingbeats.

'Lord!' Mautus called. 'There's a breach in the empyrean ahead.'

Sanguinius fought his way to the reality of the bridge. He stared at the shadow on the tactical screen. The beast taunted his fleet and killed his sons. There was a flash of primal fury. He hungered for revenge, for the brutal satisfaction of the foe's slaughter. He tore the anger from his heart, and embraced the salvation of reason. 'Fleet master,' he said to Carminus. 'Take us out of the warp. All ships, abandon pursuit and transition. *Now.*'

'So ordered.'

The trajectories on the screen changed infinitesimally. The reaction of the warp was immediate. The wake of the phantom seemed to sense the change of intent. The empyrean crashed against the fleet with renewed madness. The storm howled. The *Red Tear*'s Geller field buckled under the strain. Klaxons sounded warnings, and the air of the bridge shimmered, barely holding back the teeth of Chaos. The battleship's hull groaned, giving voice to a choir of structural and machinic stress. Carminus pushed the ship's integrity to the edge as he hurled the *Red Tear* towards the gap in the barrier between dream and reality.

At the edge of Sanguinius' consciousness, the sliver of possibility gleamed and pulsed. *Unless, unless, unless.*

The *Red Tear* plunged through the wall of the storm.

THE WORD BEARERS' Navigators died from the strain of the jump, but they kept their vow. The Ultramarines emerged from the Mandeville point inside the Anesidorax System with all ships intact. Their Navigators were exhausted, and their sanity was strained. But they had followed the leads of Nekras and Yathinius, and they had survived. Guilliman was not pleased to learn Nekras had died with a smile on her face, but he was satisfied with the result. The vow had been kept, regardless of the reason.

He had used the enemy.

He ordered the corpses jettisoned from the *Samothrace*. He left the athames in his quarters. The thought of turning them against the foe grew more insistent, but he pushed it away for now.

Thrinos appeared in the primary oculus, its orbit shining darkly with the assembled might of the Dark Angels fleet.

Beside Guilliman's pulpit, the screens lit up with the positions of the new ships emerging from the warp.

'Identified,' Lautenix said after a few seconds. 'The Ninth Legion.'

Simultaneous arrivals? Guilliman thought. He ran through a dozen theoreticals to explain the phenomenon. None satisfied. Their common foundation was the denial of coincidence.

'Hail the *Red Tear*,' Guilliman ordered. 'I will speak with my brother by hololith.'

He moved to a chamber at the rear of the strategium. The doors sealed behind him, and he climbed the plinth on which rested a hololith plate. The *Samothrace's* lithocast system was not as powerful as the one in the *Macragge's Honour*, but it would serve for ships at this proximity.

The air charged with energy. A few moments later, Sanguinius appeared before him, standing on a podium of red granite. Slight artefacting marred the perfection of the illusion of the Angel's presence. The Ruinstorm was damaging transmissions over even such a short distance.

'It's hard not to read significance in the timing of our arrival, isn't it?' Guilliman said.

'*I have no hesitation in seeing it as meaningful,*' said Sanguinius. '*I can already hear your scepticism, brother, but what can this be except fate?*' The Angel spoke with certainty, but his eyes were troubled, as if he wanted Guilliman to refute him.

Guilliman tried to formulate an answer. A good one would bring them both a measure of peace of mind, he thought. But his doubts slowed him down by a second, and before he could speak, Sanguinius completed his thought, freezing Guilliman's words.

'*We walk our assigned path,*' said the Angel.

SEVEN

Witnesses to the Pilgrimage

THE WIND OF Thrinos was cold and hard. It blew over the refugee camps, just strong enough to stir the fabric of the shelters of the more recent arrivals. They had not yet had time to build stronger, more rigid defences against its insistent, insidious touch. On the ramparts of the Iron Hands fortress, Sanguinius faced west, into the wind, looking out over the vista of misery.

'How many?' he asked Levannas.

'A few million at our last estimate, Lord Sanguinius,' the Raven Guard said. He was acting as guide to the Angel, Raldoron and the Sanguinary Guard. Guilliman had not yet descended from the *Samothrace*, and Sanguinius had chosen to learn the truths of the desperate of Thrinos before his conference with his brothers. 'More are arriving all the time,' Levannas said.

Sanguinius could feel the Lion's eyes on him. From somewhere in the keep behind him, his brother was observing. It would be against his nature to do otherwise. *To know without being known, isn't that it, brother?* Did the Lion think his interest in the refugees was a waste of time? Perhaps. But perhaps not. The Lion was not a machine.

The keep was a structure of brutal, jutting walls and jagged angles. The Iron Hands had constructed it from the remains of broken ships. It was patchwork, but it was strong. There was a funereal quality to the structure. It was constructed from the bones of loss. Once proud vessels had been gutted by the years of battle. However many engagements Khalybus' company had won, attrition was wearing them down, and eating away at their strength. The fortress was defiant, but it was just as much a last resort as the shacks and tents that surrounded it.

The refugees used whatever materials the Iron Hands discarded. Sanguinius saw constructions of plasteel and burnt, twisted shielding. A few miles to the north-east, the entire stern of a frigate, gutted of everything but the skeletons of the decks, had become the hard refuge of tens of thousands. Hundreds of fires, lit against the growing cold of the late afternoon, flickered in the huge shell.

'How are they fed?' Sanguinius asked.

'There was a colony here before our arrival,' said Levannas. 'Not a major one, but enough to have developed an agricultural industry.'

'I'm surprised,' Raldoron said. 'This does not strike me as a fertile world.'

'It isn't. Not very. The settlers are... *were*... miners. The colonists grew enough to subsist, and had a small surplus to stockpile against the years of weak harvests.'

Sanguinius frowned. 'And this influx of population is being fed by that surplus?'

'Essentially, yes,' Levannas said.

'Hardly a long-term solution.'

'No, it is not. Nothing on Thrinos is.'

If the war ever came to Thrinos, the fortress would be swept away along with everything else.

Tents and shacks stretched to the horizon on all sides of the fortress. The size of the camps was a testament to loss, Sanguinius thought. So many refugees from so many worlds had come here. As he walked, a clamour rose from below, growing louder, becoming more and more distinct from the general din of the camp. He looked down the hundred feet of sheer, ablative sheeting. A crowd was gathering at the foot of the wall; there were already a few thousand people. Their faces were upraised. They lifted their arms towards Sanguinius. They shouted and wept for joy.

Sanguinius had seen some of this behaviour on Macragge, after he had been proclaimed emperor. But word of the Imperium Secundus could not have reached Thrinos. And there was a frenzy, a desperation to the celebration that was new. 'Tell me what I am seeing,' he said to Levannas.

'After years of despair, three primarchs have come to Thrinos.'

'That isn't all, though, is it?'

'No,' Levannas admitted. 'They are rejoicing at the sight of you, Lord Sanguinius. At what you represent.' He paused for a moment. 'Your symbolism,' he added, grimacing in apology.

Sanguinius nodded. That was hardly a new experience for him, though it had always distressed him when he had encountered it before. Any sort of mystification of his being was contrary to the Imperial Truth. 'Go on,' he said.

'There is a...' The Raven Guard paused. 'A folklore,' he said. 'A mythology in this camp.'

'Oh?' Sanguinius said sharply.

'Quite a specific one, and consistent across the worlds these people have fled.'

'Myths are turning out to have a very dangerous core of truth these days,' said Raldoron.

'So we have been coming to learn,' Levannas said.

'What are the stories being told?' Azkaellon asked.

Sanguinius held up a hand before Levannas answered. 'I want to hear them first-hand,' he told the Raven Guard. 'Take us below.'

The primarch's party walked away from the wall, down a relatively wide and straight avenue, one of a dozen radiating out from the fortress and dividing the camp into sectors. The Sanguinary Guard tried to form a cordon around Sanguinius, but he shook his head and walked on. The people lined the sides of the avenue, weeping at the sight of the Angel. They held their arms out in entreaty. Sanguinius swallowed his distaste in the worship he saw in their eyes and moved back and forth, touching the tips of fingers with his gauntlets. The hope he saw spread through the crowd had value, even if he did not like its source. It was what the refugees called to him that he wanted to hear, though.

'You will save us!' they cried.

'The Emperor has heard us!'

'The Pilgrim will not find us here!'

'Shield us from the Pilgrim!'

The pleas were consistent, and Sanguinius saw the truth of what Levannas had said. The people before him were from a multitude of civilisations. No matter the skin tones and cultural encoding of their ragged clothes, they were unified in their desperate gratitude towards him and their terror of the Pilgrim.

Sanguinius rejoined Levannas in the centre of the dusty avenue. 'The Pilgrim,' he said. 'What do they mean?'

'That hardly sounds like a name for Horus,' Raldoron said.

'Perhaps one of Lorgar's zealots,' Azkaellon suggested.

'We have refugees from traitor-occupied worlds,' Levannas said. 'They don't talk about the Pilgrim.'

Sanguinius narrowed his eyes. 'So many of these people come from worlds that have *not* fallen to Horus' forces?'

'Most have not,' said Levannas. 'The majority of the recent arrivals have been fleeing something else.'

'Fleeing what?'

'I'm not sure. The stories are vague on that point. I'm not sure the people know themselves. Events have surpassed their ability to understand.' He scanned the crowd, then pointed to a cluster of figures a few hundred yards ahead and to the right. 'I suggest you speak with them, Lord Sanguinius.'

A score of men and women stood beneath the overhang of a broken girder. The metal fragment was the smallest part of a ship's framework, but it towered over this sector of the camp. It had been painted by what appeared to be hundreds of hands, endlessly reproducing the aquila. The symbols overlapped and spread up the girder's height. The group beneath were all robed. They had shaved their heads and marked their scalps with the aquila again, some with crude tattoos, others by having the symbol carved into their flesh. They knelt and bowed their heads as the Angel and his party drew near. The people around them followed their example.

Sanguinius frowned. He paused before approaching the group. 'This is a cult,' he said to Levannas.

'It is.'

'You seem unperturbed.'

'The cult's loyalty to the Emperor is fanatical. The force of these people's belief has had some positive impact on the wider morale of the camp. Given the circumstances, Captain Khalybus decided it was impractical and counterproductive to suppress it.'

'You agree?'

'I do. Stamping it out would also have involved a waste of resources.' Levannas paused for a moment. 'But you see now, Lord Sanguinius, why your appearance is having a pronounced effect.'

'I do. It is not what I would choose.'

'I understand. Nothing on Thrinos is what any of us would choose.'

'No, I don't suppose it is.'

The Angel walked towards the kneeling mortals. He signalled Azkaellon to keep the Sanguinary Guard a few steps back. He did not want these people so overwhelmed they could not speak. 'Stand,' he said when he reached them. 'I would speak to you.'

They stood. Like all the other refugees, they were ragged, malnourished, exhausted. Desperation and the terror of war had carved deep lines into their faces. There were weeping sores on their lips and on their arms. But when they looked at Sanguinius, there was more than fear in their eyes. There was hope. It was primal, almost feral. And it refused to be extinguished.

'Tell me about the Pilgrim,' Sanguinius said.

It took a moment before any of the mortals found their voices. 'It is the destroyer, lord,' said one man. Sanguinius thought he was young, but the war had added decades to his age.

'It is the bringer of ruin,' a woman said. She *was* old. Her back was hunched. Her gnarled fingers had never known juvenat treatments. 'When it comes to a world, the world ends.'

'It visited all of our worlds,' said a second man. He was missing his right arm. 'It travels, and where it passes, the end follows.'

'It?' Sanguinius asked. 'The Pilgrim is not a warrior, then?'

'No, lord,' said the woman.

'What is it, then?'

There was uncertainty again.

'It is blackness in the sky,' the one-armed man said. 'It is made of night.'

Whatever the Pilgrim was, it had been transformed in their minds by superstitious awe. And yet... Sanguinius exchanged a look with Raldoron. The First Captain concealed his worry well, but Sanguinius could see it all the same. They shared the same thought. The descriptions of the Pilgrim were disturbingly familiar.

'Is it a ship?' Sanguinius asked.

The mortals didn't seem to know. Instead of answering directly, they offered more myths. The Pilgrim was to them less a thing than an event. It was darkness, and it brought darkness. Finally, the younger man said, 'It isn't a ship, lord. It's too big.'

'Have you served on vessels?' Sanguinius asked him.

'I have. On mass conveyors.'

He spoke from experience, then. He was familiar with massive ships.

'The Pilgrim is the end,' the man continued. 'It comes, and when we look up into the dark, we are looking at the doom of our world.'

'What is the ruin it brings?' Sanguinius thought he already knew the answer to that.

There was yet another moment of silence, as if the mortals feared that their answers would be a conjuration. The old woman stepped forwards, seeking comfort in Sanguinius' shadow. She bowed her head and whispered, 'Nightmares. Nightmares that walk, and we cannot awake from the sight of them.'

'And change,' the younger man said. 'The ruin is change. The worlds are transformed.'

'Into what?' said the Angel.

'Into nightmares.'

'We thank the Emperor for you coming,' said the one-armed man. 'You will stop the dark fates, lord. You will stop the Pilgrim.'

The hope in their eyes pulled at Sanguinius. It gave him no strength. They were feeding on his presence.

HE MET WITH his brothers in the command chamber at the top of the keep's squat turret. It was a pyramidal structure on the roof. Narrow armourglass windows looked out over the camp in every direction. The walls, floor and furnishings were iron. It was a space of cold functionality. Khalybus brought the primarchs to the room, and then withdrew. When they were alone, the Lion described what had been found outside the Pandorax System.

'The way to Terra is through Davin,' he said.

Guilliman frowned. 'I understand that you believe this to be the case,' he said. 'Your message to us must have come at a great cost to your astropaths.'

'It did,' said the Lion.

'And I understand that you felt the cost we paid to answer it was necessary as well.'

'I do.'

'What I do not understand,' said Guilliman, 'is *why* you are convinced. Why Davin? How will going there, assuming we can, bring us closer to Terra?'

Sanguinius answered for the Lion. 'Because Horus fell at Davin.'

'I know he was injured there, but...'

'No,' Sanguinius cut him off. 'That is where he *fell*. Where he turned from our father.' As soon as the Lion had spoken the name of the world, Sanguinius had known his brother was right. The light coming in the windows turned brittle. The sense of onrushing fate reached into Sanguinius' hearts with its freezing touch. He felt again as he had on the bridge of the *Red Tear* with the shadow of the phantom reaching for him. The limits of his perception thrummed with the beat of fate's advance.

'Granting that,' Guilliman said, 'what of it?' He looked back and forth between the Lion and the Angel, as if eager to be convinced. That surprised Sanguinius. He expected Guilliman to hold fast to the reason. It was clear the Lion had too. He was watching Guilliman closely, as if the Avenging Son, and not the Lion, was the one bearing strange news. Sanguinius heard doubt in Guilliman's voice, and he thought it was more doubt in himself than in Davin as a target.

'The Davinites did not travel to Pandorax by accident,' said the Lion. 'Their journey was deliberate. The system was their destination. We found evidence of a ritual, and of mass sacrifice. Now the system is inaccessible. The warp storm is one of the most violent I've ever seen.'

'You infer a connection,' Guilliman said.

The Lion snorted. 'What is wrong with you, Roboute? I don't infer it. I *declare* it. We have seen too much now to embrace the dangerous fiction of a coincidence.'

'That is so,' said Guilliman, 'but nor can we commit our fleets to anything less than a certainty.'

'There was a Davinite on Signus Prime,' Sanguinius said.

The other two primarchs fell silent.

There was much he could not tell them about Signus Prime. For the sake of his sons, and the future of his Legion, the trauma of that war must fall to silence. But he would speak about some of the madness now, so both his brothers could see the path forwards as clearly as he did. Sanguinius didn't need the Lion to convince him. If necessary, he would convince the Lion. 'There was a Davinite,' he said again, 'and the daemonic attack on the entire system was massive. I saw the stars vanish. I saw a planet made over into the symbol of Chaos. The entire system was transformed. I can't know what Pandorax is undergoing inside that storm, but I can imagine it.' He took a breath. 'Horus fell at Davin,' he said again. 'This war begins at Davin. Maybe it ends there too.'

Guilliman said nothing. He looked thoughtful, doubtful, still wanting to be convinced, still unable to let go of the dictates of reason.

'Did you make any headway towards Terra?' the Lion asked.

Guilliman shook his head.

'And we were led here,' said Sanguinius.

'That is troubling in and of itself,' said Guilliman. 'It suggests we are walking into a trap. If the enemy wants us to take this path, we would be mad to do so.'

'What enemy?' the Lion asked. 'I have not encountered any of the traitor forces.'

'I have,' said Guilliman. 'I have prisoners of the Seventeenth Legion, Navigators who were more than happy to offer to guide me here.' He turned to Sanguinius. 'And who led you here?'

'I don't know.'

Guilliman paced the length of the iron table. He tapped its surface as he walked, striking a rhythm on hard, unyielding reality. 'The case for Davin is a strong one,' he said.

'Then we should accept the truth that Davin is the key to Terra *and* that it is a trap,' said the Lion. 'What better place to prepare an ambush than on the route a foe has no choice but to take?'

Guilliman stopped pacing. He tapped the table with his index finger, more slowly this time, more deliberately, as if counting off strategic postulates. 'If our fleets are destroyed, the galaxy falls,' he said.

'But if we break our foes where they are strongest, then it is our victory that becomes the critical one,' said the Lion. 'How better to storm that stronghold than with our combined fleets?'

'True,' Guilliman said, still visibly uneasy.

'This is where our path takes us,' Sanguinius told him.

'I believe you,' said Guilliman, but the admission appeared to worry him. 'The question remains whether we can reach Davin. It may be as closed to us as Terra.'

'I don't think it will be.' *Davin is inevitable*, Sanguinius thought. He could almost see the world rising above his temporal horizon. The Blood Angels had come to Thrinos through no choice of their own. Davin's pull would be even stronger. He was finding it difficult not to fall into a blank fatalism. His steps were predestined. Destiny was not negotiable. If he threw his fleet to the mercy of the warp, he would wash up on the threshold of Davin.

He turned his mind away from the lunacy of that impulse. There was a difference between arriving at Davin in force and arriving as a shipwreck victim.

You know your end, he reminded himself. *You don't know its meaning.* That might still be under his control.

'My Navigators have a fix on the trajectory we must take,' the Lion said.

'Impressive,' said Guilliman. 'I presume it would be futile to ask how they managed this feat.'

'We have our means,' the Lion said.

Guilliman sighed, but did not press the point.

'It will take more than one jump,' the Lion went on. 'I would suggest our best strategy is as tight a formation as possible, with your Navigators keyed to follow ours. We will be your beacon.'

'Agreed,' Sanguinius said, and the shadow came a bit closer. He looked out of the window. The afternoon was fading into evening. Thick clouds covered the sky, the narrow breaks between them limned by the cold, golden light of the setting sun. The shadow he sensed came from something darker than approaching night. It overlaid everything he saw, yet was invisible to the eye.

'Agreed,' Guilliman said too, after a pause.

'Your ships have taken damage,' the Lion said. 'How long before you can depart?'

'We are void-worthy. More extensive repairs are beyond what can be done here. The Thirteenth Legion will be ready at dawn.'

'So will the Ninth,' said Sanguinius.

'At dawn, then,' said the Lion.

LEVANNAS FOUND KHALYBUS on the peak of the fortress. It was a narrow spire, the platform surrounded by lethally sharp metal plates. Khalybus stood motionless, an iron sentinel looking out over the people who had come to him for refuge. He turned his head slightly at Levannas' approach and nodded very slightly.

'The *Sthenelus* departs with the Legion fleets,' Levannas said.

'It does,' Khalybus answered, his metallic voice making the curt response sound even harsher.

Levannas joined him in gazing at the refugee camp. 'We will be turning our backs on all who came to us for help,' he said.

'We go where the war takes us. We are warriors, not guardians. The battle calls us to Terra. Remaining here would be pointless.'

'The people below would tell us otherwise. They would say we are abandoning them to their doom.'

'They may yet survive.'

'Not if the Pilgrim comes here.'

'And if it does, and we are here, what good would we do?'

'None,' Levannas admitted. If half the tales the refugees told were true, a single strike cruiser would not last long against such an enemy.

'Then we are agreed,' said Khalybus.

'We are.'

Khalybus walked to the edge of the parapet. His fists closed over the adamantium crenellations. Levannas found the Iron Hands captain hard to read, even after years of combat together. But it seemed to him Khalybus was struggling with a heavy weight.

'When Atticus escaped the Isstvan System,' Khalybus said, 'he had warriors from the Eighteenth Legion with him as well as from yours.'

'You're wondering what the Salamanders would say about leaving Thrinos to its fate?'

'I know exactly what they would say. It changes nothing.' He turned away from the camp. 'I thought, when you arrived, that I would hear their argument from you.'

'Why?' said the Raven Guard. 'Remaining, as you said, would be a poor strategy.'

'I am not sure. Perhaps I imagined, because you are still more flesh than I am, that you would feel closer to the flesh below us.'

Levannas found the camp hard to look at now, too. 'You may be right,' he said. 'I knew what must be done when I climbed the steps of this tower. But if I'm honest, I wanted to hear you make the case for leaving.'

Khalybus grunted. It was the sound of gears slipping, the closest he came to laughter. 'Any hint of doubt from me is unwelcome, then. It seems we are disappointing each other.'

'The truth of the matter is, whether we like it or not, we *have* been the guardians of Thrinos these past years.'

'And now that ends,' said Khalybus. 'The flesh is weak, and that is also the truth. These people must find their strength or die.' He paused. 'But if, with the force of three Legions, we encounter the Pilgrim, that would be a battle worth fighting.'

'Salvation for Thrinos after all?' Levannas asked. The hope felt like a grim one.

With a visible effort, Khalybus faced the camp one last time. 'It is the only salvation we can offer.'

'There is one other matter we need to address,' said Levannas.

'Of course,' said Khalybus. 'You and your battle-brothers will be rejoining your Legion.'

'I have spoken with the Lion. If you agree, we shall serve out his mission aboard the *Sthenelus*.'

Khalybus was silent for a moment save for the faint hum of servo-motors. Then he said, 'You honour me, brother.'

'The honour is mine, brother.'

'Then we shall finish the long journey from Isstvan together.'

THE SHADOW CAME for Thrinos with nightfall, spreading with the name *Davin*. It covered the land, seeping into the camps and into the tortured sleep of the refugees. It clasped the fleets at low anchor. It travelled the halls of battleships and strike cruisers. The mortal crewmembers who were off shift slept as badly as the civilians on Thrinos. The dreams were not uniform. The shadow took whatever shapes twisted through the unconscious of its victims, and turned them to its ends. Dreams of loss or hope or anger, of grief or home or victory, of desperation or of faith, all were tainted by *Davin, Davin, Davin*. Premonitions descended on psykers, opening vistas of terror to them that were unformed, but threatened to acquire monstrous definition. The Dark Angels lost more astropaths, and the Ultramarines more Navigators, as the more psychically damaged of their numbers fell to the new onslaught.

But there was nothing to fight against. No enemy declared itself. There was only the sense of coming immensity, and that was enough, more than enough. The horrors in time yet to come, in distances yet to be travelled, were that strong.

The Ultramarines and the Dark Angels experienced the shadow as a tensing towards the future, of an unseen enemy probing resolution before the encounter. Guilliman kept his vault sealed, but his thoughts went to the athames, and he raged silently against the sense that every decision was foretold, every choice an illusion, even as the choice about whether to use the enemy's tools hovered before him.

The Lion sequestered himself in the chamber of Tuchulcha. He spoke to the meat puppet. He tried, and he failed, to summon answers that would satisfy him.

'Where are the barriers between here and Davin?' he asked.

'Before us,' said the servitor.

'I warn you not to trifle with me.'

'I do not,' said Tuchulcha. 'That truths displease you is no fault of mine.'

'Then give me the truths I seek. How far can you take us in a single leap?'

'To the limits of my sight.'

'That is not an answer.'

'It is still the truth.'

The Lion's eyes narrowed. 'Will you be clear, or will I have you destroyed?'

'I am as clear as blindness permits.'

'My blindness?'

'No,' said the puppet. 'Mine.'

The admission of limitations was new from Tuchulcha. It was disturbing. 'If you are blind, how do you know our way is blocked?'

'Because something will stop my sight.'

'Where?'

'My blindness is not measured by location. I know it will occur.'

The Lion went around and around with Tuchulcha, growing more and more uneasy as he became convinced the being was not trying to deceive him. He emerged from the chamber hours later, no wiser than when he had entered. He was left with only the certainty of uncertainty, and the knowledge that he was dragging his brothers down a broken path.

THE SHADOW TOUCHED the Blood Angels too. It fell on the Angel first, and spread out from him onto his sons. In the privacy of the Sanctorum Angelus, Sanguinius meditated, seeking the way to find meaning in destiny. Instead, he felt Horus strike the fatal blow. He gasped. He fell to his hands and knees. The marble beneath him did not go dark with his blood, yet every wound was real. His brother's blade sawed through his hearts. His sight greyed with the pain. A massive figure in black flickered before him, and the walls of the *Red Tear* shivered, on the verge of becoming the foulness of the *Vengeful Spirit*.

Dark. Black. Night. Everything was darkness, and so was the thing that rose inside him. It was not blood. It was nothing physical. It was not the thirst. It was something else, so black he could not know it, yet it was his. Yet it was him.

He shouted a denial. His voice rang against marble and gold. He curled in on himself, clutching hard, holding back darkness. It strained to be released. His will was stronger, and as the spectral pain faded, so did the dark. His vision stabilised. The Sanctorum became stable again. He stood up, unsure whether he had claimed a victory or suffered another blow.

Across his fleet, the Blood Angels paused in their preparations for war, and blinked at the wave of anguish that rolled over them.

With the coming of dawn, the shadow did not dissipate. It lingered in the hollows of secret thoughts and fears. It was a venomous dust in the corners of every soul on the surface of Thrinos, and in orbit over it. Mortal and Legiones Astartes and primarch, all felt it, and all moved on to confront it. The warriors of three Legions were ready to make war, and they would burn the shadow from their consciousness with the light of their righteous anger.

The mortals below did not have the same strength. They saw the saviours they had prayed for leave Thrinos. Even the Iron Hands departed, leaving the fortress empty. So there was no celebration as three fleets raised anchor. The people looked up at the vessels, at the daylight stars that stood between them and the violent sight of the Ruinstorm. Then the stars began to move away.

The lights of hope departed Thrinos, and the wail of a great mourning followed them.

PART II
THE DOMINION
OF RUIN

EIGHT

A Great Work

THE BARRIER APPEARED across the nav screens of the *Invincible Reason* a second before the fleets fell from the warp. From his throne, the Lion saw every readout collapse into static and darkness. Every one of the *Reason*'s senses was blinded in an instant, as if they had slammed into something impenetrable that spanned the empyrean. That was the only warning before the ship transitioned.

Colossal gravity seized the *Reason*. Proximity klaxons blared. The pict screens flashed and strobed, as cogitators fought to process a sudden, overwhelming influx of data. The ship jerked forwards, rushing despite itself towards the thing that had seized it.

'Shutters open!' the Lion shouted. They parted over the bridge's great oculus, and he beheld what had pulled the fleets from the empyrean.

The *Invincible Reason* plunged towards the wall of an impossible fortress. The Lion stared at the vision, and for several seconds his mind was unable to reconcile the structure with its size. It would have inspired awe had he seen it from the cockpit of a Thunderhawk. From the bridge of a ship, it beggared belief. He looked upon twisted, spiked battlements and towers of brass and iron. They rose from a wall that stretched to port and starboard as far as the Lion could see. The wall bristled with what, from this distance, looked like thorns and claws. The glow of ugly fires shone from innumerable apertures, a galaxy of pinprick flames. Light the colour of blood and hate moved over the fortifications, a nebula of horror.

The fortress filled the oculus, the wall dropping beyond the frame. There was nothing to see except the battlements, nothing to give the structure scale, but at last the Lion grasped its full monstrosity. The fortress spanned a system. The wall was tens of millions of miles high. It was billions of miles long. And though the proximity was lethal, it was still millions of miles away.

The fleets were caught in its gravitational well. They sailed across the void before it, pulled towards a collision, minute specks of dust blown at a mountainside.

'Hard to starboard,' Captain Stenius ordered. In his command throne one level below the Lion's position, he leaned forwards, pulling at the mechadendrites that linked him to the *Invincible Reason*, as if he could lend the ship greater mobility by the actions of his body.

The Lion opened a fleet-wide vox-channel, and heard the same command echoing and re-echoing. It was too late to attempt to reverse away from the fortress. But the ships might yet avoid disaster by taking the momentum into a turn, moving parallel to the barrier using a slingshot manoeuvre to break the wall's grip. The Lion shifted his attention back and forth between the monster growing larger in the oculus, and the trajectory screens for the combined fleets. The lines were shifting, slowly. The fortress was coming closer, quickly. The prow of the *Reason* shuddered before the Lion's gaze, mile upon mile of gothic majesty wrenched by forces that reduced it to insignificance.

'Hails from the *Red Tear* and the *Samothrace*,' said the vox-officer.

'Private channel,' the Lion said. His brothers wished to speak to him. As he had expected they would.

'*Where have you brought us?*' Guilliman demanded.

'I don't know, Roboute.'

'*Neither do I. We can't identify the system, whatever it once was.*'

'*If this is a system, it has been moved,*' Sanguinius said. '*But the location is not as important as its nature. This is not the work of Horus. It cannot be the work of material hands, be they human or xenos.*'

'*I suppose we should be grateful for that,*' said Guilliman.

'We should,' said the Lion. If the traitor Legions had become capable of such a feat, then the war was over. He looked at the fleet trajectories again and frowned. 'Some of our smaller vessels are not turning fast enough,' he said. The port wing of the formation was ragged. It was extending closer to the fortress.

'*Some of ours are struggling too,*' said Sanguinius. '*Their engines are pushed to their limits.*'

'*They should still complete the manoeuvre,*' Guilliman said. '*But they'll be very exposed.*'

'*Then we must hope…*' Sanguinius began. Then he stopped. The Lion heard his breath catch. When the Angel spoke again, it was with the tone of one caught in the grip of premonition. '*The structures between the towers…*' he said.

The Lion turned back to the oculus. The angle of the *Invincible Reason's* approach had become oblique, though the fortress was so vast, its expanse stretched for an eternity into the void, glowing and pulsing with its unnatural fire. Conical shapes jutted out from the battlements at irregular intervals. They were the size of gas giants. They could not be what they appeared to be.

Sanguinius confirmed the madness. '*They're war-horns,*' he said. His tone was flat, and leaden with prophecy.

The horns blared a challenge. Across the airless void, they made their terrible, warp-created sound. It travelled the millions of miles that separated the fleet from the fortress. Perhaps the cry had come as soon as the fleets had been detected and it was only now reaching the ships. Perhaps the horns had only sounded on the instant. The laws of reality had been suspended in this star system, and the Lion knew that what mattered was not how the horns cried, but that they did. The sound smashed into the *Invincible Reason*, shaking the hull. It boomed through the bridge. It was deep, as deep as the heartbeat of mountains. And it was a wail, a rising, shrieking, raging wail that harrowed the soul. The Lion winced. He made himself breathe through the blast. He leaned into it. On the bridge below, officers screamed, blood running from their ears and eyes. Servitors collapsed, spines ground to powder. The electrical systems of the ship surged and stuttered, blowing out pict screens, setting control stations ablaze. The thrum of the battleship's engines became a hammering roar, yet the cry of the horns sounded above everything.

There was a pause, as if a behemoth of Caliban's myths were drawing a breath, and then the horns sounded again. The cry was more than sound. It cut into the port flank of the formations, culling the weak like a scythe. It pulled the Dark Angels frigate *Undaunted* and the cruiser *Unsheathed* of the Ultramarines away from the fleets. The ships, miles long, powerful enough to turn worlds to glass, tumbled like leaves in a storm, massiveness made minuscule. The nearest horn sucked them in, hauling them away faster and faster, until they were streaking at a small fraction of the speed of light towards the fortification. They crossed the event horizon of the war-horn's cone and vanished into the darkness within. There was no explosion, no flowering of ignited plasma. There was the brutal severing of communication the moment the vessels entered the cone, and that was all.

The fleets continued their turn, still picking up speed, the angles of approach changing as slowly as the erosion of monuments. At last the *Invincible Reason* was parallel to the wall, and then at last its speed became the strength it needed to pull away. The collision alarms fell silent.

The Blood Angels cruiser *Excelsis* did not complete the manoeuvre. The curve of its turn was too long. It came too close to the fortress and fell against it. It did scar the void with its end. It became a long streak of flame against the fortifications. The death flare was brief and barely noticeable against the infinite expanse of the wall.

'Brothers,' Sanguinius said as the combined fleets began to increase their distance from the fortress, *'can any of you return to the warp?'*

'No,' said Guilliman. *'Warp drives are functional, but the distortion of the materium and the empyrean is too great here. That structure has a gravitational pull in the warp as well as here.'*

The Lion thought about demanding that Tuchulcha take the fleets back to the immaterium. He reminded himself about the futility of giving that order. Tuchulcha had warned him about the barrier. Tuchulcha could not cross it. 'Then we have only one choice,' he said. 'We have to breach the wall. If we can't go around, we must go through.'

'Our options for making such an attempt are limited,' said Guilliman.

'If the options are few,' Sanguinius said, 'then each must be pursued with the greatest rigour.'

'Do any of us think we can destroy it?' the Lion asked.

'We are all agreed that we must try,' said Guilliman.

The greatest single naval barrage in human history occurred less than an hour later. Hulls vibrating from the strain of engines pushing back against the pull of the fortress, the formation closed to firing range with the construct. The wall filled the oculus of the *Invincible Reason* completely. The Lion could see nothing but the iron, the brass, the flames and the thorns resolving themselves into guns taller than Olympus Mons.

The weapons systems of the Imperium powered up. When they were ready, when the synchronisation of fire was arranged, when the speed of torpedoes was calculated against the immediacy of lances, so that every hit would strike the wall at the same moment, then the Lion, in concert with his brothers, said, 'Fire.'

Fire.

The fire came to burn the void. More than a hundred ships opened up with every weapon. Macro-cannon batteries, ranks of lances, nova cannons, cyclonic torpedoes and more unleashed the anger of humanity against the obscenity before them. The raging of the Ruinstorm faded before the searing light of purest, purging destruction. It was an act of war on a scale that had never been witnessed before. If there had been remembrancers aboard any of the vessels, they would have felt compelled to record an event so monumental in song and in verse.

The barrage struck the fortress, and then it did not matter that there were no remembrancers. The action would not be remembered. There would be no songs. The immense became the insignificant. The explosions that erupted on the face of the battlements lit up the view in the *Invincible Reason*'s oculus. But the Lion made the mental adjustment, and understood how tiny the site of the impact was in relation to the wall as a whole. It might as well have been invisible, a momentary glint on the brass. *We aren't trying to destroy the barrier*, he reminded himself. *We need to pass through it. That is all.*

The flare of the blasts faded. Geysers of molten metal extended into the void. Burning gas dissipated. A crater as wide as the fleet appeared. It glowed from the heat of its creation.

'*Our auspex readings put the depth of the breach at approximately four thousand miles,*' Guilliman said.

'It might as well be nothing at all,' the Lion muttered, disgusted. The crater was a meaningless blemish on the barrier. The wall could be millions of miles thick. There was no return fire. The fleets did not even register as a threat for the things inside the fortifications.

'*This is futile,*' Sanguinius said. '*We must find another way through.*'

'*If there is one,*' said Guilliman.

'*A fortress is a barrier on a path,*' the Angel insisted. '*Its existence means we must cross it. This is the road we must take.*'

'*I will not smash my fleet against this wall to no purpose,*' Guilliman said.

'*We will cross it,*' Sanguinius told him. '*We do not end here. I must face Horus.*' Sanguinius spoke with the same certainty the Lion heard in Curze's voice. Both of them lived only partially in the present. The other part of them existed in the inexorable reality of their future deaths.

'By your logic,' the Lion said, 'a wall must have a gate.'

'*Yes. This is not a blank wall. This is a fortress. We see its features. We must find the others. Our long-range scanning shows a different heat signature to port and in the direction of the wall's base.*'

'*A base with what foundation?*' Guilliman asked.

'*Perhaps none. But the shape has meaning. The turrets declare that we are looking at the peak of the fortifications. Their existence implies the presence of a base, foundation or not.*'

'Agreed,' said the Lion.

'*We are relaying the coordinates of the heat bloom,*' Sanguinius said.

A few minutes later, the fleets began to move, descending the infinite heights of the wall. The search target was as distant from the *Invincible Reason* as Mars was from Terra. The ship shuddered as if it were passing through an atmosphere, straining to hold its position against the gravitational pull.

Stenius looked back up at the Lion as the ship passed the unending expanse of the wall, its apertures flickering with infernal red, a million eyes staring out, mocking and hungry. 'Lord,' he said, 'what is this thing?'

'It's the future,' the Lion answered. The longer he gazed at the fortress, the more the shock of its size wore off, and the more the implications of its being sank in. 'This is what the galaxy will become if we do not win this war.' *Did you foresee this, Horus?* he wondered. *Greater powers are using you. You have opened the door to this horror. I hope we have the strength to close it.*

'Can we destroy this?' said Stenius.

'Not this form. Our task will be to end its possibility.' *If we can. Father, you should have warned us.*

The Lion experienced a glimmer of hope when he saw the first sign that Sanguinius' theory was correct. *Roboute would congratulate you on the precision of your theoretical,* he thought.

There was a gate. It came into view as the fleets travelled towards the galactic east. As far as the Lion could tell, it ran the entire height of the wall. By this time, the peaks of the battlements were long out of sight. The gate extended above and below the *Invincible Reason*'s position to the limits of perception, a universe of daemonic might. The fleets increased the angle of descent, heading for the promised base.

For much of the journey, the gate seemed endless, but it had a design, and so the Lion knew it must end. It took a long time for him to make out the engraving in the middle of the portal. This close, it resembled a mountain chain, a topography as big as a thousand worlds pressed together. The mountains had lines, though. They were constructed, they were art, and so they had meaning. The Lion watched the portions of the design as it passed by the oculus. He held the fragmented visions in his head, and assembled the pieces into a whole. It was an eight-pointed star. It was a brand upon the universe. It was a wound in reality, and it was a declaration of rule. As soon as the Lion understood its contours, it seemed to look back at him, an eye more monstrous and knowing than any of the red glows in the wall. It gazed at the dust motes of the fleet, and it looked upon the Lion from inside his mind.

His lip curled in defiance. He focused on the progress of the *Reason's* journey. He promised the symbol destruction as he stared forwards. *We will hurl you from the galaxy. By whatever means necessary.*

The gate and the star slid by. The pace was agonising, though the fleet moved at full speed. The heat bloom detected by the Blood Angels became more intense and more defined in the long-range auspex scans. At last, its source became visible.

'Sanguinius,' the Lion voxed, 'we have located your foundations.'

The eastern hinge of the gate was anchored to a world. As it came into sight, the planet was tiny, barely an excrescence at the bottom of the wall. But the intersection of gate and planet flared with enormous energy, far more than the disparity in size would suggest. The bloom originated in the planet, and travelled, spreading out a long way up the height and breadth of the gate before it faded.

'So pitiful a foundation for so immense a construct,' said the Lion.

'*We have nothing to boast of,*' Guilliman said, angry regret breaking through. '*I declared the Imperium Secundus with even less of a foundation.*'

'That is gone,' said the Lion. 'Let us bring an end to this, too.'

Seconds later, the monster guns of the fortress opened fire.

NINE

The Harrowing of Pyrrhan

THE DAEMON FLAMES reached out for the fleet. Eruptions of warp energy lashed at the void. They burned and slashed, a storm and a web. The Blood Angels battle-barge *Lineage of Virtue* was the first caught in the nexus of the crossfire. Its void shields collapsed in seconds. Writhing beams of warp fire cut through the centre of the hull. Conflagrations raced across all decks. The starboard engine exploded, blowing out a fifth of the hull's length, venting thousands of crew and scores of legionaries into space. Captain Athaniel's last vox-transmission was a vow to his brothers and to the Angel.

'*Our pyre shall be your shield,*' he said, and the *Lineage of Virtue* began its turn, exposing more and more of its port flank to the fortress, taking on the barrage, blocking at least some of it from the vessels in its lee. It kept turning, becoming a torch, and as the rest of the fleet pulled further away, racing for the shelter of the southern hemisphere of the planet, one last burst from the *Virtue*'s port engine sent the ship plummeting towards the gate.

By will or chance or fate, the *Virtue* held together until it crashed into the gate. The plasma sun of its explosion destroyed hundreds of square miles of daemonic turrets. The effect was a pinprick, yet the pinprick was enough to save at least the *Blood's Son* and the *Encarnadine*, which had been closest to the battle-barge.

Four more vessels from the combined fleets died before the expeditionary force put the planet between it and the turret fire. They died too suddenly even to vox a farewell.

'*We have identified the planet,*' Khalybus voxed the primarchs. '*Enough of the topography of the southern hemisphere is unchanged. It is the forge world Pyrrhan. We had refugees from it on Thrinos. It was visited by the Pilgrim.*'

Sanguinius walked across the *Red Tear*'s bridge, taking in the portrait of the planet emerging from the combined rapid scans of the fleet as they developed on the arrays of auspex screens. It was a small, rocky world, not much larger than a planetoid, less than three thousand miles in diameter. Steep mountain chains dominated much of the south, diminishing as they approached the equator. Tens of thousands of years of intensive mining in the once-inhabited northern hemisphere had worn the peaks down. The composite images of the north showed the traces of human civilisation and industry, now twisted almost past the point of recognition. Manufactoria taller than the mountains they had replaced belched fire and smoke into the world's eternal night. A spiral pillar, five hundred miles wide, linked the north magnetic pole of Pyrrhan to the bottom of the gate. It emerged from the greatest manufactorum, a jagged monster that rose from the surrounding terrain like two gigantic, clawed hands clasped in prayer. There was no clear division between manufactorum and pillar. They flowed into one another, and the pillar flowed into the gate. The pillar shone with the light of molten matter.

Sanguinius took what he saw with him to the hololith chamber. 'Matter,' he said to the images of his brothers. 'Matter is being created at this juncture. We can observe it happening. The pillar grows from the manufactorum. The gate's being is forged here.'

'*It cannot be the planet's own matter,*' the Lion said. '*It is a speck compared to the gate. It would have been consumed a million times over by now.*'

'There is nothing about what we are seeing that is rational,' said Guilliman. His jaw was set with frustration. He said *rational* with something like bereavement. 'This fortress is already impossible a million times over.'

'Yet Pyrrhan is somehow necessary to it,' Sanguinius pointed out. 'The impossible has attached itself to something real.'

Guilliman's eyes widened in the hope of reason. 'An anchor,' he said. 'The fortress needs to anchor itself in the materium. Maybe Pyrrhan's industry, in the new configuration, is a gateway, funnelling in the warp's substance, making it into stable matter.'

'That conforms to what we are seeing,' said Sanguinius. 'The intensity of the energy suggests an important nexus of some sort. Brothers, I would thrust a sword into that heart and sever the connection.'

Guilliman nodded. 'Destroy the forge. Shut down the flow of matter. Perhaps that might destabilise the gate.'

'We are under attack,' said the Lion. 'So we must now constitute a threat. The enemy does not want us on Pyrrhan.'

'We can't move close enough to the target zone to stage a drop,' said Guilliman. 'The defences will take the fleets apart before we could launch even a fraction of the ground forces we'll need.'

Sanguinius turned to the pict screen on his hololith podium and called up the topography of Pyrrhan's northern hemisphere. 'The north-east quadrant has the potential for a clear run,' he said. 'North of the equatorial cordillera, it is primarily a region of plains.'

'I see it,' said Guilliman. 'The spaces between the foundries are wide.'

'Former transportation networks,' said the Lion.

Sanguinius changed the screen to show enemy movements on the surface. 'The activity is minimal,' he said. 'All efforts are concentrated inside the manufactoria. The land is effectively empty, it will take time for the enemy to respond.'

'A ground advance might go far before encountering resistance,' Guilliman agreed.

Sanguinius mentally traced the path from the mountains to the great forge, and the tactical situation became less important. He pictured the most savage strike he could bring to the daemons. The wounds of Signus Prime were still fresh. He would heal them with this assault. The Blood Angels would hit the daemons with maximum force. There would be anger, but no loss of control. Not this time. There would be atonement through disciplined fury. There could be a precision and a majesty in wrath.

This was the lesson he and his sons would bring to the abominations.

THE THUNDERHAWK *Karaashi's Fire* left the *Sthenelus* and plunged towards the atmosphere of Pyrrhan. Now that he finally saw it, the work of the Pilgrim filled Khalybus with both disgust and awe. Seated opposite him in the troop compartment, accompanied by five of his legionaries, Levannas said, 'The tales of the refugees did not begin to do these horrors justice.'

'The changes had only just begun when they fled,' said Khalybus. 'Otherwise they would never have escaped the system.'

'Obscene,' Iron Father Cruax growled, echoing Khalybus' disgust. 'It is an insult to the purity of the machine.'

Khalybus nodded. The forge world's transformation was offensive as well as monstrous. The *Sthenelus* had encountered daemons during its long and isolated war. The abominations were confirmation of everything the X Legion had come to despise about the flesh. They were its deformation, its corruption, its overwhelming excess. They were proof of its weakness, because it could be remade in such a fashion.

But the metamorphosis of Pyrrhan brought the same monstrosity to the machine. The great forge and its link to the gate were a brutal refutation of any kind of purity.

'This obscenity will not stand,' Khalybus said to Cruax. 'On this day, it falls.'

'That won't be enough,' said Cruax.

'No, it won't,' Khalybus agreed.

'This will not stop until we find the Pilgrim,' said Levannas.

'Then we will,' said Khalybus. 'Before Terra or after, we will hunt it, and we will destroy it.'

'So it shall be,' Levannas said.

What had been a hope became a vow.

THE LEGIONS CAME down on Pyrrhan. Hundreds of drop pods at a time burned through the atmosphere. They were a hail of iron, the sky falling upon the land in one storm after another.

'Are there any humans left below?' Kletos asked. The drop pod shook and hammered down through the thin atmosphere.

'Doubtful,' said Hierax. 'There is no sun. The only heat is from the foundries.' He shook his head once. 'No. There is nothing to save here.'

'I didn't think so.'

'Why did you ask?'

'An idle thought, captain. I wondered what they would think, were they to look up.'

'They would know they had not been forgotten,' Hierax said. 'But be assured, legionary, we have witnesses. They may not know it yet, but they are learning what their annihilation looks like.'

The drop pod's retro-rockets fired. The grav-harness strained against Kletos' shoulders with the sudden deceleration. He grinned fiercely, anticipating the bone-jarring jerk of the landing. It came, and the pod's hatch doors blew open, slamming down on the basalt surface of Pyrrhan. Kletos stormed out of the pod with the rest of the squad, behind his captain, joining the mustering of the Second Destroyers.

Overhead, the contrails of drop pods and lifters clawed the sky, scarring it with silver trails. East and west and south of where Kletos stood, the lava plain trembled with the landings and the gathering forces of the Ultramarines and Dark Angels. There were far fewer pods coming down in the north. The Destroyers were in the vanguard. The fortress was still over the horizon. The march would not be a long one before it appeared. The fleets were anchored low, almost grazing the mesosphere, and they had come as far forwards as they could while still remaining shielded from the ship-killing cannons before beginning the drops.

Kletos could remember a time when Guilliman had been reluctant to unleash the Destroyers. That had begun to change after the Thoas campaign. After Calth, he had been much freer in using the brutal weapon they were. And here was a world where the concept of mercy was inconceivable. Kletos had no illusions about the kind of warrior he was. The Second Destroyers were the side of the Ultramarines that was not celebrated in chronicles or in murals. They were the warriors of hard necessity, of scorched earth and of weaponry many would prefer not to think about. They fought with no less discipline and no less a faithful application of the primarch's precepts than any other company. But alchemy weapons and rad bombs were messy. The wars of the Destroyers were messy. There was no pretending their campaigns were anything else except the brutal extermination of the foe.

So they had proven aboard the *Annunciation*. So they would prove again on Pyrrhan. This was a mission of annihilation.

Rhinos rumbled forwards to the drop pods and lowered their loading ramps. Kletos followed Hierax into the *Blood of Honour*. The heavy armour landings were a continuous earth tremor.

Next to Kletos, Mnason grumbled, 'More sitting. No marching.'

'There will be plenty of marching,' Hierax said. 'But speed is the watchword of our advance. Tell me, legionary, are you opposed to reaching the enemy faster?'

'No, captain, I am not. Please consider me happily resigned to sit a bit longer.'

'So noted,' Hierax said. He cocked his head, listening to his vox-bead. When the loading ramp clanged shut, he banged a gauntleted fist against the bulkhead separating the troop compartment from the driver. 'Teosos,' he barked. 'The order is given. Take us forwards.'

The *Blood of Honour* lurched forwards, accelerating quickly. The Rhino was hungry for battle.

THE ARMOURED COLUMNS roared across the wide plain of Pyrrhan. Hierax opened the roof hatch of the Rhino to man the pintle-mounted storm bolter, and to witness the charge. For miles on either side of him, for many more to the rear, tanks and armoured transports in the blue and black of two Legions covered the land, and filled the air with choking clouds of exhaust. The air of Pyrrhan was thin and cold, and only the infernal heat of the foundries prevented the atmosphere from freezing and falling to earth. The smell of the engine fumes came in through the filters of Hierax's helmet rebreather. He welcomed the stench of human machinery. It represented order. It was the hard, burnt tang of reason going to war.

Half a mile to his right, the Land Raider *Flame of Illyrium* advanced between the columns to lead the charge. It was the primarch's command vehicle, and Guilliman rode in the upper hatch, pointing the way forwards, a living monument of gold and blue taking his sons to burn their way through the enemy. Hierax couldn't see the lead elements of the Dark Angels from this distance, but he was willing to wager the Lion was as visible to them as the Avenging Son was to his legionaries. Hierax's heart swelled with the pride of crusade.

'Hierax,' Iasus voxed, '*what say you?*'

Hierax glanced to his left, to where the Chapter Master rode as he did. 'I say this is a sight long past due,' he answered.

The sight was of the unity of the Emperor's loyal Legions, of determination, and of their crushing strength. For several more minutes, Hierax consciously gave himself leave to revel in the sweep and storm and majesty of the tide of armour.

Then the fortress began to appear over the horizon. The black, infinite wall ate the sky. The Ruinstorm disappeared behind it. Darkness and red flame climbed higher and higher, swallowing the sky, becoming the sky. Hierax felt its inconceivable mass pressing down. He was suddenly aware of the horror of scale. The world on which so vast a display of Legion might was advancing was less than a speck beneath the daemonic construction.

Hierax lowered his gaze, bringing all of his attention to bear on the land before him, pushing the monster in the sky to the edge of his consciousness. He stared straight ahead, a motionless sentinel. The hours passed. The Ultramarines and Dark Angels covered hundreds of miles towards their goal. The land was uneven but battered down, the rock so rounded by erosion it was a faded corpse of topography. At last, far ahead, belching smoke, the first of the forges came into view. They were pointed, twisted silhouettes. They looked like torn fragments of the night, spewing flame.

In the endless red-lit gloom, there was movement on the ground.

'*Captain,*' Teosos voxed, '*we have contacts ahead.*'

'I see them.'

The land appeared to be boiling. He was too far away to make out the details. The motion of the daemonic mass made him think of insect swarms. There was a suggestion of inhuman limbs and shapes in the jerking, flapping, skittering approach of the abominations. This was a tide too, and it was everything the Ultramarines and Dark Angels were not. It was undisciplined. Closer now, the wave of the enemy was filled with competing currents. It was chaos, rushing to repel the invading order.

Hierax closed his grip on the storm bolter. He gauged the shrinking distance between the two forces, calculating the moment he would begin to fire. He predicted the precise second the longer-range guns of the Land Raiders began to thunder. He nodded as solid lines of artillery blasts engulfed the leading edge of the daemonic charge. He could see the exact spot on the barren ground where the mailed fist of the Legions would slam into the jaws of the daemons. Without asking Teosos, he knew how far they were from the primary target.

Still far. Too far to punch through without committing to a long campaign, one that the daemons, with their infinite resources, would win. The charge had been fast. It had summoned the enemy to the battlefield. The daemons were rushing to stop the threat of two Legions.

Now was the time for the true speed of the attack. Now was the time for the third Legion.

And because it was time, Hierax allowed himself to look up once more.

The firmament screamed. The sky above Pyrrhan was filled with crimson anger. Squadrons of Blood Angels Stormbirds streaked over the battlefield in the direction of the great forge. There were so many engines howling at maximum velocity that Hierax could hear them over the grinding rumble of the tanks. The glare of the exhausts was a purging light, brighter than the baleful, flickering glow of the fortress. The gunships were the Warhawk IV model, winged giants, each carrying a hundred Legiones Astartes. If the tanks of the XIII and I Legions were a battering ram into the mass of the daemons, the IX Legion was a hurling spear into the foe's heart.

Hierax watched the flight of Angels until his internal sentinel signalled the coming of yet another movement. He faced forwards again, and opened fire with the storm bolter.

THE WARHAWK *Talon of Baal* flew over a land begging for flame. Sanguinius stood at the open side-door. He held on to the bulkhead and leaned out into the wind, looking towards the great forge and the pillar linking it to the gate. The speed of the *Talon* blurred the enemy below, turning the daemons into a grasping abstraction. Bursts of psychic fire lashed upwards at the Stormbirds. It was scattered. The daemons' attention was still concentrated on the ground attack. The manufactorum reared ahead. It had appeared at first like a broad-shouldered mountain, a volcano of warp-altered industry. The Blood Angels flew between lesser forges, large as mountain chains. They held traces of the human constructs they had once been, now distorted by immensity. Chimneys were thousands of feet high. Conduits were half a mile thick. Vaulted archways had turned into fanged maws, iron and flesh and stone indistinguishable.

The primary manufactorum dwarfed them all. As it filled Sanguinius' sight, he could see here, too, the echo of the thing it had been.

At his side, Raldoron asked, 'How will we know what to attack inside?'

'Look,' said Sanguinius. 'You can see the essence of what was taken by the enemy. The principles of the construction have some of the human in them.' The manufactorum was built of monoliths the size of hive cities, but it was still recognisable. It was still a foundry.

'They use us,' said Raldoron. 'Everything about us.'

'Yes. Do you see what that means? At some level, they need us as the foundations.' *Or our horror is simply the worse for seeing the human endeavour made monstrous,* he thought. 'What we know, we can fight,' he said. 'What we can fight, we can destroy.'

They know us well enough to fracture us along every weakness. Time we turned that principle against them.

The *Talon of Baal* angled downwards. The main gate of the foundry was visible now, illuminated by the glow of industry within. It was twenty miles high and ten wide. Its iron doors were open, vomiting forth an endless stream of daemons. They scraped against the basalt ground as they closed, striking comet tails of sparks. The movement was slow, the march of glaciers towards collision. Past the gate, the foundry was a hive of tunnels, clearly too small for the Warhawks. The squadrons of immense gunships made for the terrain immediately before the gate. At the rate the doors were closing, the Blood Angels would have several minutes yet before the way in was barred.

Hellstrike missiles flashed from beneath the wings of the Stormbirds. The hard rain became a sea of fire. Nose- and wing-mounted auto-cannons opened up, hammering the ground through the spreading fireballs. The squadrons hit with the full complement of their heavy weaponry. It was an assault that would have vaporised a human force. Clouds of dust rose, enveloping the gunships as they dropped planetwards. The downdraughts of their engines whirled the stone fragments into scouring cyclones. The Stormbirds landed on ground blackened by fire, the loading ramps coming down at the same instant that the landing gear made contact. Thousands of Blood Angels disembarked, the sound of ceramite boots on metal a pounding counterpoint to the descending whine of the engines.

The terrain for a few moments was clear of the enemy. The bombardment had melted rock. Clusters of shell craters overlapped. Everywhere

Sanguinius looked as he led the way forwards from the gunships, he saw daemons reduced to twitching, hissing pools. Carbonised bodies liquefied as they came apart at a fundamental level, losing their grip on the materium. Desultory blue and violet light, sick with the taint of the warp, flickered over the sludge.

The gunships took off again immediately. Their pilots headed back the way they had come, turning their autocannons on the mass of daemons to the rear, holding them back. Monstrous howls filled the thin air. The daemons understood the strategy being used against them, and were trying to counter it. Sanguinius hoped the Stormbirds would buy him a few more seconds during which he would only have to fight on one front.

The doors continued to close. Sanguinius looked up at them slowly scraping their way along the ground. Their edges, unnaturally straight, the tops invisible in the far heights, were less than five hundred yards apart now. The narrowing gap had slowed the rush of daemons to the battlefield, though the baying horde that ran and leapt and crawled and danced towards the Blood Angels was large enough. In the mass was a terrible plenty of forms. The monsters were things of disease and excess and wrath and unceasing change. Reality frayed at the edges of the daemon army, unravelled by their presence and their numbers.

Eyeing the ferocity of the charge, Azkaellon said, 'They do not want us inside.'

'They do not,' Sanguinius agreed. 'That in itself shows that we are on the right path.'

With the primarch and the Sanguinary Guard forming the tip of the spear, the Blood Angels charged forwards to meet the enemy, bolters and lascannons striking out ahead of them. As the first of the daemons fell, Sanguinius voxed the Legion. 'My sons, today we purge the memory of Signus Prime. Hold fast to your anger, but preserve its righteousness. Hone it. Be its master. Through it, let us thirst only for victory.' *And nothing else.* 'We will be tempted. We will not fall.'

Not again. And not with my brothers as witnesses. If we fall again today, then the war is over. The power that built this fortress will have the galaxy as its plaything.

He switched the channel to a private one. 'Amit,' he spoke to his troubled son. 'Do you hear me?'

'I do. And I understand.'

'Good. But bring justice to the abominations, Amit. Be our vengeance.' He gave license to Fifth Company and its captain. 'Tear them asunder.'

The spear of the Blood Angels plunged into the mass of the daemons. There was no pause in the weapons fire. Mass-reactive shells burst warp flesh apart. Las burned it to ash. The daemons did not fall as living things did. They kept coming, missing arms and legs, torsos punctured by wounds that should have been lethal. But they had become matter, and so were subject to destruction.

Sanguinius swung the *Blade Encarmine* through the body of a thing whose flesh was the pink of a drowned newborn. The monster's liquid howl became a doubled, burbling squall as the flesh darkened to the blue of suffocation and the two halves sprouted new limbs. The babbling maws of the beasts fastened on to his legs. As he cut them down with two swift strokes, a scream descended upon him, a scream of reason shredded, of hope turned into the anguish of doom. At its sound, the pain of his fate rose in his chest, and despair mocked the futility of every effort. The scream was a psychic javelin. It sought to transfix him, to drive his soul into the earth and hold it there, writhing, helpless before the predator.

Sanguinius defied the paralysis and jerked his head up. The two horrors had held him in place long enough to make him the target of a flying daemon. Its sinuous tail sliced the air as if swimming. Talons lined the edges of its wings. Its maw was framed by horns as long as a man's arm. Another daemon rode its back. It was the same revolting pink as the abomination Sanguinius had dispatched, but its limbs were longer, muscled. Its horned head was jewelled with necklaces of golden bones. Two of its three hands held a curved dagger and a flesh-bound book. The third was open. The daemon extended it towards Sanguinius, revealing an azure eye in its palm. The daemon cocked its head, as if in greeting, and psychic energy blasted from the eye.

Jittering lightning struck Sanguinius in the chest and wrapped itself around him. Change, hard and cold and inexorable, reached through his armour, into his marrow, into his mind. The daemon chanted, its voice twining around the scream of its mount. The words were beyond his understanding. No human tongue could make their shape. Yet they drove even deeper into the heart of the Angel's being. They called up fate, like a stone, a cold yet molten stone, diamond and lava, the unalterable and the consuming. Horus' blade pierced him once more, and beyond that pain was a darkness. It was not the abyss of his death. It was formed of the consequences of his death.

The attack, the words, the agony and the vision all took barely a second to transpire. Sanguinius shouted, defying the paralysis that pulled at his limbs and soul. *If my fate is decreed, then I do not die here.* The daemon's attack meant nothing, and with his left hand he thrust the *Spear of Telesto* upwards, impaling the winged daemon through its maw. He arrested its flight with that single gesture, grounding himself against the impact of its mass. The head of the spear tore through the upper jaw and emerged through the top of the daemon's flat head. Impaled, the abomination shrieked mindlessly. It lashed its body around Sanguinius, spines gouging the surface of his armour. The rider sank the talons of its feet into the back of the monster and kept its position. It ignored the flailing wings and tail. The eye in its hand unleashed jagged blue lightning. The daemon held the book higher, and it chanted the words of its pages with greater ferocity, and greater knowledge.

I know you, it seemed to be saying. *I know everything you will say and do, and how you will end. I know how this battle will end. I know you, and you are the one who is impaled.*

It struck downwards with its twisted blade. Sanguinius blocked it with the *Blade Encarmine*. His movement felt slow, as if he were a puppet straining against his strings. Fate was inevitable, yet change tormented his frame, seeking to bend him to a new, more terrible arc, blackening the meaning of his death, turning sacrifice into atrocity. He pushed back against the daemon. The blades scraped against each other. Crimson and violet light collided. Flames that burned and flames that sliced made war against each other. The flying daemon sank lower on the spear. Its flesh boiled away from the weapon's touch, and it wrapped the length of its tail around the author of its pain.

The horned daemon chanted, and its eyes blazed in mockery.

I know you.

Sanguinius hurled his strength against the daemon. The *Blade Encarmine* began to slice through the edge of the abomination's sword.

His peripheral vision caught movement on his right. Something huge had broken through the Sanguinary Guard. It was charging him.

Gold flashed to his left. His herald leapt past him, attacking in such a blur of speed that Sanguinius would have sworn he saw the flash of wings carrying the herald upwards. He landed beside the three-armed daemon and drove his powerblade through the side of its head. The warp light vanished. The book fell from the daemon's grasp.

The charging beast was almost upon him.

Sanguinius turned in the coils of the winged daemon with such force that he shredded the creature's muscle. The *Spear of Telesto* was caught in the monster's body, but he swung the *Blade Encarmine* over his head as he turned. He brought it down with a roar. He hit his target before he could truly register what it was. Behind his blow was all his rage at the paradoxes of his fate, its certain arrival and uncertain meaning. He struck at the powers that laid claim to knowing him and the purpose of his being. The sword hit the skull of a daemonic beast. Scarlet of hide and of armour, a single razored horn rising from its forehead, its jaws were parted in rabid rage. It had trampled one of the Sanguinary Guard beneath hooves of brass, pounding the legionary into a mass of pulp and splintered ceramite.

All this, Sanguinius took in after his blow. The blade split the monster's skull in two. The blazing eyes fell to either side, their wrath flaring once more, then fading as dissolution took hold of the behemoth.

Its legs buckled on the instant and it slammed into the ground. The sword-wielding daemon that rode its back was pitched forwards. Bolter fire took it apart before it landed. Sanguinius leaned into the collision, crushing the winged daemon's coils between his armour and the fallen beast. Daemonic flesh merged and melted. Freed, he spread his wings and took to the air.

Sanguinius hovered briefly over the melee. The herald had only just withdrawn his blade from the body of the chanting daemon. He saluted the Angel and turned back to the fray. The war called, yet Sanguinius felt compelled to watch the herald a moment longer. He had the vertiginous impression of seeing himself wade into the crush of monsters.

Amit had detached his company from the main advance, leading his men in an arc around the edges of the flood of daemons pouring from the gate. Now he took them back in, cutting across the flow before the doorway. Amit sent a flight of rockets just ahead of them. The legionaries charged into the dust of the explosions. They went in fast, reckless in fury, bolters and blades punishing the reeling monsters while the fireballs were still fading. Amit's anger was who he was, and it could take him too far, but it was not the Thirst. It was the shadow of the Blood Angels' nobility, the brutal reality of warfare. They aspired to the sun, but they drew blood too. Right now, the burst of Fifth Company's anger was the exemplar for the Legion.

The main advance of the Blood Angels was less than a hundred yards from the narrowing gap between the doors. The swirl of daemons was confused. There were fewer emerging from the manufactorum, and the ones at the entrance were striking out in every direction, momentarily unsure of the primary threat.

Sanguinius rose higher, faster, his wings beating hard against the thin air to hold him aloft, the confluence of events giving him speed.

'Lord primarch,' Azkaellon voxed. Sanguinius was pulling away from his escort.

'Be ready,' Sanguinius told him. 'We are about to take the forge. All heavy weapons,' Sanguinius voxed. 'Fire forwards, and fire now.'

Lascannons and rockets by the hundreds obeyed his command a second later. The sudden holocaust cut through the ranks of the daemons, punching craters in rock and gouging out trenches of incinerated warp flesh. Sanguinius streaked downwards, and he was another flame, a comet of war. He held the *Spear of Telesto* before him as he flew to the nexus of daemons. He charged the spear with the psychic force of the angelic war, and unleashed its judgement.

The beam was a blinding sear in the gloom of Pyrrhan. It sliced through clusters of sinuous, hooved, long-necked abominations. It turned them into ash. Sanguinius flew in on the path of the beam, wings folding back. Spear extended and blade sweeping before him, his descent was a bloody streak. He decapitated daemons with the speed and force of his strike. He was unstoppable.

He landed just ahead of Amit's company. He stood between the closing doors; their edges, wide as mountain faces, rumbled in. The ground shook without cease. Around Sanguinius, daemons of wrath closed in, swords raised. Their numbers looked thin. Too many had rushed forwards to try to counter Fifth Company. Before Sanguinius were the mouths of thousands of tunnels, blurring in the great heights above. The daemons had stopped their advance. They were on the defensive, guarding the entrances. Some capered, eager for the Blood Angels to make their assaults. The creatures of disease rang bells, so many that the funereal clamour rivalled the grinding thunder of the doors.

Sanguinius attacked the abominations trying to encircle him. They stalked forwards on hoofed legs that angled backwards. With their long, curving horns and crimson skin, they truly were the daemons of ancient Terran myth. In the crimson of their hide, though, Sanguinius saw a dark mirror of his Legion's colours. The daemons came to fight angels, but in their snarling rage, they were the image of the angels' threatened fall. Sanguinius fought them in a sweeping run, hitting them like a scythe. He deflected swords and cut abominations in half. The *Spear of Telesto* flashed again, burning purity sending the rage that walked back into the abyss of the warp.

The deep thudding of bolters and the snarl of chainswords drew closer. The din of war echoed up the edges of the doors. Less than two hundred yards of space remained. Fifth Company broke through at the same time as the Sanguinary Guard. Amit and Azkaellon converged on Sanguinius. Amit's armour dripped with ichor. His breathing rasped from his helm grille. It was almost a snarl.

'Captain Amit,' Sanguinius said. 'Are you the master of your anger?'

'I am, lord.' The breathing became slightly more regular. 'We all are.'

'That is well. Then we go forwards.'

The main body of Blood Angels was between the doors now. The legionaries marched shoulder to shoulder, their boots tramping in unison. They were a single mass, indivisible, unstoppable. They left a stinking, dissolving wake of foulness behind them. The Stormbirds maintained their bombardment, concentrating their fire on a smaller area as the closing doors hampered the attempts of the daemon army to return to the manufactorum.

The IX Legion moved at a brutal run between the doors, racing to get through before they shut with crushing finality. There was a mile of open floor between the doors and the tunnel mouths. The surface was metal, though it looked like knotted flesh. With the Sanguinary Guard as point again, Sanguinius crossed the threshold in the manufactorum and directed the phalanxes to the left and right.

'We take the widest halls,' he ordered. 'One company in each path. Captains, choose your terrain to fight upon.'

'*What are we looking for?*' Raldoron asked.

'We'll know when we find it,' Sanguinius answered. 'Believe that this is still a manufactorum. We can destroy its ability to function without having to destroy the structure itself. Go now, for Baal, for Terra and the Emperor!'

He was running forwards as he spoke. His army was spreading out behind him, escaping the doors. He chose the central hall for the Sanguinary Guard and First Company. Halfway across the floor of the towering vestibule, Sanguinius looked back. The doors were almost closed. The last of the Blood Angels were inside. He could just see a narrow slit, flickering with the flames of the battle outside the manufactorum. 'Brothers,' he voxed Guilliman and the Lion, 'we are inside.'

'Well fought,' said the Lion. *'We will scrape the land clear of the abominations for your extraction.'*

'Does the interior suggest how you can shut the forge down?' Guilliman asked. *'I would think–'*

Vox contact with the exterior of the manufactorum cut off. The doors closed with a tectonic boom.

As Sanguinius led the march to the central tunnel, to where daemons gibbered and snarled and chanted, a psychic shudder rippled through the immense forge. It passed over Sanguinius. It was the touch of malevolent sentience. It felt like a welcome.

TEN

The Cleft

THE MANUFACTORUM BREATHED. It was metal and stone, a monstrosity constructed on a framework of brass and iron girders the size of cities that gave shape to the bones of the planet. It was a work built in the materium, of the materium, and yet it breathed. The taint of the warp oozed from every crack in the metal, every pore of stone. The floor beneath Sanguinius' boots heaved up and down with the slow inhale and exhale of lungs. It slithered too. Footing was treacherous. The metal felt as if it were covered by a thick, viscous slick of ichor. It was not. It was dry. Serpentine tremors moved through it, shifting and pulling, the surface changing from rough to smooth in the space of an instant.

The manufactorum bled. Where bolt shells or daemon claws struck the walls, rotting blood ran. The wounds puckered and sucked like hungry mouths.

And the manufactorum sang. The conduits were the pipes of an organ. Whatever moved through them summoned notes of cancerous music. The deeper the Blood Angels ventured into the forge, the more complex the song became. The mouths of open conduits had teeth, and tongues lapped at their edges. They shaped themselves to the demands of the tune. The tongues vibrated. The octaves of the sick melody plunged so far beneath hearing, the vibrations would have shattered a mortal's skeleton. They rose so high, Sanguinius tasted blood. The music was a polyphonic symphony of dark industry and darker intent. It was a hymn to ruin, and a threnody for hope. In the complex nodes that developed, he thought he heard the formation of a whisper. It was at the edge of perception, unwilling to declare itself yet. There were no syllables. It was the hesitation that came before a familiar word was pronounced.

Sanguinius was not alone in hearing the whisper. Raldoron spoke to him when First Company and the Sanguinary Guard broke through another horde of the corpulent, plague-bearing abominations. *'Something is speaking here.'*

'And it wants us to listen,' Sanguinius said. 'Shut your ears to it. There will only be poison in the words.'

They were in a hall hundreds of yards wide, and they had a clear run for at least a mile. The space was lit by the conduits. They ran in thick clusters along the walls and the ceiling, two hundred feet up. Each was almost as wide as a Rhino, and they glowed, lit from within by the burning fusion of warp and matter they carried. They tracked their way down the curving tunnel like veins, their lines irregular, merging and branching but always feeding deeper.

'The voices want us to advance,' Raldoron said. *'They are pulling.'*

'And we must advance for our reasons too,' Sanguinius said. 'There are matters where we have no choice. There are actions we are bound by destiny to take. That does not mean the consequences of the action are preordained.' He needed this to be true. *Please, Father, let it be so.* 'The foul song of this place may want us to go deeper. We will, and we will overwhelm the power within. It will rue its desire to lure us in.'

The tunnel curved sharply. Its immensity sighed. A great choir resounded, and the hall opened up into a chamber of even larger dimensions. Filling the centre was a nexus of conduits. They arrived from a score of corridors, from multiple levels. They tangled with each other, forming a gigantic knot.

'A nerve cluster!' Sanguinius shouted. It could be nothing else. The unwholesome light within flashed with maddening intensity, illuminating the chamber with a blinding stutter. 'This monstrousness mimics life, and so makes itself vulnerable. Teach it pain!'

The song of the manufactorum became a wail, punctuating each flash with the celebration and lamentation of the materium twisted, and the impossible made real. Hundreds of the pink-fleshed daemons gathered around the base of the nexus, adding their babbling to the chorus. They turned at the sound of the Blood Angels' arrival. The daemons sent a wave of warp sorcery ahead of them. The Sanguinary Guard and First Company hurled themselves through it. It washed over armour, boiling ceramite and melting it. The wills contained within were strong, made stronger by the crucible of Signus Prime. The Blood Angels withstood the wrenching attempts of change and blasted the abominations out of existence. They waded through the twitching mess of blue matter that remained, and gathered, squad by squad, around the nexus.

Raldoron joined Sanguinius before the mass of the conduits. 'Melta bombs?' he asked.

Sanguinius smiled. 'It seems so mundane a means of destroying the extraordinary, doesn't it?'

'Yes,' said Raldoron. 'If the myths of the past are real, it seems they should be banished by rituals too.'

'Naturally.' Sanguinius was conscious of the feathers of his wings trembling very lightly in response to the vibrations of the manufactorum's song. He knew more than he cared to about myths. His life had been a constant struggle to avoid becoming one. 'Only rituals banish nothing. Actions do.' He swept an arm, taking in the smashed and burned remains of the daemons. 'They have become material, and so can be destroyed by material means.' He examined the nexus a moment longer. 'Melta bombs,' he agreed, then said it again, voxing the order to the company.

Howls came from the other tunnels. They grew louder in the time it took to set the charges.

Azkaellon drew the Sanguinary Guard more tightly around Sanguinius. 'Reinforcements are coming,' he said.

'Indeed.' Sanguinius scanned the tunnel openings, choosing the next path. He settled on a corridor on the opposite side of the chamber from where the Blood Angels had entered. It was as large as the passage they had left, and had as many conduits. He saw now that not all of the pipes fed into the nexus. Perhaps not even all those that did were bringing material *to* the junction. They might be carrying something away, too.

There was another consideration. The roar of an approaching mass of the enemy was louder down that tunnel. If a larger force was coming, it might be from something worth defending.

There was a score of melta bombs, keyed to a single detonator, placed on the nexus when the company moved on. The junction was that big. The Blood Angels moved down the next tunnel, retreating from the blast they would unleash, and advancing on the foe. Raldoron ordered Sergeant Vahiel to hold the rear, trigger the detonator and note the results. The noise of the daemons was deafening, though still subsumed to the song of the manufactorum, but they were not yet in sight when Vahiel set off the bombs.

'*Detonation*,' Vahiel reported. '*It looks like–*'

The sound that cut him off was greater than the explosion. Sanguinius heard the deep-throated thunder of the blast. He pictured the nexus shattering, the conduits flying back in shards as the energy they transported was unleashed when the melta bombs ruptured their integrity. That was the material explosion. It was barely audible beneath the other sound. That sound, the one that silenced Vahiel and daemons alike, was the sudden wail in the heart of the song. The symphony of the manufactorum broke into a momentary cacophony. The words crumbled before they could finally be spoken. A mountain screamed. The dark miracle that fed the great gate above the planet stumbled in its operation. Even Chaos could be disrupted, and it was now. The shriek of the music ended quickly. Junctions elsewhere took on more labour, and the work of destroying reality resumed.

In the space of those few seconds, though, for the duration of the wail, Sanguinius felt the complex shudder like a stabbed animal. The pain went deep, much further than the immediate vicinity of the nexus.

After the shriek, the mournful insanity of the song resumed. From the rear came the rumble of collapsing stone and metal.

'The chamber is gone,' said Vahiel. 'There's been a major collapse.'

Sanguinius voxed the captains of the other companies. 'Our strategy is bearing fruit. Destroy the large junctions.' The desert scorpion of Baal was a juggernaut in its armour. A single spear could do nothing against it. But strike it with many, and it would fall. Enough spears would kill the foundry too.

'We have our prey,' Amit responded. 'You will hear our blow very soon.'

The tunnel split ahead, the equally large branches turning left and right. The left-hand path took a steep descent. The roaring of the daemon horde came from there. Sanguinius chose it, wondering why there was still no sign of the foe. The Blood Angels had travelled two miles since the first blast. The volume of the howls was no longer increasing.

'Lord primarch, are they retreating?' Azkaellon asked.

'It doesn't sound as if they are, does it?' said Sanguinius. It was more likely an auditory distortion created by the web of tunnels. There was so much unnatural about the manufactorum, a deceptive quality to the sound would hardly be surprising.

Perhaps he had been wrong to think a daemon army guarded this path. At least the conduits were as numerous as the first tunnel. Sooner or later, there would be another junction.

The terrible song hesitated again, and then again. Two other companies of Blood Angels had destroyed their first targets. Both times, Sanguinius heard and felt the deep tremor shake the manufactorum. 'We are damaging this terrible place,' he voxed the Legion. 'It knows us. Soon it will fear us, because it will know we have come to kill it.' But how many spears will it take? he wondered. For all that the Blood Angels had advanced quickly, they had barely broken the skin of the huge forge. There could be hundreds of miles between Sanguinius' current position and the core. If there was a core.

The slope became steeper. The floor writhed. Sanguinius listened to the song more carefully, hoping to find that it was waning, a hint that the damage was starting to matter.

He found something else instead. The whisper was emerging again, more distinctly than before, as if the wounded animal were desperate to cry out. The words would not be stopped. There were syllables now. They were so slow, long seconds passing between each consonant and vowel, that their refrain was hard to distinguish.

At the next intersection, Sanguinius paused. He listened for the whisper now. It seemed more localised than the rest of the song. The full symphony did not change in volume depending on the route taken. It was the voice of the entire manufactorum, and its voice was everywhere. The whisper was getting louder. And it was getting faster. It slipped out between the pause in the manufactorum's intakes of breath with such sudden clarity that Sanguinius wondered how he could not have known it for what it was from the start.

It was his name.

'Lord primarch?' Azkaellon asked as, with a wounded snarl, Sanguinius plunged down the left tunnel in pursuit of the voice.

'Can you hear it?' asked Sanguinius.

'The song, my lord?'

'No, the whisper.'

Azkaellon said nothing for a moment, listening. 'I hear no whisper.'

'Raldoron?' Sanguinius called. 'Can you still hear the voices?'

'No, my lord.'

'Then it is for my ears alone. The enemy is preparing a more insidious attack.' The thought came that the daemonic power that held the manufactorum might not be on the defensive at all. Sanguinius dismissed the pessimism. The wounds were real. The music had fractured.

Sanguinius followed the hissing syllables of his name. It summoned him, and he answered. *I do not die here*, he thought. *My end will come, but today, I am the one who brings the end.*

Daemons roared in the distance, always in the distance, always around the next bend, but never arriving.

At last the corridor narrowed and made a sharp turn to the right. It ended in another nexus chamber. In the chamber was a single abomination; it stood before the junction of conduits. It was kin to the one Sanguinius and the herald had fought outside the manufactorum. It was taller, its horns longer, but the muscle-pink of its hide was the same. It carried a staff instead of a sword, and this it held at the vertical. Its other two hands held a book. Sanguinius did not know if it was the same tome or not. He didn't care. The daemon appeared to want him to care. It held the book open. It held it forwards, arms extended, an invitation Sanguinius would decline.

A nimbus of warp energy surrounded the daemon. It dissipated as the Blood Angels came into view. As the energy vanished, the sounds of the daemon army fell into silence. The illusion of the multitude evaporated.

'So this is our ambush,' said Azkaellon. 'A single foe.' He sounded very suspicious.

'Kano?' Sanguinius asked. He advanced slowly into the chamber. Several hundred yards separated him from the daemon. He saw no other abominations lying in wait.

'*I sense only the one we see,*' the Librarian voxed.

Sanguinius hesitated. The daemon was motionless. It did not attack. It held the book, and that was all. It had lured him here. It must know what he planned to do. It could not think it would be enough to stop the entire company.

His choices were few. He had come to destroy the nexus. That imperative had not changed.

Sanguinius halted less than fifty feet into the chamber. He would not be part of the design being woven. 'Fire on the nerve cluster from this position,' Sanguinius commanded. 'Ignore the daemon.'

The sorcerous light returned, and a sudden nova burst from the book. It shot up and behind the daemon, striking the nexus.

'*Back!*' Sanguinius ordered.

The conduits disintegrated. Coruscating, murderous light burst from them. It formed a contained ball of energy, blinding in intensity, its convulsions scraping at the mind like claws. It fused tighter, drawing in on itself. It imploded, and now, where the junction had been, was a single point of warp light.

Oh, Sanguinius thought, and then the light came for him.

The beam struck him in the eyes.

There was a moment of absolute void and then there was a maelstrom of creation, an uncontrolled explosion of being without form. He dropped down its eye, into dark. He fell through blackness veined with red and green and blue and violet, the colours of ruin entwined and cutting into his mind like wire.

He did not land, but he stopped falling. He floated in the black. The darkness became mist, gathered definition, and became the bridge of the *Vengeful Spirit*. He was there again, as present as he had been when he had slipped between realities on the *Red Tear*. And again, Horus struck him down.

The pain again. The pain of final dissolution. He felt himself die, and he felt the grief at treachery and the grief of failure, the grief that his death was meaningless. There was no doubt now. He died, and Horus won, and that was all.

He fell into the dark, and light pierced it again; it became shadows and then substance again, and once more Horus towered over him. Once more, Horus slew him.

The pain, the grief, the futility... It was all there *again*.

And then again.

And again.

And again.

He lived his final moment over and over. The pain never diminished. Each iteration of his doom was as excruciating as the last. He tried to turn his head as the *Vengeful Spirit* materialised. He was confronted with the same perspective. He groaned, and with a wrenching effort of will, he turned his back on Horus. He spun himself away from the vision, though he heard the sound of his boots against the deck.

The effort was futile. He turned and turned and turned, and he died and he died and he died. There was no escape, no meaning, no hope. Each time Horus killed him, he saw a trace of the future that would come. Every death brought its consequences. None were repeated. All were terrible. Horus was endlessly triumphant. All that changed was his immediate route to power.

Sanguinius spun faster, the movement no longer of his volition, and he saw endless iterations of his fate at once, as if he were in a mirror corridor, with the same image reflected to infinity. But this was more than an image. It was real. He died a thousand times at once, and the pain was a thousand times amplified.

A new blackness rose. This one was his. It came from within. It was anger that dwarfed the pain. Its jaws were immense, jagged with fangs, breathing flame and hatred. It consumed him, and yet the jaws were his too. With them, he would repay the treacherous galaxy with blood. He roared in an agony of wrath as the images of his death endlessly repeated. Darkness within lashed at the darkness without. Deep in his mind, buried in the agony, a sliver of his identity protested. It did not want this thing he had become. It rejected the black monster that claimed him as its father. His last piece of rationality reached out in desperation for any trace of hope. It flashed through the deaths upon deaths upon deaths, becoming weaker and dimmer as it looked for any meaning, any sign of doom leading to consequences other than eternal night for the Imperium.

At last, the hope appeared. In the infinite variations of the battle against Horus, there was one that challenged predestined death. One vision was different. Only one. In it, Sanguinius dodged the death blow. Horus put so much power into it that he overbalanced when he missed. There was a fraction of a second of hesitation as he sought to correct his momentum. Sanguinius seized the chance, and drove the *Blade Encarmine* up. It found the weakened point in Horus' gorget. It pierced his armour.

It pierced his throat.

It pierced his skull.

This was the outcome Sanguinius had never even dreamed of, because the entire foundations of his destiny were built upon its denial. In this one vision, the terrible blackness withered, collapsed and broke apart into whirling ash. Here, and only here, there was hope. Here, and only here, the Imperium did not fall. Here, and only here, the Emperor's dream lived on.

Like the coils of a monstrous serpent, the continuum of dooms gathered around Sanguinius. They came to strangle the single hope. They came to destroy the thing that turned them from certainties into mere possibilities. The visions formed a knot around Sanguinius and the image of light. It tightened. The wrenching anger rose once more, fastening its grip on his being. When the knot closed, the light would be gone, and there would only be the fury.

Sanguinius felt the imperative of decision. He made his choice. He refused the blackness and chose hope. He lunged towards the light. He raised his sword and plunged into the vision. He became the Sanguinius who slew Horus. The sword killed Horus, and it cut through his evil dream. It sliced through the knot. The visions fractured, mirrors broken into shards. They fell away into the void.

Now Sanguinius was falling again, but he was not done with the sword. After driving the *Blade Encarmine* through Horus' skull and through the knot of fate, he brought it down. There was so much strength in the blow, it cut through unreality itself.

The blade sank into the flesh of the dream void. It tore the warp fabric open with fire. Light appeared beneath Sanguinius as he fell. He was leaving the realm of visions, but had not yet returned to reality. He was in a nether zone, neither dream nor real, but linked to both states. The light was another knot, another nexus. It looked like the intersection of the manufactorum conduits, only the conduits themselves were absent. It was the flow of warp energy and material mined from the interior of Pyrrhan, the unreal colliding with the solid to form the gate. Searing, impossible creation whirled through the convulsions of the nexus. It was the forge of the new reality of the galaxy. Sanguinius descended, wings outspread, to cleave the knot in two.

He passed through the nexus. In his wake, creation ended. The energy screamed. The uncontrollable explosion spread though the void. A dome of conflagration unfurled above Sanguinius.

Still he fell, still powered by the single sword blow. Another knot of energy appeared, and he cut it, and then the next, and the next, and the next. He had chosen to live, and so had torn destiny open, and with that rupture was slicing apart all the coils with which Chaos sought to entangle him. He was dealing a death blow to a creature he barely understood, whose size he could not grasp, and yet had defeated.

Down, down, down, the great sword blow of hope cutting through all the knots of ruin, a streak of red unleashing the flames of purification, until he cut his way back to reality. The void peeled back. The light of deliverance engulfed him. It blinded him with the blood-red fire. He blinked, and the flare vanished. He stood in the chamber from which he had first fallen. The daemon was at his feet. Its body was cut in two. As was its book and its staff. Weapons and corpse curled at the edges, dissolving from the materium. Violent light filled the chamber. A sea of liquid fire roiled across the ceiling. Currents of flame strove against each other. Maelstroms formed, melting everything above. Metal and stone dropped in blinding streams to the floor of the chamber. Everything was shaking, cracking, breaking apart.

'Lord Sanguinius?' Azkaellon was at his side, half reaching as if unsure whether or not the Angel was an illusion.

Sanguinius looked around, trying to get his bearings. He felt the solidity of the floor beneath his boots. The surface quaked, but did not flow away into dream. He looked at his sons. The Blood Angels were more or less as he had last seen them. More of the company had

entered the chamber, but that was the only change in their disposi-
tion he could see. They were solid, unwavering in their reality. 'What
happened?' he asked.

'You vanished,' said Azkaellon, alarmed.

On the *Red Tear*, he had fought visions, but they had been *visions*.
He had not fallen into an *elsewhere*. The fusion of dreams and reality
made him dizzy. 'How long was I gone?'

'A few seconds. You and the daemon.'

It had felt like hours. A lifetime. As long as death.

His vox-bead vibrated, erupting with the reports and interrogatives
of his captains and Chapter Masters. He listened to them now, putting
together what had happened during his absence. He realised after a
few moments that he was the author of the new situation in the forge.
What he had cut apart in that netherzone was now destroyed in reality.
Tangles of conduits all over the manufactorum had exploded, far more
than had been targeted. The complex trembled. Its song was broken
beyond repair. The manufactorum screamed now. It howled a chorus of
final pain and terror. Machines and power were tearing each other apart.

In the hail of reports coming over the vox, a fragment broke through.
It was a single word. *'Brother.'* The rest was lost in static. But the voice
was Guilliman's. The Blood Angels were no longer isolated from the
other two Legions.

The tremors were growing more violent by the second. The forge's
scream rose higher, losing coherence, becoming a thunder of catastrophe.

'We have triumphed!' Sanguinius voxed to the Legion. 'The enemy's
works fall before us.'

At his nod, Azkaellon ordered, 'All forces, withdraw immediately.'

Spear held high, he led the turn away from the chamber. The tunnel
beyond roared. Liquid flame consumed its ceiling too. The conduits
split, bleeding energy. Uncanny lightning forked across the width of
the corridor. It burned glowing crevasses into the walls and floor.

The Blood Angels raced to keep their victory. The mountainous forge
was about to fall in on itself.

We do not die here, Sanguinius thought. *My end is not yet.*

And then he wondered, *Are you sure?*

He wasn't. And the uncertainty elated him.

WHEN THE BLOOD Angels entered the manufactorum, they dropped into silence so complete, they might have been swallowed by the grave. Daemons abandoned the other manufactoria to flood the land. Under the shadow of the daemonic fortress, on a battlefield so long that the combatants at either end were over the horizon from each other, the Legions struggled against the abominations.

The Lion led his legionaries to the regions before the closed doors of the forge. The formations of Dark Angels were walls of black iron. The daemons hurled themselves against the barriers. The Dark Angels refused to give up a single step of the land they held. Their heavy artillery bombarded the swarms of monsters, and the infantry advanced methodically, the walls of iron crushing the enemy.

While the Warhawks of the IX Legion launched strafing runs against the manufactoria, cutting into the hordes as they emerged from the gaping doorways, and Khalybus led his Iron Hands against the daemons emerging from the foundry closest to the primary manufactorum, Guilliman struck from three centres. After being part of the vanguard in the initial run to the great forge, the Destroyers turned back, driving a wedge through the centre of the mass of daemons at the same time as Guilliman took *Flame of Illyrium* and the Invictus Bodyguard in a stiletto-jab through the body of daemons besieging the Dark Angels. Towards the middle of the battlefield and at the southern end, the greater body of the Ultramarines attacked in two radiating movements. Phalanxes cut into the enemy like so many swords. Guilliman forced the daemons to contend with multiple fronts and kept them on the defensive. They sought to repel the invaders and take back the land. The Ultramarines had no positions to hold. All they needed to do was keep moving, and destroy everything in their paths.

The Destroyers threw themselves into the fight with an enthusiasm that might have troubled Guilliman in a different context. When he monitored the communications between Hierax and his company, he heard tones verging on savage joy. Yet the discipline of their attacks never wavered. What he heard was the brutal satisfaction of no longer fighting a defensive war. He understood. When he pumped the *Arbitrator*'s double stream of bolter shells into the abominations, when the explosions vaporised warp flesh, he felt the same satisfaction. And when the Destroyers pulverised the heaving mass of the enemy with rad artillery barrages, there was more satisfaction. The worst of weapons for the worst of foes. That logic was unassailable.

Then use the weapons you have acquired. You know what the athames can do to these beings.

He brushed the thought aside. The daggers were in the vault aboard the *Samothrace*, beyond the reach of temptation. There was no need of them here. The weaponry of the Ultramarines was effective in destroying the abominations.

Then Gorod, marching with Guilliman beside the *Flame of Illyrium*, challenged his certainty. 'Chainswords and axes are felling these things more readily than bolters,' he said.

'We've seen this before,' Guilliman answered. 'But they are falling quickly enough.'

'I could almost wish we had brought even more primitive weapons.'

Guilliman didn't answer. He punched the *Gladius Incandor* through the skull of a glistening pink monster, then finished it with two more stabs as it tried to divide itself.

FOR MORE THAN one hundred hours, the battle raged. Then the manufactorum cried out. A mountain chain of infernal creation screamed with a throat of stone. Fissures snaked up the heights of the walls. Chimneys three miles high wavered. Their bases crumbled, and they dropped like broken spines into the pyres of chaotic lightning. The fissures widened. Howling light burst from them. The warp lightning punched holes through the towering doors. The daemons in the field moaned as one, and abandoned the attack. Their reduced army melted away, flowing back into the secondary foundries. Soon the high towers on both sides of the battleground began to flash. Streaks of corrupted light shot upwards to the base of the fortress.

'They flee,' the Lion voxed.

Guilliman turned to the primary foundry's doors. They were still closed. 'Brother,' he called to Sanguinius. 'Can you hear me?'

There was no answer at first. It wasn't long, though, before one came. When a huge split appeared the entire height of the doors, Sanguinius' voice reached Guilliman. 'We are coming out, Roboute. We have done what we came to do.'

'I can see that.' The manufactorum was a volcano about to be blown apart by its internal forces.

'Can you clear the terrain for the Stormbirds to land?'

'That will not be a concern. They have quit the field. Focus your efforts on escaping the site of your triumph. Don't let it be your tomb, Sanguinius.'

'It won't be.'

Guilliman was struck by the ringing confidence in Sanguinius' voice. He had become used to hearing his brother's iron fatalism. Sanguinius sounded different now. For the first time since they had been reunited on Macragge, Guilliman heard the Angel speak with real hope.

The manufactorum convulsed. A series of explosions mounted the pillar joining it to the keep's gate. They began as pinpricks on the umbilical length, then became a pulsing river of fire. A blast at the base of the fortress gate was larger than Pyrrhan itself. The terrain before the manufactorum shook with constant tremors. A widening web of fissures extended from the foundations. To the south, for as far as Guilliman could see, clouds of dust erupted as the ground cracked.

'Withdraw, brothers,' Sanguinius voxed to Guilliman and the Lion. 'This battle is finished, and greater victories will come.'

'*You saw something in there, Sanguinius,*' said the Lion. He sounded almost accusatory.

'*I did,*' said the Angel. '*I saw hope. We are not slaves to fate, brothers.*'

THE END OF the manufactorum arrived as the combined fleets came over the horizon, putting them once more in the line of fire of the keep's guns. The surface of Pyrrhan flared white. Coronas of warp energy whipped up the pillar, growing vaster with every slashing coil. Pyrrhan imploded, vanishing in an instant, the tiny growth at the end of the pillar sucked into the climbing disintegration. Blasts the size of miniature suns rocked the pillar, and then the dissolution reached the gate itself.

The gun emplacements on the gate fired briefly. They did not destroy their targets before destruction came for them. On the bridge of the *Red Tear*, Sanguinius watched the holocaust. Warp-infused flames hundreds of thousands of miles high consumed the gate. The structure lost coherence. It disintegrated. Shrapnel as big as planets spun away from the main body. Solid matter millions of miles thick became vortices, hurling streams of incandescent rubble into the void. The trailing edge of one stream hit the Dark Angels cruiser *Claustro*, turning the vessel to burning gas. The greatest vortex appeared in the middle of the gate. The eight-pointed star spiralled into fragments. The breach spread wider with ferocious speed. The colossal structure consumed itself like burning parchment, the edges peeling away from the centre, ash that could smash a battleship to dust billowing to the galactic east and west. The sides of the ruined gate glowed, molten. Between them now was a passage millions of miles wide. The void, stained by the Ruinstorm, was visible on the other side.

Engines powering up to maximum speed, the fleet began the long crossing between walls of infinite fire.

ELEVEN

Resonance

WHEN THE GRAVITATIONAL hold of the fortress weakened, and the fleets prepared to enter the warp again, Sanguinius called Mkani Kano to the Sanctorum Angelus. Sanguinius looked at the golden sculptures that made the space into an oasis of meditation, unable to draw peace from them.

'Do you know how we won on Pyrrhan?' Sanguinius asked.

'I do not,' Kano confessed.

Sanguinius told the Librarian a version of what he had experienced. He was circumspect about the visions. 'I saw visions of defeat,' he said. 'I found a single one of victory, and chose it.' He described the great fall, and the cleaving of the knots.

'Then you destroyed the manufactorum,' Kano said, awed.

'And by extension, the fortress gate itself. With a single blow. What I saw has given me great hope. But the implications trouble me, too. I must not believe I wield such cataclysmic power. No one should. The idea is corrupt and corrupting.'

Kano shook his head. 'The things we are seeing are beyond anyone's experience. The scale is simply too vast for easy explanation. They seem more symbolic than real.' He paused.

'Yes,' said Sanguinius. 'Symbolism. That is a key somehow. In the Signus System, that symbol of the eight-pointed star covered a planet. And
there are patterns to the beings of the daemons. They represent things.'

'Then perhaps so did your victory,' Kano suggested. 'We can use their
nature against them.'

As they do to us, Sanguinius thought. 'A single blow can change the
galaxy, then,' he said. *Or a single choice. That came before the blow.*

'For the better.'

'In this case.' Sanguinius was not satisfied. Too much still flowed from
his actions. He dreaded the constellation of circumstances that might
grant him even more power.

'More reasons to be on guard,' said Kano. 'Even so...' He trailed off.
Blood drained from his face. His eyes widened in sudden pain.

The *Red Tear* jerked, a toy in the hand of a giant. The drop from
the warp was as violent as it had been before the fortress. The sound
pierced the hull in the next moment. High-pitched, vibrating, like a
tuning fork struck against madness itself.

Sanguinius supported Kano from the Sanctorum, fighting through
the thrumming in his own skull. He felt warmth on his neck. Blood
was running from his ears.

'WHERE ARE WE?' Guilliman called. He wiped the blood from his nose
and ears.

On the bridge below the pulpit, officers clutched their heads in agony.
One man's teeth had chattered so violently they had splintered. Servitor movements were jerking, spasmodic, unpredictable. The resonance
hammered through the hull. The *Samothrace* rang as if the vibrations
would shake it to powder.

'Where are we?' Guilliman repeated. The system was not Davin. Much
more than that was ceasing to have meaning in this region of the galaxy.
Guilliman called for the information to force purpose into the crew, to
give them a way forwards through the pain of the unceasing resonance.

The crew responded to the command in Guilliman's voice. More officers collapsed, but others found strength in duty. The cogitators were spitting out gibberish scrap data, and the auspex array had to be shut down and restarted. At last, Nestor Lautenix spoke, his voice thick with pain. 'Episimos,' he said. 'It's Episimos.'

'Thrinos again,' said Prayto. The Librarian had grasped the railing overlooking the bridge. His posture was straight, but only through a massive effort of will. As painful as the sound was for Guilliman, it was much more harmful for the psyker. Blood droplets had formed on Prayto's forehead. 'There were refugees from here,' he said.

'Yes,' Guilliman said, sparing him further effort. He had made the connection too. Episimos IV had been well represented in the camp on Thrinos.

The evidence of the Pilgrim's passing was obvious.

Enormous constructs filled the system, dwarfing the worlds. The vessels of the fleets once again had to fight from being captured by the gravitational pull of the gigantic bodies. The objects were so immense, their shapes extended far beyond the limits of the Episimos System, beyond the range of the scans. They might, Guilliman thought, reach as far as other systems. They might be light years in size.

Objects. Shapes. Constructs. Guilliman hunted for words of greater precision, words that would describe the immensities he saw, and give him a measure of control. The whining, spine-grinding sound made it hard for him to think, but even in silence, language would have failed him. There were no names for these things. The daemon fortress at least had been recognisable. Its obscenity had been in its size. The constructs in the Episimos System were geometry run amok, angles building on and into other angles. On the nearest mass, the side facing the *Samothrace* was dominated by a formation that seemed to be both an extrusion and a depression. The pounding in Guilliman's head grew worse when he tried to force sense onto the formation, and he turned away.

'Analysis,' he said, maintaining order on the bridge.

'Warp,' said Prayto, breathing hard.

'Granted. But what is the materium correlative? The fortress was stone and brass. The abominations have something we can recognise as flesh. What is this?'

Guilliman spoke with more frustration than he intended. The surfaces appeared to be smooth. The objects were carved from single blocks millions and billions of miles on a side. Colours swam and rippled across them, deep rotten violets and greens. Patterns like the scales of reptiles appeared and disappeared. The constructs had hides, or they were ice, or they were a dream. Lines curved and straightened, a language of monsters preaching its lessons to the materium. The meaning of the lesson crawled inside Guilliman's chest. He tore his eyes from the flowing runes before he could understand them and be wounded.

He was not sure how many of the constructs there were in the system. A few floated alone in the void, serene in their lonely horror. Others were linked to one another, forming complexes so vast, they extended beyond the range of the scanners.

Even more than the fortress, these monoliths were the death of reason. There was no logic to the structures. Their material was the reification of madness. Their foundation was the bones of the Emperor's dream.

'What are they?' said Drakus Gorod. His question had no expectation of an answer. It was an expression of frustrated anger.

Guilliman gave him an answer all the same. 'They are the consequences of the loss of this war.' He wondered if Horus or Lorgar really understood what they had unleashed. Was this what they wanted? They could not rule here. There would be nothing to rule. They would be the slaves of these powers.

'The sound,' Prayto said. 'They're making it.' He pushed himself back from the railing, wiping blood from his face. He worked through the pain with grim determination. His psychic hood crackled as if he were fending off an attack. 'There are lines,' he said. He was speaking with difficulty. 'Psychic lines. Between the constructs. And between them and the worlds.' He winced. More blood appeared on his brow. 'I can see it. It's a web...' His voice trailed off. There was a flare from his hood, and then he was steadier again. 'It's holding us here.'

From below, one of the ship's tech-priests, Byzanus, looked up. 'With respect, Librarian Prayto,' he said, his bionic larynx hitching and popping with static, 'this seems unlikely. We cannot detect any source of energy from the constructs. They are inert.'

'Their being is enough,' said Prayto. 'Their shapes, their positions... The web is created by their conjunctions.'

'So we have no enemy to combat,' said Guilliman. 'What is our status?' he asked Turetia Altuzer.

'Almost immobilised,' said the shipmaster. 'The warp drive is inert. We have some power in the engines, but not much. We can manoeuvre to a limited degree, but if we get much closer to any of those objects, I'm not sure we'll be able to resist their gravitation.'

The back of Guilliman's skull throbbed with pain. If the mass, shape and position of the constructs was creating the sound, then he had to disrupt those conditions. But the constructs were too large to destroy.

'My lord,' said Terrens, 'vox activity coming from Episimos Three.'

'Human?'

'Yes.' Terrens stabbed at the screen before her. 'It's broken up badly. They appear to be hailing the fleets.'

'Take us closer,' Guilliman ordered. He looked at the fleet positions. The Dark Angels were nearest to Episimos III. 'Contact the First Legion,' he told Terrens. 'I will speak to my brother.'

The vox traffic between the ships was rough. The Lion's voice scratched in Guilliman's ear, but he could understand the other primarch well enough. The Dark Angels had picked up the same transmission. At their location, closer to the source, it was clearer.

'The Imperial forces planetside are under siege,' the Lion said.

'I'm impressed they've held out this long,' said Guilliman.

'I believe their time is growing short. They're asking for liberation.'

EPISIMOS III WAS a blackened skull. Its two great hives still burned, embers glowing in eye sockets. Further from the sun, Episimos IV had been the cooler, more temperate heart of the system. Now its surface was a writhing mass of grey flesh. Thin lips pulled back over a continent-wide smile. Teeth showed, then vanished, and another parted, running across the fading scar of the first maw. The world had become hunger. Episimos III, though, still fought. It still screamed.

'We have made contact with a Colonel Eleska Revus,' the Lion told Guilliman. 'We will relay the substance of our communications.' He had hesitated before making that commitment, then decided it would be better for his brothers to know what was being said. In this instance, he would want them to understand the reasons for the actions he sensed he would have to take.

'Who is in command of your operations?' the Lion asked Revus.

'I am,' she voxed back. '*Our lord governor is dead. General Palher dropped out of contact a week ago.*' Her words were slurred with exhaustion and horror.

'And your current situation?' He could foresee what the import of the answer would be. *Liberate us.* That was the cry that had first come through on the vox. If there had been any trace of hope in those hails to the fleet, it did not sound like the sudden expectation of victory. The Lion had been careful to use the same word when he spoke to Guilliman. *Liberation.* Not *reinforcements.* Sitting in the throne above the *Invincible Reason*'s bridge, he knew that he was, in this moment, a judge more than a military commander.

'*Our resistance is confined to isolated pockets.*'

'Is there any chance of linking up?'

'*No. Even if we could, it would be pointless.*'

'Do not try my patience with defeatism, colonel.'

'*I am not, my lord. I am stating facts. Ever since the Pilgrim came...*' Revus trailed off, the horror in her voice growing so strong that it strangled her words. '*It destroyed everything in orbit. We couldn't escape. Did anyone from Episimos Four get away?*'

'They did,' the Lion told her.

'*Oh. Oh good.*' She sighed with dark joy. '*Then our culture will survive.*'

Perhaps, the Lion thought. The refugees on Thrinos were cut off from the rest of the Imperium. Their long-term survival was doubtful.

'What was the Pilgrim?' the Lion asked. He had to, though he did not expect to get an answer any clearer than had been found on Thrinos.

He was right.

'We don't know,' said Revus. 'It came like a ship, but it was much too big. It brought the change...' Her breathing was ragged. 'Nothing is real any more,' she whispered to herself.

'Colonel,' the Lion snapped, breaking into her thoughts before she disappeared into them, reminding her of her duty.

'Yes, my lord. I'm sorry. My troops are holding a block of the underhive. We might have a few more days. But there is nothing to break out to. The land is turning against us. We lost contact with the southern continent when it attacked the regiments there. These... things... these... My lord, there are billions of them. They cover the land. And there's a disease, or a corruption. I don't know how to name it. Our people are changing. This needs to end while any of us are still human.'

'Are you clear about what you are asking?' the Lion said.

'I am, my lord. Save our souls.'

The Lion frowned. Revus was loyal to the Emperor, but in their extremity, she and her people were failing in their loyalty to the Imperial Truth.

'Exterminate the monsters,' she said. 'Send us to the embrace of the Emperor.'

The Lion was silent for a moment. The endless whine sawed its way through his skull. Then he said, 'Very well. Make your preparations.'

'Thank you, my lord.'

He silenced the channel, then reopened communications with Guilliman and the Angel. 'I am ordering the use of cyclonic torpedoes on Episimos Three,' he said.

'You said there were loyal forces still fighting there,' said Guilliman.

'I did. This is the liberation they request.'

'This is precipitous,' Sanguinius protested. 'We did not know definitely there was a key to breaking open the barrier of the fortress until we were inside the manufactorum on Pyrrhan.'

'The situation is different,' said the Lion. 'There is no victory here. Episimos Three is overrun with daemons. Nothing more. Or have you perceived something else, Sanguinius?'

'*No,*' the Angel admitted.

'No. There is nothing to save here.'

'*Except the loyal troops themselves.*'

'Nor them. They are falling away from our father's path. Their sacrifice is the last, best demonstration of loyalty they can still make. They know this. The planet is diseased. It must be purged.'

'*By that logic,*' said Guilliman, '*we should destroy the entire system.*'

'I would if I could,' said the Lion. 'I will shatter a world sooner than stand by and let it be corrupted. So Episimos Three will die.'

Neither Guilliman nor Sanguinius answered.

'Your silence is consent,' the Lion said. 'Captain,' he turned to Stenius, 'prepare cyclonic torpedoes for launch. Full barrage. This world is corrupt to its core. Let only dust remain.'

The command felt like a counter-attack against the malevolent resonance. The *Invincible Reason* had manoeuvred to place Episimos III directly before it. The smouldering planet occupied the centre of the oculus. At the edges of the Lion's view, the corners of the great shapes intruded. He spared them a glare of hatred before he focused his attention on Episimos III. They were foul mysteries, secrets that he could not pierce, and he knew better than to try. The depths of the unknown were a reminder of the risks he was incurring in the relationship he was forging with Tuchulcha. A reminder so pointed, it was an accusation.

What would you have me do instead? he asked in a prosecutorial voice that sounded a lot like Guilliman's. *Would you have us still lost on the edges of Ultramar?*

I will not. I will do what we must.

The torpedoes launched.

'Vox,' he said, 'contact Colonel Revus again.'

'The channel is open,' the vox-officer reported, 'but she doesn't answer.'

The Lion listened to the noise flooding from the vox-speaker. There was static, the distant sounds of battle, screams human and inhuman, a rising clamour of voices shouting a language that formed a chorus with the resonance.

'Close the link,' the Lion said. *Farewell, colonel*, he thought. He wished her the good fortune of hearing the torpedoes arrive.

The first two torpedoes hit the besieged hives. The final bastions of Episimos III disappeared in a blaze of light thousands of miles across. The guttering eyes shone with a flare of vengeance. The intensity of the blast faded, then, but its spread kept growing. The atmosphere caught fire. The flame clouds reached around the globe like the peeling back of flesh to reveal the burning blood beneath. The second stage of the bombardment hit a planet that was already dying.

The *Invincible Reason* was close enough that its auspex array was able to filter most of the distortion caused by the resonance and register the process of the planetary crematorium. The initial torpedoes had split the crust. The wounds went deep, convulsing the mantle, triggering seismic upheavals that tore continents to shreds. In the southern hemisphere, the land screamed with the voice of a living thing. The second wave plunged through the wounds and hit the planet's core. The pressure wave of the blasts pushed outwards in every direction. It could not be contained. The surface of the planet was invisible under the flaming atmosphere, but the upheavals were so violent, it vibrated before the Lion's eyes. Arcs of magma rose thousands of miles. For a few seconds, the planet resembled a star. But the image was a lie. It was unsustainable. The pressure wave reached the surface, and Episimos III exploded. The raging heat of its annihilation caught the fragments of crust as they were propelled into the void. They melted, collided, disintegrated. Before the shockwave of the planet's explosion buffeted the Dark Angels fleet, the Lion's command had been executed. Nothing but dust remained.

The mind-scraping whine scaled new, acute, peaks in the moments of the world's final agony. The Lion winced, and blood started flowing from his ears again. But when the planet shattered, the sound stopped at once. The silence was startling. For the space of a heartbeat, the Lion thought he was deaf.

He stood up from the throne.

'My lord,' the vox-officer called, 'hails from the *Red Tear* and the *Samothrace*.'

I'm sure there are, he thought. 'I will tell you when I am ready to answer.' He strode from the bridge. There was something he had to do first. Someone else he had to speak with first.

In the chamber of Tuchulcha, the servitor was waiting for him. It had degenerated noticeably since the arrival at Episimos. The resonance had sunk into its flesh like rot. It had lashed at the body with a whip. Mottled skin hung from its legs. The musculature was spongy. The stench was thick. The Lion tasted its viscous quality at the back of his throat. The meat puppet's scalp was splitting. It oozed yellow and green pus. Its eyes were filmed, but the will of Tuchulcha focused them on the Lion as if they were las sights. Blistered lips moved.

'Do you wish to travel again?' Tuchulcha asked through its proxy.

'Can we?'

'We can. You did what was necessary.'

So simple? the Lion thought. He caught himself. He must not trivialise the destruction of an entire world. 'We did not damage the constructs,' he said.

The servitor shrugged. 'You altered the configuration of the system. The alteration is sufficient. They cannot hold me here now.'

'And where will you take us this time? What nightmarish impossibility awaits us now?'

Tuchulcha did not respond to his sarcasm. 'Where do you wish to go?'

'Davin.'

'As you will, it shall be done.'

The old formulation again. The words Tuchulcha had last spoken when the Lion had thought to travel to Caliban.

The Lion walked slowly back to the bridge. He was barely aware of Holguin's presence. He hadn't realised the Deathbringer had followed him to the entrance of the chamber. Holguin kept his peace until they were in the hall leading to the bridge. 'Is the way clear, then?' he asked.

'So it seems.'

'How?'

'One of Guilliman's Librarians believes it was the arrangement of shapes in the system that created the resonance. We removed a shape.'

'That was...' Holguin stopped.

'Easy?' the Lion asked.

'I did not mean to suggest that.'

'But you thought it.'

Holguin nodded once, visibly uneasy.

'Our sense of scale has been affected,' said the Lion. 'Inevitably.' The hall through which they walked was high-ceilinged. Marble columns formed its vaults. Monumental statues commemorated the extermination of the Beasts of Caliban. The light from the wall sconces could not pierce the dimensions of the hall, and deep shadows draped the walls. The architecture was designed for awe. The Lion felt the presence of the constructs pressing in, invisibly, through the hull. They made the hall insignificant. They made everything the Lion knew insignificant.

Yet he had defeated the trap. The fleets were about to leave the daemonic constructs behind. It did not matter how vast they were. They were the things that had lost their significance, and the Lion had taken it from them.

'There is a lesson here.'

'What lesson, my lord?' Holguin asked.

The Lion shook his head. He hadn't meant to speak aloud. 'Ignore my incomplete thoughts,' he said.

Only they were more complete than he admitted. The destruction of a world had punched a hole through an immaterial net. The Lion wondered how far he could extend the principle.

The vision was tempting in its simplicity. Horus and the rest of the traitors could not rule if they had no bases. The Lion pictured a programme of deliberate, systematic annihilation. If a world had fallen to the enemy, a campaign to take it back was a waste of resources.

Break the worlds and break the foe, he thought.

The Lion suppressed a smile as he and Holguin entered the bridge again. *How do you like this theoretical, Roboute?* he thought. He would shortly have the opportunity to put it to a practical test.

He sat in the throne once more. He looked through the oculus, at the debris field that had been Episimos III. He nodded to the vox-officer, who opened channels to Guilliman and Sanguinius.

'Brothers,' said the Lion, 'our path forwards is clear. Let us take it.'

PART III
DAVIN

TWELVE

The Embrace of Bone

SANGUINIUS FELT THE shadow before Jeran Mautus reported the contact. His shoulders tensed. His wings straightened, preparatory to a flight of combat. The presence of the shadow pressed on his spirit. He raised his eyes to the shuttered bridge windows as if he could see through them and perceive the enemy beyond. The Angel sensed the shadow was much nearer. Its presence seemed heavy enough to crush the hull of the *Red Tear*. When Mautus called out, Sanguinius asked, 'How close?' Space was a lie, yet battles could still be fought on the foundation of this illusion.

Mautus worked the controls of the auspex array, lips tight with frustration. 'I can't get a consistent reading.' On the screens, the readings of the vague mass of the shadow kept changing. The phantom raced ahead of the fleets, then it was stalking them from behind, then keeping pace on different flanks.

The vox-channels between the bridges of the three flagships were now open continuously. 'Brothers,' Sanguinius said, 'are you detecting an intruder?'

'*We are,*' Guilliman said. '*Is this the same contact you had before?*'

'It appears to be.'

'*The readings are nonsense,*' said the Lion. '*It is now between my forma-tions and yours, Sanguinius.*'

The changes in the shadow's position were rapid. At the same time, there was a sinuous flow to them. Instead of blinking in and out of existence in its impossible locations, the spectre moved like a river, like a current, like a serpent. Sanguinius began to see it less as a pres-ence, more as a manifestation of malaise, encircling and weaving its way through the fleets, spreading its influence by the fact of its pres-ence alone.

'*You fought this,*' Guilliman said.

'To no effect, though we lost some ships.'

'*Combat is futile,*' said the Lion. '*There is no target. This must be a phan-tasm of the immaterium.*'

'Do you think so?' Sanguinius asked. He took a breath. It grated with the effort. A huge stone weighed down his chest. 'Are you telling me you can't feel its presence?'

'*Perhaps,*' Guilliman said after a pause.

'*That is nothing we can fight.*' The Lion's evasion betrayed his unease.

His brothers' uncertainty disturbed Sanguinius. It was possible for them to view the phantom as a mirage. He could not. 'Do not dis-miss it,' he said.

Before he could continue, the shadow appeared directly before the *Red Tear*. Elongated, made of night, it dwarfed the battleship. It fired a single shot. The defensive scans of the *Red Tear* recognised the attack, but not its nature. It appeared on the screens as a line, direct as lascan-non fire, but it was dark, a lightning strike of black hitting the battleship.

The Geller field flickered. The failure's duration was less than a micro-second, but the shot came through. It pierced the shielding. It slashed onto the bridge.

A thin beam. Black as despair. Precise. Unerring.

It struck Sanguinius in the chest.

☩ ☩ ☩

THE SHADOW PASSED over the Night Haunter in his cell. He caught his breath. His eyes widened, staring into nothing, and in that nothing he felt dread. He had foreseen the shadow's arrival, but now that it was here, the future turned into a cascade of doubt. Possibilities multiplied, then winked out. The certainty of the implacable succession of moments vanished. They were replaced with a blank.

Nothing.

Curze frowned. He shook his head, the only movement he could make, trying to clear the amorphous, mocking fog that billowed through his thoughts. Anticipation, the bleak, remorseless companion of his consciousness, fell silent. He fell into limbo. The future left him.

He gasped. His body convulsed with psychic pain. He had foreseen the arrival of ignorance only in the last few seconds before it descended on him. He had thought he was mistaken. He had not believed in the loss of the fundamental principle of his life, of the nightmare bedrock of his existence.

Yet it had come. And he did not know what came next.

'You're a barrier,' he whispered to the shadow. 'You conceal, but you change nothing. There is nothing that can be changed.'

The tremor of a memory ran through him. He saw himself again on Macragge, the Angel transformed with rage, descending upon him to kill with his bare hands. He had lost the thread of the future in those seconds. The stream of futures had stuttered, paused. The moment of his death, the absolute that defined all others, had begun to slip from his grasp. For those terrible seconds, fate had seemed mutable. He had been confronted with the horror of a universe that not even fatalism could explain.

But then the Lion had materialised in the chamber. He had stopped the execution. Curze had fastened his grip on the future again, and the moments to come had begun hammering through his skull once more. It was the closest thing he had known to relief in decades.

Now, though, the future was blank. He strained against his manacles, as if he could physically force himself through the barrier and see once

more. 'Nothing changes,' he said. 'Nothing changes. Nothing changes.'
Beyond the barrier to his vision, the future unfolded as fate had determined it would. That was the lesson he had learned from his arrested
execution. He had been wrong to doubt then. He would not doubt
now. The shadow blinded him, but that was all, and it would pass.
'Nothing changes,' he said.

But the fog lingered. The seconds passed, one after another whose
form he did not know before they came. And he did not know when
the fog would lift.

Without foreknowledge, he could not act. The blindness was worse
than his physical shackles.

'Nothing changes!' he shouted in defiance. The blankness remained.
It was a barrier, he told himself again and again. It was not a slate waiting for fresh script. 'Nothing changes. *Nothing changes!*'

The scream echoed back and forth along the prison corridor. It fell
into the background noise of the deep hum of the ship's engines. Curze
shrieked his defiance again. The barrier remained. On the other side,
the future resided, hidden from its darkest prophet.

MKANI KANO WAS nearest to the Angel when the psychic beam struck
him. Sanguinius staggered, stumbling off the command dais to the
main platform of the flying bridge. He doubled over, clutching his
chest. Kano rushed to his side. Azkaellon and the duty squad of the
Sanguinary Guard were a few steps behind.

Kano put his hand on the Angel's shoulder. 'My lord?'

Sanguinius reared upright with a sudden jerk. His wings spread wide,
pinions shaking with anger. His eyes glistened black. He turned to
Kano, his face a perfect marble carving of rage. For an instant, he was
indeed a statue, the nobility of his bearing transformed into the aspect
of a predator. Then his lips drew back over his fangs. Hatred consumed his features. The air around him crackled. Kano smelled burnt
ozone. On instinct he raised a defensive psychic shield. Sanguinius
lunged but Kano was too slow. None of the Angel's sons would have

been fast enough. Sanguinius seized him by the gorget and lifted him high. The Angel's jaw opened and closed as if straining to speak. The tendons of his neck stood out, taut as iron cables about to snap. No words emerged from his throat. The fury was too great. Snarling and groaning at once, Sanguinius threw the Librarian down. Kano slammed through the nearest cogitator stations to the dais, crushing a servitor and sliding fifteen feet across the deck.

Sanguinius pursued. He leapt over the wreckage of the cogitators, and landed before Kano. He took the Librarian by the chest plate and hauled him up. Kano's training warred with his loyalty. He could not strike his primarch. He tried to pull away, but Sanguinius lifted him above the deck and drew the *Blade Encarmine*.

Azkaellon grabbed the Angel's arm. Sanguinius lashed back, hurling Azkaellon away. His eyes never left Kano. 'My lord,' the Librarian pleaded, trying to break through the haze of fury. The black orbs stared through him, unblinking.

Another hand arrested the blade. It was the herald's. Kano did not know when Sanguinius' proxy had arrived. He had not been on the bridge a few moments ago. The Angel yanked his arm free, dropped Kano and turned, snarling, on the herald.

He froze.

Primarch and herald faced each other, motionless. Psychic energy burned around the edges of the Angel's wings. The herald said nothing. Sanguinius held the blade high, but it did not descend.

Kano saw the primarch's face reflected in the mask of the herald, snarling fury mirrored in unchanging serenity. The Angel froze at the sight, and then the black dissolved from Sanguinius' eyes. His breathing slowed, no longer gasps of rage. He lowered the sword. He blinked, looked around, and after a moment of incomprehension, his face contorted with understanding and grief. He went to Kano's side. 'Are you injured?' he asked.

'I am well, my lord,' Kano said. 'Do you know what happened?'

Sanguinius paused before answering. 'Not entirely, no. Enough to be on my guard.'

'Was it the Thirst?' Kano asked. The symptoms had been different, though the overall effect, of insane violence, was similar.

'No. This was different.'

Sanguinius returned to the command dais. He looked out at the bridge, at all the witnesses of his madness, both Blood Angels and mortal. The unaugmented officers were pale. They had seen worse on Signus Prime, but the reminder of the madness on that world was disturbing to mortals and Blood Angels alike.

On the auspex pict screens, the position of the phantom continued to fluctuate. It seemed to be pulling away now.

'By injuring one, I have done you all an injury,' Sanguinius said. The savagery Kano had faced was gone. All the nobility of the Angel had returned, austere in its acknowledgement of pain. 'But the attack by the enemy failed. It was repulsed.' He nodded to the herald. 'The foe that has destroyed our ships has suffered its first defeat.' He paused. 'I am not invulnerable. None of us are. We have faced this truth, and with that knowledge we are more determined, and stronger. Despair and hubris are the paths to defeat. And we will not be defeated.'

Since Signus Prime, and during the period of Imperium Secundus, every word Kano had heard Sanguinius speak had been tinged with melancholy. The burden of his tragedies was a heavy one. Kano found it difficult to hold at bay dark thoughts about the Legion's destiny. How much harder, then, for the primarch? He had to contemplate the reality that tainted blood was his gift to his sons. Since the victory on Pyrrhan, though, Kano thought he had detected a change. Now he was sure. Sanguinius' eyes were still marked with care, their gaze fixed, it seemed, on a distant point, eternally considering how the present moment and a future end aligned. What was different was his voice. He sounded as if he had encountered something he had considered impossible, and he had been renewed. The weight of concerns had not lifted, but new possibilities had opened before him, and he was eager for the challenge. Though the Angel, too, was disturbed by what had just happened, the attack had run up against a core of hope that was stronger than before.

Kano wished he felt more reassured than he did.

Sanguinius looked at the silent crew and legionaries. His face was shadowed with concern again. 'I will be in the Sanctorum,' he said to Kano, and withdrew from the bridge.

The Angel was still in meditative mood several hours later, when the fleet translated back to the materium.

'I have the coordinates,' said Mautus. 'This is Davin!'

At last, Kano thought. He felt a sharp stab of premonition as the shutters parted.

Silence descended on the bridge again as the system came into view. The Blood Angels gazed upon an immensity of death...

A GREY SPHERE surrounded the Davin System. At first, from the point of translation, it had appeared almost featureless, except for a porous quality that made the Lion think of dilapidated stone. Its gravitational well was weak, barely pulling at the fleet.

'Why do I feel like I'm looking at a grave?' Holguin asked.

'Not a grave,' the Lion said as the fleets moved closer and the details of the sphere resolved in the oculus. 'An ossuary.' He shook his head in disbelief. 'This thing is made of bones.'

The *Invincible Reason* came within a thousand miles of the surface of the necrosphere. Auspex scans zeroed in on small areas and projected magnified hololiths on the tacticarium screens. Individual bones and complete skeletons interlaced, creating a cracked, knobby plain. There were bodies of humans, eldar, orks – of every xenos race the Lion had ever encountered, and an even greater number he did not know.

Abyssal solemnity radiated from the necrosphere. It was perfect stillness, the quiet of the end of everything. Beyond it, the frenzy of the Ruinstorm was more intense, and the bones appeared to float in a sea of agonised colours. The materium bled around Davin, and the system was death lurking at the centre of the wound.

The Lion ordered an exploratory bombardment. The *Invincible Reason*, the *Honoured Deeds* and the *Intolerant* fired nova cannons. It was like shooting through fog. The beams cut through the necrosphere. Vast clouds of debris rose into the void, and a chasm opened, wide enough for the combined fleets and stretching for tens of thousands of miles.

'What does this barrier mean?' Holguin wondered.

'At this moment,' the Lion said, 'it signifies only its own weakness. Death falls before us. We will not be stopped.'

The Lion took the Dark Angels into the necrosphere. The other fleets followed, descending into the endless grey.

THE PHYSICAL PASSAGE through the necrosphere was easy. The mental one was less so. Guilliman, Prayto and Gorod marked the journey in Guilliman's chambers. They stood before a floor-to-ceiling window. As the *Samothrace* journeyed through the shell, the nature of the necrosphere became clearer. Grey remains, broken from their moorings by the blast, floated past the vessels. The boneyard of the infinite contained more than the skeletons of beings that had once been alive; there were the skeletons of dead vessels, of cities and of worlds. The inanimate had turned to bone. Iron and stone, alloy and gas, everything was bone and cold and grey. Planets had ribcages now, and cities had skulls, the better to show that they had died.

Other corpses were harder to identify. Some had the shapes of colossal beings, human and xenos. Others had crystalline forms. Still others were spheres themselves, smooth as the back of skulls.

'Are those statues?' Gorod asked.

'They are still bones,' Guilliman said. 'They are something that has died.'

Prayto grunted in psychic pain. 'Hopes,' he said. 'Dreams. Philosophies.'

'The forces we have been combatting favour symbolism in their attacks,' Guilliman said. Prayto was speaking from a more visceral knowledge, but Guilliman could see the possible meaning in the copses Gorod had pointed out. If statues represented abstractions, the skeletons were the demises of those ideas. It was as if, in their death, they had been given flesh to rot away, and bones to mark not the promises that their existence had made, but its futility.

'*Contact!*' Lautenix's voice buzzed from a wall-mounted vox-caster. Then, a moment later, '*Correction. I was mistaken.*'

'Mistaken in what?' Guilliman asked. 'What sort of contact?'

'*I thought there was movement, lord primarch,*' said Lautenix. '*There is nothing in the scans. Perhaps it was more floating wreckage.*'

Wreckage. Not *remains.* Lautenix was using distancing language. All the bridge officers were. They were keeping the reality of the necrosphere at bay. Guilliman understood. That was their luxury, as mortals. If they turned away from the reality, just enough to blunt its meaning, yet not so much as to create a misleading picture of what they were confronting, he would not correct them. He did not have the same flexibility. His lot was to look at the real directly. He must face all truths in all their horror, or he risked basing crucial theoreticals on a lie.

He worried that he had already done so. The sin of Imperium Secundus was a heavy weight he could not set down. He had not found atonement yet on this crusade. Instead, he had found this embodiment of absolute death.

Gorod drew his attention back to the window. 'Look at that,' he said, pointing to one of the dead dreams. It had a human head. A halo of spiked bones radiated from its crown. 'What was that, I wonder?' he said.

'What it was no longer matters,' Guilliman answered. 'It is the ones that are not present that matter. They still live.' He believed what he said, though he felt staggered by what he was seeing. The necrosphere was the final extension of the theoretical transformed into the practical. The ossuary took his guiding principles, and turned them into a mausoleum. 'The dream of the Imperium is not here,' he said. 'It is not dead.'

He wondered, despite himself, if he might see Imperium Secundus entombed here.

This is the death of all dreams. The voice was authoritative, proselytising. It did not feel like his. It felt like the whisper he had heard in the fight against the Word Bearers. *Past and present and to come, all the hopes are here. Their murder has happened, the promises are over. This is their silence. The end of words.*

'Lord primarch,' Altuzer broke in on the vox. *'Lautenix has seen the intruder again. I have as well. The auspex readings are too fragmentary to be of use, but that may be due to the material of the sphere limiting the reach of the scans. The sighting is definite. We are being shadowed.'*

Guilliman looked out into the grey tunnel down which the fleet was travelling. There was a flare in the distance as the Lion's vessels fired again, punching deeper into the shell. He could see as much as a few miles into the sides of the tunnel. The bones were loosely clumped together. The fabric of the necrosphere broke apart easily. It revealed nothing but more skeletal remains, the grey stillness extending forever until lost in the shadows.

'Where is it?' said Gorod.

'There must be other passages through the shell,' Guilliman said. 'Sanguinius' warp phantom is in the materium now too.'

'If that is a single ship,' Prayto said, 'it travels with suspicious ease. The Blood Angels have been encountering it since they left Macragge.'

Guilliman stared at him. Prayto's choice of words made pieces of the dark mosaic fall into place. 'It travels,' he repeated. 'A pilgrim.'

'You think it might be the cause of the constructs we've encountered?' Prayto asked. 'If so, can it be fought?'

'Maybe not the cause,' Guilliman said, thinking over the tales Sanguinius had described hearing in the refugee camp. 'Perhaps a catalyst. The witnesses said its arrival marked the beginning of ruin. It brought change with it. They saw that. None of the survivors of Pyrrhan mentioned the fortress – that happened after they fled. After the Pilgrim had passed.'

'I like that theory better than Titus',' Gorod said.

'So do I,' said Prayto. 'We still don't know what it is, or how to fight it.'

Or even if it's here, Guilliman thought. Only the Blood Angels had had any true contact with it. It was a ghost, cruising through warp and minds. Its being was indefinite. It hovered between myth and threat.

The Pilgrim was uncertainty itself, neither real nor illusion, lurking just beyond the horizon of the observable. From there it spread doubt.

Guilliman wondered if it had already targeted him. He pushed the question aside. It was another trap of uncertainty. He would not construct theoreticals on an absence.

A shadow. A phantom.

The bridge became an assembly of sentinels. The word went out across the fleets to watch for the Pilgrim. The scans were continuous. The guns of three Legions pointed at the depths of the surrounding tunnel walls. The hours passed. Guilliman stood at the pulpit, staring into the grey sepulchre. The stillness went on and on and on. There was nothing but the bones of life and hope and reason. The universe beyond ceased to exist. The temptation arrived, insidious as it was insistent, to believe that there never would be anything except the grave. The fleets had willingly entered the trap. There would never be anything to fight. The Legions would journey through the infinite grey until they too became still, became bone.

Quiet crept onto the bridge. The hum of the engines, the whine of servitor joints and the clatter of keys at data stations became a fading background. The voices of the mortal crewmembers as they queried and answered each other fell below murmurs. The quiet was grey. It was dust falling, burying light, burying hope.

Guilliman watched the bones. He did not waver. If this was the last thing he witnessed, then he would stand guard until death.

The grey did not go on forever. It was, in the end, what it had appeared to be, a shell. It was a few million miles thick, a hair's breadth in comparison to its diameter. The fleets emerged into the encircled void of the Davin System. For the first time since it had begun to rage, the Ruinstorm was invisible, hidden behind the necrosphere.

We're in the eye of the storm, Guilliman thought. The calm here was a lie.

Ahead, centred in the oculus, glinting in the grey darkness, was Davin. The shine of its reflected light was the cold of the most profound death.

THIRTEEN

Scorched Earth

THE PRIMARCHS GATHERED in one of the smaller strategiums aboard
the *Invincible Reason*. The chamber was dark, and despite its narrow
dimensions, it seemed to Sanguinius that the walls withdrew from the
tacticarium table, draping themselves in secrets and shadows.

The table's hololithic display was of a massive crater on Davin's surface. It was surrounded by a jagged mountain chain. In its centre stood
a temple. The fane was the largest construct the scans had detected,
and its position within one of the most distinct geographic features
of the planet signalled its importance. The reports sent from Davin by
the XVI Legion, the sanitised, misleading records, called the structure
the Delphos.

A narrow gorge ran from the crater, cutting through the mountains.
The scans had picked up other human artefacts along its length. Statuary, Sanguinius deduced. The gorge looked like a processional avenue
to the Delphos.

At the edge of the mapped region, a lone, conical mountain rose
from a plain, like an inverted image of the crater's formation. It had
a building of some kind on its peak. The construction was smaller,

though, making it a secondary target. Pict screens on the periphery of the table summarised the auspex readings of the rest of the planet.

'There is nothing down there,' the Lion said.

Sanguinius pointed to the temple. 'I hardly call that nothing,' he said. 'We know the Davinites were primitive – the ships you found were proof of that. They had to rely on poor salvage. This temple is a work of monumental construction.'

'Granted,' said the Lion. 'But there is nothing unnatural about it. After what we've encountered, how much weight are we going to place on something built of stone, by human hands?'

'Are we going to ignore it?'

'No. My point is the absence of any activity. The planet is deserted. All evidence points to a total exodus.'

'To Pandorax,' said Guilliman.

'At least in part. Perhaps elsewhere too. But there is no one here. That makes our course of action clear.'

'Does it?' Guilliman asked.

'I'm surprised you haven't already proposed it, Roboute. We should launch cyclonic torpedoes without delay. If we destroy Davin, we open the way to Terra.'

Sanguinius shook his head. 'It cannot be that simple.'

'It was in the Episimos System.'

'You don't pretend the situations are identical.'

'Identical, no. Comparable, yes.'

'Because of the necrosphere? Because there are huge daemonic constructs in both cases?'

'Other than size, the nature of the objects is quite different,' Guilliman pointed out.

'The principle stands,' said the Lion. 'We have seen it twice already. We cannot destroy the objects themselves, but on the correct target, the devastation we unleash must be total.'

'I disagree,' Sanguinius said. 'You think we should have destroyed Pyrrhan rather than assault the manufactorum?'

'With hindsight, yes.'

'No,' said Sanguinius. 'No.' He leaned his fists on the tacticarium table. He stared at the hololithic representation of the Delphos, willing it to reveal its secrets to him. 'If we had done that, we would still be trapped on the other side of that gate, or vaporised by its defences.'

'You sound very sure,' said Guilliman. He was being unusually reserved, holding back his own tactical views. For the time being, he seemed to be limiting his role to that of the doubter.

What troubles you, brother? Sanguinius wondered. *It is something that runs deep, I think.*

'I am sure,' he said to Guilliman. He felt the muscle memory of the sword blow that had carried him through fate and destroyed the manufactorum. He had severed the ties of destiny and darkness. 'What I experienced in the forge...' He thought about what he could say, even to his brothers. 'We did not triumph through brute force. We have been confronting the symbols. Our successful attacks have been symbolic too. They have been the only ones possible, and targeted at the heart of what opposed us. This war has taken us far beyond the realm of the rational. And think about why we are here at all. Why do you think destroying Davin will defeat the Ruinstorm? Because this is where Horus fell, and this is where the war began. The logic is symbolic. Very well, then. We must follow the symbolism to its end. We must stand on the spot where Horus fell.'

'I accept your argument about Pyrrhan,' said the Lion. 'The nature of what happened in the manufactorum escapes me.' He was clearly displeased by the mystery. 'That it played a critical role is clear, though. But there was an enemy on Pyrrhan. This planet is deserted.'

'I wonder if Horus was as confident in his assumptions when he came here.'

The Lion glared. 'I am not Horus.'

'No,' Sanguinius said, keeping his voice level. 'You are not. And you are not what he has become. But remember, brother. Remember what he was. I remember. I remember how wise I thought our father was to make him Warmaster. I remember Horus' doubts, how he wondered if he was worthy of the task. How could this brother turn on us? Remember that none of us saw his treachery coming. Our *father* didn't see it coming. Remember all of this, and remember that *here* is where Horus fell.' He paused. 'Now tell me you are certain there is nothing below.'

'He's right,' Guilliman said. 'I would like to know what happened to Horus.'

'You think I don't? And if Sanguinius is correct, what then? Is our strategy to replicate Horus' error?'

Guilliman turned back to Sanguinius, an eyebrow raised.

'Where do you stand, Roboute?' Sanguinius finally demanded. 'Why won't you tell us?'

'I wanted to hear you both out. We have a lot of data, but it does not point in a clear direction.' He gestured towards the exterior of the hull. 'We have just come through unambiguous evidence of the importance of Davin. But the necrosphere tells us nothing about how we should deal with the problem this world presents.' He drummed his fingers on the table. 'On balance,' he said, 'I agree with the Lion. Our enemy isn't here. It is somewhere in the necrosphere. You saw it, Sanguinius. You've done battle with it already.'

More than you know, the Angel thought. 'We can't fight it until it declares itself,' he said.

'I agree. Destroying Davin may bring it out. In any event, I think a landing here will be a distraction.'

'It will not be,' Sanguinius insisted. 'We have to know what is down there. We have to go.' He stared at the centre of the map, thinking about the journey, how barriers immense beyond comprehension had tried to stop them, and how they had broken through. Their victories appeared to him as both impossible and inevitable. *We are going planetside*, he realised. *We have no choice. Fate decrees it.* The moment the thought crossed his mind, he doubted it. He had been doubting fate since Pyrrhan.

He was torn between certitude and hope. He didn't know which to embrace. He looked back and forth between the Lion and Guilliman. Neither of them had his experience of time. Neither had lived their own deaths. Neither could truly perceive destiny concretely. They didn't fully understand the implications of being here, now, where everything had begun. They thought they did. They could appreciate the symmetry of returning to the source of the war. But they could not feel, viscerally, the chains of inevitability and fate that were drawing them to this nexus, this singular point in space and time.

Where fate might be in flux.

No. They could not understand. There was someone who would, though.

'I must speak with Konrad,' Sanguinius said.

The Lion snorted with surprise. 'You think he will convince me?'

'No,' said Sanguinius. 'Nevertheless, I would speak with him.'

The Lion shrugged. 'My decision is made.' As Sanguinius reached the strategium's door, the Lion said, 'I will take action. Without delay.'

'You will be wrong to do so,' Sanguinius said, and left.

HE SAW THE future again. The barrier to his vision fell when the brain-piercing whine had ceased. There was certainty again. The charnel house of the universe unfolded before him, every step known in the moment before it arrived. There was no comfort in this. There was no comfort in anything. Comfort was the delusion of the weak. There was, though, satisfaction. Curze could look upon the morbid farce of time and once again share in the humour.

For a long period, humour was all he had. The moments succeeded each other without change. The ship travelled. It entered the warp. It translated back into the materium. Curze sensed the changes, but they meant nothing. His cell might as well have been a stasis field. Anonymous guards changed shifts. The Lion did not return to speak with him. Time stagnated. There were no actions for Curze to take, no decisions in the physical limbo.

At last, limbo ended. He looked up, cracked lips peeling back over the stumps of his teeth. Before the boot-steps sounded, the Night Haunter was smiling. This was much better than a second conversation with the Lion. Much better.

The cell door ground open and Sanguinius entered. He stood before Curze, saying nothing.

Don't you know how to begin, brother? Curze thought. *Then let me help you.* 'So,' he said, 'you have come to free me.'

'Have I?'

'Do you doubt my insight?'

'I doubt your honesty.'

'You know better than that. I have never lied to you, Sanguinius. The truth is a great weapon.' He twitched his fingers, numb from the pressure of the manacles. He wanted his claws. They were the truth given form. They cut as it did. They were as deaf to entreaty. Still, the truth of darkness was always there. It was always his. And in the end, it would do the cutting, the severing and the slaughter, whether he was able to pronounce it or not.

'Do you know where we are?' Sanguinius asked.

'The Lion did not consult me about the itinerary,' Curze said. And then he heard Sanguinius' next words in his mind before the Angel spoke them.

'We are in orbit over Davin.'

'Ah. I'm fascinated to see why that is the reason you're going to free me.'

Sanguinius ignored him. 'What is down there?' he asked.

'Haven't you taken the trouble to scan? Roboute must have. I would check with him.'

'The scans show nothing. What is waiting for us there, Konrad?'

And suddenly there was ambiguity. The potential futures multiplied around the word *us*. In one branch, Sanguinius meant himself and Curze. In another, he meant the triumvirate. The futures divided, splitting again and again before rejoining at critical junctures. Death was the constant. It drew the strands together. But a fog of potential lingered around it.

'I don't know what is on the surface,' Curze said. 'How could I? I didn't even know we were at Davin until just now.' He did not expect to have that knowledge. His certainties were centred around his end, and the immediate moment. No, he would never expect to know what was on Davin. Yet the fact he didn't bothered him. His ignorance was a reminder of the earlier blankness. There was no reason to connect the two, yet he felt the link, and unease wormed its way into his veins again. His lips pressed together, turning his smile into a grimace. This was not the way of things. He was the Night Haunter. He was the bringer of nightmares, the murderer of sleep. Unease was his to bestow, not his to suffer.

'I believe fate is down there,' Sanguinius said.

'Whose? Yours or mine?'

'Horus' was.'

'You didn't answer my question.'

'I think it might be fate itself.'

Curze saw himself answer before he did. The inevitability of his words made them true, though he did not know why. 'I think you're right,' he said. Truth and uncertainty collided. The unease grew.

Sanguinius cocked his head, listening to something on his vox-bead. His eyes hardened. 'Roboute is returning to the *Samothrace*,' he said.

'I can see this concerns you.'

'The Lion plans to bombard Davin with cyclonic torpedoes.'

Again the import of the words registered with Curze before they were said. The unease reached a point of crisis. The future rushed in, blazing at a point of critical disjuncture. Sanguinius stood on the surface of Davin in one branch. In another, the planet flew apart under the Lion's bombardment. There was another branch, too, murkier, far more uncertain, hovering on the edge of potential. It blurred the future's divide. It made both possibilities true.

'Why have you come to free me?' Curze asked. That Sanguinius was going to take him from the cell had suddenly become imminent, turning into a concrete inevitability in the last few seconds. Sanguinius' reasons remained beyond his reach as they flickered and changed in microseconds, caught in the tempest of the Angel's uncertainty.

A klaxon began to sound. The doubts lifted from Sanguinius' face. His eyes hardened with determination. 'Don't you know?' he said. 'Because you do not die on Davin. And neither do I.'

Sanguinius left the cell. He turned to the guards standing a few yards down. 'I am taking the prisoner with me,' he said. 'Prepare him for transport.'

The two Dark Angels hesitated. 'Lord Sanguinius,' one of them said, 'we have received no orders about this from the Lion.'

'Nor will you.' The klaxon boomed through the corridors. The *Invincible Reason* was manoeuvring into position for the bombardment. 'I have no authority over you. Nevertheless, I am giving this command. I will not be opposed in this.'

Sanguinius placed his hand on the hilt of the *Blade Encarmine*. He did not draw it. The act was less a threat than a reminder. He had no intention of harming the legionaries. Physically opposing him, though, was more than they could do. He spread his wings, lifting them high. He filled the corridor. He towered over the Dark Angels.

'Do what your honour demands,' he said. 'Know that the responsibility for what happens now is mine, not yours. These events are beyond your ability to control.'

The legionaries did not move, but they did not raise their guns.

'Know this too,' Sanguinius said. 'What I do, I do for the Imperium. So does the Lion. Nothing that happens now changes this fact.'

'We cannot let you pass, Lord Sanguinius,' the other guard finally said.

'I understand,' he said. 'And you have my respect.'

Sanguinius drew the *Blade Encarmine* and smashed the blade against the helm of one guard, splitting it open and staggering the Dark Angel. He whirled and seized the other guard before he could fire. He raised the Dark Angel and slammed him against the wall. His breath hissing with anger at the necessity of what he did, he struck both guards with the flat of the blade, hammering them into unconsciousness.

'Forgive me,' he said. He turned from them to a small chamber a few paces further up the hall. It was the guard post. He entered it, yanked open a plasteel vault, and took the chains and neuro-manacles he found inside. He returned to Curze and worked in silence as he transferred the Night Haunter from the wall shackles to the new restraints. The beats of the klaxon continued, counting away the time before Davin's annihilation.

'No threats?' Curze asked. 'No warnings that I will die if I try to escape?'

'Escape to where, Konrad?'

'Well said. There is no escape for any of us, is there?'

Perhaps not, Sanguinius thought. He was not certain, though, and so he felt hope. Destiny was tightening into a knot on Davin. He could feel his actions being dictated by events that marched forwards, unstoppable, to ends he could not perceive. But on Pyrrhan, he had cut through such a knot. There was a possibility he did not wish to articulate, for fear of extinguishing a frail and precious flame. Soon, he hoped, it would be strong enough for him to speak of it.

He took Curze down from the wall. He shackled the Night Haunter's hands behind his back, but left his legs free.

Curze cocked his head at the sound of the klaxons. 'I hear the blaring of your time running out,' he said.

'There is time enough,' Sanguinius said. He thought of what Curze had done to his sons. He thought of the dead of the Sanguinary Guard on Macragge, and of Azkaellon's severed arm. He faced his rage at his brother's crimes. Then he did what was necessary for the Imperium, and for his father. He yanked on the chain attached to Curze's neck and hauled the Night Haunter into a run down the corridor.

Curze laughed as they ran past the fallen guards. 'You do your very best to bring me joy, brother.'

'*Sanguinius,*' the Lion shouted through the Angel's vox-bead. '*What are you doing?*'

'What I must. As you are. But you are wrong.'

'*You are setting us against each other. This is madness.*'

'No. It is necessary, and it is fated.' He shut down the channel, cutting the Lion off mid-roar.

Sanguinius opened a vox-channel to his Chapter Masters, grateful for the preparations he had made before taking the Thunderhawk to the *Invincible Reason*. 'Launch drop pods,' he ordered. 'Immediate landing in the vicinity of the temple. All forces away, *now!*'

He and Curze ran down the halls of the Dark Angels battleship, racing for the bay where his gunship waited. The Night Haunter kept laughing, and laughed harder as the Lion sent troops to stop them, and Sanguinius battered them down. With every Dark Angel he harmed, Sanguinius felt the knot of destiny closing, growing tighter, choking off one future after another. He did not know how far the Lion would go to stop him. Sanguinius was pushing him hard, risking the fragile trust that existed between the brothers. *We only really trust ourselves*, he thought. *If we can even be said to do that.*

'The Ninth Legion is landing in force,' Holguin observed.

The Lion gripped the arms of his throne. He took a breath, forcing himself to see clearly through the red haze of anger.

'Sanguinius must be mad,' Farith Redloss said.

'Launch from bay thirty,' a servitor's mechanical voice intoned. The flat announcement signalled the flight of the Thunderhawk *Vyssini* from the *Invincible Reason*.

'Auspex,' the Lion said, 'give me a trajectory.'

'Towards Davin, my lord.'

'What are your orders?' Stenius asked.

Do we shoot my brother down, you mean? the Lion thought. Wood creaked beneath his grip. *Damn you, Sanguinius. Damn you for forcing that choice on me.* 'Track it all the way down,' he said. He knew where the Angel was heading. He gave the command solely because one was needed.

'Why did he take Curze?' said Holguin. 'What sense does that make?'

'None,' said Redloss. 'Is he mad?'

'He acts according to his convictions,' the Lion said. 'He is wrong. And we must act for the Imperium.'

'The fleet is in position,' Stenius said. 'Bombardment targets locked.'

'So noted, captain,' the Lion said.

Then Guilliman was voxing. *'You can't fire now,'* he said.

The Lion killed the vox.

'My lord,' Holguin began.

'I will have silence,' the Lion told him.

The noise of the bridge fell to a murmur. Davin filled the oculus, its atmosphere streaked by the fires of the drop pod descents.

The decision loomed before the Lion. He had to make it now. The madness of Sanguinius' actions convinced him even more firmly of the need to destroy Davin. The world was dangerous. It was attacking them even now, even though all the scans still showed no activity of any kind. Perhaps its existence was enough. It was a foul thing, and had to be purged from the galaxy.

Is this what I must do, then? Destroy it, and kill Sanguinius? Precipitate war with the Ninth Legion? And possibly the Ultramarines as well?

That would serve Horus well.

And what is the alternative? Stay my hand, and let this madness play out? Allow Davin to wreak havoc? Reach this point only to fall into a trap?

The destruction of Davin was an absolute imperative. If he had had any doubts left after Episimos, they would have been burned away by Sanguinius' actions. The corrupted worlds must die, and Davin was the source of the corruption.

'The *Vyssini* has entered the atmosphere,' said Stenius.

Give the order, said the inner voice of brutal necessity. *You know what must be done.*

The Lion nodded to himself. 'Captain,' he said. 'Prepare to…'

He stopped.

His blood froze at the enormity of what he was about to say.

'Cancel the bombardment,' he shouted. 'Prepare for a massed landing. We are taking Davin.'

The Lion stormed from the bridge. He marched through the corridors, his fury warning all, legionary and mortal, from his path. He did not stop until he reached Curze's cell. He dismissed the guards. He had no good reason for having come here. He hadn't consciously known where he was headed at first.

He stood in the cell and faced the wall, staring at the empty manacles. He blinked, and held up his right hand. There was a faint tremor in his fingers.

'So close,' he whispered. He had come within a word of murdering his brother. A word.

A malign influence has been working on me.

An influence too subtle for him to feel its effects and resist them. Slowly and patiently, it had been leading him to ruin.

The Lion closed his eyes for a moment. When he opened them, the cell seemed too welcoming, as if he had come here to condemn himself. He grunted and stepped into the corridor. He slammed the door closed behind him.

He felt no freer. There were chains around him, all the stronger because he was not sure of their nature.

He voxed Guilliman. 'Roboute,' he said, 'you must beware.'

'What have you done?' Guilliman demanded. *'You can't bombard–'*

'I am not,' the Lion interrupted. 'But I almost did.'

Guilliman fell silent, absorbing the implications.

'Roboute,' the Lion said again, 'beware of yourself. Do not trust your impulses. Be sure of your decisions. I almost destroyed us.'

The Lion walked on. His steps were heavy. Horror at what he had almost done warred with his anger at Sanguinius, and his mistrust of himself. He longed to strike a blow against the enemy that had manipulated and shamed him. Perhaps the foe was the shadow Sanguinius had seen in the warp.

Unwillingly, he looked back at every step of the journey since Macragge. Everything he had seen, every battle and every victory had led to this point. Events had shaped him. Events had shown him the need to destroy Davin.

He didn't know what he was fighting. He marched faster to prepare for war. He could not escape the shadow that followed him, eroding every certainty, spreading doubt like plague.

Beware of yourself.

Though the Lion's words were intended as a shield, they stabbed like daggers.

'Ready our ships,' Guilliman ordered. 'We launch for Davin immediately.'

'What should we prepare for?' Gorod asked.

'The worst.'

He left them then, and made for his quarters, where the athames waited. He had kept his turmoil from his face and words. The effort had been considerable. His blood was running cold. *Be sure of my decisions?* he thought. *You have no idea how long I have been second-guessing them.*

And he had been right to do so. The Lion had almost made the worst possible one. *We are so fragile. We command this much might, and we can fall so easily.*

He touched his neck where Kor Phaeron's dagger had pierced the flesh. He reviewed decisions, questioned logic and saw the pattern. The reasoning that was pushing him to ruin was always strong. Its strength was its temptation. It disguised its true nature.

Some decisions he might never be able to judge properly. Imperium Secundus would, he was sure, pursue him with doubts until his death. Others, though, he saw clearly in this moment of crisis. He had used the Word Bearers' Navigators, and because he had used the enemy's weapons successfully once, the urge to keep the athames had grown stronger. He wondered how long the voice in his head had been speaking to him, shaping his thoughts even though he did not hear it.

He arrived in his quarters and opened the vault. He turned off the stasis fields and took out the daggers. He handled them with care. They were inanimate, simple crude daggers, and yet much more than that. He placed them on the central flagstone of the chamber's deck.

Behind his desk was an iron door. It was embossed in blue and gold.

The aquila embraced a gleaming sword with its wings. Guilliman pulled the door open and entered his private armorium. The weapons before him were the opposite in every way of the athames. The daggers of ruin were crude, ugly things. They would pass beneath notice were it not for the dull, light-killing menace of their blades. The weapons of Guilliman's rule were works of majesty. They were the summits of the weaponsmith's art. They were tools of war, of death, of destruction, but in the service of reason and light, and their intent was as clear as that of the athames. They brought purity to the battlefield. Their means were war, but their ends were peace and order. Gazing at the intricacy of the engravings on the barrel of the *Arbitrator* and the hilt of the *Gladius Incandor*, Guilliman felt clarity. His path was clear now.

We all walk the assigned path.

No. He walked according to his duty, but his will was his own.

Guilliman reached for the *Hand of Dominion*. The power gauntlet was the purest expression right now of his will, and of the action he knew he must take. He pulled the gauntlet on and made a fist. A blue nimbus of lightning crackled around the fingers. It was the light of purity, the power of duty.

The equation before him was simple. *Theoretical – the athames are a poison. Practical – destroy them.*

Guilliman knelt over the athames. He raised the *Hand of Dominion*…

And the thought occurred that his action was predictable. It would be the simplest thing to manipulate him into taking precisely this action. In the name of purity, he was about to deny himself, his Legion and the Imperium insight into what they fought, and weapons that were as dangerous to the daemonic as any he knew.

Strike a blow, and you harm yourself.

His fist was suspended. Caught by a web of doubt.

Beware of yourself. Do not trust your impulses.

What impulse had been more forceful than the urge to destroy the athames?

He thought of the Lion, poised on the brink of committing the

unthinkable, convinced that he was acting to save the Imperium, preparing to kill his brother and open a new front of the war between
the Legions. If he had not pulled back in that moment, three Legions
would have burned inside the sphere of bones.

The *Hand of Dominion* wavered.

The currents of destruction swirled around Guilliman. The storm
had him, he knew it, and he could not see his way out of the raging
dark. The storm had rushed the Lion to a monstrous choice, and it
had pushed him to take action on a gigantic scale. The tempest had
caught Guilliman in a more intimate trap. Instead of forcing him to
recklessness, it had him caught in doubt and indecision. The action he
would take or not would have no immediate effect outside his quarters.

The range and skill of the attack took his breath away. The enemy
moved against him and his brothers on the smallest and largest battle-
fields at once. Its precision was lethal. He could see the attack now,
yet he did not know how to counter it, and the enemy was still invisible, untouchable.

Sanguinius, he thought. *How has it attacked you? Are you aware it has?
Have you already made your choice? Have you doomed us?*

His thoughts wandered. He began to analyse the Angel's actions from
the end of the Imperium Secundus until now. He unclenched his fist.
The Lion is right. Be sure of your decision before you make the wrong one.

He would return the athames to the vault.

His blood froze. He saw what he was doing. He saw himself falling
to inaction and keeping these malevolent, corrupt knives. If he did not
act now, he would never get rid of them.

A storm surge of doubts crashed against him, but his arm was moving. There was too much force in the blow to arrest it. In the fraction
of a second before the *Hand of Dominion* struck the athames, he was
torn between hope and dread. He tried to stop himself, and he fought
that effort. He cried out, the roar of the self at war shaking the walls
of his quarters.

Thunder boomed. Guilliman raised his fist. The hilts of the athames were flattened, twisted metal. Their blades had shattered into dozens of shards, all of them sharper than darkness.

Guilliman tore through the thoughts that tried to hold him back. Roaring still, hurling himself into the frenzy beyond reason, he smashed the blades again and again. He created another storm in his quarters, one of purging lightning and a thunder of desperate rage. He beat the deck, buckling it, sending tremors through the ship. The shards of the athames became dust, and then less than dust. The remains vanished. He kept going until the roar ended, and he fell back, exhausted.

He was numb. That was better than the acute edge of doubt.

Guilliman staggered out of the crater. He returned to the armorium and took the *Arbitrator* from its bronze case. Then he crossed to the chamber's entrance. The frame of the doorway was warped and cracked, holding the door shut. One blow with the *Hand of Dominion* knocked the door free and smashed it against the far wall. Gorod and a squad of Invictus were running down the corridor. They halted when Guilliman emerged.

'My Lord Guilliman?' Gorod asked.

'I am well, Drakus.' *Well enough, at least.*

'What happened?'

'I fought our first battle of this campaign. I was victorious.' He would hold to this position until forced to relinquish it. 'It is time we descended to Davin,' he said, 'and stood by the side of my brothers.'

FOURTEEN

Delphos

ON THE CRACKED esplanade of the temple, before its huge gates, Sanguinius said, 'This is, truly, the eye of the storm.'

Guilliman and the Lion looked sceptical.

Curze smiled, reptilian. 'You are feeling lyrical,' he said. 'Does that mean you're ready to be swept away by the winds of fate?'

'We will defeat the storm,' Sanguinius told him.

'Nothing will be defeated,' the Lion said, 'because there is nothing here.' He spread his arms wide, taking in the temple, its grounds, and the entire crater. 'This is what you risked so much for, Sanguinius. Is it worth it?'

'Not yet,' said the Angel. He felt serene. He had since the moment he and Curze had set foot on the soil of Davin. He felt more certain, more eager for the future than at any time since he had first known how he would die. He and his brothers were standing on the threshold of culmination, and he was ready.

Even though the Lion was right. There was nothing. The landscape appeared to be beyond calm. It was as dead as the necrosphere.

The drop pods of all three Legions had come down in the crater, and hundreds of Legiones Astartes had taken up positions at the end of the causeway leading to the Delphos. Blood Angels, Ultramarines and Dark Angels surrounded the esplanade. With no sign of threat, they did not know if they came as invaders or defenders. Half the guns pointed towards the crater rim, ready for a foe to come over the peaks of red stone, or through the valley that led to the crater. The other half were trained on the temple. Squadrons of Thunderhawks and Stormravens flew above the crater on escort missions for the columns of heavy armour rumbling through the valley. Big as the crater was, it was too narrow to land the larger transports. They came down in the plains to the south, disgorging the tanks and thousands more troops. The first vehicles were arriving now, and the bowl of the crater was slowly filling with the might of three Legions.

Twilight had fallen. There was no wind. The roar of engines and the tromp of boots against stone seemed thin, unable to crack the stillness of Davin. The Delphos was a colossal octagon, built from monolithic blocks of red stone. A tower rose from each corner. A dome covered the central mass. The spires of two of the towers had fallen to the esplanade, and the dome was cracked. A fissure, gaping darkness, ran from the crown of the dome to its base. The primarchs stood beside a wide basin. It had been a pool, but it was dry now. The once-smooth sides of the basin were flaking and pitted, and the bottom was covered in a thick layer of dust. A canal running along the base of the temple wall had once fed the basin. It too now held only dust and crumbled rock.

Tall columns ran on either side of the staircase to the esplanade. They were eroded, as if ferocious sandstorms had blasted their features away. A few isolated patches of gold scale were still visible on the serpents that coiled around the pillars. The sockets of their eyes were deep and hollow. The serpents gaped with blind ferocity at the army below.

Two colossal iron doors formed the entrance to the temple. They were rusted. Their engraving, of two serpents entwined around a spreading tree, was worn down, its details fading into the metal's decay. The doors were open. The left had dropped from its great hinges. It leaned against the entrance, a corpse fossilised in the act of falling. Great sconces dotted the esplanade, their flames long extinguished. Everything was cold. Everything was still.

The dust was red, the stone was red, but in the gloom of the evening, all was grey. Overhead, the lights of the fleet glimmered. They were the only stars above Davin.

'So much silence,' Guilliman said. 'The galaxy burns because of this world, but there are not even embers here any longer.'

'These ruins mark its history,' said Sanguinius. 'I feel its weight. I feel the corruption that shaped every stone. Don't you?'

'That history is finished,' the Lion said, but he was looking intently at the ruins, as if studying them for the secrets they held within the rock.

'Our presence here begins another chapter,' Sanguinius told him.

'I'm not sure.' Guilliman looked up at the pervasive grey of the necrosphere. 'Histories have died here.'

'Ours will not. The Imperium's will not.'

'We risk our histories if the true threat is in the necrosphere and this landing is a distraction.'

'It isn't,' Sanguinius said. He faced the temple's broken gate. 'Look at the decay,' he said.

'What of it?' the Lion asked.

'This was a place of worship when it was pacified. You saw the records from before Horus' arrival. This is a ruin, but the early surveys said it was intact.'

'You think it decayed since then?'

'Yes. So much erosion in a period of a few years? This is the work of centuries. Horus was brought to an unnatural place, and it is unnatural still.' He walked towards the doors. 'Let us face the enemy,' he said. He pulled Curze along at the end of a length of chain. The Night Haunter regarded the Delphos with interest. Sanguinius thought he saw a frown cross Curze's face. It was gone before he was sure. Curze's pallid features were shadowed, unreadable.

The primarchs walked at the head of a contingent of their elite warriors. Squads of the Sanguinary Guard, the Invictus, the Deathbringers and the

Doombringers followed. The Ultramarines marched between the Blood
Angels and the Dark Angels. The men of the I Legion glared at those of
the IX. The Blood Angels did not react, but Sanguinius could feel the tension in his sons. They did not share the serenity that had touched him
here. They were alert, wary, braced, as they had been since Signus Prime,
for an attack that might come from within as easily as from without.

The darkness beyond the gate was heavy, dry. It was a husk. Helm
lights pierced it, revealing eroded walls. They looked as if sandstorms
had blown through the temple's chambers. Reptilian frescoes were faint
dying whispers of images. Their content was a mystery, though what
remained slithered against the eye.

The rooms were deserted. The echoes of marching feet bounced dully
against the walls. The primarchs and their guards moved deeper and
deeper into the Delphos, deeper and deeper into nothingness. The
Lion muttered under his breath with each succeeding empty chamber.

'This is a waste of time,' he said at last.

'Patience, brother,' Sanguinius said.

'Patience until what?'

'I don't know. But it will come.' He was certain. The knot of fate was
tight before him.

'Konrad,' Guilliman said. 'What do you see? Is Sanguinius right?'

'What should I tell you?' Curze answered, his rasp hissing against the
stones. 'Something you would believe, or something true?'

'Maybe I should break your back again,' the Lion said. 'I might believe
what you said then.'

'My answers would be the same. So, I think, would your disbelief.
You can't accept the absence of hope.'

'You can't accept its presence,' Sanguinius said.

'You keep disappointing me,' said Curze. 'You, of all our brothers,
should know better.'

The frown appeared again. This time Sanguinius was sure.

In the centre of the Delphos, they found a room that had been
secret. There were no iron doors over its entrances. Instead, there were

openings in the walls where masonry had fallen in. There were faint patterns of dried blood on the floor.

'We are close,' Sanguinius said.

'To what?' Guilliman asked.

'I'm not sure.' He looked at the Avenging Son. 'Can't you feel it?' The temple's air had been stagnant and dead since the main gate. In the last few minutes, it had grown charged, as if building up to something.

'I don't feel anything,' said Guilliman.

'Nor do I,' the Lion added.

Sanguinius wondered if he was wrong, if his conviction was manufacturing anticipation.

Curze was silent, his expression closed.

On a level directly up from the hidden room, under the dome, they found an altar. It was the first object they had seen. It was in the centre of a chamber so narrow it was more like a cylinder. The walls went up a hundred feet to the dome, but the floor was less than twenty feet across. The primarchs entered by the single doorway. Their legionaries waited in the larger hall outside. The altar was a single large slab, over ten feet long and five feet high. It was a much deeper red than the rest of the stone of the temple. It was almost black. There were stains on the surface too. Unlike the pattern in the chamber below, these appeared to be the pooling from a wound.

Sanguinius stopped on the east side of the altar with Curze. Guilliman and the Lion stood on the west. The gaze of all four alighted on the stain, and lingered.

'He lay here,' said the Lion.

Guilliman nodded.

Sanguinius said, 'This is where his fate took shape.' He struck the altar with the pommel of the *Blade Encarmine*. The ringing of metal against stone was loud and hollow. 'Here,' he said again. 'The war began here.' He wanted to say the war would end here too. He could not. Yet there was symmetry at work in the presence of four primarchs here. The journey from Macragge was a descent further and further into the very heart of the war.

They were there now, at the fulcrum of space on which the galaxy had turned and fallen into flame.

The air should have trembled with the import of this moment. Instead, there was nothing. The event Sanguinius anticipated did not arrive. He considered the possibility of self-delusion, and discarded it. This was where he and his brothers were meant to be.

And yet.

Stale air hung in the chamber. The altar was covered by the layers of the past.

'Sanguinius,' said the Lion, 'we have been deluded again. Both of us.' For the first time since he had arrived on Davin, he spoke without anger. He was grave. The altar and what it meant weighed on him too. 'The Delphos is dead. Davin is dead. You were wrong to bring us here. I was wrong to believe in the imperative of destruction.' He sighed. 'This world was corrupt. Now it is a corpse. What happened here is reason enough to destroy it, but there is no military reason to do so. It will not get us any closer to Terra.'

'You were the first to show us the way here,' said Sanguinius. 'The road to Terra led to Pandorax, and from Pandorax to here.'

'I know,' said the Lion. 'And the means to breaking through the Ruinstorm must lie in this system. It is simply not here, on Davin. Can't you see, brother? Davin's history is done. All that would ever happen here, has already happened. This world corrupted Horus, and its population left to spread more ruin. Its task is done.'

'An entire world bent to a specific purpose,' Guilliman said, his face troubled.

'We have seen enough to know such things must be true,' said Sanguinius.

'Tasked by whom?' Guilliman asked. 'By what?' There was pain on his face, and he held up a hand before Sanguinius answered. 'I know. I resist the idea that we are at the mercy of gods. I resist *them*. I will not abandon reason without a fight. Horus had a choice. All of us do.'

'Do we?' said Curze, his tone a reptilian mix of bitterness, amusement and despair. 'Do you? The future is written, Roboute. You can shake the bars of our cage all you want. They will not bend.'

'Our problem is not whether fate has brought us here or not,' said the Lion. 'Our problem is what to do next.' To Guilliman he said, 'If there is nothing here, then we must consider the shadow we saw in the necrosphere. The enemy must be hiding in the shell.'

'I had hoped our presence here would lure it out.'

'We have learned otherwise. We must hope it is not too late to change our deployment. I will halt our landings. We must leave.'

'No,' said Sanguinius. 'Our task here is not done.'

'How can you be so fixated on this distraction?' the Lion demanded, exasperated. 'The enemy is the one *you* saw first, the one *you* fought.'

Sanguinius circled the room. 'There is something we are missing,' he said. As he walked, he looked at the walls, the ceiling and the sides of the altar. Everything was old, eroded, dead. The traces of runic murals were little more than patches. They did not even hint at what forms the runes might once have had. The power that had circled the room, a serpent on stone, was gone.

'Accept what you see,' said the Lion. 'Nothing more of significance will occur on Davin. All that matters has already happened.'

'*Everything* has already happened,' Curze snarled. 'Not just here. Everything is written. Nothing can change.'

Sanguinius stopped his pacing. 'You are wrong, Konrad,' he said. 'I know the future can change.'

Curze looked at him with genuine unease.

The Angel approached the south end of the altar. He rapped it with his fist. 'This was a fulcrum,' he said. 'Fate pivoted here. Horus fell, but why did he fall? Something turned him, but it did not *transform* him. He is still Horus. When he betrayed my Legion and sent us to the trap of Signus Prime, he fooled me because he was our brother. He is not a changeling. He embraced his descent into darkness. So however hard he was pushed, tempted or manipulated, he must still have made a choice. There was a decision.' He looked at the Lion.

'You faced a decision too. You might have killed me. Was it fated that you did not?'

'Of course it was,' said Curze. 'You disappoint me, Sanguinius. I thought you were beyond trying to wriggle free of the hook. I thought inevitability was why you brought me here. You and I do not die on Davin.'

'Don't we? Is there no chance that we might have? I wonder. Remember how near to death you came on Macragge, Konrad. You felt certainty slip away then. Destiny was on a pivot, and it almost turned.' Sanguinius turned to the Lion again, pushing his brother. He felt the charge in the air again, and it grew stronger as he moved closer to revelation. 'How close did you come to giving the order for the bombardment?'

'Close,' the Lion said. He hesitated, then continued, 'My reason was clouded.'

'Yet you did not give the command,' Sanguinius said. 'Where is the victory of Chaos, Konrad? The universe acted to spare us.'

Guilliman said, 'I faced a decision too.'

'A fateful one?' Sanguinius asked.

'Yes.'

'Do you see the pattern?' Sanguinius realised he was breathing faster. An enormous possibility was opening up before him. He would articulate it this time. He would make it real. 'The Davin System is a fulcrum of destiny. Brothers, you chose well. Horus fell, but you remain standing. We have been brought here to be tempted, just as Horus was.'

'If this is so, then you too must face a decision,' said the Lion. 'What is it?'

'I perceive it imperfectly, but I encountered it on Pyrrhan.' He paused. 'Konrad knows when and how he will die. I, too, know the moment of my death.'

Guilliman looked stricken. The Lion's face darkened with surprise and anger.

'I *did* know the moment,' Sanguinius continued before they could speak. 'On Pyrrhan, that changed. In the manufactorum, I confronted visions of the future. In all of them but one, I died. That was my moment of decision. I could accept what I had long known, or reject it. I chose the vision where I lived, and we triumphed.'

Next to him, the clink of Curze's manacles and chains ceased.

'Why are we here?' said the Lion. 'You made your choice on Pyrrhan, and we made ours in orbit. No one except Horus made a decision on the soil of Davin. There is nothing here except the traces of what happened to him. If this altar had a purpose, it has served it. There are relics of tragedy on Davin. That is all.'

'So it would seem,' Sanguinius said. 'The world is deserted. Too much dust has gathered. Too much has eroded. The system is enclosed by bone. Is it not extravagantly dead? As if gods were determined to convince us that there is nothing?'

'None of this advances us strategically,' said Guilliman. 'We have come here, Sanguinius, and we have seen. I feel the weight of this place, but this is getting us no closer to Terra. There is an intruder in the system, and we have the bulk of our forces planetside. We must leave.'

Sanguinius shook his head. He was not going to be deflected now. Not when understanding was so close, not when he could finally lay claim to the hope that had been denied him for so very long. 'The way to Terra is here, Roboute. In this chamber. I am sure of it. This is still a fulcrum. It...'

He stopped. His eyes snapped wide in awe. He understood what he had been arguing. He understood the full implications of his words. He understood that Pyrrhan had only been a prologue. 'Fate can be altered here,' he said. 'This is where Horus' destiny was created. It was not inevitable that he would come here. Don't you see?' he pleaded. 'Our father was not blind. He could not foresee Davin, because here is where the future changes. Here is where we will change it.'

Revelation blazed. He saw all the threads of possibilities, the severed and the chosen. He saw the knots of fate, and how they choked or were undone. 'I will!' Sanguinius shouted. 'I will change the future!'

And his words summoned light.

The Lion cursed. He and Guilliman stepped back from the altar, weapons in hand.

A vertical slit opened in the air before the north wall. It ran from the dome to the floor, thin as a las-beam, and as bright. A second tear grew horizontally from its centre, arcing halfway around the cylinder wall. Diagonal lines lashed out, forming a star. The tear widened, turning from star to sphere, burning with white light. Sanguinius stared into brilliance. He beheld the ferocious energy of life and possibility.

The sphere stretched downwards, taking on the shape of a doorway. Something moved deep within the gate. Sanguinius thought he saw a flutter, as rapid, constant alterations. He thought of the blurring succession of visions when he fell through the breach in the real on Pyrrhan, and he knew what he had to do.

Guilliman and the Lion were at the back of the chamber, squinting against the light. Their guns were trained on the portal.

'This is a trap, Sanguinius,' Guilliman called. 'There is nothing else it can be.'

'We were manipulated,' said the Lion. 'The enemy misleads you, too.'

'You do not understand what I have seen,' Sanguinius told them.

Curze still hadn't moved. He was staring at the portal, though his face was a mask of agony.

'I know what I must do, brothers,' Sanguinius said. 'This is the fulcrum. I will forge us a new fate.'

'You cannot do this,' said Curze. His voice was barely a whisper. There was something in his tone that was alien to the Night Haunter. His face was transformed. It took Sanguinius a moment to recognise what he was seeing and hearing in Curze.

It was horror. Horror that the Angel might destroy the bedrock of Curze's existence. Horror that Sanguinius might prove the future was not written.

'I must,' Sanguinius replied.

He entered the portal.

The last thing he heard before the light enveloped him was the Night Haunter screaming.

FIFTEEN

By Eight, By Four

THE PORTAL FLARED with slicing, frozen brilliance. Then it faded, the edges pulling back until only a vertical tear remained. It suffused the chamber with dim light that cut the eye like a razor. Guilliman stopped with his right hand a hair's breadth from the portal. He had lunged to grab Sanguinius and missed. He cursed. He looked back at the Lion. 'This is impossible. Where is he?'

'The warp?'

'Impossible,' Guilliman repeated. 'This is madness.'

From the hall beyond the chamber, the Sanguinary Guard had pushed forwards. Azkaellon stood in the doorway. 'Where is our lord?' he demanded.

'Beyond our reach,' said the Lion.

Azkaellon rushed towards the portal.

'*Hold!*' Guilliman commanded.

The voice of thunder stopped Azkaellon. He faced Guilliman, shaking with fury. 'I will not abandon my primarch.'

'I do not abandon my brother,' Guilliman said, his words rumbling still through the chamber. 'But a blind leap through that portal does him no good. He made this decision. Respect it, and prepare for what may follow. He went in. You know what may come out.'

'Daemons,' Azkaellon growled. The word came to his lips more easily than it did to Guilliman's.

'Withdraw and stand ready,' Guilliman told him. 'We shall expect an enemy attack from this gate.'

After another hesitation, Azkaellon obeyed.

Curze was shaking his head. He staggered against the altar. He looked as if the light had dealt him a mortal blow. He was staring at the portal, his sunken eyes glittering with anger and horror. Guilliman advanced on him. 'Tell us what will happen,' he said.

Curze looked up at him with contempt. 'I don't know.'

The Lion seized his chain. He bent Curze backwards, arcing his back to the breaking point. 'You don't know? You know I won't kill you,' the Lion said. 'And you know I will make you wish I would. Answer my brother!'

'*I don't know*,' Curze roared. His anger and confusion were real.

'He's telling the truth,' Guilliman said.

The Lion threw Curze back against the altar.

The Night Haunter struggled to stand. He was a ragged shadow in the hard light. 'If I knew he would fail, I would throw it in your faces. You're all fools, and he's the greatest fool of all.'

'Why?' Guilliman asked.

Curze whispered, 'Because he might succeed.'

CORRUPTION DRAPED THE halls of the ship. Sanded skins hung between iron spikes that reached from the walls like claws. Sanguinius tasted his blood, and the viscous slick of the air. He smelled scorched ozone, expended fyceline, burning flesh and the stench of rotting souls. The hull of the *Vengeful Spirit* rang with the clash of blades and the roars of men. A huge icon, the eye of Horus, stared down on Sanguinius as he crossed the threshold into the throne room.

Horus was there, waiting, as he always was, as he always would be until the end finally came.

The brothers fought, and warm blood coursed down inside Sanguinius' armour. He struggled against the sluggishness of his limbs. His lungs struggled to pull in the foetid air. His hearts beat like pounding stones in his head.

Most acute of all the sensations was the agony of Horus' blows. Sanguinius knew every step of the fight, every strike and parry and counter-attack. Though his body reacted to the immediacy of the duel, his mind looked at each moment with the despair of total familiarity. Each second was a painting he had studied to the minutest detail.

And still the death blow came as a brutal shock.

Sanguinius died, and then he fought again, and died again, and died again. Death was a terrible refrain. He was trapped in a hymn to the triumph of dark gods.

But on Pyrrhan he had found a way out of the trap, a way of disrupting the refrain. He reached for that memory. He seized upon that single, precious future where he killed Horus, and he made it real. For the second time, he experienced the impossible victory, and the surge of hope that came with it renewed his strength. He slew Horus and grew stronger yet. The weight of countless repetitions hurled his death at him once more. In rage and determination, he fought back.

Horus died. Sanguinius died. Reality flickered between the two alternatives. The deaths came faster and faster, agony and triumph turning from instants into constant states of being. Time thrummed, vibrating. Darkness and light took form in Sanguinius. States of being took on definite contours. The darkness was rage. Betrayal and pain fed into an anger that blinded him in his final moment, the wrath so consuming it seemed to burst from within and take on a life of its own independent of Sanguinius. The light was justice. It brought an end to Horus' treachery. It brought the revival of hope. The darkness had the strength of many futures, yet they all ended with the last blow. The light shone in the one destiny, the one series of actions that saved Sanguinius and killed Horus. Through that light, time continued. It described his future beyond slaying Horus on the *Vengeful Spirit*.

Sanguinius chose the light. He chose it and he chose it and he chose it. It grew brighter. He grew stronger. Victory's radiance dazzled. It overwhelmed the darkness. The endless cycle of death stuttered. It weakened. The anger of betrayal lost its grip. Sanguinius pulled himself away from rage. His justice was cold, and it was implacable. The light of the *Blade Encarmine* and the light of victory fused. They were the same, and the light grew and grew. The reality of the *Vengeful Spirit* faded. Soon there was only the light. It intensified, blinding, and it became the piercing white of the portal once more.

Sanguinius soared through the featureless brilliance.

But the dark would not release him willingly. It surged back. The light faded. The rewritten future slipped away from his grasp. A black tide rose beneath him. It tainted the light. His wings beat against limbo. He tried to climb. The darkness was faster. It rushed up, a deluge. It swallowed him. He choked on it. It filled his lungs. It filled his eyes. It filled his mind.

This is the choice. Let me guide your hand against Horus. Turn from me, and behold what will come.

The voice was not his. It spoke without sound. He thought that, if he could hear it, he would recognise it.

He breathed again. His lungs pulled in familiar, dusty air. Wind whipped against his face, stinging, scouring. The darkness dropped from his eyes, and he was on Baal. His armour was torn open. His chest ached. The pain of his death lingered. He stood on the highest spire of the monastery-fortress of the Blood Angels. The sky was black with smoke. Below the fortress, the landscape of canyons and jagged ridges was strewn with the guttering remains of tanks, transports and mobile artillery. Clouds of ash billowed on the wind. War had come to Baal, and war had ended.

The aftermath was cancerous. Screams of madness and rage rose from inside the monastery towers. Sanguinius gasped in the agony of recognition. The Thirst had come for his sons. Reflected in the windows of the spires, he caught glimpses of beasts. They wore fragments of battle armour. They fought and killed each other. They tore the bodies of mortals apart and lapped their blood. The wind carried the howls over the land; the animal wailing of a Legion's death. Soon blood ran from the windows. It streamed in torrents down the towers. It pooled in the courtyards and at the base of the monastery. It poured in great cataracts, becoming a lake, becoming an ocean. The fortress became an island. The blood kept rising. It reached the ramparts. It flooded the keep. Crimson waves broke against the towers. Still the blood cascaded. Storm-tossed, the ocean rose. The screams of the monsters were cut off, smothered beneath the blood.

Sanguinius groaned. He cried out against the flaw. He spread his wings to fly away from the rolling swells of grief. He could not. The blood lapped at his feet. His wings folded and he sank to his knees.

The sea of blood took him. He choked, drowning. The darkness filled him again.

Again he dropped through the smothering night. Falling, falling.

This is the choice. Turn from it.

Falling. The red of flame streaked the dark. He breathed again. The air burned.

He was on the ramparts of the Imperial Palace. The sky boiled with flame. The prow of a battleship plunged through the clouds. The vessel bore the gold and black of the Imperial Fists. It had broken in two. Wreathed in fire, a slow comet, the forwards half of the ship dropped to the Imperial Palace. The earth shook. A terrible sunrise filled the night. Huge fragments of domes, towers and great halls were specks of black in the fireball.

The streets were in tumult. Millions ran in panic before the advance of the enemy. Mutated Titans, spikes running down their spines and limbs, strode over hab blocks and smashed through the walls of Administratum palaces. War-horns blared, the cries of frenzied predators. They turned their weapons on the streets, making the ground molten.

If there were still defenders, Sanguinius could not see them. The enemy marched in shadow. They were the night beneath the night.

Their war-chants were incantations of madness. A great wailing of fear greeted their arrival. A great wailing of grief remained in their wake. The chorus of woe resounded against the crumbling walls of the Imperial Palace. It hit Sanguinius with a force greater than the death of the battleship and the war-horns of the Titans. The wailing was the sound of his failure. It felt like Horus' blade sawing through his hearts again. He had failed his Terra, the Imperium and the Emperor. His death was meaningless. He had been willing to embrace it, if, by dying, he saved his father. He would sacrifice himself on the altar of salvation. But Terra had fallen. The Imperial Palace was burning. The Emperor must be dead, for surely He would have been fighting the invaders. Where the Master of Mankind should be, there was only absence.

His sacrifice was for nothing.

This is the choice. Fall to Horus, and the light falls with you.

The Imperial Palace crumbled like sand. Sky-piercing spires toppled. Walls disintegrated. The wailing and the flames reached higher and higher. Domes and vaults collapsed into ruin.

The rampart cracked beneath Sanguinius' feet. He tried to fly, but the weight of his failure was too great. Stone turned to dust, and he fell. The world faded into darkness. Soon there was only screaming and fire. Then even that was consumed by the dark.

Sanguinius did not know when he spread his wings, but he had. His feathers rippled with the currents of the dark.

This is the choice, said the voice, and when the dark receded, this time it was to show him the full torment of his father's dream. Sanguinius flew through star systems, skimmed the surface of planets, and shot into the intergalactic void, where he looked down on the spiral arms of the galaxy. The Ruinstorm exulted in its infinite power. It had become a maelstrom that turned the stars themselves. The galaxy writhed in its grip. Sanguinius saw planets carved into the idols of worship. He saw daemonic fortresses rise up to eclipse suns. The walls towered above the galactic plain. He saw tangles of architecture that devoured stars. The blood of planets ran down the lengths of great arches. Worlds convulsed with the riots of daemons. Billions of mortals suffered and died in nights of fire and days of blood. He saw citadels of brass and cities of plague. He saw rivers of bodies fused in the paroxysms of excess. And everywhere was change, everywhere was flux, everywhere the triumph of Chaos.

He did see mortal battlements. From them flew the banners of the traitor Legions. He saw signs of what he thought might be Horus' dark empire. But the hints were few. The signs were scant. It was as if the possibility was not truly considered, or the fact not important enough to register more strongly in the mosaic of insanity.

Reality was dead. Its corpse lay open to the devouring jaws of the warp. The blood of the materium flowed in the form of a million shrieking worlds.

This is the choice, said the voice, *if you refuse my aid.*

I will not choose this, Sanguinius thought. *I will not allow it.* He turned his eyes from the great ruin. He turned into the great dark, and he struck into it with the *Blade Encarmine*. He stabbed it as he had stabbed Horus in that one future where there was light.

He tore the dark and the light rushed out, enveloping him, restoring him. He welcomed the blindness that came with it. It pulled back to the sound of a great fanfare.

He saw the triumph of the Imperium.

The loyalist forces turned back the tide of the traitors. Terra was triumphant. In orbit, its master dead, the *Vengeful Spirit* was a gutted shell. On the Avenue of Reason's Victory, Sanguinius stood over Lorgar's body. He had impaled the primarch of the Word Bearers through the chest with the *Spear of Telesto*. Behind Lorgar, the wreckage of Land Raiders and Rhinos of the XVII Legion formed hills of twisted, smoking metal. The corpses of Word Bearers were uncountable.

Perturabo kneeled before Sanguinius. His armour was shattered. Within and without, the iron had been smashed.

In the distance, Sanguinius saw Guilliman and the Lion leading more of their fallen brothers in chains, bringing them to the site of their surrender.

Loyalist forces freed world after world. The fleets were even larger than during the Great Crusade, so massive was the Imperium's response to the traitors, so decisive its retaliation. Ships of crimson and of gold, of blue and of white, of black and of grey, of all the colours of fealty, all of them shining with the light of justice, stormed through the void. In their collective might, they were a sword. They were his sword, striking across the entire galaxy. His blow rescued his father's dream and burned away the desolation of Horus. The ascendancy of the dream was assured now. Eternity was subject to the rule of the Imperium.

This is the choice. Follow me to triumph.

Sanguinius followed the golden road of this future. There was an end to the war. There was an end to the Crusade. And now he was on Terra again. He walked with the Emperor in a cloister adjacent to the throne room. It was a small space, reached by a door unnoticeable in the grandeur and colossal scale of the chamber. Sanguinius had no memory of being here before. The colonnade enclosed a garden of fountains. Each sculpture was a bronze and gold orrery of the star systems of the Emperor's loyal sons. Streams of water leapt from the centre of one orrery to another, forming a web of connections. In the gaps where the fountains of the traitor primarchs had been, there now stood silver trees. Their trunks were engraved with the names of the decisive battles of the war. Their branches linked overhead, creating another web. The garden was the strength of the Imperium. It was resilience and the bonds of loyalty.

It was also peace.

'I have tarried long enough,' the Emperor said.

'I understand,' Sanguinius said. 'Your great work cannot be left unfinished.'

'Not if the Imperium's future is to be considered. The Crusade is complete. Now, our vigilance to preserve what it accomplished must be eternal. We have prevailed against the forces that would have destroyed it, but we have not destroyed them. Their jealousy is great. They will always be outside the gates.'

'They came very close to breaching them.'

The Emperor bent His head, acknowledging the justice of the mild rebuke. 'I thought I could raise walls of psychic defence so high they would shut out Chaos forever. I knew that awareness of the daemonic was dangerous in and of itself. I hid that knowledge from all of you, thinking I was protecting you and all we had accomplished together. I was wrong. My hubris has had a terrible cost. At least you know, now, why I cannot remain amongst you.'

'I do, Father.' The admission was difficult. He did not want to admit that the joy of being at the Emperor's side again was to be short-lived. He did understand, though. And there was comfort in knowing that the purpose of the Legiones Astartes was assured. They would always be needed. They would be the eternal guardians on the material and psychic ramparts of the Imperium.

'Then I think you know what I am going to ask of you.'

Sanguinius caught his breath. He stopped walking in a corner of the colonnade. The Emperor walked on another few steps, His great stride taking Him almost halfway down the shorter end of the quadrangle. He paused and looked back at the Angel. His smile was kind. His eyes were solemn.

Sanguinius forced his legs into motion. He caught up to the Emperor. 'Father,' he said, 'we cannot repeat history.'

Water leapt from fountain to fountain. The sound was the murmur of duty.

'We are not making the same mistakes,' said the Emperor. They began walking again. 'You are not Horus. And I am not asking you to be Warmaster. The time for that role has passed.'

'What are you asking?' Sanguinius asked. He knew, yet he did not believe.

'I am asking you take up a mantle you have already borne. You must be Imperator Regis.'

Sanguinius shook his head. 'The Imperium Secundus was a mistake. It was a sin against you.'

'You acted in error, but you acted correctly. What would have happened had you refused Guilliman's plea? By accepting, by being my regent, you forged the unity between the three Legions that led to the victory over Horus. The Imperium would be lucky to experience more such errors.'

'Why me, Father?'

'Because you have already proven yourself worthy. You took up rule reluctantly, and set it aside with gratitude.'

Sanguinius sighed. 'I am still reluctant.'

'Good. But it is not merely that you are not a usurper, Sanguinius. You are also the leader the Imperium will need. You have the strength. You have the power. You defeated Lorgar. It was to you that they bent the knee in surrender.'

'You were fighting elsewhere.'

'That is my point. Even they recognised who stood in my stead. Your destiny is to be my regent.'

This is the choice. This the path you must accept. I will guide your hand at the crucial moment.

Sanguinius recognised the voice in his head now. It was the Emperor's. It had been all along. Even now, he heard no sound, but he recognised the authority, the wisdom, the knowledge and the power behind the words.

The Emperor had stopped walking. The water murmured. A breeze disturbed the Master of Mankind's raven hair. He looked at the Angel expectantly.

Sanguinius' consciousness divided. He stood before the Emperor in the Imperial Palace, and a part of him looked on from within the radiant limbo of the portal, conscious that this moment had not happened yet, that this was the future he must bring about. He had to break the bonds of fate, to make this possibility a reality. He had to strike the blow, through the knot of destiny and through Horus' skull. To reach that moment, he understood now, he had to accept the guidance of the voice. And why wouldn't he listen to his father?

The Emperor read the determination on his face. He smiled with pride. 'You are surprised to have reached this juncture, Sanguinius. That is to your credit. It is to my shame that I did not realise from the start what had to be done.' He shook His head sadly. 'I was blind when I named Horus the Warmaster. It should have been you. It should always have been you.' His eyes looked off into the vague distance, pained by the vision of the billions of lives lost in the war, and then back at Sanguinius. They grew bright with joy. 'You are the Angel,' he said. 'You have the wings of divinity. Long may the Imperium soar with you.'

'I will serve...' Sanguinius began. He stopped. The Emperor's last words rang false. He had never heard his father use the word *divinity* in that fashion. It had always been a term of contempt, a reminder of the ignorance that was humanity's lot before the Imperium shone the light of reason across the galaxy.

Joy stuttered. Hope wavered. The visions of the triumphant future fractured. A flaw ran through them. On Terra, when the traitors surrendered, why *had* he been the one receiving their capitulation?

The loyalist fleets retaking the fallen worlds and completing the work of the Great Crusade, how had they grown so large in so short a time? As he examined the memory, Sanguinius saw what he had not taken in before, or perhaps had expected too easily. The fleets of the IX Legion were the greatest of all.

'What's wrong?' the Emperor asked.

The light of the future radiated from Sanguinius. His actions brought victory. His blow shaped the Imperium. Traitors and Emperor alike recognised him as the ruler of the order to come. Every triumph flattered his pride.

Sanguinius looked around the cloister. He was sure he had never seen it before. That did not mean the cloister did not exist. But the lack of memory disturbed him. The colonnade and the garden of fountains were too perfectly suited to this conversation.

A conversation where the Emperor was too deferential to Sanguinius, too quick to blame Himself for the tragedy of the war. His majesty was lacking. Sanguinius had felt so much joy to be in his father's presence again that he had not questioned the presence. And again, his pride had blinded him.

A cold trickle of dread ran through his blood.

'What's wrong?' the Emperor asked again.

'Everything,' said Sanguinius. 'This is not real.'

'No, it isn't,' the Emperor agreed. 'Not yet. It falls to you to make it real.'

'You are not my father.'

The breeze over the garden grew cooler, stronger. Sanguinius' wings rustled.

The Emperor nodded. 'This is not real. We do not stand here. I am not your father. All of this is promise to come. Its possibility is fragile. It comes from you, and it is up to you. If you wish me to live, if you wish this reality to *be*, and for the Emperor to stand as I stand, and speak to you as I do, then you must decide. Yours is the hand that must change your destiny.' The Emperor looked solemn. 'It would be easy to let time unfold as you have long believed it would. So many events pull us to your death and mine. The resistance is difficult. You must push against currents that serve gods.'

'No,' Sanguinius said, though he was uncertain. 'There is too much here that flatters my pride. '

'You cannot divorce yourself from your perception of reality, or of many realities. You are your own filter. I am as you see me because this is how you see me.'

Sanguinius took a step backwards. He brushed against a column. The contact of shoulder against marble was reassuring. He wanted to believe what the Emperor was saying.

It is because you want to believe it that you must not.

This is the choice. The whisper in his mind was urgent. This time, he did not know if the voice came from without, or if he was speaking to himself. The voice was telling the truth. What might be a lie was the way the choice was presented.

'You are the salvation of the Imperium,' the Emperor said. 'Your pride and the truth are not opposed. Embrace what must be done.'

'I am not its salvation.'

'Will you doom the Imperium, then? Will you compound the sin of the Imperium Secundus by turning away from your duty? Will you not answer my call?'

The wind grew stronger. The light in the garden dimmed, staining with grey. Sanguinius wrestled with confusion, and he gripped the column. It cracked. 'You said Imperium Secundus was not a sin.'

'You are the source of the contradictions,' the Emperor said. 'I cannot speak except as you think I would.'

The column cracked again. Dust drifted to the ground. The breeze became a wind. Spray blew from the fountains. Their streams became erratic, splashing against the sides of the basins. Grinding came from the clockwork mechanisms. The planets shuddered in their revolutions. The reality of the cloister was eroding. It was turning to sand beneath Sanguinius' fingers, eaten away by his disbelief.

'You are a lie,' he said to the Emperor. Uttering those words felt like falling on his sword.

The figure before him was his father in every detail. He remained solid even as the cloister's reality softened. Fragments of stone fell from the ceiling, onto the Emperor's shoulders. He brushed them away. He looked up at the spreading cracks, then down at Sanguinius. The face of nobility became one of profound sadness. 'Is that your belief?' the Emperor asked.

'It is.'

The ground trembled. The world swayed in the wind.

'If you believe I am a lie,' the Emperor said, 'then it is clear what you must do.' He took a step towards Sanguinius. He spread His arms, hands open. He lifted His head, exposing His throat.

Sanguinius gripped the hilt of the *Blade Encarmine*. He did not draw it yet.

This is the choice. This is the choice. This is the choice.

Will you kill the Emperor?

'You must act on the truth,' the Emperor said. 'You cannot permit a lie to stand. Here I am. If I am a lie, strike me down. Do not hesitate.'

Sanguinius hesitated. The enormity of the act was too great. In the garden, the fountain of Baal toppled. The pillars were crumbling now. Sharp chunks of marble dropped from the arches, shattering against flagstones. The wind keened with grief.

The Emperor did not blur. His reality was strong. If anything, it became stronger as the cloister fell apart. How, Sanguinius wondered, could he be an illusion? The presence was not as he remembered his father, but it *was* a presence, more definite than any he had encountered since entering the portal. The bloody realities of Horus, so absolute when Sanguinius lived his death and his triumph, now seemed like pale simulacra. Perhaps it was Sanguinius' memory of the Emperor that was faulty, blinding him to the truth in front of him.

The Emperor nodded. He lowered His arms. 'Yes,' He said. 'We have all been blinded. Horus was. I was. You were, but are no longer.' He smiled. 'You do not strike the blow because you can see at last. You are making the choice, and it is the right one.'

There was a moment of gratitude. A moment of hope. A moment when the disintegration of the cloister stopped. Then Sanguinius tightened his grip on the *Blade Encarmine*. He drew the sword. The Emperor did not move. Sanguinius raised the *Blade Encarmine* high.

'Will you kill me?' the Emperor asked.

Sanguinius howled. He charged at the thing that could not be the Emperor. The presence was real, but the image was not. That was what he had to see. That was what he must believe, but all he knew as he screamed was that he aimed his blow at the neck of his father. The evidence of his eyes declared him the greatest of traitors. He, not Horus, struck at the Emperor. He attacked with desperate faith that he had made the choice at last, and that it was the loyal one. He attacked what could not be his father. But he could not see past the appearance. His soul cried out at the crime he saw himself commit.

Father, forgive me, for I know not what I do.

The Emperor did not move until the sword began its descent. Then He moved suddenly to block it, and He changed.

Everything changed.

The cloister melted. Columns and fountains bent and flowed. A web of fissures split the fountains and colonnade. It split the water and the air. Ferocious, roaring light of violet and red and green erupted through the fissures. All form vanished, and the cloister became a maelstrom of dark and light. The wind shrieked, a hurricane blowing reason and matter into madness.

A staff stopped Sanguinius' blow. Its head was a cluster of nestled, savage blades, and they held the sword fast. The hand that clutched the staff was huge and clawed. It was on the end of an arm thick with scaled muscle and deadly with curved spines down its length.

The Emperor was gone. In His place, a daemon towered over Sanguinius. Multiple twisted horns framed a skull with monstrous jaws and eyes that were blind yet filled with awful knowledge. Its torso was covered in eyes. Some gazed at Sanguinius with hunger. Some with amusement. Some with anger.

The daemon parted its jaws. When it spoke, a tongue long as a serpent uncoiled to taste the Angel's pain.

'By paths of eight and gods of four, I am Madail the Undivided. By fates of eight and edicts of four, you shall serve. You shall be the Angel of Ruin.'

The maelstrom slowed. The rush of non-being coagulated. It became real. It became nightmare. It became the interior of a ship.

SIXTEEN

The Shattered and the Returned

THE STHENELUS CUT through the void partway between the necrosphere and Davin. Its full auspex array was directed at the bones. Khalybus paced slowly back and forth across the width of the strategium, his bionic legs taking strides of perfect, mechanical regularity. His gaze never left the oculus. He watched the slowly shifting view of the necrosphere. At this distance, all he could see was a wall of grey lined by faint, broken, jagged veins of black. The lines were huge topographical features, the bones pushed together in mountain chains larger than worlds.

All dead. Everything was dead. Except something waited in the necrosphere. The auspex had picked it up several times during the transit through the shell. The first reading came just seconds before the primarchs alerted the fleets to the presence of an enemy. The last time was as the *Sthenelus* had emerged from the shell into the Davin System. None of the contacts had lasted for more than a fraction of a second. Never long enough to triangulate the foe's position, its size, or its nature. Just enough to confirm its existence. There had been no contacts since the frigate had reached the void inside the necrosphere.

Khalybus was patient. He would wait for the enemy to move again. While the three Legions travelled to Davin and began their landings, he held the *Sthenelus* back. Alone, the ship prowled, hunting the Pilgrim.

He had ignored the glowering stare at his back for hours. He finally grew tired of it. Without taking his gaze from the oculus, he said, 'I know what you are going to say, Iron Father. My orders will stand. But speak, and I will listen.'

'I do not speak for the benefit of outsiders,' said Cruax. His voice sounded like stones rattling in a hollow iron case.

'I'll withdraw,' Levannas said. He stood at the starboard end of the strategium. The Raven Guard kept himself still, merging with the shadows pooling at the base of the wall. It was easy to forget he was there. Cruax made a point of never forgetting. The years of fighting alongside Levannas had done nothing to temper the Iron Father's dislike. The XIX Legion had failed to support the Iron Hands at the crucial moment on Isstvan V, and for Cruax, the sin of the primarch was the sin of the entire Legion. The stain could never be expunged, no matter how vital a role the remnants of the Raven Guard had played in the survival of Khalybus' company ever since.

'No,' Khalybus said. 'Your place is on the bridge.' He had no great love for the XIX, but he had learned to value Levannas' strategic mind, and his friendship. The war was too long and too desperate to turn from any winning strategy, and any true ally. Khalybus had adapted the company's tactics to the new war. He believed that he had not betrayed the tenets of the X Legion. And he had Cruax to keep him honest.

The Iron Father grunted, displeased. Then he said, 'Our vigil here is for nothing. Meanwhile, three Legions are on the surface of Davin. We are not where the war will be.'

'I think you're wrong,' Khalybus said. 'There is no fighting yet on Davin. I believe the attack will come from here.'

'From where?' said Cruax. 'We are patrolling less than a sliver of that surface. We have wasted enough time.'

Khalybus glanced Levannas' way. 'Do you agree?'

'I think our presence over Davin would be redundant. Here we might make a difference.'

'I think so too.' He wasn't sure why he was so determined to hold a position close to the necrosphere. Cruax was right. It was highly unlikely that the *Sthenelus* would scan just the right region when the enemy moved again. He did not like to admit that he was compelled by something like intuition. That was not a proper rationale. It was too human, too beholden to the weak flesh. Even so, he obeyed his instinct. Just beyond the edge of perception, there was something familiar. He did not know what it was or how it could be, and he would not speak of it to anyone.

'We will meet the Pilgrim at last,' Levannas said, sounding as certain as Khalybus felt.

'And we will fight it alone, in the end.'

Khalybus watched the necrosphere. Waiting.

He thought *Now* the moment before the shout.

'Contact!' Seterikus called from the auspex station. Legionaries manned all the critical systems of the frigate; very few mortal officers had survived this long into the war. 'There is movement in the shell. It's big.'

'I know,' said Khalybus.

The monster moved so fast, it broke through the shell seconds after being detected. And Seterikus was right. It was very big. It did not appear so, as it emerged from the inconceivable vastness of the necrosphere, but as it entered the system and made for Davin, its scale became clear. At last the enemy had a shape. It was a warship. It was gigantic, far larger than any battleship Khalybus had ever seen. It dwarfed the likes of the *Red Tear* and the *Invincible Reason*. Yet its silhouette was familiar.

'We are being hailed,' said Demir.

'Let us hear it,' Khalybus said. 'One second only.'

He expected the daemonic electronic howl, the screech trying to break up his rational thoughts. What disturbed him more was the tone underneath the scream. This was what was familiar. For all the distortion, the signal was still that of a specific vessel. The daemonic forces that had created the monster wanted it to be recognised. They wanted the pain that came with that knowledge.

Demir cut the sound after a second. Smoke rose from one of the vox-casters. Silence fell on the bridge. The daemon ship grew larger in the oculus. It was moving fast. Its form became clearer.

'Captain,' Demir began. He too had a bionic larynx. It was not suited to the expression of emotion. Such displays were not part of the culture of the Iron Hands. The machinic ideal was cold, not easily moved. Yet Demir's voice cracked in horror.

'I know,' Khalybus said. It was hard to speak. 'Warn the fleets. The Pilgrim is here. It is the *Veritas Ferrum*.'

Secondary auspex and pict screens lit up with green confirmations, even as the primary screens were flashing red with warnings. The cogitators of the *Sthenelus* had recognised the *Veritas* too. Its transponder signatures were beyond doubt. The outline of the ship was familiar. Enough remained for the mockery to be apparent. This was the strike cruiser of Captain Durun Atticus. It had survived Isstvan V, exacting a steep price from the traitors as it made good its escape. It had destroyed the Emperor's Children battle-barge *Callidora* and its escorts. Khalybus had followed the traces of the *Veritas Ferrum*'s heroic war. He had searched for years to find it and its captain again.

He had found it. He hoped no remnant of Atticus was aboard the abomination.

'Magnify,' Khalybus ordered. Swallowing his disgust, he studied the vid screen displays in the strategium, taking what he could to learn the nature of the foe. Levannas and Cruax joined him.

The *Veritas Ferrum* had grown many times its original size. Colossal spikes of iron and brass jutted from its hull. Its flanks bubbled with pustules and sores a hundred yards wide. They swelled, burst and grew again.

Levannas said, 'That disease might be a weakness.'

'Yes,' Khalybus began. He looked more closely. 'No,' he corrected. He pointed to a blister that had just burst a quarter of the way down from the prow. 'Look. That did not leave a crater. The plates are thicker now.' As he spoke, another sore split open. Molten fluid spread outwards, then solidified. The ship was growing stronger.

The *Veritas Ferrum*'s statuary had turned into gnarled gargoyles. They moved, jaws snapping and claws raking the void for prey. They were huge, each of them the size of a frigate, though against the colossal scale of the swollen *Veritas*, they were comparable to the statues, battered by the years of war, that still stood proudly the length of the *Sthenelus*. The gargoyles of the *Veritas* were in the mould of its figurehead. The prow was a horned skull. Jaws that could snap an escort in half opened and closed, hungry, raging, laughing.

The guns of the ship had grown too. They looked like jagged, broken bones forged from brass. Flames licked up from their barrels. Acidic blood ran down their length, in defiance of absent gravity, scoring the guns with lines of strange, shifting meanings.

Khalybus exchanged a look with Cruax. The Iron Father nodded. 'Our struggle has been a long and honourable one,' Cruax said. 'I am proud of what we have done.'

'As am I,' said Levannas.

'What are your orders, captain?' Cruax asked. He spoke with grim acceptance of what was coming.

'They are what they must be,' Khalybus said. 'We attack.'

VOX COMMUNICATION WITH the surface was erratic. Carminus had no trouble reaching the Chapter Masters in the field outside the temple, but it took him many attempts to reach the forces inside. The Chapter Masters were having the same difficulty. The armies were in a state of limbo. There was no enemy to attack on the surface, but the prolonged silence from the primarchs had the commanders on edge. Now an enemy was coming, and there was nothing the planetside forces could do.

The fleets, at least, could act. The flagships of the Dark Angels and the Ultramarines joined the *Red Tear* in pulling out of orbit. Three vast wedges of ships took shape, pointing towards the approaching *Veritas Ferrum*. Davin was already diminishing to the rear as the fleets built up speed.

'More contacts,' said Mautus. 'They're coming out of the necrosphere behind the *Veritas*.'

'Identification?'

'None yet.'

'Vox, are they hailing?'

There was a pause. 'Yes,' said Neverrus. Then, with more excitement than dread, 'Captain, vox signals from inside the temple.'

It was Azkaellon. The vox stream kept breaking up. Static bursts swallowed words. Carminus heard '...*vanished*...'. That told him what he needed to know.

'I hear and acknowledge, Azkaellon. The enemy has emerged. It is the *Veritas Ferrum*.' He had difficulty believing the gargantuan auspex contact could ever have been an Iron Hands strike cruiser, but he had to accept the report from Khalybus. He had never heard a legionary of the X speak with horrified grief before. 'There are more ships with it,' Carminus went on. 'We are closing to attack. I am leaving the *Victus* and the *Scarlet Liberty* in orbit. They will await your call for a forced evacuation.' *If they hear it.* The thought came before he could suppress it. 'Please acknowledge.' When he received only static as a response, he repeated himself.

This time, he heard fragments of words, isolated syllables, '...*ledged*...'.

There was an electronic shriek in the signal, and the vox cut out. Carminus frowned at the abruptness. He did not think Azkaellon had broken communications voluntarily.

There was nothing he could do. His duty was clear. He must not dwell on what was happening below. He must not think of the absence of the primarch.

He turned back to Neverrus. 'The hails,' he said. 'One second. No longer.' Premonition told him to follow the example of the Iron Hands.

Neverrus did as he ordered. When she looked back at him, her face was pale with shock. 'The *Sable* is out there,' she said.

'More contacts,' Mautus warned. 'There's a lot of movement.' He paused. 'There's too much movement.'

'What do you mean, too much?' Carminus said.

'Attempting to resolve the data, captain.'

While Mautus worked his station, trying to make sense of the information pouring in, Carminus looked through the bridge oculus. The *Red Tear* was leading the Blood Angels fleet. To starboard, he could see the leading edge of the Ultramarines formation, the *Samothrace* at their head. Past them, beyond his sight, the Dark Angels were moving out too. The tacticarium screens to the left and right of his command throne updated the positions moment by moment, hololithic diagrams arranging themselves into a shape that was both a triple-headed spear and a moving wall. Three aimed their might at a single target. The auspex returns of the *Veritas Ferrum* defied belief, but no matter how huge the ship was, even with its escort it was outnumbered.

Or so Carminus had thought until a moment ago. He looked straight ahead. The *Veritas* would not be visible for some time yet. He was staring into the grey-tinged void, anticipating the fires of war to come, and waiting for the worst news.

Carminus blinked. There was nothing to see, yet he had an impression of movement. He turned his head, using his peripheral vision to capture more light. The feeling intensified. Movement, too vague and pervasive to define. 'Auspex,' he said to Mautus, 'tell me what is happening out there.'

'Resolving,' Mautus said. His voice was hoarse.

The first symbols to appear on Carminus' screens were more ships pouring out of the shell behind the *Veritas Ferrum*. The *Sable* was one of the first. It had not become gigantic, though the data on the auspex returns showed grievous deformation in the cruiser's shape. The vessels kept coming, and so did the identifications. The Ultramarines reported the presence of the grand cruiser *Virtu* and the battle-barge

Eternal Rampart. The Dark Angels saw the return of the strike cruisers *Judgement of Night*, *Recurve* and *Voulge*. Mautus identified ships from other Legions as well. There were many from the forces that had been scattered after Isstvan V. Ships lost to the Salamanders, Raven Guard and Iron Hands returned, corrupted courtiers to the *Veritas Ferrum*.

'There is a pattern,' Mautus said. 'None of these ships were destroyed in engagements. They have been listed as missing or lost in the warp.'

The *Veritas'* escort kept growing in number until it became a squadron. Then a strike force.

'The Pilgrim has been busy,' Carminus muttered.

Past the ships, the displays disintegrated into a fog of lines. 'Mautus,' Carminus said, 'what is the other movement?'

'It's the necrosphere,' Mautus said a few moments later. 'It's contracting.'

'How fast?'

'Variable speeds, fleet master.' The schematics on the tacticarium screen still showed a fog at the edges of the system. It had vectors now. 'Some of it is almost as fast as the ships.'

The spatial geography of the conflict took shape in Carminus' mind. Based on the relative speeds of the opposing forces, the collision would occur at a point less than half the distance between Davin and the original position of the shell. The wedges of the fleets were aimed at an amorphous swarm of daemonic ships. And coming behind them, a closing fist.

'The *Sthenelus* is engaging,' said Neverrus.

'Tell them we are coming,' Carminus told her. 'Tell them they do not fight alone.' He advanced to the command pulpit, as if the few steps from the throne would bring him closer to the conflagration.

The grey-black of the void swirled, tightening. In the centre of the view, a star twinkled. It was Carminus' first sight of the onrushing monster.

THE SEALED GATEWAY behind the altar pulsed, a vein of bloody light mixing with the vertical white line. A few minutes after the pulse, Azkaellon brought word of the *Veritas Ferrum*.

The Lion cursed. He punched the altar in frustration. It cracked along its full length. Beside him, Curze was motionless. He was a statue of night and bone, draped in rags and chains. He had not moved or spoken again since the Lion and Guilliman had questioned him. Frozen in horror, he stared at the portal, his eyes fixed on a point beyond the wall, beyond the present, waiting for the possibility that Sanguinius might triumph. The Lion had never seen the Night Haunter so bereft of certainty. All his mockery and taunting knowledge had drained away. Curze had made himself into a monster, reflecting the abattoir he saw the universe to be, and anchoring himself on the inevitability of fate. Even that pillar was crumbling before him now. The Lion could almost have pitied him. The memory of Curze's victims prevented the Lion from seeing anything other than a first touch of justice descending on the crow.

He would have drawn more satisfaction from Curze's plight if he wasn't trapped in uncertainty himself.

Guilliman grunted.

'Tell me you see our way forwards,' the Lion said. The inaction since Sanguinius vanished stabbed at him. He was stymied. He had been convinced the Angel had been mad to step into the portal. Now he had proof.

'I don't,' Guilliman said. He pointed at the gateway. 'But I wonder if the change we see there coincided with the emergence of the *Veritas*.'

'Damn Sanguinius!' the Lion roared. 'Damn him for the fool he is. I was right to begin with. We should have destroyed this cursed world as soon as we entered the system.'

'I don't think that would have advanced our cause,' Guilliman said. He was studying the gateway as if he could divine answers from the flow of colours in the light. 'I think Davin *was* dead until the portal opened. Now there is something active again.'

'You're suggesting we evacuate and destroy it now? Assume Sanguinius is dead?'

'Do you think he is?'

The Lion shook his head. 'I don't. His passage is too…'

'Inconclusive?' Guilliman suggested.

'Yes. We would know. I cannot believe his death would not even cause a ripple.'

'You are sounding like Sanguinius now, but I agree. For no reason I can call rational, I agree.'

'So we are condemned to wait in this trap,' the Lion said. 'Our forces stranded while our fleets engage.' He approached the portal. He slashed at it with his *Wolf Blade*. The chainsword's teeth scraped against stone, then flashed when they touched the rip in the materium. Energy leapt in an angry arc, then subsided. The vertical line had no width at all.

The Lion eyed the chainsword. Coils of smoke rose from its black length. He had caused a response, no matter how momentary. He exchanged a look with Guilliman. 'We cannot wait any longer,' he said.

Guilliman nodded and flexed the *Hand of Dominion*. 'We have run out of time and options. Forwards then, if we can.'

The Lion called to Holguin and Redloss. When they entered the chamber, he pointed to Curze's chains. 'Take him out of here,' he said. 'Hold him fast. Don't be gentle.'

They dragged Curze out to the hall. He did not resist. He barely seemed to notice them. His gaze never left the portal, and even when they pulled him through the doorway, there was no change to his expression.

The Lion turned back to the portal. He brought up the sword with both hands. It snarled, the silver teeth sparking light. The hexagrammic patterns in its hilt glowed an angry red. He nodded, and together they struck the line of red and white light. They hammered craters into the wall on either side of the portal. Rock splinters flew across the chamber. The portal shrieked at them. The energy unleashed by the weapons clashed with the power of the warp. White and crimson lightning flashed across the chamber in clusters. The Lion looked up the hundred feet of the cylindrical chamber. The tear in the materium vibrated. It thrummed. With anger, he thought. With pain, he chose to believe.

'The gate feels our blows,' he said.

'We will make it bleed yet.'

The Lion and Guilliman struck faster, hammering the portal to fury. There was no pause in the lightning now. Stones fell from the far wall. The energy burst arced up the height of the cylinder. Light the colour of blood and bones spiralled to the ceiling and dropped again in zigzag patterns, blasting the ancient stonework to powder. Fireballs of violet plasma blew straight out of the portal, shattering the altar forever. The monument where Horus had fallen was now a pile of charred rubble.

Dust and shrapnel rained on the Lion's shoulders. A blast of daemonic light hit him in the chest, scarring his armour. It forced him back half a step. Electric pain shot through his torso. He shouted in anger, and lunged forwards with even greater force. The flare when the blade hit the portal was so bright, so wide, this time there was no damage to the wall. The sword seemed to cut into the flesh of the realm beyond.

He thought again of how perfectly he had been manipulated. How close he had come to damning himself as completely as Horus. He had set out to conquer the Ruinstorm. In his hubris, he had almost been swept away by the tempest. Here, now, each blow felt like he was beating down the barrier between himself and redemption.

He barely heard the alarm of the legionaries in the hall. Movement in the corner of his eye made him turn his head for a moment as he brought the sword back again. Azkaellon and Drakus Gorod had pushed their way into the chamber.

'Hold your positions!' Guilliman commanded. 'Stand ready, but leave us.'

'This task is ours,' the Lion said, and he felt the truth of those words with the force of an oath of moment. There was no space for anyone else to enter the fray. There was also a necessity to the act. One brother had entered the portal. Two others must struggle for his salvation. The Lion knew the strengths of myth on Caliban. He valued the light of his father's reason above all superstition, but he understood the power of symbolism, and of the foundational truths that could animate it. The barriers the Legions had fought through on the journey to Davin had been as much symbolic as they had been physical. There was a principle to the warp and its denizens that the Lion could still see only imperfectly, but appeared to be in the order of a reification of the abstract. Ideas became things. Symbols became fortresses. And so he had to fight the daemonic on the very grounds that gave it so much awful power. His attack had to have symbolic strength, too. If anyone other than Guilliman and himself struck the portal now, they would dilute the strength of the moment.

He and Guilliman were hitting the portal with more than their own strength and the power of their weapons. They were turning the force of meaning against it. Meaning had almost destroyed them. They had pulled back from the edge of their ruin. They fought back in the hope of saving Sanguinius from his own fall.

'The enemy wants him,' the Lion said. He hit the portal again, and cut an even deeper wound. Psychic fire burned the length of the sword and up his arms. The pain was ferocious. His fury was greater. He ripped the chainblade savagely from the portal and Guilliman's power gauntlet hit again. The flare became a fountain of violet flame that washed over them. It burned, and it was proof they were striking home. 'This trap was for Sanguinius.'

'We were secondary targets,' Guilliman agreed. 'Why?' And he struck again.

The Lion thought about the height of the fall, greater still than Horus'. He thought about the power of symbols and of meaning. 'Because he is the Angel,' he said.

They struck again, and again. Their attack turned the chamber into a furnace. The walls began to glow. The heat was monstrous. Ethereal flame surrounded the Lion. It wreathed his armour. It seared his flesh and it cut like knives. Blood coursed down his face. Guilliman was as badly off. His lips were pulled back in a determined, wrathful grin. The Lion saw his emotions reflected in his brother's face. Each blow was retaliation for the way they had been manoeuvred. The raging bursts from the portal were the wounds of the enemy. They were finally making it pay. The action was so small compared to the destruction of the fortress gate of Pyrrhan, yet it felt more real. On Pyrrhan and in the Episimos System, their actions had been planned by the enemy. Sanguinius' triumph in the manufactorum was a lie. Now they could see the trap. Now they were fighting back in earnest. Now the battle was finally joined.

The Lion cut through the portal from left to right, its light bleeding over the blade's hilt. The scream from the portal was sound as well as light. The wall behind tore like flesh. The flash from the other side bathed the entire chamber in a sheet of coruscating red and searing white. Guilliman was a barely discernible outline beside the Lion. He slammed the *Hand of Dominion* into the explosion.

The second blast was larger yet. Violet flames roiled within. It hit the Lion and Guilliman with the force of a hurricane. The portal howled. It roared. It was a dragon of myth, breathing fire against its tormentors. They leaned into the fury, and the Lion saw the portal open once more. It was the jaws of a wounded beast. The light of uncreation and madness shrieked in torrents through the chamber. The far wall cracked. Its stones turned molten. The Lion's skin blistered in the volcanic heat.

The portal tore wide open. The jaws of the monster opened as if to swallow the materium. Then there were shadows in the light. There was heaving, scrambling, leaping movement. Unclean shapes charged down a tunnel of nothingness towards the chamber. They were moments from taking on form. The Lion braced himself for their arrival, the sword crackling with power eager to burn the daemonic to ash. Guilliman raised the *Arbitrator*.

Another shadow appeared behind the others. It was much larger, a mountainous shape that strode over the smaller beings. It was powerful, gathering material form to itself faster than its kin. It appeared to rush forwards suddenly, and its bellow of rage preceded it out of the portal. The silhouette became defined. The Lion saw six massive legs, arachnid in shape yet machinic in their angularity, supporting a massive torso. It swept a forelimb ahead, and the claw smashed clear of the portal. Muscle and metal were fused in the shape of a vice larger than a man. It caught the Lion full in the chest. It knocked him across the room, then slammed into Guilliman's flank, hurling him into the flowing stone of the left-hand wall.

The towering daemon forced its way through the portal, its sheer size smashing the walls of the chamber. Its horned head looked down on the primarchs twenty feet below. Its gnarled, muscled flesh was the crimson of rage. Its other arm held a sword twice the height of a man. One of its legs came down on the remains of the altar and smashed them to fragments. Roaring its challenge, the daemon charged the primarchs.

SANGUINIUS WAS IN a cavernous hall. There were mountains ahead of him. Their flanks rippled, worms under flesh. Eyes opened and closed down their length. Maws gibbered at their base. Tongues thirty feet long licked up at the eyes. The mountains heaved. They were living things, yet there was metal in them too. They were engines, larger than a capital ship. The hall was a nightmarishly huge enginarium.

The waves of the warp maelstrom withdrew. Sanguinius was in the materium again, inside a reality that was losing the war for its sanity. He and Madail were in the middle of a miles-wide deck. Its stones were smouldering skulls. It was surrounded by scores of levels of galleries, rising a thousand feet high and more. Their railings were brass, encrusted with red and black growths, tumours of metal. Banners of sanded skin hung from the railings. Each bore a single rune daubed in dried blood. Four different symbols repeated hundreds of times around the enginarium: a twisted, waving tear; a triangular assemblage of arrows and circles, like the face of an insect; a diagonal intersection of lines like a closed fist; a pendulum embraced by a scything curve. The banners were flags of allegiance, acts of fealty to murderous gods. There was a fifth rune. It dominated all the others. It was carved into the deck, taking up its entire width. It formed the dome of the enginarium. It was an eight-pointed star. The spears of its arms extended from a spiked circle. Its radiant lines came to embrace the eye and gather the universe within its shredding embrace.

Far to Sanguinius' right, to port, near a wall so distant it should not have been part of a single vessel, a line of white and red light rose from deck to dome.

Hordes of daemons crowded the galleries, chanting, jabbering, snarling. Thousands more had gathered on the deck. An army surrounded Sanguinius. Monsters lithe and corpulent, armoured in brass and rotting with disease raised a chorus of damnation as Madail pressed its advantage, its huge staff forcing the *Blade Encarmine* back.

There was a rush of movement behind Sanguinius, the slithering of reptiles over stone. Clawed hands and talons seized his arms and legs and wings. The sheer mass of daemons toppled him onto his back. He fell against a struggling mass. The abominations pulled him up a slope of their own bodies until his boots were off the deck. A four-legged behemoth whose hide was brass armour pressed a paw onto his chest. It snarled, and the breath of a blast furnace washed over Sanguinius. It lowered its head. Dual horns in the shape of axe blades scraped against his gorget. A female creature stabbed one of its pincers into the side of his neck. The daemon smiled. It whispered to him. He did not understand the words. They felt like barbed wire slicing through the inside of his skull. And they sounded like a welcome.

Immobilised, Sanguinius held fast to the *Blade Encarmine* and the *Spear of Telesto*. The weapons felt as if they were stuck in a quagmire of scaled and pustulent bodies. He had no leverage. He could move his head, and that was all. But he held the weapons. He was not disarmed. He strained against the grip of the abominations, testing their strength, searching for the weakness.

When the daemons pulled the *Blade Encarmine* beneath their mass, Madail straightened. It planted the end of its staff on the deck and stood over Sanguinius, a monster of sickening majesty. The blank eyes of its skull glowed incandescent orange. The eyes of its chest looked down at

Sanguinius, contemplating. He saw now that some of them bore scars, and a few sockets were empty. The daemon had been wounded. The sight gave Sanguinius strength. *I will make you bleed anew*, he thought.

'*You shall serve,*' the daemon told him again. '*Serve by reigning. Serve as power.*' Madail lifted its arms in praise. The monstrous assembly wailed, shaking the hall. '*You have seen the wonders. You have seen the works of faith. The works of my faith. I travel in glory, and glory blossoms where I pass.*' Its voice rumbled, the depth of mountain roots grinding over skulls. And its voice was high too, soaring to the heights of madness, scraping thought with claws of pain. This was a being very different from Kyriss and Ka'bandha. It preached. When it turned its body and gazed upon its flock, it looked upon all the daemons in the same fashion. And all the factions of daemons looked to Madail with the same ecstasy. There was unity in this hall. There was nothing like the fault lines that had split the daemonic efforts on Signus Prime. The huge daemon was wreathed in a monstrous charisma. It spoke, and its words mattered. Reality itself was compelled to listen. '*By wrath and change, by vice and plague, I am the bringer of truth and the proof of belief,*' Madail said. The daemon leaned in, and though its words thundered through the deck, it seemed to be speaking for Sanguinius' ears alone. '*I mark the path and forge the way. By eight, to four, I bring the Angel. I am the unity of Chaos. I serve Tzeentch and Khorne and Slaanesh and Nurgle. I am the conduit of a single purpose. I am the prophet, and you are the fulfilment of the will of the gods.*'

Sanguinius spat. Acid dripped down Madail's chest and into an eye. The orb shut against the burn. There was no other reaction. 'I am not what you will have me be,' Sanguinius declared. 'I am he who will destroy you.'

Madail hissed its amusement. Its left hand made a pass over Sanguinius, the talons crooked in blessing. '*You would choose death? You would embrace the emptiness of defeat, and fall at your brother's feet? This is the choice. This is the choice.*'

'I will fight Horus with my own strength. I will not choose the lie you have shown me. I would give my life for my father a thousand times.'

'*To what end? To no end.*' The daemon rocked its head back and forth, mocking him in sing-song rhythms. '*To what end? To no end.*' It stopped. '*You shall serve. You will see the glories, and you shall serve. It is written.*'

'I have been tempted before,' Sanguinius snarled. 'I did not fall then. I will not fall now.' He tried to lift his sword. It would not move. The female daemon tapped his neck, warning him to cease, inviting him to try again.

'*Tempted,*' said Madail. '*Tempted by the divided. You shall be, as I, the undivided. Before was not for you. Now is for you. Now is destiny. Now is the truth of fate. Become what your form decrees. You are the Angel of Ruin.*'

'I will not.'

'*No? You will embrace futility? You choose death? To what end? To no end. No, you will not die.*'

'I will,' Sanguinius declared. 'I will die before I betray the Emperor. I will die before I bend the knee to foulness.'

'*Bend the knee. Bend the knee.*' The daemon's eyes blinked at his foolishness. '*You do not comprehend. You do not see the path. I will show you. I will teach. You will follow.*' Madail turned around, embracing the colossal space of the enginarium. '*Veritas Ferrum,*' it said. It stretched the syllables out, the inhuman voice mocking the mortal language and savouring the irony of a name made into a greater, more appalling truth than its makers could have guessed. '*Behold the transcendence. Ship of glory, ship of legend. What was it before? A thing among many. What is it now? Shaper of worlds, breaker of real, destroyer and sovereign. Kill Horus, the imperfect vessel. Become perfection. Chosen of all, beholden to none.*'

Madail raised its staff. The blades glowed blindingly. The daemon pointed them at Sanguinius, and the light shot into his eyes. Visions assailed him, and he knew they were visions. He was living the reality of the future. He was seeing the promises of the daemon. At first, the visions were vague. He felt triumph. He was surrounded by a golden haze, and the sound of fanfares. Then there were figures in the haze. They were kneeling. Gradually, they resolved themselves into Lorgar and Perturabo. The vision became defined. It was the surrender at the Imperial Palace again. Sanguinius pushed away from the vision. He struggled to tear himself free. The daemons held him down, but the vision obeyed his command. It disintegrated. Other images took its place. He sat upon a high throne, receiving the tributes of a million worlds. He marched across fields of battle, and his enemies fell at his mere gesture. He reached out, and armies burst into flame. On another world, he lifted a hand and he summoned towers of silver into being.

He encompassed the galaxy with his wings, for he was a god.

No, no, no, no. This is not my fate.

He struggled harder. His anger grew with the succeeding visions. They came faster and faster, probing his reactions, seeking the future that would be the key to his acquiescence. There would be none. The effort was futile.

But when I thought my father stood before me…

When I thought He made me regent…

When I thought I would save the Imperium…

He had almost submitted then. If he had continued to believe, he would have made the choice the daemon wanted.

The visions became more intimate. He saw his loyal brothers, alive. He saw the Emperor, alive. He saw his sons, shining and perfect. Flawless.

In the distance, there was a sudden boom, as of a knocking at an iron door. The visions trembled. The images became jagged. The booming repeated. It did not relent. It was so insistent, so real, it cracked the visions. Their lies were obvious, and he rejected them.

He was on the monstrous ship again, and Madail stood above him. The daemon leaned down. Its jaws were wide, its tongue snaking out to capture the remains of the vanished dreams. **'Will you die, then? Will you die?'**

'I will.' To live, he would have to become a greater monster than Horus. To save the Imperium, he must die.

The booming was louder. It drew Sanguinius' attention away from the daemon. He twisted his head to the right. The vertical line of the portal was deforming. It shuddered to the rhythm of the thunder. Multicoloured lightning circled it and struck across the gulf of the enginarium. The daemons nearest the portal snarled in alarm.

Madail ignored the sounds of a battering ram smashing at fortress gates.

'You will let Horus triumph.'

'I will not.' Sanguinius cursed his uncertainty. He could not see behind his fall. His sacrifice might be in vain. His death might be empty of meaning. Horus might triumph. The daemon's long manipulation had weakened Sanguinius' confidence in everything he had held as true.

Madail leaned closer. The armour-plated monster moved out of its way. *'Will you die? Will you die? Will you die?'* The daemon repeated the question over and over, as if to a child.

'I will!' Sanguinius shouted back.

'Do you understand?' It straightened again. It called to the congregation of abominations, its tremendous voice drowning out the intensifying blasts of the portal. *'Praise to the carnage, praise to the change, praise to gifts of the flesh and the plague!'* The choir shrieked in ecstasy. *'Feed on the blindness, you children of Ruin. Lap the blood of the unknowing dream. By eight and by four, he chooses his fate. By eight and by four, he will have the consequence.'* Madail paused. It looked down at Sanguinius again. *'Take the consequence, or take the lesson.'*

What consequence? That was the question the daemon wanted him to ask. He burned to ask it. But the hammering from the other side of the warp distracted him. It took him out of the web the daemon's words wove around his consciousness. Consequence? No consequence could be so momentous that he would swear fealty to Chaos. It was all lies.

Sanguinius heaved against the arms holding him down. He heard the crack of breaking bones as he snapped the fingers of the daemons holding him. Madail turned with a snarl to face the portal. It gestured with its staff. The legions of abominations on the deck turned from

Sanguinius and approached the portal. Madail made another gesture, as if parting the veil of the real. The portal opened wide. The daemons poured into its maw. A huge abomination, a construct of flesh and machine, commanded the charge. The daemons leapt from the galleries in an avalanche of monstrosity. An army vanished from the ship, leaving an army behind. As many stayed to worship and to witness Sanguinius' surrender.

His frame vibrated with anger. The fury was an alloy. It was forged from so many causes, so many crimes of the daemon, so many mistakes Sanguinius had made to bring himself to this pass. There was a darkness too, the darkness he had encountered before. He was wary of it. It had consumed him briefly on the *Red Tear* when the *Veritas Ferrum* had struck him. He had no memory of those moments, only impressions of dark and fury. It had made him dangerous to his sons. It had made him a beast. But at this moment, he did not fight it. The dark scraped at the edges of his being, still amorphous, a thing unclear. It could not distract him. His focus was Madail. His fury was concentrated on that single foe. It had annihilated billions. It was the author of his and his brothers' doubts. It had given him false belief, and treacherous hope.

The roar built in his chest, then escaped, so loud it seemed it would bring down the great dome of the enginarium.

The *Spear of Telesto* flashed with power. Its crimson light enveloped Sanguinius, igniting the flesh of the daemons. Their limbs turned to ash, and their forms melted. The horned juggernaut howled. It stumbled backwards, its head engulfed with flame. The female abomination's claws shattered.

The Angel tore his right arm free. He raised the *Blade Encarmine*. He sliced through the bodies of plague daemons. The monsters fell apart, halved, and the sword shone brightly in the foul air of the enginarium, ichor dripping from its length.

The Angel rose in his terrible wrath. He spread his wings, hurling the monsters back. The blast of the spear haloed him, and they could not touch him.

Temptation could not touch him, for there was no glory he desired. He fought for Terra and for Baal. He fought for the Emperor and the Imperium.

Death could not touch him, for he was the lord of the Blood Angels, and in this heart of the enemy's domain, it was he who had come as death.

The Angel launched himself into the air. With sword and spear, he fell on Madail. The daemon snarled and raised its bladed staff to counter.

The weapons clashed with the flash of suns.

SEVENTEEN

The Reaping

THE STHENELUS CAME in from below towards the *Veritas Ferrum*. Helmsman Kiriktas guided the frigate towards the belly of the monster. On Khalybus' orders, he had taken the *Sthenelus* far beneath the plane of the ecliptic even as he had begun to turn the ship for the attack run. The *Sthenelus* rose now in a steep diagonal with respect to the *Veritas*. A cloud of daemonic ships was approaching, some of them in line with the *Sthenelus*. Beyond them was another cloud, the billowing thunderhead of the contracting necrosphere.

The *Veritas'* escort was almost in range. 'We have time for one attack before we are destroyed,' Khalybus said. 'Let it be our most ferocious. For Ferrus Manus and the Tenth Legion, for Durun Atticus and One Hundred and Eleventh Clan-Company, we will strike against the corruption of the machine.' He paused, watching the *Veritas Ferrum* grow larger in the oculus. Already it was so huge, the bottom of the hull covered the stars. The *Sthenelus* was rushing towards a ceiling in the void. The ceiling had eyes and mouths. It slavered with hunger.

At least it had no guns.

'Helmsman,' Khalybus said. 'We fire, and then we withdraw.' The command left a foul taste in his mouth. It was contrary to the design and the spirit of the *Sthenelus*; it was not made for a darting attack. He had no choice. The scale of war had changed. In head-on confrontation with the colossus the *Veritas Ferrum* had become, the *Sthenelus* would not last long.

The machine is adaptable, Khalybus thought. *The tool is shaped for the task, or else it fails.* He had adapted since Isstvan V. He had sacrificed his strike cruiser *Bane of Asirnoth* in a run that had only appeared to be a retreat, but had been a trap to destroy an entire fleet of the Emperor's Children. This time, the flight would be genuine.

One strike. *I will gut you if I can*, he thought.

The *Sthenelus* rose higher. The *Veritas Ferrum* filled the oculus. The auspex screens in the strategium flashed red as the first of the escorts came in range.

'Fire,' Khalybus said. *Fire everything*, he thought. *And burn, you foul thing. Burn, for defiling your name and the memory of the heroes you have betrayed.*

All banks of torpedoes launched. Every battery of cannons opened up. The entire forwards armament of the *Sthenelus* fired. A swarm of projectiles streaked towards the behemoth. The plasma batteries discharged moments later, their fury timed so their blasts would hit the *Veritas* at the same time as the ordnance. Khalybus counted the seconds of the barrage. The moment of the first pause came. He shouted, 'Hard to port and down!'

'Port and down,' Kiriktas confirmed.

The view in the oculus changed slowly. The shells and torpedoes and focused plasma blasts hit the *Veritas Ferrum* before the turn was well underway. The explosions flared in the upper left of the oculus. The flash overwhelmed the view. For several beautiful seconds, the daemon ship vanished, hidden by the incandescence of the barrage. Khalybus watched, willing the attack to have opened a gaping wound in the enemy's hull.

The flames boiled away. A giant eye in the hull was punctured. It oozed a sea of ichor over the hull, spreading armour. The surface of the *Veritas* swirled at the impact sites. Storms formed in the daemonic substance of the ship, then passed. There was no breach. There was no damage.

Khalybus witnessed his opening salvo in the void war turn into an empty gesture.

The *Sthenelus* turned from the site of futility. It angled down and away from the *Veritas*. It was prey now, and it began the race away from the predators.

'Captain,' said Seterikus, 'auspex readings of the *Veritas* are changing. There's a deformation in the lower hull.'

Khalybus turned to the pict screens in the strategium. The rear sensors assembled a hololithic rendering of the enemy. Below the snarling bow, a new spike protruded.

Levannas said, 'It's growing a gun.'

'Hard to starboard,' Khalybus ordered. 'All power to the engines. Kiriktas, get us out of its line of fire.'

The deck vibrated with the sudden strain on the engines. Kiriktas, silent now with his entire consciousness melded to the machine-spirit of the *Sthenelus*, pushed the ship to its limit. The hull groaned with the turn. The manoeuvre threatened to break the frigate's spine. Klaxons sounded as stress damage spread the length of the ship.

Khalybus exchanged a look with Levannas. The Raven Guard nodded. They braced for the inevitable.

The run had been a long one since Isstvan V. *The fight has been a worthy one*, Khalybus thought.

The *Veritas Ferrum* fired. Lightning blacker than the void flashed from the spike and struck the stern of the *Sthenelus*. It cut the ship open. Warp flame erupted, a firestorm of night and green enveloping every deck of the rear third of the hull. The spine snapped. The frigate broke in two. A greater blast came. The material and the immaterial destroyed each other, and the explosion hurled the two portions of the ship away from one another. The blackened shell of the rear tumbled down, guttering and disintegrating, into the dark below the plane of the engagement. The blast sent the forwards section into a spin. Uncontrolled, helpless, the *Sthenelus* turned and turned, drifting, as the giant predator closed in.

The jaws of the *Veritas Ferrum* gaped wide.

Khalybus and Cruax yanked Kiriktas from the throne. The helmsman's limbs spasmed. Neural feedback from the mortally wounded machine-spirit shook through his body. They pulled the mechadendrites from his spine. They made for the stairs to the main deck of the bridge, supporting him between them until he could walk again. Levannas was one step behind.

There was light on the bridge from the pict screens and emergency lumen strips. Some secondary generators were running yet. In its dying moments, the *Sthenelus* fought to remain on duty. Smoke poured into the bridge through the main doors. The wavering glow of flames came from the main hall.

'Abandon ship,' Khalybus ordered. His battle-brothers were already on the move. 'We make for the gunships.'

'We fight still,' Cruax growled.

Or so we will tell ourselves, Khalybus thought. 'Yes,' he said. 'We fight still.'

Levannas echoed him, and so did the legionaries of the 85th Clan-Company as they abandoned the bridge.

WHEN THREE THUNDERHAWKS left the only functioning launch bay, Khalybus muttered the words to himself again. He looked through the viewing block of the *Karaashi's Fire* at the end of the *Sthenelus*, and the defiance felt hollow. The frigate turned and turned, a broken femur, as the *Veritas Ferrum* bore down on it. Ignited gases flickered at the edges of the stump of the hull. Minute flashes were larger chunks of wreckage. The bodies of lost legionaries and hundreds of serfs were falling through the void too. They were invisible. The Thunderhawks were specks in the void, beneath the notice of the daemon ship.

Khalybus waited for the jaws of the monster to crush the remains of the ship. The *Veritas Ferrum* snarled, closing in. Then it clamped its jaws above the frigate. It passed over the *Sthenelus*. The last of the frigate's lights went out.

The immensity of the *Veritas* was above the Thunderhawks now. Mile after mile of horror sped on, seeking the larger prey of the fleets. It glowed with a putrescent light. The blackness of its hull was broken by the red shine of the eyes and maws. The barrels of the huge cannons were bright with infernal fire. It moved through the system like a diseased sun, bringing its own light. It was the bearer of terrible revelation.

Khalybus looked up at the Pilgrim, and understood the superstitious awe it had created on the worlds it had visited and transformed.

A large mass rose through the dark to meet the ruin of the *Sthenelus*. Strapped into the grav-harness next to Khalybus, Cruax uttered a guttural cry when he saw what was happening. Khalybus felt the cold touch of anticipated horror. He was not surprised by what he saw. Now that it was happening, it seemed inevitable.

The mass was the stern of the *Sthenelus*. It matched the spin of the forwards half of the ship. Metallic tendrils reached across the space between the two portions of frigate. They met, fused, multiplied. The *Sthenelus* reformed itself. With unity came corruption. The hull bubbled. Its plating squirmed. Foul light blazed from the superstructure, silhouetting the transformations of the statuary into grotesquery. Eyes opened on the flanks. The frigate became a pitted, gnawed-bone reflection of the *Veritas Ferrum*. Dwarfed by the bleak majesty of the great monster, the *Sthenelus* was a ghoul, a thing to feast on the leavings of its master. The engines flared to life, slowing the spin, then stopping it.

The *Sthenelus* moved forwards again. It bore down on the escaping Thunderhawks.

The port cannons fired. Green energy flashed. It vaporised the *Forge of Will*.

There was no point in flight now.

'Kiriktas,' Khalybus voxed. The helmsman was piloting the *Karaashi's Fire*.

'Captain.'

'Turn us around. Open fire on the *Sthenelus.'*

'So ordered, captain. It has been an honour.'

'The honour has been mine.'

The two remaining Thunderhawks reversed course. Guns blazing, they hurled themselves at the revenant *Sthenelus*.

'We fight still,' Cruax said.

'We do,' Khalybus said. 'To the end.' He detached his grav-harness and stood. So did the other legionaries. They would meet the end on their feet.

At his side, Levannas said, 'We have made a good war.'

'We have,' Khalybus said. The end had not come at Isstvan V. They had fought long. They had bled the enemy. They had taught the traitors that the Iron Hands and the Raven Guard were not extinct.

Levannas extended his hand. 'The flesh is weak,' he said. He and Khalybus clasped forearms.

'Victorus aut mortis,' said Khalybus.

Levannas' smile was grim. 'That is certain,' he said.

Khalybus raised his bolter. When the end came, he would fire.

He did not wait long. The forwards section of the Thunderhawk peeled back for him. He had time to pull the trigger before the flames of night engulfed him.

THE FLEETS OF the three Legions fired first. The capital ships trained their biggest guns on the *Veritas Ferrum*. A third of the other vessels did as well. The rest of the fleet hammered the resurrected ship's escort. The barrage was simultaneous, coordinated between the flagships. The daemonic fleet sailed directly into explosive hell. The salvo vaporised four of the *Veritas'* cloud of escorts in an instant. The ghoul ships returned to oblivion, skeletons shattered into fragments. A curtain of blasts spread out behind the enemy fleet as lance fire reaching past the ships smashed approaching fragments of the necrosphere.

On the bridge of the *Samothrace*, Shipmaster Altuzer said, 'They can be destroyed.' Carminus shouted the same words on the *Red Tear*. Across the fleets, in hundreds of ships, a roar of defiance met the success of the bombardment. The great barrage at the gate over Pyrrhan had led to nothing, but here, enemy vessels vanished. Others limped on, broken, on the edge of falling back into the tomb that had spat them out.

The triumphant refrain lasted as long as the *Veritas Ferrum* was obscured by the star-death brilliance of scores of plasma blasts and multiple nova cannon hits. An angry dawn bathed the void. Then the abomination emerged from the fire. Streams of flame ran along its length and wreathed the huge, moving gargoyles. The silhouettes jerked in anger. The skull of the prow gaped wide, its roar raging across the psychic aether and resounding in the minds of every soul in the Imperium's ships. There were craters on the hull. Portions of superstructure slumped like candle wax.

But the craters vanished, filled in by the flowing excrescences of disease. New pillars of brass and bone shot up around the superstructure, reinforcing it, rebuilding the massive fortress of clustered, jagged towers. It weathered the barrage and drove on towards the fleet, its speed undiminished, its hunger growing with its wrath.

The daemon fleet returned fire. A storm of warp energy scythed through the Legions. The barrage took the form of entwined lightning and flame. The void tore open at the passage of the blasts, filling the space between the closing formations with clouds of blood. The storm hammered void shields and triggered emergency activations of Geller fields. Where the defences fell, metal burst into unnatural fire and hulls warped into carnivorous life. The huge jaws of the *Veritas Ferrum* vomited black flame against the *Samothrace*. The Ultramarines battleship ploughed into a burning maelstrom that swept over the entire hull. The void shields shrieked with strain, flaring like suns. A chain-reaction collapse began as the *Samothrace* came out of the fire. Its prow turned up gradually, and the ship, trailing smoke and burning gas, began to rise above the direct line of fire of the skull.

The flagships took the brunt of the first daemonic salvo. There were losses in the fleets, mostly frigates, a first culling of the smaller ships. But the numbers of the Legions were vast. The ships of the Imperium outnumbered the daemonic several times over. The formations were undiminished. They tightened up as the moment of collision approached. Unscathed vessels drew up beside the damaged ones, ready to draw fire and support their comrades.

The *Veritas Ferrum* appeared to lunge forwards. It came at the Legions with the speed of nightmare. Its path was a straight line, as if the ship was too massive to manoeuvre, or too powerful to divert. It battered through the lance beams and cannon fire. Wounds opened and closed on its hull. The mouths on its flanks chanted a psychic chorus that came ahead of the ship like a bow wave. The choir shouted in triumphant wrath as the *Veritas* plunged into the heart of the Ultramarines wedge, its guns firing to port and starboard.

The *Samothrace*, already rising, narrowly avoided a collision. The behemoth passed just below its stern. The barrage of warp fire had the effect of a supernova in the heart of the fleets. Multiple beams burned through the *Glory of Fire* and the *Legendary Son*. The ships seemed to freeze in their forwards motion, transfixed by a hundred spears of night. Their atmospheres vented in moments, gales blowing out of multiple killing breaches in their hulls. The *Glory of Fire*'s engines went critical. The shockwave from the plasma detonation crashed against the void shields of a dozen ships, breaking open their defences, leaving them vulnerable to a new deluge of enemy fire. The *Glory of Fire* vanished in its self-immolation. The *Legendary Son* went dark. Tears half a mile long raked its hull. Its engines were silent. Its decks had collapsed and fused with one another. Tens of thousands of crew were crushed to a thin slick of pulp in fused ruin.

The *Veritas Ferrum* was a bludgeon, breaking open the wedge, forcing the vessels into evasive action, the impact rippling out over the entire span of the fleets. As the shockwave from the *Glory of Fire* had expended its fury, corrupted light ran down the length of the *Legendary Son*. Its hull grew spines, and it accelerated again, turning its guns on the *Unbroken Vigil*. The other ships hit by the daemonic barrage also transformed into corrupted wraiths. They attacked, burning the vessels that had come to their aid. The formations of the Ultramarines collapsed. Disorder grew exponentially. Ships that had not yet died succumbed to the infections of their festering wounds. Machine-spirits screamed in madness. They fell into oblivion, but the madness lived on, and summoned them forth again, transformed into monsters. Metastasising cancer reached more deeply and widely through the ships of the XIII Legion. The attack that had begun from the front was now coming from every direction.

The charge of the *Veritas Ferrum* disrupted the forwards movement of the Imperial fleets. The daemonic ships multiplied. Immediate, proximate fire forced the Legion ships to turn away from the advance and bring their weapons to bear on the revenant vessels. The wedge formation turned into a melee.

The *Veritas Ferrum* moved deeper into the formations, spreading ruin with its monstrous broadsides. Its escorts followed closely. With the Ultramarines stalled, the Dark Angels and the Blood Angels used the forwards momentum they still had to bring the angles of their attacks inwards. Their crossfire decimated the rearmost ships of the daemonic fleet. Behind the enemy came the great swarm of bones. The shell had fractured into clusters ranging in size from a single grave to planetoids. The arriving storm drew the focus of the I and IX Legions. The shell disintegrated under fire, but the storm was infinite. For hundreds of thousands of miles, the void was grey with rushing death. More than half the ships had to use their guns to keep the battlefield clear. And still some of the larger chunks came through. Meteors of bone slammed into flanks and superstructures. The skull with the spiked crown, larger than a hive city, smashed into the bridge of the Blood Angels *Nine Crusaders*. The collision destroyed the skull and decapitated the ship. It surged on through the void, rudderless, its officers dead. It disappeared into the grey tempest, battered into darkness, at last dying in fiery paroxysm.

The *Samothrace* climbed above the *Veritas Ferrum*, then came about. Altuzer expected the *Veritas* to have put real distance between them by the time the *Samothrace* had finished its turn, but the daemon ship had slowed. It was where it sought to be, in the midst of its prey. Everything was lesser before it, and everything died, only to rise again as a hideous disciple, spreading its message of devastation.

'All ships,' Altuzer voxed across the fleets. 'If you are crippled, enact self-immolation.' The *Glory of Fire* had not risen from oblivion. Its destruction had been complete. 'Take the enemy down with you.'

The *Veritas Ferrum* was in close range. It was under fire from every ship not already engaged. The efforts were futile. The salvoes were small, and impacts healed as fast as they formed. If the initial strikes had had so little effect, it would take something catastrophic to break the spine of the beast.

The desperate idea came to her in the moment huge batteries on the stern of the *Veritas* turned and fired at the *Samothrace*. There was no question of evasion. She winced at the light from the void shield flares. They deflected the worst of the initial damage. Then the black, burning lightning seared its way through and struck the *Samothrace* amidships. The armour of the upper hull erupted. Ruptured plasma conduits launched geysers of flame into the void. Altuzer felt the depth of the wound without a damage report. The deck shook as if the battleship were staggering, a giant of legend struck and bleeding from the abdomen. She knew the controls were sluggish. She knew they were losing velocity. The rhythm of the engines changed.

Ahead, the *Veritas Ferrum* began to come about. It was slow, a world changing orbit. As it gradually turned to port, the jaws of the bow were half-closed. The skull appeared to be grinning. Soon the *Veritas* would be broadside to the *Samothrace*, half its batteries trained on the Ultramarines flagship. And it was still moving forwards. When the *Veritas* fired, the ships would be at point-blank range.

'Launch cyclonic torpedoes,' Altuzer said.

'Shipmaster,' Lautenix began, 'this close in...'

'We will achieve at least one of two ends,' Altuzer finished. 'Single-stage torpedo. Give me detonation on impact.'

The *Samothrace* launched its planet killer. Altuzer and her officers stood to attention to witness the end of their tragedy. The torpedo hit. The entire length of the *Veritas Ferrum* convulsed as if it had turned liquid. A maelstrom took hold of the ship's hull.

Then came the great fire.

GUILLIMAN AND THE Lion dived through the doorway ahead of the collapsing walls, then turned to meet the immense daemon's attack. The monster's charge threw rubble across the hall. The altar room was gone. The portal covered the north wall, the materium screaming at its edges. The portal unleashed a flood of daemons into the temple. They swarmed before the giant and around its feet. It crushed the slew beneath the slow, grinding iron of its legs.

Dark Angels, Ultramarines and Blood Angels met the daemons with a battle cry of vengeance. The hall boomed with bolter thunder and the purifying blaze of power swords. The fury of the legionaries broke the daemonic tide, and the space beneath the dome became a maelstrom of slaughter.

'Loyal sons of the Emperor,' Guilliman called, 'now we shall make the enemy fall!'

The primarchs ran at the great monster as it reached for them. It smashed its colossal sword at Guilliman. He rushed under the swing. The sword buried half its length in the flagstones. They melted into gibbering flesh. Warp flames rushed outwards from the gap. Guilliman fired upwards with the *Arbitrator* into the daemon's wrist. He struck the limb with the *Hand of Dominion* at the same time. Muscle and bone parted. Ichor gushed into Guilliman's face, bubbling his skin with acid. Severed from its master, the sword exploded with a wave of uncontrolled energy.

The daemon screamed and struck at Guilliman with its immense claw. Guilliman threw himself to the side, but the edge of the limb clipped his shoulder, smashing him down. His fall drove a groove into the floor. He rolled to his left just as the huge arm came at him again, pulverising stone, shaking the walls of the Delphos.

As Guilliman regained his feet, the Lion leapt onto the back of the beast. Shrieking in rage, it whirled its giant mass, trying to shake the primarch off. It horns slanted backwards over its head, and the Lion had seized one of them. His cloak billowed behind him as he clung on with his left hand. His right raised the *Wolf Blade*. 'I hunted greater beasts than you on Caliban,' he shouted, 'and I slew them all!' He sawed into the rear of the daemon's neck. It reared up, scuttling backwards on four of its legs. It slammed into the temple wall, crushing the Lion between its bulk and the masonry. The *Wolf Blade* kept snarling. Gouts of ichor and shredded flesh splashed up on the stone.

The daemon looked straight up. Serpent and lightning, its tongue whipped out of its mouth. The hall strobed with violet and green light as the tongue lashed behind the daemon's head. The wall burst into flame. It limned the silhouette of the Lion as he drove the *Wolf Blade* deeper into the daemon's neck.

Guilliman pounded over the floor after the great daemon. Whirlwinds of fire and flesh tried to stop him. He held the trigger down on the *Arbitrator*. The stream of explosive shells shattered their forms, clearing his way.

Above him, two of the creature's massive, piston-driven legs flailed in the air. They clashed together, and when they did, lightning flared again.

The movement of the legs, the timing of the collisions, the height of the daemon and the arc of a jump were the givens of an equation. Guilliman saw the vectors of force and momentum. At the moment of his leap, the equation was resolved.

As his legs bent, he maglocked the *Arbitrator* to his side. He jumped, and reached up with his now free right hand. He grabbed the end of a leg as it rushed inwards, and used its momentum to launch himself at the daemon's chest. With all the force of his flight, he drove the *Hand of Dominion* into the monster's thorax. The power gauntlet annihilated daemonic matter. The huge body collapsed below the neck. The monster's roar was cut off. It slashed out one more time, then disintegrated. The body tried to heave back, but the *Wolf Blade*'s growl rose in a rattling crescendo, and the sword ripped all the way through and came out the throat.

The daemon slumped down. Its fall crushed a score of lesser abominations that had rushed forwards, shrieking, as their leader was destroyed.

Guilliman and the Lion jumped down from the body. Foul smoke lifted from it, hacking at the throat with razored claws. The metal and the flesh began to lose substance. The primarchs waded into a streaming rush of daemons. The portal disgorged them without cease.

'There are too many to stop,' Gorod voxed.

The abominations were a tide flowing past the blocks of Legiones Astartes and out of the hall.

Guilliman blasted the head off a four-legged fiend with a scorpion's tail. 'Are you in contact with our forces outside the temple?' he asked.

'Not since the portal opened.'

So be it. He trusted the Chapter Masters of all the Legions to do what had to be done. And stopping the incursion was a distraction, not the goal. The three Legions were not here to reclaim Davin.

'We fight to hold our position,' he said, answering Gorod but voxing on an open battle channel. 'We stay in this hall. There is no retreat.' Two crimson daemons, wielding swords, attacked him with simultaneous swings. They were far too slow. The *Hand of Dominion* crushed the skull of one abomination, the *Arbitrator* cut the other in half.

A monstrous wave of force blasted from the portal, disintegrating the daemons on the threshold. The floor of the temple heaved upwards, splitting into uneven plates of stone. The dome cracked open and rained masonry. The walls swayed, buckled and leaned in towards each other.

The tremors rolled on. The Delphos groaned. From inside the gateway, Sanguinius roared.

To a man, the Sanguinary Guard turned at his voice, plunging into the abominations with renewed fury.

'Now the battle is truly joined!' the Lion called.

Side by side, Guilliman and the Lion fought their way through the tide of daemons towards the portal, marching steadily over the pitching and rising floor. The portal flashed and raged. The temple rocked back and forth, buffeted by the clashing, unseen waves of a struggle beyond Guilliman's reach.

THE FLAME BURST swallowed Sanguinius and Madail. The conflagration ate at the Angel, turning his matter into energy. Lightning flashed outwards from the tips of his wings. The daemon snarled in anger, its many eyes narrowing. It slashed to the side, twisting the *Blade Encarmine* in Sanguinius' grip and throwing him to his left. He made the flight his, catching the momentum with a beat of his wings. He rose into the air of the enginarium. The abominations below raged at him. Clawed hands reached for him from the galleries. Winged monsters circled the dome, their mindless screams piercing through the clamour, but they did not descend to meet him. The gathered army of abominations was not intervening. His struggle with Madail had an audience, and, for the moment, nothing more.

Madail looked up at him. *'You do not die here,'* it said, confirming fate. Its voice was tremendous, drowning out the thousands of horrors bearing witness. *'Death is later, forged in futility. Here destiny is remade. Here you will serve!'*

Flames coursed through Sanguinius' blood. The mercy that tempered his spirit had fled. It was not wanted here. He dived towards Madail, and answered the daemon with the *Spear of Telesto*. Blazing gold struck the daemon full in the chest.

Madail roared. The priest of Chaos Undivided who saw the hidden, who looked into the depths of primarchs and Legions, recoiled, and for a moment, its eyes were shut. It was blind. The blank eyes of its skull erupted with sheets of warp flame. Madail turned its head from side to side, sweeping the enginarium with the fire. It caught the shrieking abominations in the dome during the burn. They tumbled downwards, their bodies given over to sudden change, their forms losing all coherence and then cohesion, until they were a rain of ash upon the deck.

Unbound from the chains of the daemon's lies, Sanguinius soared on the wings of his freedom. He swerved around the blasts from its eyes. He would fell this priest. He would cleave the Undivided.

Sanguinius turned in a sharp angle away from the daemon. He arrowed his flight to the canyon between the masses of the engines. The mouths gabbled in anger, and their tongues lashed out for him as he passed. The immense, heaving walls called out for their master. With a ferocious beat of his wings, Sanguinius veered right, coming in close to the port engine. He plunged the *Blade Encarmine* into the wall. He flew even faster, dragging the sword through the fusion of metal and flesh. He slashed open a wound fifty feet long. The wall screamed in pain. Ichor and promethium gouted, and then there was a burst of ignited plasma. A curtain of flame billowed down the length of the canyon, washing over Madail as the daemon strode into the gap.

Sanguinius rose above the flames, wheeled around and came back at Madail, gouging the port wall. The screams of the engines redoubled. Explosions overlapped and fuelled each other, shaking the canyon. From the midst of the developing firestorm, Madail struck out wildly, blasts of warp energy stabbing up in every direction. Sanguinius soared over the roiling core of the explosions that marked the daemon's position, then dropped, racing back low as the fires began to fade. He swung the sword at the daemon's neck. Madail turned at the last second, and the *Blade Encarmine* sank into the spined, chitinous armour of its shoulder. Sanguinius' blow split the plate and cut deeply into the daemonflesh beneath. Madail snarled, and its immense talon seized the Angel, arresting his momentum and hurling him against the engine. The wall's teeth gnawed at his armour and sank into his pinions. Jaws parted in fury, Madail raised its staff and aimed the weapon's points at Sanguinius' throat.

Then it hesitated, remembering itself.

You do not dare kill me, Sanguinius thought, feeling the balance of power shift his way. With a burst of fire from the *Spear of Telesto*, he broke Madail's grip and launched himself upwards. He climbed high, streaking towards the dome of the enginarium, and at the peak of his flight, prepared to fall upon the daemon like a meteor.

But Madail had not finished its sermon. *'Be the Angel of Ruin, or the other ruin will come. It reaches for you now.'*

Sanguinius hesitated at the moment of descent. The words of the daemon stabbed through his anger. They did not diminish it, but his awareness grew of the blackness that flew with him. The thing was of him but not yet with him. It was of the future, though seeded in the past. It had no shape yet, but it was strong, and it made him strong. He could not shed it, and so he used it. Though he felt it eat at his self-control, he used it. He burned with justice. He was the fire of loyalty. The Thirst grasped at his consciousness too, and he subsumed it to his great and perfect rage. He dived.

His moment of hesitation was enough for Madail to recover. Arms outstretched, the daemon shouted, its hymn of praise to the gods it served louder than the choirs of thousands that surrounded it. A warp vortex, a burning wind made visible, gathered at its command. The vortex spread wide, a spinning cone of destruction. It lifted the daemon at its apex. A beast upon a throne, Madail rose to meet Sanguinius' flight.

The Angel unleashed another strike of light from the *Spear of Telesto*. The daemon deflected the blast with its staff and trained the blade at Sanguinius. The head of the weapon crackled with energy the colour of nightmares. Sanguinius folded his wings, accelerating into the dive. He struck with the *Blade Encarmine*. The blow would have cut a Rhino in two. The daemon took the sword in its shoulder. Sanguinius spiked and cut deep through the armour plating of the hide. Madail hissed, turning, and thrust its staff at Sanguinius' chest. It stabbed through his armour and through his flesh. In the moment before the full shock of pain and warp fire seized him, Sanguinius stabbed the *Spear of Telesto* into the abomination's central eye.

Angel and priest trapped the other's weapon in their body. The vortex spun them. Power burst around them. They clashed in the heart of a crucible where reality was made and unmade, where futures birthed and died. The enginarium vanished from Sanguinius' sight. The spike in his chest, the icon of the priest's office, sent the torments of the future through him. Psychic waves shook him, seeking to detach him from purpose and throw him into an abyss of unfettered pride. He balanced between two tempests, abstract storms of triumph and of the fall into the blackness. He could barely make out the shape of the daemon before him. He held on to the reality of his foe. He cut deeper with the *Blade Encarmine*. The spear grew hot in his grip as it burned the daemonflesh.

'*The choice remains,*' said Madail. At last there was pain in the monster's voice. There was the first hint of desperation. '*Fall and rise, or stand and fall. To fall is written. Fall to power. Fall to glory.*' Its staff flared again. The blackness rushed closer. The dark thing was not just part of him, it was linked to his choice to stand against Madail.

Cracks appeared in the armour of his purpose.

Madail laughed. It reached out with its free hand. Its huge talons seized Sanguinius' skull. '*See and know!*' the daemon bellowed. '*See and choose!*'

The blackness took him. His rage transformed. His consciousness split. He disappeared into the dark, and he remained detached from it, a sliver of his identity preserved in the suspension of choice. He split into madness and agony, because now he saw the true nature of the darkness.

'*This is the consequence,*' said Madail. '*Wrath of the future. Flaw of origins. Doom of sons.*'

The fate Sanguinius had declared he would accept unfolded again. Horus killed him again. This time, he looked on at his death from a remove. Even so, he felt the fatal blow. As he saw himself die, he witnessed the birth of the darkness. It was a howl of rage, summoned by betrayal, forged from that which was broken in his blood. It was a rage of terminal darkness, and its shriek of birth sounded down the long millennia, to be heard by all his sons, until the final Blood Angel should fall. The moment of his death froze. It became eternal. It could never be expunged. It was the final expression of his soul. It was his scream, his anger, his fury at betrayal, and it would live in the blood of his Legion forever. His lost time on the *Red Tear* returned to him.

He remembered.

He remembered holding Mkani Kano, and not seeing the Librarian. He had seen Horus. He had not seen the bridge of the *Red Tear*. He had seen the *Vengeful Spirit*. From the abyssal depths of fury, he had sought vengeance for his death by changing time. He had been about to kill Kano, hallucinating him as the author of a crime yet to come.

That was his legacy for his sons. The Black Rage would come for them and tear reality from their grasp. Roaring hate, they would slip to the moment in their past that marked the beginning of their long fall. They would seek vengeance upon Horus, and see him in whoever stood before them. Their fury against evil would turn them into mad butchers.

'This is the choice!' Madail boomed. *'This is the choice!'*

Sanguinius had thought his sacrifice was his alone. He had stood at the precipice of despair at the thought his death would have no meaning. But it would. It would have dreadful meaning. He did not know if through his death Horus would be stopped. He did not know if this choice meant the fall of the Imperium. He did know that the sacrifice would be that of his entire Legion. If he accepted his fate, the blood of his sons and of those they would kill would be on his hands.

The Angel screamed in agony, and the daemon grasped its prize.

And suddenly there was thunder.

EIGHTEEN

The Choice

THE THUNDER DESTROYED the real and the immaterial. It blasted through the vortex. It hurled the daemon and the Angel apart. They plummeted to the deck. The enginarium twisted and flowed. The huge dome began to spiral. Skulls and metal and stone blurred with one another. The thunder shattered all thought, all consciousness, all struggle. The *Veritas Ferrum* shuddered. Its existence trembled on the edge of dissolution. The colossal engine casings split, peeling back like flesh. Blood and ichor flooded the deck. The galleries collapsed. Daemons fell and thrashed. Their jaws gaped with screams that could not be heard. There was only the thunder.

Sanguinius landed at the edge of the portal. It was unstable, and howling energy slashed from its maw, jagged strikes rupturing the bodies of daemons with uncontrolled change.

Sanguinius pushed himself up. Madail's staff had fallen from his chest, and blood pumped from the wound. He cried out again from the greater injury to his soul, shaking with horror before the new curse that would fall on his sons because of him. Even to breathe felt like a condemnation, but he saw his foe fallen before him, and he found the strength to fight on. Madail thrashed, the *Blade Encarmine* and the *Spear of Telesto* embedded in its torso.

The thunder was passing, rolling away in rumbles like the fall of mountains. The walls of the *Veritas Ferrum* began to stabilise. The ship had been hurt, but it was not dead. A growl began to build in the wake of the thunder. It came from a vast distance forwards, vibrating down the length of the ship. It was the snarl of a vengeful beast, about to strike back.

The fading of the thunder was the measure of the moment Sanguinius had before him. He lunged at Madail and grabbed the hilts of his weapons. He sank them deeper into the daemon, then pulled the impaled daemon towards him. He could feel the portal at his back. The material and empyrean warred with each other. The ocean stormed, waiting to swallow him one more time. Madail reared up. Sanguinius held tight to the weapons. His anger was desperate now. The storm of his destruction threatened to overturn his reason. Despair pushed his wrath to the edge of the blackness. Grief swamped him. His choice was nothing more than a choice of dooms. He would doom his sons and perhaps the Imperium if he accepted his fate, or he would *be* the doom of the Imperium if he surrendered to Madail. Hope had fled. He forced himself to think no further than the next second, the next gesture. He followed the path of blind duty, though it seemed even that might abandon him too. And so he dragged the weapons towards him, and his wretched fury was still enough that the *Spear of Telesto* burned the daemon again.

Held, half-prone, Madail lunged, its staff abandoned. Its giant claws grabbed the Angel by his wings. **'YOU WILL SERVE!'** Madail bellowed, and the air shattered like glass. The daemon's grip was iron on Sanguinius' wings. It was still moving forwards. Sanguinius threw himself backwards. Madail, in mid-lunge, went with him.

They fell into the portal.

There was the jolt of a huge disjunction, of two realities forced together, yet separated by the blade of the empyrean. Sanguinius plunged through the violence of the portal. He landed, and his torso was on the floor of the Delphos. His legs were still on the skulls of the *Veritas Ferrum*'s deck. The daemon held his wings, and he held his weapons. They were caught between the realities, and the warp ran through the centre of their beings. They thrashed. The tip of the *Spear of Telesto*, embedded in the daemon's chest, was inside the portal. There it held Madail, transfixing the abomination.

Sanguinius was held too, by more than the daemon's grip. He was suspended in grief, trapped by fate. He saw his brothers approach over quaking rubble. Azkaellon and the Sanguinary Guard were right behind them. They cut down the daemons that remained between them and the portal, and then they were with him.

They seemed so far away.

Guilliman crushed Madail's wrist with the *Hand of Dominion*. The daemon's claws splayed in pain. The monster struggled, unable to pull free from the Avenging Son's strength. The Lion brought the *Wolf Blade* down on the daemon's pinned arm, grinding through the armour plating of its hide. Guilliman slammed the *Hand* down again, and the daemon's hand went limp. Flames licked up and down the wounded limb. The daemon released Sanguinius' wings and slashed at the primarchs. Its claws cut deep gouges into their armour, but they would not be stopped. The Lion's sword chewed into the daemon's flesh. The monster screamed. With a sickening wet crack of gristle, the Lion severed the arm. A deluge of ichor spilled into the temple.

Madail screamed, and the eyes of its skull bathed the temple hall with fire. The walls wavered, shifting back and forth between stone and flesh. They burned and bled, and the broken dome slumped lower. The blast threw the Sanguinary Guard back and swept over the Dark Angels and Ultramarines. The great daemon's power was overwhelming. Its flames coursed over and through the legionaries' armour, burning bodies and souls. Azkaellon cried out in pain and determination. Leaning forwards as if against a hurricane, he staggered back through the fire towards his primarch, fighting for every step.

Unbowed in the heart of the furnace Guilliman and the Lion redoubled their blows against Madail. Sanguinius could barely see them. The foul brilliance of the fire turned them into silhouettes. Madail slowed them, but could not stop them. They were jagged shapes, indomitable in their attacks, striking through a firestorm with immense blows to smash open the daemon's body. They were titans of war, and with their features hidden, they were myths, embodiments of strength and courage raining down judgement on the terrible priest.

Yet Madail moved. Its skull eyes still spewing fire in an unending torrent, it heaved itself up. Sanguinius jammed his spear and sword deeper into its chest, holding the daemon down. Tremors ran through its body, growing stronger. It was drawing the energy of the warp into it. It would rise again. It was imprisoned for the moment, caught between two points in the materium. It must not free itself. It must not cross to one point or the other. As long as the portal was open, the daemon was a threat.

On the threshold of the portal and the temple, Sanguinius saw what he must do. Here time changed. Here the Warmaster fell. Here the Angel was tempted. Here the galaxy pivoted.

Azkaellon reached the threshold. He hunched against the blasts, wracked by pain but no less determined than Guilliman and the Lion.

'Free your primarch!' Guilliman shouted.

Azkaellon reached forwards in the vortex of warp and materium. Layers of his armour peeled away in the storm. 'My lord,' he cried to Sanguinius, 'give me your hand!'

'No,' said Sanguinius. 'I must stay here.'

Azkaellon froze, rigid with horror.

'Roboute,' Sanguinius rasped. Speaking was difficult. Battered by the instability of the portal, he was weakening. He clutched the seconds as they went by, holding them with the slender, silver thread of hope that was all that remained to him. 'Leave me. Leave Davin now. I will hold the daemon as long as I can.' He looked at the Lion. 'Now is the time. Destroy this world.' The portal linked Davin and the *Veritas Ferrum*. The planet had been dead, but now it was convulsing with power.

Sanguinius writhed in pain. He dared not wonder if he could last until the evacuations were complete. He could not think of the hours. Only of the seconds. One by one by one. He would hold for this one. Then he would fight to hold for the next.

Madail strained futilely against the *Spear of Telesto*. *'This is not your fate!'* it raged. *'Fall or rule! You do not fall here!'*

Sanguinius ignored the daemon. He had to. The hope for a meaningful death was too precious. *'Go,'* he pleaded with Guilliman. He turned his eyes to Azkaellon. *With my last breaths, I will spare my sons,* he thought. *'Go!'* he roared.

Azkaellon took a step away. His face was a mirror of Sanguinius' agony. He could not disobey his primarch, but the order was condemning him to the unthinkable.

The Black Rage crawled into the back of Sanguinius' skull, coiling, ready to spread its cancer through the millennia. He was sparing his Legion nothing. His death would still be the trauma that would bestow his legacy of madness. Whether his sons relived his death at the hands of Horus or on Davin, the result would be the same. The doom was in his blood.

Curze was right. His fate and that of the Blood Angels could not be altered.

Perhaps Curze was wrong, too. If Sanguinius could not save his sons, he might still preserve the Imperium. His death could have meaning. The sacrifice of his Legion could have meaning. Here and now, in this act, there was meaning.

There was also no choice. Curze was right there, too, if not for the reason he thought. Madail and Davin must be destroyed. There was no other action open to Sanguinius. There was the duty of the second, and he held fast.

The thoughts flashed through Sanguinius' mind in the time it took for Azkaellon to retreat a single step.

The rest of the Sanguinary Guard, and beyond them Ultramarines and Dark Angels, had formed a wall, blocking access to the portal. No more daemons were coming through it. Instead, those still in the hall had turned back, trying to reach their fallen priest. The tremors continued to shake the temple. Two storms battered the hall. The portal raged at the edge of extinction. The struggle beyond created a curtain of sorcerous fire, exploding shells and ignited promethium. Legionaries and daemons destroyed each other.

'Go,' Sanguinius pleaded.

A new armoured figure knelt before him. It was his herald. He had not seen the legionary approach. Had he marched with the Sanguinary Guard into the Delphos? Sanguinius couldn't remember. He was there now, as he had come to the Angel on the *Red Tear*. As, indeed, he had answered the first need on Macragge. His power sword upraised, he held his hand out to the Angel. He said nothing. His gesture was eloquent.

I will take your place. Let this burden be mine.

Sanguinius looked up into the helmet of his unknown son. His path became clear. His duty could not end here. He could not protect his sons from their doom. His duty would be to fight until the appointed end came for him. Theirs would be to fight on, and bear the dual burden of Thirst and Rage until salvation or oblivion would come for them.

He did not hesitate. He had no doubts now. This too, was fate. In the depths of his pain, he experienced a bleak hope, and a bitter joy. He had always been meant to stand at the juncture of timelines, and though there was flux, though there was possibility, he had always been meant, too, to reach this point, and to receive this offer from the one Blood Angel who could make it. There were too many symmetries, too many echoes, for the meaning of this moment to be otherwise.

Once before, on Signus Prime, a son had taken the place of the father. Meros had sacrificed himself. He had become the Red Angel. He had embodied the Thirst, becoming the worst of the Blood Angels' nature.

On the *Red Tear*, the herald had banished Sanguinius' madness. He had confronted the primarch with the best of what he was.

The best was there now. He would suffer for the Angel. He was the perfect offering to the fates.

'No choice,' Sanguinius gasped. The pain of the truth was as great as the physical agony that wrenched him across the portal.

Sanguinius turned his back on ruin. He nodded. The herald raised his sword, both hands wrapped around the hilt, the blade pointing downwards. He stepped forwards.

'*Save your servant,*' Madail cried, '*who trusts in you, oh Four!*' It snatched at the herald. As its great claws came together, the air burned around their contours. It tore the fabric of the materium in the frenzy of its effort. With the power that had shattered worlds, that had enveloped a system with a boneyard, it hurled itself against the gates of destiny.

And found them closed.

It seized the herald, but the herald was already leaning forwards, plunging the sword into the portal. Madail's grasp moved the Blood Angel into the position determined by fate, and the blade struck the daemon at the point where it was bisected by the portal, into the wound struck by the *Spear of Telesto*. The herald stabbed the sword down to the hilt, holding the daemon.

Madail screamed with a voice of a thousand agonies. The shriek clawed down the vault. Rubble by the tonne collapsed into the centre of the hall, crushing the daemonic horde even as the abominations recoiled from the scream, moaning their despair. The roof of the temple was suddenly open to the air. The daemon's torso reared up. Its eyes were wide and staring, and they were as blank as the orbs in its skull.

Madail was blind.

The daemon screamed again and again.

When Madail arched its back in pain, Sanguinius rose. He yanked the *Blade Encarmine* from the daemon's shoulder. He pulled the *Spear of Telesto* from the monstrous body. The weapon burned in his grip, and the spearhead glowed white. He staggered back from the portal. The herald stood in the midst of the portal, neither in the temple nor in the *Veritas Ferrum*. Bestriding realities, enveloped by the storm of the warp, he should not have been visible any longer. He should have vanished the moment he entered the portal.

His silhouette was visible, bent over of the body of the daemon, his sword transfixing the Undivided. The edges of his outline trembled, as if the immaterium sought to eat away at his being. His stance over the writhing daemon was strong. He was motionless, already a symbol more than a warrior of flesh and bone. He would stand until his work was done.

'We have little time,' Sanguinius said to his brothers. 'We must act while my son holds fate at this crossroads. We must honour his sacrifice.' It felt like a crime, like a new form of treachery, to turn his eyes from the herald and the miracle of that silhouette in the portal. At the last moment, he witnessed the greater miracle. He saw the outline of wings spring from the herald's shoulder.

A new angel was coming into being.

'Son of my blood!' Sanguinius cried. 'Son of my hope!' And the angel blazed with gold.

Sanguinius forced himself to turn and face the hall. The battle was over. The bodies of Blood Angels, Ultramarines and Dark Angels lay in the near approach to the portal, some mutilated obscenely by daemonic claws and sorcery, others crushed beneath the fallen stone. Despite the losses, the formations were intact. The wall of ceramite stood around the primarchs. The daemons here were finished. Their burned, shattered remains covered the visible portions of the floor. Smoke rose from liquefying masses. Screaming shapes half formed in the smoke, vanishing as it spread wider in the air.

The hall was a mass of rubble. The walls were buckling. Pillars had fallen, and the ones still standing were cracked, stone dust falling from the crevasses. There were ways through the wreckage, though. Where doorways were blocked by collapses, new breaches in the walls opened other passages. The tremors went on and on. The Delphos was shaking itself apart. It had failed in its last task, and the failure was destroying it.

'There is no time,' the Lion corrected. 'We are in contact with the fleets again.' He glanced up through the broken roof. Sanguinius followed his gaze. The night was greyer than it had been when they entered the temple. The void flashed. Stars blazed and died. There was war in the void, and the firmament itself seemed to be drawing closer, cracking, closing in on the world. 'The *Veritas Ferrum* is laying waste to our fleets,' the Lion said. 'It has withstood cyclonic torpedoes.'

'Not easily,' Sanguinius said. He thought of the eruption inside the ship.

'Easily or not, it lives. And every ship the daemons kill becomes one of their number.'

Sanguinius moved forwards. His legs were weak. His chest felt like a ruined shell. Pieces of him, physical and psychic, had floated free and were grinding against each other like bone. If he confronted all the ways in which he was broken, he would not walk at all. 'Davin is the target,' he said again. 'The ship is vulnerable through its master, and we hold its master.'

'Then we must withdraw our forces while we still have fleets to use,' said Guilliman.

As they moved away from the portal, Madail called to Sanguinius. *'The Rage will come!'* The daemon said no more, roaring in helpless anger at the herald. The last shout fanned the flames of grief in the Angel's breast. He glanced at Azkaellon. *Will I warn you of the curse that will fall on our Legion?*

I cannot. Not without revealing its cause.

He could not tell Azkaellon that the loss he had faced a few moments before was inevitable. He could not destroy the hope of the Blood Angels in the midst of war.

The primarchs and their guards made for a breach in the eastern wall. Sanguinius paused at its threshold. He could feel time slipping away. From outside the temple came the thunder and angry rattle of combat. The armies of the three Legions had engaged the tide of daemons. In the sky, ugly blossoms of fire marked the deaths of more ships. And the void was filled with a grey fog, the shell of bones completing its contraction, coming to enclose Davin in its final tomb. There truly was no time. Even so, he paused. He looked back at the portal. It twisted on itself. Wave after wave of mutating fire bellowed from the interior. A storm had turned on itself, and was lashing out with the force of its ruin. In the heart of the maelstrom, the herald stood bowed, his sword planted. He radiated his own light. The silhouette shone golden. At the last, just before he turned away, Sanguinius was sure he saw the shape of wings spread from the herald's shoulders once more.

THE RED TEAR came about through the ignited plasma fog that had been the *Sable*. The cruiser had died a second time, but not before inflicting fratricidal wounds on the battleship. The scars of the daemonic burn festered on the lengths of the hull. Carminus turned the *Red Tear* away from its run at the *Veritas Ferrum*. The huge abomination had recovered from the wound inflicted by the *Samothrace*. It was accelerating again. Its salvoes were frenzied, indiscriminate. It was a maddened predator, attacking as if it would destroy the entire fleet on its own. Carminus thought it might yet succeed. The combined fleets had lost a third of their ships. They had held the daemon fleet at a constant size, but that was not even stalemate. That was a slight delay to defeat. And the bones of the necrosphere smashed though the battle zone, breaching hulls, shearing off cannon batteries, ramming through sterns and destroying engines. When they hit the daemon ships, they stuck like tremors to the hulls, accumulating grotesquery and strength.

Carminus had brought the *Red Tear* parallel with the *Veritas*. He vowed to sell the life of the vessel and its crew with honour. They would hurt the monster again, even if they could not kill it. The *Samothrace* had set its pyre, and had died well. It was ash in the void now, and had not come back. The *Red Tear* was not alone in making a last, bloody stand. The formations had collapsed into disorder. The near space of Davin was a cloud of individual battles. The commanders of the three fleets saw the end coming, and the vessels that could do so converged on the *Veritas Ferrum*. It welcomed their sacrifice with jaws agape.

Then the call had come. Sanguinius had returned. The ground forces were withdrawing in haste. The order was given by all three primarchs. Return to Davin and destroy it.

The *Red Tear* changed heading. It turned away from the *Veritas Ferrum*. Carminus' hope raced ahead of the gradual turn of the battleship's prow. His hope ran before them, seeking time they did not have. The void shields flared again and again as bone clusters battered the hull.

'The *Veritas Ferrum* is altering course,' Mautus warned. 'It is closing with us.'

'The enemy senses its end,' Carminus said. 'It is desperate.'

Not as desperate as we are, he thought. He could feel the shadow of the daemon ship pressing down on his shoulders.

Not soon enough, Davin came into view. Not soon enough, he saw the transports and gunships rising from the atmosphere, heading for the vessels that had remained on reserve. The stream of the departing ground forces would not be done soon enough. Carminus' will joined his hope in urging the gunships to greater speed.

'The *Encarnadine* is gone,' Mautus said.

The cruiser had been a short distance ahead of the *Red Tear* before the turn. The *Veritas Ferrum* bit it in half.

Carminus cursed the treachery of time. 'Target cyclonic torpedoes on the temple valley,' he said. Then he waited for his primarch's signal, or for the death ship to devour the *Red Tear*.

THE VYSSINI WAS among the last of the ships to leave the corrupted world. Sanguinius ordered it to fly a holding pattern over the Delphos until the evacuation was complete. The outer walls of the structure fell at last, exposing the portal. Sanguinius stared at the raging wound in reality, and knew that the herald still held Madail in place. Had the herald fallen, the daemon would have commanded the hordes of lesser abominations in the land beyond.

Caught between Davin and the *Veritas Ferrum*, Madail formed a link between the ship and the planet. Davin had been inert when the primarchs had come to the temple. Now it was violently alive in the place where the fate of the galaxy had been altered once before. Now there was an unstable fusion of the materium and the warp, and fate hung in the balance once more.

At last the *Talon* rose from the crater blackened by tens of thousands of rampaging abominations. The *Vyssini* turned away from Davin. Ahead, the *Veritas Ferrum* loomed behind the *Red Tear*. The ship was so vast, it seemed much closer than it was. There were other vessels between it and the Angel's flagship. They were insignificant prey before it. Sanguinius had seen the interior of the monster. The exterior was a new form of horror. The malevolence of the vessel surpassed the will of Madail. It did not need its master. It would ravage the galaxy forever. It was coming now to destroy the Imperial vessels before they could destroy Davin. It would finish what its master could not. It would swallow whole the remaining hope of the Imperium.

'Brothers,' he voxed Guilliman and the Lion. 'It must be now.' They were on gunships that had started their climbs at the same time as the *Talon*.

Azkaellon, a few paces away, said, 'My lord, we are barely free of Davin's gravity well.'

'We must run the risk.'

'*I concur,*' said Guilliman. '*The moment is about to pass.*'

Sanguinius saw the moments to come. He saw the *Red Tear* murdered and transformed. He saw the turning point join them, and the fleet falling quickly to the plague of revenants.

Is this what it is like for you, Konrad? he thought. *Always to see, always to know, what will and what must be?*

Everything was too close to Davin now. The density of conflict turned the vicinity of the world into a charnel house. The immense guns of the *Veritas Ferrum* unleashed a continuous barrage. Vessels died off its port, starboard and bow. The first of the bone clusters were falling on Davin, taking out transports and gunships in fiery collisions.

'Launch the torpedoes now, Carminus,' Sanguinius shouted. 'Do it now!'

The *Red Tear* fired its cyclonic torpedoes. So did the *Invincible Reason* and so did the *Gauntlet of Glory*, and the *Ultimus Mundi*, and the *Intolerant*, and the *Decimator*. A superabundance of death burned through Davin's atmosphere. Three Legions struck at the world with the fury of a last, desperate hope. They struck with anger, determined to see the cursed origin of Horus' rebellion annihilated, erased forever from human sight.

They struck, because it was written they must, or on this day three fleets would perish, and then the Imperium would surely fall.

The cyclonic torpedoes hit the site of the temple. The Delphos and all its surroundings vanished, the initial blast flashing the region to dust. Then the more terrible wounds came, one after another. The entire surface of the planet turned molten. The core was hit by overlapping blast waves, creating a destructive force many times greater than the one that had broken Episimos III. Davin exploded. The bane of the Emperor's dream hurled its death cry outwards. The shockwave and the burning fragments of its crust slammed through the near space. The last of the gunships, those that had not been able to dock with the retreating vessels, took frantic evasive action. Some fell to luck, or fate, and died with the planet. The blast strained the void shields of the great ships. The Dark Angels grand cruiser *Culverin*, its hull badly damaged by a strike from the *Veritas Ferrum*'s cannons, blew up. The fireball exploded from the bow, and the ship drove forwards, disintegrating, into its own flame. The entire combined fleet rode the wave of annihilation, ships in a storm. They were tossed by the violent ocean of forces they had unleashed. Some sank. Most survived.

The torpedo salvo caused two explosions. The destruction of Davin was the weaker of the two. The greater blast did not touch the vessels of the Imperium. The souls aboard them felt its passage, and they witnessed it. Sanguinius gasped as the wave passed through the *Vyssini*. It felt like a huge severing. Fragments of time, present and to come, bled and died, and he sensed a falling away of possibilities. Enormous destruction and the final creation of a single future were one and the same.

The second overlapped with another, birthed at the same moment. The Delphos vanished, and the *Veritas Ferrum*. The huge maw at its prow loosed a monstrous scream. In the *Vyssini*, the Blood Angels staggered. Sanguinius winced. He stood firm against the sound in his skull. He heard the voice of Madail, and the voice of the monster the daemon had created. The resurrected, corrupted machine-spirit of the *Veritas Ferrum* raged against its end. The howl went on and on, and the ship swelled. The skin of its hull cracked opened, bursting with the pressure of the conflagration within. Violet unlight speared the void. The *Veritas Ferrum* flew apart. Wreckage of mouths and eyes and bones raced ahead of the expanding ball of inchoate warp energy, and the scream went on.

At the centre of the explosion, the void was torn, and the immaterium reclaimed its own. An implosion began. Its energy ball reversed its growth, shrinking in a single moment to a point. It caught the fleeing rubble of the ship, and pulled it all in. In its absolute violence, the implosion unleashed the second shockwave on the aether. It collided with the first. In their intersection, they reduced the daemonic fleet and the swarm of bones to dust.

The scream faded as the revenant ships returned to oblivion. Deprived of the force that animated them, their bonds broken, they lost substance. They became ragged phantoms sailing through the uniform void of grey. Then they were shadows. Then echoes. Then only memories in the minds of those who had seen them.

The destruction of Davin and its works rushed outwards from the system, further and further, carried by the agony of the warp, transforming the materium at speeds far greater than light.

Sanguinius looked out through the viewing block of the *Vyssini*, and he saw the wound before he heard the new cry. With the necrosphere gone, the Ruinstorm was visible again, and it was in agony. The aurora of madness still twisted across the galaxy, but there was a gap. A chasm of untainted void broke up the storm, as if a break had been blasted through a firestorm. Or a spear thrust through the body of a great beast.

Sanguinius tightened his hold on the *Spear of Telesto*, feeling the

muscle memory of his strike. The blow he had struck on Pyrrhan, slicing through the knots of fate, had been a lie. His blow on the *Veritas
Ferrum* had been an act of truth. It reached just as far.

Davin had died as the forces linked to it tried to shape his path and
the Imperium's. The convulsion of power and destinies had cracked
open the barrier of the Ruinstorm.

There were stars in the gap. Sanguinius could see the face of the
galaxy again. Among the stars was the brightest light. He could not see
it, but he felt its return like the sudden warmth of dawn after a flood.
Its light was the cause of the new cry, the one that came on the vox.
The cry was voiced first by the Navigators of every surviving ship, and
it spread to every member of the crew, and every legionary.

'Terra!' came the cry as the Astronomican blazed. 'Terra! Terra! Terra!'
A shout and not a scream. A chorus of triumph.

'Terra! Terra! Terra!'

Sanguinius closed his eyes. The shouts washed over him like a balm.
There were no screams, for now. He had purchased the triumph at the
cost of a scream in the future. He listened to the roar of his sons. He
tried to forget what that roar would sound like when fate came to col-
lect its ransom, the Black Rage in its claws.

EPILOGUE

THE WAY TO Terra was clear, and it was not.

The primarchs met once more aboard the *Red Tear*. They spoke in the Sanctorum Angelus. 'The astropathic messages paint a disturbing picture,' Guilliman said.

'I am grateful that we are receiving them at all,' said Sanguinius.

'We are receiving intelligence,' said the Lion. 'That is very much to the good. But I agree, the news is far from reassuring.'

'Multiple blockades,' Guilliman mused. 'If Horus didn't anticipate we would defeat the Ruinstorm, he was leaving nothing to chance.'

'Your Navigators concur with ours?' the Lion asked.

'They do. A single warp jump to Terra is impossible. The empyrean is still too unstable.'

The Lion drummed his fingers on the hilt of the *Wolf Blade*. 'They'll tie us up,' he said. 'They seek to entangle the fleets and delay us until Terra has fallen.'

'Our information is far from complete,' Sanguinius pointed out. 'We don't know the full scale of their deployment.'

'We know enough,' said Guilliman. 'We know they are more than

three Legions. Our brother is correct. Even if we hit them with our combined force, that will be nothing more than what Horus wants us to do.'

Sanguinius hissed with frustration. Then he closed his eyes for a
moment. He calmed himself with the knowledge of what had to be.
'The blockades do not stop me,' he said. 'I will reach Terra, because I
must fight Horus. It is written. The fate of the Imperium will be decided
then. Even the daemon believed that.'

Guilliman and the Lion exchanged a look. Guilliman was no happier with the idea of predestination than he had been on Macragge.
There was far less resistance in the Lion's expression.

'Then we must learn how we achieve what we are fated to accom-
plish,' said the Lion.

Guilliman's brow furrowed in sudden pain. 'You reach Terra,' he said
to Sanguinius. 'That does not mean we do.'

'I don't know. I have never seen you or your Legions in my visions.'

Guilliman nodded slowly, looking off into a future that already
caused him agony. 'There is a way,' he said. He turned to the Lion.
'But after all this, we will not reach Terra. We will not fight at our
father's side. We hit the blockades ahead of the Blood Angels. *We* tie
Horus' forces up instead of the other way around. We run interference for Sanguinius.'

The Lion thought for a moment, then said. 'We can also draw some
of their strength away.'

'How so?'

'By applying the lesson I have learned at Episimos and Davin. Your
fleet is the largest. I will attack their bastions, Roboute. I will destroy
their home worlds. That is the judgement that awaits them. Let it
come now. Burn the corrupted planets. How many of our treacherous
brothers will stay with the blockades if their worlds are directly threatened? Not all of them.'

'Very well,' said Guilliman. 'It makes sense for my Legion to be the
battering ram against the blockades.' He turned to Sanguinius. 'We will
open the way for you.' He sighed. 'I never thought, if Terra still stood,

that I would not be at Father's side in the struggle. Perhaps this is my expiation.' The pain in his eyes was hard to look at.

The Lion was expressionless. Sanguinius wondered if he might not be finding some real satisfaction in his path, in being the hand of judgement.

The three primarchs stood in silence for a few moments. The paths were set. The moment of the Triumvirate's dissolution had truly arrived. They would fight for the common cause, but separately now.

'When shall we three meet again?' the Angel said.

But he had told his brothers what waited for him on the *Vengeful Spirit*, and they did not answer.

THE CHAMBER WAS dark. Though it was not a cell, it could easily have been. The vault door at Sanguinius' back was sealed. Azkaellon and a full squad of the Sanguinary Guard waited beyond it. Azkaellon had been reluctant to leave Sanguinius alone with Konrad. 'His bonds are strong,' Sanguinius had told him. 'They are about to become stronger.'

The stasis coffin stood against the far wall. It was open, angled backwards, waiting for its occupant. It was embedded in a generator that protruded into the room, bulking like a mausoleum's vault. Energy coils sparked, their power contained, ready to generate the field.

The Night Haunter stood in front of the coffin, unconcerned. 'You think your faith has been rewarded,' he said.

Sanguinius thought for a moment. Then he said, 'I believe you are speaking for yourself. You must be pleased, Konrad. We march towards the ends we both know. Nothing has changed.'

'Nothing ever could.'

'Really? I don't think you believed that on Davin.'

Unease, that emotion so strange to see on the Night Haunter's face, appeared again. He covered it by glancing back at the stasis coffin. When he looked back at Sanguinius, his contempt was in place once more. 'So now you take me back to face our father,' he said.

'You will answer for your crimes.'

'He isn't going to execute me. We both know that.'

'We do,' Sanguinius agreed. A new possibility occurred to him. He turned it over and over in his mind before he allowed himself to consider it more than wishful thinking. It rose before him, not a sudden epiphany but a slow dawn. Forged in darkness, tempered in despair, it was hope, thin as a blade, but oh, how it might serve the light. How it might be salvation.

In the midst of its lies and manipulation, Madail had spoken a truth. There *had* been a choice. It *was* possible to alter fate. The question was whether that chance had only occurred on Davin.

Sanguinius put his hope to the test. 'Father won't have you executed,' he said. 'I believe He should, but you're right. He won't.'

'Prison will be very dull,' said Curze. 'I'll miss our conversations.'

Sanguinius ignored the taunt. 'Father might do worse,' he said. He watched Curze's face closely. 'He might forgive you.'

He struck home. Curze's mask of contempt fell. The unease returned. The reptilian eyes widened as they saw destiny enter a state of flux. In the storm of emotions that passed in micro-tremors over the Night Haunter, Sanguinius saw anger and doubt. He saw horror again at the thought that the universe really was not as Curze had known it to be, for so long, and so absolutely. And Sanguinius saw what he was looking for. He saw the rarest of all things in Curze's eyes. He saw hope.

That was what he needed. That was confirmation.

He pushed Curze into the stasis coffin. The Night Haunter fell back and lay prone, helpless.

'He might forgive you,' Sanguinius repeated. 'I don't. You cannot have that redemption. I won't let you. Rest certain in your destiny. You will have it. I am not taking you to Father.'

'You can't kill me either. I die at the hand of Father's assassin.'

'I'm not going to kill you. I am going to jettison your coffin into the void. The assassin will find you when the time comes. It may be millennia, Konrad.'

The hope vanished forever from Curze's eyes, replaced by a different form of horror.

'You claim destiny can't be altered,' Sanguinius continued. 'So be it. Yours will be as you say.'

He stepped back and depressed a pad on the side of the coffin, generating the stasis field. It froze Curze in mid-scream.

Sanguinius turned from his brother. He moved to the vault door. He did not open it immediately. Before he saw Azkaellon, before he looked upon any of his sons, he thought about his fate and hope.

He would meet Horus on the *Vengeful Spirit*. He accepted the inalterability of his fate to that point. But he had learned that destiny could change. Perhaps there was still a choice to come, only it was not his.

Horus was not Curze. What he had been was too magnificent to be lost utterly. Sanguinius would summon it again. He had passed through the Delphos and triumphed. He would save Horus. The spear thrust that had felled the Undivided and pierced the Ruinstorm was not done yet. He would see it unmake the dark to come.

He reached for the vault door, ready to see his Blood Angels. His decisions were clear, his path shining. He would walk this road, and save his sons from the Black Rage.

Metal ground against metal as he opened the door. The sound was high-pitched. Its reverberations sounded oddly down the hall, as if they were the echoes of a scream yet to come.

ABOUT THE AUTHOR

David Annandale is the author of the Horus Heresy novels *Ruinstorm* and *The Damnation of Pythos*, and the Primarchs novel *Roboute Guilliman: Lord of Ultramar*. He has also written *Warlord: Fury of the God-Machine*, the Yarrick series, several stories involving the Grey Knights, including *Warden of the Blade* and *Castellan*, as well as *The Last Wall*, *The Hunt for Vulkan* and *Watchers in Death* for The Beast Arises. For Space Marine Battles he has written *The Death of Antagonis* and *Overfiend*. He is a prolific writer of short fiction set in The Horus Heresy, Warhammer 40,000 and Age of Sigmar universes. David lectures at a Canadian university, on subjects ranging from English literature to horror films and video games.

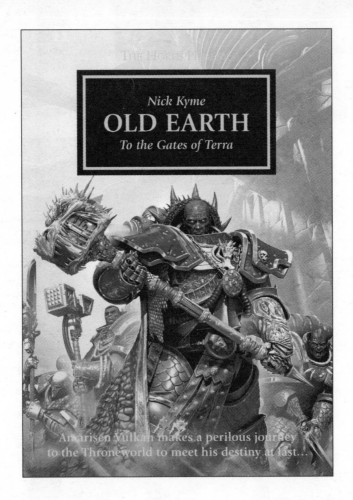

Nick Kyme

OLD EARTH

To the Gates of Terra

An arisen Vulkan makes a perilous journey
to the Throneworld to meet his destiny at last...